RISE OF THE ORACLE
NIGHT OF THE RED SKY

About the author

L.B. Mayman lives in the Mount Dandenong Ranges in Victoria, Australia with his partner, Meghan. *Rise of the Oracle: Night of the Red Sky* is his debut novel.

L.B. MAYMAN

RISE OF THE
ORACLE
NIGHT OF THE RED SKY

LAMP
HOUSE
INTERNATIONAL

First published by Lamp House International, Australia, 2012.

Ordering Information: Quantity sales. Special discounts are available on quantity pur-chases by corporations, associations, and others. For details, contact the publisher at www.lamphouseinternational.com

National Library of Australia
Cataloguing-in-Publication entry

Mayman, L.B.

Rise of the oracle: night of the red sky / L.B. Mayman.

ISBN 9780987393005 (pbk.)

A823.4

Cover image by © iStockphoto.com/AlexRodavlas
Cover design by © Lamp House International

For Megs,
The greatest thing that I ever did
was to find the wonderful person behind that smile.
Always and forever

PART I

Chapter 1

The old man scampered around in the kitchen fretting over the leaks in the roof of his ageing house. He had rounded up every pot or jug he owned and put them down to catch the rain drops that were falling from the ceiling; even though, the pursuit was ultimately hopeless. The old man had known that heavy rain was coming for quite some time even if the news or officials did not have any idea it was coming; however, he had not the inclination to get the roof fixed in time. The main room that led to the kitchen at the back was littered with a collector's feast of small tin toy robots that the old man had made himself. Thousands of them lined shelves on every available wall space. Every now and again he would take them to the street market that was held on the forth Sunday of every month and told their stories to the children on how they came to be. Every child in the area had heard the old man's stories. He had told the same stories to George Underwood who now sat crossed-legged on the floor and who was attempting to get the old man's attention but failing miserably in competition with the rain drops from the roof.

Underwood said to himself as he took down one of the tin toy robots, "The robot army will rise up when The Oracle is no more."

As the old man went from pot-to-pot and emptied its contents out on the street through the window he sang a familiar song that Underwood had heard before.

"The Chief is strong and wise. The Farmer is careful but loyal.

The Librarian is smart and skilful. The Mother is desire and playful. The Warrior does not know its enemy. The Chronicler does not know its story. The Archaeologist does not know its history. The Diplomat will bathe in glory-"

"And The Oracle," interjected Underwood, "Will save them all."

With this the old man finally looked up at Underwood and pointed to him with a shaking finger, "You know the song but not the words, my friend. I knew you would come back. What did you find?"

"If you are talking about Tibet then what I found was nothing short of an abomination."

Underwood had in fact just come straight from there and what he had found had begged even more questions than he knew he could find answers.

"Oh, come on, come on, my friend. You find what you seek," said the old man with a gleeful look on his face.

"I found mountains," replied Underwood.

"And what was inside these mountains?"

"I found people. Hundreds of thousands of people."

"Ha-ha! What did I tell you! What did I tell you?"

Seemingly satisfied with this answer the old man went about his managing of the water flow into his pots ignoring the agitation on Underwood's face. Underwood though needed more than just vindication of a tale that the old man had told which led him to mountains.

"What are the people for?" asked Underwood but the old man continued with his pots mumbling to himself as he went, 'The Chief is strong and wise. The Farmer is careful and loyal…' and yet Underwood would not be denied, "Where are those people from? Why would anyone keep thousands and thousands of people in suspended animation inside a mountain? Are they for an army? What is the UFA?"

The last question must have struck a chord as the old man dropped a pot that splashed all over the floor and he came rushing toward Underwood waving his finger.

"What you know of this?" said the old man his tone of voice and mannerism changed somewhat from happy to annoyed.

"Nothing, only what you have told me," replied Underwood.

"I tell you nothing. Got that!"

"If you have told me nothing then why did you send me there? You must have a reason?"

"I need no reason."

"Or, do you mean that you do not know the reason, Oracle?"

At hearing his name the old man lit up and came closer to Underwood than he had ever come before. He had made it a point in their previous meetings to stand on the other side of the room to where Underwood was standing and forbid him to come any closer.

"You listen here and you listen good. You know nothing. Have never known nothing. You find too much and give reason for all enemy to know what you know. Is not a good thing."

It was then that an uncontrollable urge succumbed Underwood to grab hold of the old man's hands. His movements were so quick that the memory of the movement happening was simply a blur. He could only recall that he had taken The Oracle's hands in his which caused a look of absolute shock and terror on the face of the old man even though the touch would have only been for the briefest of moments. But, to Underwood, the touch was a whole new reckoning; a surge went through him that he could only describe as an electrical current flowing through him. He was acutely aware of the surrounding room and all the toy robot figurines on the walls that seemed to be warning him of something. A little army of tin scouts that told him to run for danger was at hand. And then he could see them. The mercenaries surrounding The Oracle's house and their intent to kill. The sensation was something that Underwood was used to and had grown to be able to control; but, this time he saw it with a clarity that he had never experienced.

It was then that everything around him seemed to slow down.

Almost on cue, the door at the other end of the room was kicked in and bullets were littered throughout the room; but, Underwood already knew their trajectory. Underwood dragged down the old man to the floor and when the shooting stopped briefly his only thought was that he had to run. He kept low heading for the kitchen where he dived through the window where the old man had been emptying his rain water pots smashing the glass as he fell through to the other side and landing on some kind of small shrub. The twigs and leaves dug into his back as he turned and lifted himself onto the fence all in one motion and vaulted over into a back alley. More bullets followed him but missed their target as he ran down the alley and came out into a busy street.

Underwood's only thought was that they had found him. They had found him and he did not know what they would do with The Oracle. And yet, a small part of him realised that the old man would be safe; that the pursuers were only after Underwood. But why they wanted him dead, Underwood did not know.

Chapter 2

Tim Marshall was lamenting the fact that this would be the last time that he would be making this journey. He sat in the Miami International Airport waiting for his flight to Caracas, Venezuela amid a flurry of late passengers trying to stretch the patience of the check-in and ground crew alike. Marshall himself was early. He was always early for airports. It took a great number of good intentioned people to make a long distance trip as less stressful as possible and the majority of the time the staff really did do a good job. It was the least he could do to be punctual and organised to ensure that he was less of a burden as possible.

Marshall also travelled light. He had learnt this from his previous journeys from North to South America. He never took anything with him that couldn't be taken onto the plane as carry-on luggage which included a change of clothing for the journey. He didn't like the idea of being unable to control his personal belongings. Knowing exactly what was in them, who would look in them and what they could put in or take out of them. Marshall thought that it was best to buy things when you got there or have them flown in by professionals. At least courier companies took some responsibility for your luggage; a damn site more than the good intentions of baggage staff on minimum wage.

The stresses of the travelling people around Marshall were amplifying his own tensions of that day. Usually, travel didn't bother him.

Marshall loved the journey, especially knowing where he was going and that it was somewhere different from the everyday. He didn't care for people who had an unrelenting urge to worry about everything on the journey. Will the plane be late? Will I like the food? Will they lose my luggage? Will this, will that! The reason for Marshall's own stress stretched to the meeting he had not four hours earlier. Marshall hadn't intended to depart that day; however, it was a burden of circumstance. The meeting was called because there were many unanswered questions which needed to be settled; even though Marshall feared they were questions that no-one could answer. Still, he had come for one thing and that was to secure the continued support of his financiers, Globe Corp.

At the meeting, all Marshall could do was remind them of the facts as they were. Marshall led a team of scientists whose pursuits were to find that which did not want to be found. He couldn't answer their questions on how long this and that would take to complete. As Marshall saw it he was either going to find what he set out to achieve or he wasn't. It was simply a fifty-fifty bet either way.

However, Marshall knew that the reason he was dragged into this meeting was not whether he would complete his task as agreed. The former contact of his financier had moved on and left a gaping hole unfilled which meant the bean counters were asking the questions now and not the dreamers. Marshall knew, for instance, that they did not read the long winded brief that he had prepared to secure the finance in the first place. Especially, Norman Rogers, who supposedly was leading up the investigation. Rogers had asked Marshall what it was he was trying to achieve flashing his smile and brandishing a gold tooth.

"Exactly what I wrote in the brief. If you'd care to look," Marshall had responded.

"Then you wouldn't mind going through it with us. I mean, this was written some years ago–"

"And the goal is no different. The procedure stays the same."

"You're not offering me much in terms of return on investment here, Mr. Marshall?"

"A return?" Marshall was perplexed. What return did he think there would be on something that either was or wasn't?

"This is not an exact science," said Marshall, "I can't give you a result sheet here with boxes ticked to appease the board that all was carried out as planned. Because there is no plan to this, it's organic. We are only learning through trial and error here."

Rogers had chewed on his lip. Maybe that would shut him up, thought Marshall; however, Rogers was only bridging the silence to build up to deliver his address of the situation.

"You do understand why it is a company like our own would be interested in your discovery, Mr. Marshall? We manage risk, that's what we do. Now if your hypothesis has any credit you would be able to present to me some kind of fixed data on what it is you've been doing down there. But you can't. All I needed to see was on the numbers sheet and the amount of expenditure this company has been footing while you are doing god only knows. Now, clearly, we have spent the money getting you this far so we are not going to be pulling out straight away; however, there will be some substantial changes to our agreement with you until we start seeing real results. The first thing will be that a documentary team will be sent to film the discovery. If it does happen, we want it to be big. If it gathers the press, we'll sell the footage rights which will compensate us for the losses we have incurred. Second, you've been operating independently and away from any formal structure within the organisation that monitors the progress of our investments; we feel that this was a grouse oversight by the last administrator and will be sending auditors in regularly to provide us with a detailed account. And, as these requirements are necessary for our continued support, which I assume is something that you continue to desire, I call an adjournment to this meeting, Mr. Marshall."

With that Rogers stood and left, dropping a manila folder in front of Marshall. He flipped open the manila folder and read before him the new terms of the agreement if it could be called that. It was everything that he hated about such endeavours: clause this and clause that subject to this and subject to that. In the end, it meant nothing. The original agreement that Marshall had signed was only a single page which went along the lines of Globe Corp agrees to pay an agreed sum per month until complete to Marshall Discoveries for the endeavour entitled 'Classified'. The new agreement sort to make Marshall's business public, something he could ill afford and the very thing that the previous administrator understood could bring down everything they set out to achieve.

Marshall wasn't proud of the fact that his next course of action involved the fire department, a cigarette lighter and a bin with the manila folder he received from Rogers burning as he left the Globe Corp building. However, he had come to the decision to be nonchalant as one could be with such demands a long time ago and he had no intention of starting now – not when he was so close to the end.

What was to follow was an hour of unprecedented negotiation on Marshall's part that he had never endured. His first point was to book a flight on the next plane to Caracas, the second was to arrange for a storage company to move all his belongings on the next ship to Panama; third, was to transfer the two-million dollars US out of the accounts that had been established as emergency funds, which Marshall was the sole assignee, to be redirected to off-shore accounts under the name of the members of his team. The last act, and most important, was to contact his previous administrator at Globe Corp, Charles Harrison.

Marshall pulled out his PDA and sent Charles Harrison a message to alert him to the fact that he had been right. As it seemed, Harrison had correctly anticipated that the company was set for a buyout. Harrison had then guessed that Marshall's exploits would come under close scrutiny and he set about discretely pointing Marshall in the right direction to keep the expedition afloat. As it turned out Harrison knew a lot of things and was trying to warn Marshall of the impending crisis; however, the remoteness of the operation in Venezuela meant that Marshall did not receive word of the impending storm for at least a week. It was all too late, the winds of change had swept through and Marshall's party was a mere clean up in the aftermath by men like Rogers.

However, in his last communication with Harrison, Marshall had not at all been absolutely truthful and it played on his mind now with everything that Harrison had done. As it turned out, Marshall and his hapless team had happened upon a chance encounter that was making the seemingly fruitless exercise seem every chance a possibility. It had seemed like a long time since they first set out and most of his team had lost sight of the bigger picture. But, that all changed two weeks ago and it was an unfortunate set of circumstance that coincided with the upheaval at Globe Corp that Harrison was not sharing in their success at this moment.

While he didn't like leaving the team at this critical stage, if he hadn't appeared before Rogers face-to-face, Globe Corp would have sent someone after him which would have caused even greater concern. At least this way they knew what was coming. Marshall predicted that he had bought himself a day or two before they would send someone after him and close down the whole operation. It would take them some time to decide what to do and more time before they would try to find the right people to carry out the job. There would be delays while the Caracas office gave them the run around on Marshall's orders and further delays finding where it is his team was located. While his operation was mobile and could move whenever they pleased; right now, they were closer to the goal than ever before and it was paramount that everything continued as it had been progressing.

Marshall's flight was finally called for boarding. He wasn't the type to run to the front though and he needed the spare five minutes anyway to send a final note to Harrison. But upon inspecting his PDA Harrison had beat him to it:

'Marshall, old boy, you must accept my sincerest apologies for any inconvenience caused. I dislike it when I'm right as my predictions are often the cause of great anguish for the recipient. But knowing you, you've already taken the necessary course of action as advised in our previous discussions. As you could appreciate, I shan't be able to offer you any further assistance in wisdom or kind as our contact will be heavily monitored and the wheels of change are turning more progressively as we speak. I understand that your confidence has waned of late but rest assured that your little undertaking is of vital importance in the larger scheme of things and never forget that we are relying on you to produce the goods. Thus, it is with deepest regret that I sign off until both our successes lead us together which, evidently, I know will be the case...it's up to you now, Tim.'

The message was full of the same charm that Marshall had come to expect from Harrison. He would be astute to the last and Marshall often felt a sense of inferiority for some reason. His own abilities in lateral thinking were inadequate at best and Harrison had always been able to offer the alternative in a manner that didn't condescend Marshall's direct way of thinking. However, not having Harrison to fall back on was a daunting prospect to say the least; but, Marshall knew he would manage, he always did.

But there was something that was still bugging Marshall and he didn't think it was possible to keep Harrison in the dark as he now stood in the queue to board the flight to Caracas. He needed to let Harrison know that he could see light near the end of the tunnel. As the attendant checked his ticket, Marshall decided that he would risk the final contact. At the most, they'd be able to track him to the airport which Marshall was sure they had figured anyway and as he made his way down the race, he hit reply to Harrison's original note and typed:

'Sorry, but this couldn't wait...we're closer than what you think.'

Or, perhaps Harrison already knew that, Marshall thought as he hit send dropping the PDA into the bin for used head phones.

Chapter 3

The last thing that Tenashi wanted to do was to kill a man.

Tenashi was a pacifist for the better part of his childhood where he had spent most of his days toiling in the waste dumps of rich western hotels finding half eaten steak sandwiches and discarded soft drink bottles. His adolescence was spoiled in waves of crime robbing tourists until finally this led to the kidnapping of the daughter of a wealthy export manufacturer that they had ransomed for one-million US dollars. It was a disaster of course. Under planned and overzealous the operation was doomed from the beginning.

His long time friend, Amatsu, a second rate drug dealer who owed a local drug baron more money than he could earn learned of the tycoon's presence in the hotel where he worked as a chef and there the plan was hatched. They were high of course, sitting as usual in Amatsu's small shack that backed onto an open sewerage drain and smoking the cheapest thing men like Tenashi and Amatsu could afford to forget their woes and lack of opportunity in their world, gungy, which was the root of a common forest plant in tropical parts of Asia. Amatsu was pacing the room as his mood was beginning to turn into an angry rage. He described how they could easily sneak into the room and take her while she slept as the house maid had told him the tycoon was out most nights. He had stolen a colleague's security pass and they could easily obtain maintenance clothes from the laundry where most of the laundry girls bought their gungy from Amatsu and had owed him a favour or two.

And this was exactly how it played out. Amatsu sweet talked a young laundry girl with half a stick of gungy. The security pass worked without a hitch and they entered the room of the tycoon without being noticed. The room, three times the size of Tenashi's own house with separate sleeping rooms from the main lounge area; however, was still occupied by the tycoon when they entered sitting on the couch with a young girl not much older that Tenashi having intercourse.

The tycoon didn't flinch at their presence and started yelling at them, "Finally, I have been calling the front desk for hours! Fix that damn air conditioner! Can't you see I have busy work to complete here?"

The girl tried to hide as she buried her head into the couch as the tycoon lit up a cigar and poured himself a drink.

"Where is the air conditioner?" Tenashi asked.

The tycoon grunted and pointed down the corridor and Tenashi and Amatsu wheeled the waste trolley they had planned to smuggle the girl out of the hotel with in that direction. They found the girl awake sitting at the end of the bed watching cartoons and Amatsu in his drugged state snapped up the girl in the laundry bag and put her in the cart. Surprisingly the girl was silent, almost submissive in the whole affair and made it easy for the tycoon not to notice what was happening right under his nose. Tenashi made an excuse for not having the right tools for the job and they quickly exited the room without delay.

When they got back to Tenashi's house they put the young girl into his bedroom and Amatsu made the ransom call to the hotel. Unfortunately, the receptionist was unwilling to trouble such an important guest at that hour and suggested that he could only leave a message. However, it was not until later in the morning that they received a return phone call from the tycoon; the young girl was seemingly not at the forefront of his mind.

"Thank you for picking her up," said the tycoon, "Could you please bring her back to the hotel?"

"Are you joking!" said Amatsu at the suggestion, "We have your daughter! We want your money! One-million US dollars or she dies!"

Amatsu hung up the phone and stormed into the kitchen. He grabbed a knife from a drawer and made his way to the bedroom. He took the young girl's long black hair and sliced off one side very close to the scalp which left a patch of pale skin. Amatsu gave the hair to Tenashi and told him to mail the hair back to the tycoon so that they would know they were serious. Tenashi thought at this time that they would do nothing to hurt a little girl and that this would be a simple exchange. He first refused to do such a thing and said that they should return the girl and plead that it was all a misunderstanding. But Amatsu would have nothing of it and gave Tenashi the ultimatum to obey or be killed while Amatsu held the knife to his throat.

Tenashi had been friends with Amatsu for years and he had been an influential person in his life to a stage where he was dominated by him. He didn't necessarily want to smoke gungy or make a meagre living by stealing. However, Amatsu had led him down these unwitting paths and it was now Tenashi's time to dominate.

"I will take her hair to the hotel myself," said Tenashi, "It could take days before we get a response if we send it in the mail. I will pass myself off as a delivery man."

And this is what Tenashi did using the security pass they had used previously he made his way up the stairs to the level of the tycoon's room and he was confronted by two police on guard. Tenashi offered that he had information for the tycoon about his daughter; however, the police recognised him at once. You didn't walk around town selling gungy on the side and have the police not know about it. Besides, most of them were in on the take. The tycoon for his part identified him as the air conditioner repairman from the night before and the detectives handling the case put two and two together. Tenashi was there to give himself up and yet the police still beat him with their batons. The tycoon sitting in the lounge watching the display said nothing and only sucked on his cigar while the detectives took turns at whacking Tenashi with the backs of their hands. The punishment continued even after he gave up the whereabouts of the young girl and Amatsu and it was not long after this that she was returned to the tycoon. Tenashi watched this through puffed and bloodied eyes while the young girl was told to go to her room. Her emotional state was not even taken into consideration as she walked back down the corridor.

For Tenashi, however, there would be no trial. He was instantly transported from the place where he had spent all his life to a place he determined to be a detention facility. He was hooded through the entire journey punched and kicked every so often. He was only allowed to see light again when the journey was complete and he was locked away in isolation in what appeared to be a cell with no windows. For months on end men would come to his cell dressed in fatigues and beat him all but an inch from his life. The beatings became his only sense of time as there was no clock or sun light by which to pass the days and eventually he learned how to anticipate when his tormentor would come into his cell for what Tenashi gauged was his weekly round of violence.

However, eventually, the violence became more and more random which put Tenashi off balance until he could stand no more and he struck back at his tormentor. The tormentor at first was stunned and wiped his mouth revealing a gold toothed grin. The tormentor left without a word and for the first time since the kidnapping he had felt a sense of jubilation that he had not experienced since his last hit of gungy. However, this feeling was short lived. Suddenly the door was smashed open and a group of military looking men entered the room flanked by barking canines.

"Time to move," shouted one of the men and forcefully removed Tenashi from his cell as one of the canines tried to take a bite of him. They pushed him down the corridor past other cells that Tenashi could see and opened the door at the far end pushing him into a smaller cell. One of the military men tore off the rags that had become his attire for the entire time and at the far end of the room there appeared a sealed door when there was suddenly a high pitched warning alarm and the door started to rise slowly up. Tenashi could see what appeared to be a vacant lot strewn with housing debris, burnt out cars, stacked worn tyres and burning oil drums. Was this to be his freedom, Tenashi thought? And yet, nothing could be further from the truth as he walked out into the open area. He looked left and right and saw that there were other doors opening up and equally beaten men standing naked slowly entering the area.

The first bullet whizzed past him like a silent train. He moved into a state of flight trying to crouch behind whatever kind of cover he could find along with the other hundred or so people. It became preverbal musical chairs of sorts as those who did not find cover were indiscriminately shot dead. Once they were tagged by a bullet and knocked to the ground whatever that was firing upon them finished them with a targeted volley of quick fire shots. One man who dared to peak over the hood of the car they were hiding behind was shot straight through the head. His remains spilled uncontrollably onto Tenashi who was completely horrified and without thinking stood up. It was lucky that the next bullet was off target and Tenashi managed to crawl behind a burning oil drum before another barrage came toward him.

When the gun fire stopped Tenashi peaked around the oil drum. From his position he was in the middle of the area and could see large tubes being thrown over the high cement walls from the other end that bounced along until one exploded. Tenashi recognised that they must have been grenades and noticed that many more were being hurled into the area exploding in a wave toward their position. The other men were pinned down behind their cover and Tenashi decided that he would make a run for where the grenades had already exploded. He moved fast with his eyes closed; however, he tripped landing face first sliding underneath a small cavity in the ground covered by broken bricks. When the first shockwave came through he felt all the air in his lungs being ripped out from inside him and he struggled to fill them again. When he opened his eyes, he saw the spot where the other men were taking cover and the vehicle exploded scattering the men around it like nine pins. None survived.

Tenashi then had crawled with his face to the ground finally making it to the far wall where he found another door. Tenashi tried the door handle and found that it opened to a small room filled with razor wire scattered on the floor which Tenashi assumed was more appealing than the area behind him. Slowly and painfully he moved through the razor wire. At one point he misplaced his footing and landed heavily on the wire which sliced the bottom of his feet like butter. A warm pool of blood on his foot made it difficult to manoeuvre; however, he eventually made it to the other end of the room where another alarm sounded and the door opened into an adjoining corridor.

The corridor was dark and its walls were covered in mould. A single light at the end drew Tenashi toward it and as he got closer he saw that lying on the floor was a hand gun. Tenashi himself had never handled a firearm before and it felt cold. He could not tell if it was heavy from weight or the burden of what could be done which such a device. He briefly contemplated taking his own life with the weapon before anyone else could. If what had transpired previously was any indication on what would be behind the next door then surely it would be a decision that he would not regret.

His train of thought was again broken as an alarm sounded and the door slowly slid across revealing a room with a glass panel in front of it. There was a small hole as large as a man's fist that was drilled in the centre and behind the glass was his friend, Amatsu, hanging in chains sporting a placard reading, 'Kill me and it ends!'.

Tenashi was quick to understand what needed to be done. He did not want to kill a man, he didn't know how; even though, he held the means to write his own destiny. If he could only conjure enough courage to kill another human being what seemed to be a nightmare would be over. But, Amatsu was his friend. They had only had each other their entire lives. Without Amatsu, Tenashi did not know what would become of him and after all it was wrong to kill another man regardless of the circumstances.

As he was standing contemplating his next move a door opened behind him and out stepped his tormentor with the gold tooth. He smiled confidently walking toward him and the sudden urge fell over Tenashi to raise the gun toward the man.

"You will kill me but you will not kill someone that has used you your entire life!" said the tormentor.

"You know nothing about me!" replied Tenashi.

"Oh, I disagree. We know what we need to know. Your friend here told us how it was your idea to take the girl. He begged for his own life and gave up yours to save his own neck. What kind of friend is that?"

"I don't believe you!"

"It is sad the lengths a man will go to when his own mortality is in question. These are things I know."

"How can you know? You just beat people and don't tell them why."

"Well, there is always a reason. I beat you not to punish you but to release you."

"Release me. Release me from what?"

"From the safety of your life, from the confines of drugs and into a position where you can control your own destiny."

"My destiny! There is no destiny when you ask me to kill an un-armed man. There is only murder."

"At this point you are the only one that is armed, my friend. You have a choice. Kill me and you can leave this place through the next door and go off into the jungle; however, you will be hunted and always running in fear. Or, kill your so called friend and we will teach you to become a warrior never to be controlled by anyone ever again."

The weapon in Tenashi's hand was now scalding hot; however, he gripped it tighter. Tenashi never wanted to kill a man. He only ever wanted to live without poverty, without the fear of not knowing when his next meal would be coming, whether he would have shelter over his head. He wanted to laugh with friends and be in love with a girl. But these things in Tenashi's world were not available to him. He was born poor and thus a slave to be utilised by anyone who cared to profit from his misfortune. And yet, he could not justify killing his own friend in his heart. If he killed the tormentor then he could easily justify that to himself as being an act of self defence. But a friend who he knew every-thing about, his hopes and dreams, his fears and loves was something else all together. This was a life he would mourn.

"Take the decision you know to be true," said the tormentor,

"Become a man that grows above the poverty and into the world as a hero."

"No, I cannot."

"Then you choose to be a mouse. A fearful scavenger living off scraps from the wealthy!"

"I am my own man!"

"Then pull the trigger, Tenashi. Kill him and it ends or you die a worthless ant carcass, forgotten, unknown to anyone but your own stupid self and this rodent you call a friend...Kill him!"

Tenashi could not recall what he was thinking when he unloaded the clip of the pistol through the hole in the glass and into the helpless Amatsu. Tears flowed freely and his vision was contorted into a reddish hue from the blood splattering on the walls. He kept pulling the trigger until there were no more bullets and his legs fell from under him resting on the ground where his muscles, aching with the emotion, were unable to function.

He recalled the tormentor patting him on the head and grunting in laughter, "The first step to becoming a warrior is getting over the emotional attachment of life. One's first kill is always the hardest. In the past, warriors from around the globe felt empathy for their enemy and could not kill them despite having not known who they were, not even their name. But now, we have learnt that a man that can kill his friend can kill anyone."

Tenashi's muscles suddenly conjured enough energy to whip the pistol around at the tormentor and he pulled wildly at the trigger. The weapon was of course empty, the chamber echoed in defeat as he finally let go his grip and gave way to exhaustion and blacked out under the muffled laughter of the tormentor. Tenashi's final thought was that he had not only killed a man - he had killed his only friend.

PART II

Chapter 4

It was in the twilight hours of the day when Harry Lockley wiped the sweat from his brow. He had been hard at it all day fencing a paddock; but, there were only a few more meters to go before he would call it a day. A truck driver had passed out at the wheel, veered off the highway and proceeded to tear off three hundred meters of the fencing that was herding his cattle. Luckily no-one was injured, the load remained on the trailer; but, his fence was squashed flat and curled all through the eighteen wheels of the semi-trailer. Lockley had received a call around five in the morning from the local police as the cattle were moving dangerously to the highway and grazing on the lush grass beside the black top.

It had taken him the first two hours rounding up the herd into another paddock before he could fully assess the extent of the damage. He was astonished at where the truck had come to a stop. It was a straight patch of highway popular with local youths for their fast cars; but, it wasn't the first time an accident had been here and torn down a fence. The only thing stopping the momentum of the truck would have been the thin wire and rotting posts which had been a mere feather trying to hold back a fully loaded truck. But, Lockley had worked through the day and it was almost complete as he had enlisted the help of his neighbours, who had owed him a few favours; but, he'd let them go home an hour ago as he could finish the rest off himself.

Lockley wondered whether or not he would see the insurance money the driver had assured him would come through. Lockley held his doubts. Every second day, some kid with a brief case would haul his shiny sedan up the dusty three mile track that was his driveway to his home and try to convince him on the potential of bad days ahead. But, how could any one company really insure against the unpredictability of the land? He'd yet to see an insurance policy that didn't have the words, 'excludes', or, 'does not cover' in them. The only true insurance policy that would work for his situation would be one that said, 'we cover everything, no exclusions'. Because, that was the reality of working life on the land in the Australian bush where everything and anything happened.

Lockley twisted a clamp on the wire and reached for the water bottle. It was still cool from the cooler that his wife, Mabel, had brought down and he was thankful for her thoughtfulness. As he tilted his head back, he caught a glimpse of something from the corner of his eye. He lowered the bottle from his lips and listened to the wind. A car roared by on its way through. The sound lingering until it passed the rise. He could see its headlights in the distance and momentarily he found it difficult to focus in the low light. He blinked until he could form shapes against the clear night sky with the quarter moon casting a ghostly ambience across the plain.

He often found himself alone on nights like this looking at the stars. They were an enigma to Lockley, a formidable entity, holding onto their pattern of movement as they slowly arced across the sky. He'd seen many things out of the ordinary in the sky at night. Some things he could explain, others he couldn't. He'd grown accustomed to how the sky looked at night and the position of stars and how cloud formations would sweep through the hills and down into his land. He'd learned how planes silhouetted in the night sky and how a helicopter descended beyond the horizon. But when he saw what came at that moment from the corner of his eye he felt nothing but the unknown.

It reminded him of a time when he was younger as he and few of his buddies were returning from the river where they were swimming. They were following the train tracks home and they had decided to cross the train bridge instead of walking around to where the highway cut over the river. There was something that Lockley sensed that day that told them not to cross the train bridge; and yet, two of his buddies decided they'd risk it. They didn't have a chance as the goods train coming from the coal mines came hurtling at top speed around the bend onto its only path, the bridge. The only thing his buddies could do was jump from thirty feet and hope that the river below would break their fall. One missed the river and rolled in agony on the grassy bank with a broken leg. The other managed to make it to the water; however, the shallowness of the water made him fall awkwardly and it was the last step he ever took.

And here now, Lockley sensed something coming again.

There was a moment of complete silence, even the crickets were held in a refrain as several low flying objects the size of a bus skimmed over head. They kept coming in waves of four, one after the other as Lockley stood there astonished, paralysed by fear. He couldn't quite make out their shape; however, they weren't shaped like any conventional flying machine he had seen and at speeds that he was certain could not be achieved by any modern airplane. What was most astonishing to Lockley was how quiet these things were. Moving at those speeds, Lockley thought, would require a pretty hefty engine to propel something at that magnitude. But there was nothing. The only thing he could discern from his stationary position was that the wind resistance lasted a whole half second as these machines sped by.

And then on cue, after the last of them moved by, the crickets returned to the chorus and a wide eyed Lockley already making as fast as he could for his pick-up truck. His tools and the remaining fence posts discarded, the fence forgotten and Lockley thinking to himself, not again.

Chapter 5

Harvey Amsterdam strolled slowly around the casino floor. He had canvassed the room in his usual way first perusing the slots where an elderly lady clapped and cheered from one of the machines. He had then moved onto the Black Jack tables and watched for a time as two men of Asian descent lost hand after hand and the dealer raked in practically all of their chips. Watching as they lost gave Amsterdam the innate belief that he could fight the urge that prevailed inside – that if they were losing then surely someone would be granted the privilege of winning. It didn't make sense that everyone would lose as the casino wouldn't allow such an aura of negativity to spiral out of control and give the impression that they were there only to take your money. So, maybe it was his turn, for once. After all, if there was only losing, then what would lure the masses.

But, these were the thoughts of the old Amsterdam. He had managed to curve the addiction that once had promised to take everything away. His entire life had been transformed from one of happiness with his wife, Ginger, and their two children, Rachel and Nathaniel, to one of absolute distress caused entirely by him and the addiction. He very nearly lost it all until he found the courage to seek help and counselling which gave him hope that one day he could change his ways and make good on the life he had promised for his family.

One of the techniques Amsterdam had found worked most of all was to walk around the casino and look at the people and their faces. There were the drones of the slot machines; expressionless and dazzled at the same time that appeared to be caught in a loop of routine like a factory worker on the production line. There were the card goons and barons who gave off a sleazy air of resentment in the dealer and other players on their table; cautiously eyeing the motives of those around them like paranoid schizophrenics in an asylum ward. And, not forgetting, the roulette and craps players who were an ever excitable bunch caught in a collective trance like some religious cult calling to the heavens. It was then that Amsterdam would reach for his wallet and open it to a photo of his family. It was taken three years prior at Christmas time when Rachel and Nathaniel were about to become teenagers and they still had that look of innocence in their eyes that said maybe Santa was real after all. He looked at his wife, Ginger, and how her eyes sparkled as she held their two children in her arms. It was one of the best times of his life and comparing that with the drones, goons & cultists of the casino there was no question where he would rather be.

It was stress that had been the prime cause of his addiction and he had found gambling relieved the pressures of his life. It allowed Amsterdam to escape into a world where it was only himself versus chance, albeit for a brief moment; that, in the end, became more and more alluring a proposition than facing reality. It took some time to understand what it was that was causing Amsterdam to experience this heightened state of stress. At first he had thought that it had been the pressures of family life such as the mortgage, bills and his children's education which had caused him to seek refuge. He had assumed this because he often found himself drawn to the casino after his working day when he had the choice of coming home or taking a punt. The theory was broken when he was on a family vacation and had found that he didn't have the urge to want to gamble at all. Amsterdam then understood that the stress had primarily surfaced due to his work as a journalist for *The Gazette*. It had made sense given his responsibility as the senior journalist on the staff and the high requirement he had been given to provide compelling copy that sold newspapers.

While the connection was obvious now, Amsterdam had not considered the possibility at the time as being a journalist was all that he had ever wanted to be and had found contentment in pouring over a deadline, discovering a lead or exposing a crook authority figure. He had spent time in practically all the departments; however, discovered his main passion was in writing feature articles that provided the opportunity to flesh out a story in full. The problem was that feature articles were increasingly hard to come by and the Internet had made his job even harder again as the real-time news cycle had taken over providing endless breaking news coverage which didn't leave much scope for feature articles. However, this time, Amsterdam had the scoop and he had spent the last three months investigating the story that would put his career on the historical map. It was a story like no other and one that even Amsterdam had difficulty comprehending. Unfortunately, the editor of *The Gazette*, Roger Evans, had not seen it that way nor had senior management or the board, he was informed; and, Amsterdam had taken the news very badly indeed. He found no other solace that could prevent him from descending into a pitiful sense of dejection; so, he escaped to the casino if only to remind himself of the place that he didn't want to be.

Satisfied that his fix of renewed hope had changed his perspective he decided to head on home. As he was walking out he noticed that the elderly lady who had won previously had vacated the machine and Amsterdam thought to himself, 'what the hell one more try for old time sake, I've earned it,' and he jammed in a dollar that had been floating in his pocket into the slot and tapped on the screen randomly. Much to his surprise, he had a win. As the credit title on the screen counted up to the desired amount Amsterdam could feel a sense of overwhelming clarity: if he could take the chance now on a slot machine what could he achieve with one more try with Evans? Who knew what it could lead to? For old time sake, he had to be reasonable; after all, the story was quite compelling and Evans had said so himself. Amsterdam couldn't understand what was holding him back and decided then and there that he would make his way back to the office and confront Evans on the issue. He would be there for sure, even at this late hour, a fitting testimony to his work ethic being the first there in the morning and the last to leave at night once the presses started rolling.

Amsterdam cashed out and left for good this time. He had a vision perfectly in his head of how the conversation would play out with Evans: there would be a heated discussion and condemnation on the way each other worked; Evans would say that his hands were tied, that he didn't have the authority to overrule the editorial direction of the board; Amsterdam would throw around the possibility of leaving for *The Post* or *The Herald* (Evans understood that approaches had been made) and then Evans would compromise on a deal to keep them both happy. The image was very clear to Amsterdam; but, the reality was that he had never been in disagreement with Evans and they had mainly seen eye-to-eye on most decisions throughout both of their tenure at *The Gazette*.

In the cab on the way back to the office which was on the other side of the city, Amsterdam had noticed how cold the city streets seemed at night and how quiet and hollow they seemed without the teeming individuals that swallowed it up during business hours. He looked at all the windows holding objects that gave their owners wealth and was intrigued with the thought that those items were some persons way of life; providing them food, water and shelter. He felt that he may have had the beginnings of a story there. He even thought of the title, 'Wealth, possessions and the great divide', where it went from there was anyone's guess; but, this was the beauty of working as a journalist that he adored so much. And, quite often, the stories themselves came to you; but, sometimes, there was not much to write about and a good journalist had to keep a scrapbook of ideas to fill in the gaps between big and slow news days. Amsterdam's own pile had collated into at least a dozen exercise books and now this one would also make the grade graduating from a mere thought to words on a page.

As he passed through the security checkpoint of *The Gazette* building the security guard, Mike, gave him a smile. Mike, who was a portly fellow, wore a blue uniform and dark blue tie with a badge on the left shoulder in the shape of a police shield which said, 'Security Saints' and he also sported a beard and thick rimmed glasses.

"Got another deadline to meet, Mr. Amsterdam?" said Mike as he checked in his security credentials.

"No, but maybe a date with destiny, all things being equal. Is the boss still in?" replied Amsterdam.

"Does he ever leave? I didn't notice?" answered Mike with a wry smile as he handed back Amsterdam's security card and he headed toward the elevators.

While the design of the building on the outside had aged significantly and was in dire need of an upgrade, the inside was somewhat modern and had been recently refitted to catch up with the new digital age. The foyer itself was a testament to modernity with flashy vertical screens extending the length from floor to ceiling highlighting the top stories of the day down a corridor which led to the elevators. The floor itself, a highly polished black marble reflected the image of the screens in reverse designed to give the impression of a printing press in the years gone by. At the end of the corridor was the office of their Chief Executive Officer at a somewhat strange position; however, Amsterdam had never seen him or his assistants grace the floor with their presence.

As he clicked the button to go up the elevator his phone began to ring in his pocket. He took it out scrunching up his brow as the number read 'Blocked' on the caller ID. One thing he knew as a journalist was never to be too hasty to dismiss the opportunity of a story. This meant that he had to deal with all types of people, some that most would not bother to provide the time of day for; but, he made sure to keep an objective frame of mind as everyone had a story, no matter how ridiculous and it was his job to filter out the good from the print worthy.

"Amsterdam?" he said answering the phone.

"Harvey, this is Arch." Archibald Worthington was the lead source of his story that he was about to lay his career on the line for with Evans. This type of call at the eleventh hour usually meant that the source usually had cold feet and wanted out of the arrangement. Arch was an Officer in the Royal Australian Air Force for over twenty years and commanded the central air traffic control unit for the military in Canberra called the 'Birdcage'. It was from the Birdcage that Amsterdam had learned that all air traffic was controlled and had the powers to override any domestic or international flights as well as keeping tabs on the skies all over the planet. However, it wasn't the level of power that the Birdcage welded which was the story they were trying to expose.

"Arch, this is not a secure line."

"I know. I just couldn't wait. I thought that maybe you could help get the word out. It may be a lost cause but I thought I would risk it anyway."

"I'll do what I can, Arch. What have you got?"

"We've been dismissed, Harvey. My entire unit has been dismissed from duty without any explanation. We were given our orders at thirteen-hundred to stand down from our posts and remain in our barracks until further instructions were provided. "

"What? That can't be. They shut down the Birdcage?"

"That's the thing, Harvey. It's not just the Birdcage. I mean, it appears that a defence wide stand down order has been issued."

"Defence wide? Can they even issue such a thing?"

"Apparently so, several of the officers and I decided to go ask some questions and found that our superiors were nowhere to be found. We got word from the ground-crew at the Griffin Air Force Base that an unmarked 747 flew in around thirty minutes ago and loaded senior political ministers and military staff. The Prime Minister then came in his pyjamas and they took off a short time later. But, right now, the entire nation is defenceless and the hierarchy has flown the coup."

As the elevator opened Amsterdam was finding it difficult to comprehend what it was he was hearing. From what Arch was describing, the story that they had been trying to expose was rolling out in front of their very eyes.

"Arch, what do you make of it?"

"Looks an awful lot like K29K to me."

"It's as we feared then."

"Unfortunately, I'm inclined to agree. Harvey, are you a god-faring man?"

"Never had time for religion, Arch."

"Me neither. But, somehow, I wish I did."

With that Arch closed the line and Amsterdam entered the elevator. Surely, Evans had to listen now.

Chapter 6

When Tenashi woke he was in clean clothes. His wounds were all but gone and he could only recall snippets of memory from what had transpired. He managed to see a doctor's chart hanging beside his bed and counted the dates where the nurse had initialled her rounds. He counted forty-nine dates. Had it been that long? Tenashi's only visitor for the day was the tormentor which he recognised instantly. There was a sudden moment of realisation from Tenashi of what it was he had dodged and the memory came flooding back, a memory of horror, that he had killed his only friend.

"Good," said the tormentor from the end of the bed, "I can see from your eyes that you are remembering your first kill. Your life has changed forever. You will kill many men, women and perhaps children but you will always remember your first. Every time you take the life of another you will always see his face and you will want nothing more than to kill again."

Tenashi did not answer him. He would not look at him for many weeks while he fully recovered from his ordeal. Tenashi could not bear the thought of gratifying the tormentor by listening to one of his many speeches at his bed side. The tormentor would talk about victory as if it were the only thing worth living for; however, failed to tell Tenashi exactly who their enemy was.

His last words from the tormentor were something that he would never forget. He leaned in close to Tenashi's ear, "Do not search for God. He has forgotten you. But you will hunt God. In every kill you will be just that one step closer to be called to His stage and there you will have your revenge. There you will battle for His will and only by defeating God himself will you be able to be free from the anguish that you will face. It is a day that you will learn to look forward to. Every morning you will wake praying that it be your last and that every kill is in preparation for what you want most. No man knows just how many men one needs to kill to have this honour. It could be hundreds, thousands, even tens of thousands before your turn is up. You will know when you are ready Tenashi. A time will come when clarity of your destiny will overwhelm you and you will see nothing but the anticipation of your own demise."

The role of the tormentor in Tenashi's life had seemingly ended. The next group of military men were less philosophical and proceeded to besiege Tenashi with a wealth of knowledge. Everything from hand-to-hand combat to complicated assassination techniques and weapons. It was a flurry of death where anyone less prepared to accept the ideas that were presented to him would have found them grotesque. And yet, Tenashi held his own as every day he grew stronger and more proficient in dealing death blows and becoming the complete warrior he was promised. Throughout his training Tenashi did not have the thought to ask questions of his captors. He did not think to ask who it was he was fighting for or with or even who it was his enemies were. Every day was a continuation of the next directed by the fatigue wearing men whose stern voices commanded his every move.

However, they did not take all of his thoughts like most of the men who were also in training with Tenashi. Most of these men were zombie like and did not communicate with anyone even when they were allocated free time of which they devoted themselves to more physical strength training or meditation. Tenashi had adopted the latter to fit in with the group and concentrated his thoughts on the tormentor. He had decided that every man, woman or child that he killed would be in search of the day where he would again confront his tormentor. On this day he would take the tormentor's life and then his own and together they would go to war in death against the God that had brought them into the world of such destitution and sorrow. He played the event over and over in his mind as the days past and his training had come to an end.

At their graduation speech, a General of whom Tenashi did not know spoke of the coming days of dominance and power. He spoke of the day where the superiority of the East would rule the world and that all races and cultures would bow to the will of the United Federation of Asia. The General told them that they were all crucial to the plan which had been decades in the making and would serve in a war to end all wars. The General served Tenashi's first orders strangely enough as an order to stand down. That they would be marched to a facility deep in the hills of the Himalayas where they would wait in a state of suspended animation ready to be used when the time came. With that the ten thousand strong military machine was dismissed and ordered into transport vehicles seating twenty at a time. Luckily, Tenashi received a seat at the end of the vehicle and looked out in awe over the convoy stretching for miles on end as it travelled without impediment through neighbouring countries and entered the foothills of the Himalayas.

The entrance to the facility itself appeared to be nothing of consequence. It was nothing more than a simple Buddhist Monk temple adorned with the usual religious symbols which lead to a road with an entranceway only large enough to fit the vehicle. The entranceway led to a tunnel that quickly descended into the side of the mountain and the men were ordered to put on oxygen masks to combat the exhaust fumes.

Eventually the tunnel opened out into a cavernous landing the size of a football stadium where the transport came to a halt. The men were ordered out and Tenashi being the first out stood and assisted the other men in the transport with their gear. He had a moment to scan his surroundings and looked across to where the other men in the transport were being directed in front of a queue where one man entered what appeared to be a standing coffin shaped device. The door would close in a swift hissing sound and attach itself to a conveyor belt moving the coffin down a tube inside the mountain. The sight would turn any man cold and a flash of anxiety clouded Tenashi momentarily before reason brought him back to reality. Why would they train us to be killers only to end our lives at the end of it all? The notion made no sense at all; however, nothing since all of this started would have made sense to Tenashi's previous life. The moment of truth kicked in when it was Tenashi's turn to enter his coffin. There was a small port hole the size of an Orange on the front with a bar code and serial number: F-E-143-33.

Tenashi, surprisingly without question, accepted the direction of the Officer who was providing instruction on the coffin unit.

"Your number is FE-143-33. What is your number soldier?"

"F-E-143-33, Sir!" Tenashi replied.

"Good, do not forget that number. Now, put your gear in the hold and step into the SAC." On cue, a drawer opened on the bottom of the coffin that fitted perfectly with the dimensions of his baggage. He placed it in the hold as directed and used the drawer to step inside.

The inside of the capsule was padded on each side and Tenashi had difficulty manoeuvring to take a last glimpse back into the cavern as the lid of the coffin sealed shut with that swift hissing sound he had heard earlier. Everything in his training was pointing to the idea that he had to escape this situation. He was simply locked in a cage with no exit and it gave him a feeling of desperation. Should he fire his sidearm through the lid of the coffin and make a break for it? It was a valid question at the time; however, the folly soon decimated as an image of the same General at his graduation appeared on the screen of the port hole and the coffin jolted onto the conveyor belt.

"Soldier F-E-143-33. Here are your orders. Await here in this SAC unit until further advised. We have made preparations for your deployment for a time that is classified and yet will aid in the vision of our ultimate success. That is all."

The image of the General flickered out and was replaced with the image of a smiling woman of substantial beauty. Her face was perfectly proportioned with bright dark eyes and straight teeth.

"My name is Lupei, soldier F-E-143-33. I will be directing you through the features of this Suspended Animation Capsule or what is commonly referred to as SAC. The SAC is designed to keep you perfectly sustained both physically and mentally while your deployment is being determined by your superiors. I will be monitoring your life signs constantly and reporting updates frequently to central command. When your orders are activated you will be released from this suspended state instantly retaining your current age and body mass. The facility has the capability to house tens of millions of SAC's and can sustain life in suspended animation indefinitely."

A thought suddenly fell on Tenashi that he could be in this state for thousands of years. What would the world be like then? What would humanity become?

"I am detecting a level of anxiety soldier F-E-143-33. Do you require me to administer a relaxing stimulant while we complete the suspension procedure?"

"Ah, no." Tenashi lied. He could kill for a gungy hit right about now but felt the need to keep control of his faculties.

"Fine. I understand that there may be some reservation about the procedure that will soon be performed. Your superiors have been testing and perfecting this procedure since the end of World War Two and have now come to a stage where life is perfectly preserved inside the SAC. You will not dream or be hampered by the needs of your bodily functions."

With this Tenashi felt the SAC slip from the conveyor belt and slide into position. He could hear a mechanical noise that must have resulted in a clamp holding the SAC in place as a definitive click eerily ending Tenashi's ascension from squaller rat to a warrior. He could barely look outside of the port hole and he strained to see in his field of vision there was another SAC that must have been stacked beside his and could only make out the serial number F-E-143-32. A sudden flash of light filled the port hole of SAC F-E-143-32 which gave Tenashi a fright pushing forward the need for him to concentrate his energies to meditate on the path he had been and the path that would one day lead him to his tormentor. However, his time was not long enough as the voice of SAC, Lupei, suddenly began to countdown to the final stages.

"Okay, soldier F-E-143-33. Preparations are ready for Suspended Animation in 5-"

"Wait!" Pleaded Tenashi.

"4...3...2...1"

A flash consumed Tenashi eyes and then nothing.

...and then a man of African descent and a muffled voice say, 'So this is where The Oracle led me. I will help you overcome your tormentor, soldier. If you will help me overcome mine. There is a moment in time someday soon that will turn the night sky red. Find me after then and I will grant you your wish.'

...and then another flash and Tenashi was gulping for air.

A sound beeped inside the capsule and the image of Lupei blurred into Tenashi's vision as he blinked reactively to focus.

"Welcome back soldier F-E-143-33. Please wait while I conduct preliminary scans on all of your vital signs."

"What happened? Where am I?" asked Tenashi as he flexed his muscles, fingers and toes but found they were moving without pain.

"Authorisation denied," replied Lupei, "Information classified. There, your vital signs are all reading to normal levels as expected prior to suspended animation. Stand-by to receive orders."

Lupei's image flickered out and was replaced again by the General as Tenashi could feel the SAC move forward.

"Soldier F-E-143-33 you have been activated under guide lines specified under the United Federation of Asia code Long March and will move to immediate deployment under the command of General Marshall Huwei of the 34th Field Battalion."

The General's image flickered and was replaced by another military man.

"Thank you Master General Marshall Jao. Soldier F-E-143-33 I am General Marshall Huwei of the 344th Field Battalion. We have been established as a forward post heading up key invasion points for the Long March. You will be equipped with the IA5 combat unit which has been designed to protect you from many forms of enemy assault. Communication and weaponry will be provided as per mission details. Your first contact from suspended animation will guide you through the necessary requirements of the IA5. Once you are armed further instructions will be delivered. That is all."

Tenashi could feel the SAC move at a rapid pace; however, could not see anything but another SAC in front of him to get any sort of bearing. He looked at the back of his hands but could not detect any signs of ageing. He ran his hands through his hair and it was still as thick as it had always been; however, nothing would answer the burning question he had on how many years had he been in this state.

"Lupei?" he asked. Her face appeared again in the porthole.

"Yes, soldier F-E-143-33"

"How many years have I been here?"

"Information classified," she replied.

It was an answer he half expected to receive; however, it was enough to focus himself. Whatever the reason he was brought back to do a job and no matter the year people still needed to be killed.

"...the first kill is always the hardest..." the Tormentor's words coming back to him in a frenzy of rage. And then he was ready.

Lupei announced, "Stand by for deployment in 5, 4, 3, 2, 1."

The SAC doors hissed open and Tenashi stepped out and was greeted by an Officer.

"Attention!" he yelled and Tenashi dutifully responded.

"State your identification soldier."

"Soldier F-E-143-33, Sir."

"Soldier welcome to the Long March. Hunt and destroy. Kill without prejudice. Make your way down the red line to check point one."

Tenashi moved without further instruction down the path as directed by a red line. He hadn't had the time to even look where he was or gather any kind of bearing on his environment and he felt his body move along with the order of following the red line without a hint of question. It was only once he reached the end of the line where a queue of soldiers standing on the red line had formed that he even thought of taking his focus from the job at hand. And even then the surrounds made little sense. It was a hangar of some description. He could see behind the line of soldiers what looked like to be some kind of ship. It had a cabin at the front with a line of glass that you could see through but the shape of the ship looked like an upside down yacht.

The line itself moved swiftly and in no time Tenashi was confronted by another Office.

"Identification soldier?"

"F-E-143-33," replied Tenashi.

"You take the yellow line now and meet up at rally point F."

"Yellow line and rally point F."

Tenashi looked down and saw the line the officer was pointing at. It ran underneath the ship he was observing earlier and he made as quickly as he could with his head down until the yellow line ended and yet another Officer stood to offer direction at a ramp leading into the ship.

"Orders?" asked the Officer.

"Follow the yellow line to rally point F, Sir."

"Identification?"

"F-E-143-33., Sir."

"Head on up soldier."

Tenashi obeyed and walked up the ramp. In the sides of the ship stood what he could only describe as large metallic humanoid robots. They were human in shape with limbs similar to his own and a head which was covered with some kind of helmet. They lined both sides of the ship ten to a side with one standing in the middle.

An officer stood up at the top of the landing holding an object with a screen attached to an extended pipe. At the end of the pipe flashed a light and the officer held it up to Tenashi's eyes. It beeped and the Officer brought it down to his side.

"Soldier F-E-143-33 on the left side of the vehicle and stand in front of the second IA5 from the front."

As he got closer to the mechanism he could tell it was grey in colour. The height it stood was taller than an average man at around seven feet at a guess. Tenashi had found it odd that it was without markings or codes to identify it. He had discovered that the military was fond of the way its ordered regime was managed down to the finest detail. There were no markings of rank or symbols to define the platoon or squad that it belonged to of any kind. Indeed, the only thing that Tenashi could see was a small horizontal bar code on its left arm.

He stood at ease and looked toward the centre of the ship where the sole IA5 stood at the front. The ship slowly filled to capacity as one by one another soldier entered and stood in front of their respective IA5. There was no discussion by the soldiers who looked straight forward not making eye contact with the other. There was just a steely gaze forward waiting for a superior voice to command their next move.

Thankfully, this would not be too long to wait. A burly looking Lieutenant marched in with authority and made a line for the IA5 in the middle of the ship.

"Attention!" the Lieutenant ordered, "I am only going to tell you this once and once only so listen up. Behind you is the IA5 combat unit which will be deployed in this mission. As all of you would not be familiar with this unit I will detail the necessary operations. Point one is that once you are in the unit it is designed so that you cannot exit the unit. Bodily functions are catered to internally so you will eat, shit, piss, and sleep all without the need to remove the unit. Take a good look around boys and girls this will be the last time your body is exposed to the elements of nature. The greatest advantage of the human condition is also its weakest. This is no more. To enter stand and face your IA5 unit."

Tenashi and the rest of the squad did just that.

"Announce your soldier number and seek permission to come aboard."

Simultaneously, the squad responded as well as Tenashi, "Soldier F-E-143-33 permission to come aboard."

Suddenly, the docking station of the IA5 whirred into life. Its arms like tentacles on an octopus opened up the body of the IA5 revealing a cavity humanoid in shape.

"Step on to the unit right foot then left foot. Spin your body around using your hand to guide yourself in and rest your back down as you would sit on a chair. Position your arms and legs in the holders."

As Tenashi did so the tentacles of the docking station whirred into life again replacing the coverings in position over his legs arms and body. He let the weight of his body be taken by the suit which then relieved the pressure he was feeling as he was dangling their like a star fish.

"I won't lie to you. This next part is going to tingle."

Suddenly, Tenashi felt the wind being sucked out from his lungs and he heard a scream from the other side of the ship. He could not tell completely but suddenly his legs and arms went cold and then he felt a flash of heat at his shoulders and groins. And then the docking station whirred again and his legs and arms were removed from their positions on his body.

The soldiers in the ship were a picture of shock as all their limbs were removed. People began screaming in fear whirling around their heads in the body of the IA5 distraught at what had just happened. Tenashi could not breathe overwhelmed with emotion. And yet, there was no pain nor were there pools of blood dripping under his hanging body where one would expect to see such things. The Lieutenant himself was calm. His eyes were closed until the screaming subsided and he again began to speak.

"The IA5 is fitted with the latest exoskeleton technology. Your arms and legs made with skin and bone are vulnerable and will be replaced with indestructible metals and robotic functions that are linked to the motor functions in your brain. You will be stronger, faster, and more aerobic than you could ever be with muscle and cartilage."

The docking station whirred again and Tenashi could not help but think that his neck was next to be removed from his body. Surely, the internal operating system that was his heart, lungs, liver, kidneys, stomach and intestines were more vulnerable to decease and wounds. The experience was starting to become a slaughter house of Hollywood proportions; however, Tenashi accepted the situation and focused on the benefits. Tenashi himself was not a big man. Nor, did his body react well under excruciating physical activity. No matter how hard he tried his muscle mass remained the same leading to intimidation from other men much larger and more powerful than he. Now, he would be on an equal playing field.

As the fear subsided he saw the robotic limbs being placed into position onto his torso. A couple of quick electrodes zapped at his shoulders and groin and an immense flow of energy stretched through his torso. He felt a slight twinge and from the corner of his eye could see the robotic digits of his hand start to twitch. Tenashi concentrated harder on the end of the finger tips and closed his hand making a fist. And in that instant his hands and legs were back again. His mind blocking out the distress of dismemberment had renewed strength and dexterity.

"Now you are all over the initial shock of the procedure we are now moving into the critical body functions. That's all your insides for you jug heads out there. There's going to be little robots slicing you up inside the torso attaching your organs to all kinds of electronic wizardry. So suck it up soldiers and ride the pain." The Lieutenants face squeezed like he was constipated as he held his breath.

Tenashi didn't get it initially. Then he felt movement on his body like a pair of monkeys fighting with each other. What was really happening below was a surgical master piece. The quick sharp pangs Tenashi interpreted as monkey nails scratching him were in fact quick jabs of strategically positioned needles filled with local anaesthetic.

After that he didn't feel a thing really. He could sense movement like kneading bread dough and in some instances he was gasping for breath as his lungs were repositioned; but, all in all, he blocked the pain out by concentrating on his enemy, the tormentor. He remembered those gold teeth and the arrogant look in his eyes. He thought about the way he moved looking for weaknesses as he was sure they would meet in a bloody hand-to-hand combat death match.

As Tenashi's mind drifted he felt comfortable enough again to look around at the other soldiers. Clearly, this was an experience dealt with at an individual level much in the way that one deals with ones on death in their own way. It was then that the lights changed to fill the room with a red colour and Tenashi could feel the ship move. He looked toward the front where the pilot was and saw from the window that the ship was turning around. But not like any airplane he had seen before. This seemed to turn on its axis on a full one hundred and eighty degrees. A slight rush of momentum and then they were off.

The bright light of the fading sun filled the room from the pilot's cabin and Tenashi was relieved to think that it still existed. He still did not know how long it had been since his own eyes had seen the sun light but it rejuvenated him in warmth. He managed to catch a glimpse of the hangar they left and was astonished to find that they weren't in the Himalaya's anymore. In fact, he couldn't see any land mass at all. What he saw was nothing short of amazing as a giant ship seemingly floated in the air.

"That wasn't so bad now, was it?" announced the Lieutenant, the question was of course rhetorical, "The procedure that was just performed on you ensures that your body will never be burdened by the inadequacies of common man. You have made yourself into a being of evolution right before your very eyes. What nature took billions of years to accomplish you have achieved to transform into a super human in a few measly seconds. The mind is evolution people. Once trapped inside an animal you are now free to accomplish absolute greatness. Now, your organs will be housed in this torso plate individually separated so that one critical hit will not kill you instantly like before. Not that much will be able to penetrate through the outer shell that is. The IA5 is designed to withstand blasts from any standard explosive. While you won't survive a nuclear explosion you'll survive the fallout as it is rated to withstand all forms of radiation. Take a good look behind me people; this will be your last look at the sunlight. Once the helmet is in place the connection is liquefied and becomes a seamless entity. This means that it is stronger and more flexible to react to the natural movements of your body that your mind is familiar with. The down side is that it cannot be removed as it will connect to sensors on your brain controlling the life support functions of the IA5. This final step will involve the mind turning itself off for a time. The dramatic trauma that you will experience, while not fatal, is not something a sane person can withstand. I know what most of you must be thinking, why didn't they just do that in the first place? In the early stages of the IA program we discovered that the human mind took many months of recovery when it awoke anew as it were. It had difficulty synchronising with the IA unit and terminated the test case out of sheer unwillingness to accept the new being it had become. As it turned out, the mind can only accept what it knows as truth."

There was a final whir of the docking station and Tenashi looked at the mask that would keep him hidden from the outside world. It fell into place on his shoulders and for a brief moment there was darkness. He felt something wrap around the back of his head and around his eye line. He was relieved when the familiar face of Lupei appeared smiling on what could only be described as a screen and behind her face he could see everything inside the ship in a new light.

"Hello, soldier F-E-143-33. Your final transition will be complete in 5, 4, 3, 2, 1..."

It was like a lightning bolt. An overwhelming experience like drowning would have felt like as the water consumed your entire body. And then, Tenashi felt something wrap itself around his head building up pressure until he could stand no more and he was gone.

Chapter 7

Roger Evans' office was not what one pictures when they think of the editor of a newspaper. It was neat, orderly even; with a small laptop and simple phone handset. The only personal touch that was provided was a picture of his family sitting on the right hand side of his desk. The walls were bare of accolades or artistry and the whole room could be best described as minimalist in the extreme; and yet, his own chair was an old leather dinosaur that appeared to be circa nineteen-twenties. It was a room that Harvey Amsterdam found himself in often and even more often than not he found himself pleading his case on the reason as to why a story needed to be told; and, today was no exception. The crux of this story was that there existed an evacuation procedure known internally by the government and military as K29K; whose sole purpose for existing was to ensure that the heads of government and military were provided an avenue of escape in the so called unlikely event that the borders of the nation were breached by an unstoppable force. An evacuation that Amsterdam had just been informed was enacted only a few hours before.

"Harvey, it's late. The presses are running and I'm going."

"Roger, this is important. That story I want to run. We have to get it out there as soon as possible."

"I've made up my mind on that, Harvey. There's no point in wasting your breath anymore. Unless, like we said, you are prepared to give up your sources, we can't even entertain the possibility of running an attack on that magnitude. You know the rules as well as anyone for crying out loud."

"This one is different, Roger. You've got to trust me on this. If I could, you know that I would reveal all, I always have in the past, but it's too hot for exposure."

Evans took a sigh and fell back into his leather chair reaching for a piece of paper from his briefcase which he held up and began to read aloud.

"The Gazette has learned from its source within the Royal Australian Air Force that the government has recently developed a procedure to evacuate the entire senior government ministry, including high-ranking members of the military, if the threat of invasion is imminent on the borders of Australia. The Gazette, has also learned by its investigations that these allegations have been verified by an inside government official who also proclaims that the evacuation procedure extends not only to the government and military but also to wealthy business tycoons, celebrities and academics who have received significant peer recognition. The government official also indicated that the list of individuals is finite and over the course of time has changed to include the most up to date celebrities, academics and wealthy and that those removed from the list have been advised to keep their knowledge of the existence of the evacuation a secret in the possibility that they be readmitted in time...Should I go on? I mean, Harvey, come on; think about this from our perspective. Are you seriously suggesting that there is a conspiracy to hand pick individuals to save on some kind of Noah's Ark? And the people, people that you have then pointed the finger at are an A-list of the best and brightest in the country. Have you any idea on the size of the law suit that would be hurled our way if we even decided to print an abridged version of this in the funny section? "

"You're forgetting the *why*, Roger."

"Oh, that's right, it gets better; this guy that you call *The Chief* and his merry militia men proclaiming that the military has been preparing for something of great significance. It's always the same with these quacks, Harvey. They proclaim that on such-and-such a date that such-and-such will happen and the world will never be the same. I've heard it all before and this, this is no different. What I'm most disappointed about is that you've been sucked in to this, Harvey. You're one of the most experienced writers out there on my staff and should be able to tell the difference between a scoop and a hoax."

Amsterdam was beginning to sweat with the dressing down he was receiving from his friend and colleague. There was little he could do to defend himself or put the story in any higher regard. The facts were plain and simple and Amsterdam knew it; but, it was impossible to reveal his sources even though it would absolutely without an ounce of doubt confirm the legitimacy of his story.

"It's not a hoax, Roger. In fact, I have reason to believe that the evacuation order has been given. I have just received a call from my source in the Air Force advising that their unit has been ordered to stand down. That the entire defence force has been ordered to stand down, Roger. He also confirmed that the Prime Minister has been flown out of the country."

"Oh, really. The Prime Minister has been flown out of the country. That might be a blessing given his current polling."

"Call it in, Roger, and find out. You always taught me that there is always some truth to any story and it's our duty to be diligent."

Another deep sigh and Roger reached for the phone dialling a number on loudspeaker which started ringing, "You're going to make me regret this, Harvey."

The croaky voice on the other end that picked up seemed to have been awoken from his slumber and immediately launched in to his tormentor.

"Evans, this better be bloody good. I told you that we'd get the scoop on the Prime Minister's office and we did so can't you give me a break already?" The voice was that of Steve Pendelsen, their political correspondent in Canberra.

"Keep your shirt on, Pendelsen," replied Evans, "This is something else. You got the number of that pimple headed advisor to the PM handy?"

"Of course I do. Roger, what's this all about?"

"I've got Amsterdam here saying that the PM has left the country."

"Amsterdam! That clown! Of course that's absolutely preposterous. The PM couldn't get up and move that quickly without anyone knowing about it."

"That's what I thought. But I'd like to have it checked if I can."

"All right, I'll make it my first agenda item in the morning."

Amsterdam interjected, "If I'm right, Steve, then it'll be too late by then."

"Listen, Amsterdam, if you think that I'm going to waste my valuable, but slim, contact list on a hunch then you've got another thing coming!" replied Pendelsen.

"Just get it done, Pendelsen," said Evans, "Make the call now and conference us in."

There was emptiness on the line for a moment and breathing, "All right, Evans," Pendelsen began, "But you better get loose with that cheque book because this kid is savvy and plays a pretty tight game. I can't guarantee that he'll answer."

There was a series of grunts, knocks and what sounded like the microphone on the phone being dragged across a gravel road until there sounded a ringing sound.

"Hello, Stevie boy, that didn't take you long to make a booty call!" The person that answered was a male but the effeminate voice had identified in no uncertain terms how it was Pendelsen was able to get inside the Prime Minister's office.

"Hi, Gerald. No unfortunately my call today is in relation to your good boss, the Prime Minister."

"Oh, that's disappointing, Stevie. I thought that you weren't one of the boring types who only wanted me for my contacts."

"I hope that I can prove that to you a little later, but, I have a question. Where is the Prime Minister now?"

"Come on, is this a trick?"

"Gerald darling, unfortunately not. You see, we have reason to believe that the PM has left the country and I'm sure that something like that wouldn't have left your watchful eye?"

"You are a charmer, Stevie. Of course not. He's sound asleep tucked up in the Lodge where I left him earlier this evening. If anyone needed to move him they would firstly advise me and then I would go get the PM. Unless, of course, there were bombs falling from the sky and I tell you that isn't happening tonight."

"Well thank goodness. You know we often get weird and wonderful tip offs and we do need to check them out from time-to-time. So, no-one has advised of any changes to the PM's schedule?"

"Not a one."

"That's settles it then. Thank you for your time, Gerald. I promise that next time I call will be for something of more tangible quality."

"That's okay, Stevie. Bye now."

There was a click as the other end was hung up followed by the severe, angry voice of Pendelsen, "Now are you happy, Evans! I want that Amsterdam's head on a platter by the morning!"

"We'll discuss it later. Goodbye, Steve," Evans pressed a button on the phone handset and the line went dead putting his hands together he slowly looked up at Amsterdam.

"I'm sorry, old friend. It appears that what you've been told was a lie. You heard it yourself. From what I hear the PM doesn't take a shit without asking that guy what paper to use."

"But it's hardly concrete," replied Amsterdam, "It wasn't like he checked with the security team?"

"I'm going home, Harvey. I suggest you do the same."

With this, Evans stood picking up his briefcase and patting Amsterdam on the shoulder as he left the office. Amsterdam had failed to convince anyone, yet, that the story had merit; nor, been able to warn of the threat of something that was happening right now. He sat there thinking of the situation and what it was that he had done wrong. His only failure was his inability to risk those that gave him the story in the first place. But, now unless they wanted to be heard they would need to shout it out from the heavens. Either that or go rogue. He was confident enough that Arch would not mislead him into something that did not exist. After all, it was someone very close to Amsterdam that had introduced them and made the connection and it was that person now who he must speak with and try to confirm everything before he took his next step. Unfortunately, that meant there would be probably be dire consequences for his wife, Ginger.

Chapter 8

George Underwood stood on the deck of the cargo ship, *Isora*, looking at the glowing horizon of San Francisco. It was the first time that he had seen his home town for some time and he felt an overwhelming sense of nostalgia. Even at night he could recognise the spot where he and his father would go fishing on a small pier that butted out from the shore along the cargo route. It was where he had decided that he would jump ship to avoid customs on his return back to America and he gripped the railing tightly as he gained enough courage to haul himself overboard.

This wasn't the first time that Underwood had entered a country in such a way. A cargo ship was the cheapest form of unregistered travel that he could buy his way onto. He simply found a ship, tailed some of its workers while they were on shore leave and negotiated a price at the appropriate time. Getting out of the country was not an issue; however, getting into one was a whole new ball game. He could have bought his way off; however, returning to the United States would have been tricky given that you still needed to the run the gauntlet of convincing customs officials that you were who your forged passport said you were. Underwood's preferred method was a whole lot easier and cheaper; and, as he had done it a few times, he no longer had the fear of falling into the water and never coming back up.

There were some important measures that Underwood had to undertake; however, to ensure that he could perform the feat safely. For instance, it was crucial that he knew the water. It had to be deep enough so that you could survive the fall and while most cargo ship routes allowed for deeper water there were often ports whose channels were so narrow that a meter either way would be the difference between life and death. He also needed to ensure that he didn't jump too early otherwise he would drown on the swim to the shore. The cargo ships that came into San Francisco followed a path that brought it only a hundred meters or so to the shoreline where the pier was so he had a small window of opportunity to get this right.

As Underwood began to brace himself he sensed a presence behind him. He saw the face of an African man as he closed his eyes and when he turned around he saw the man standing there wearing a large coat, "You best not be doing what I think you're going to be doing?" said the African man in a thick accent.

"Just admiring the view," replied Underwood.

"Oh really, at night?" said the African man, "My name is Musoke."

He held out his hand and Underwood shook it, "George," he replied.

"Now why would an American man such as yourself want to enter into the United States illegally, I wonder? My guess is he's run away from something and that coming home would not be so easy."

"I guess you could say that."

Musoke smiled, "I've been watching you, George. You're not like all the other greased up monkeys on this ship. Much like myself, you have a purpose about you."

"And what would be your purpose, Musoke?"

"To live in America, of course," replied Musoke, "You see I've been travelling for the last fourteen months on these godforsaken ships. I went to Greece first, then Oman and then South Korea. I got on this ship in Japan finally to come to America."

"Why not just get on a ship and go straight there?"

"That is what most people do and it is why most people get caught. Usually, a well-meaning relative alerts the authorities and they track you down fairly easily."

"I haven't seen you around much?"

"I keep myself a low profile. Besides, one can never be too careful when one is trying to enter a country illegally."

"I can understand that. Well, I'd love to stay and chat. But, there's some stuff that I need to take care of. So, I'll be seeing you."

Underwood grabbed the cold metal railing and made to bound over the edge. His window was closing fast as he watched the shoreline begin to get further away; however, he felt the arms of Musoke grab him and keep in on the deck.

"Whoa, where do you think you are going, George. There is another way, my friend. There is another way!"

Just then, two men walked by speaking what appeared to be Russian to Underwood's ears and they briefly glanced in their direction.

"I need to get to shore and fast!" pleaded Underwood as the Russian men moved from earshot.

"And what of the Coast Guard, George? This isn't like entering some desert wasteland. When a ship comes into an American port they keep a very close eye on the whole thing. I have a better way, but I need your help!"

"I thought you said that you could never be too careful?" replied Underwood.

"I have papers. Papers for an American man. This ship is carrying cars down below and the papers are for an American worker to drive the cars off the ship. But, there's a man there who checks the papers and since my accent is far from American I think I would have a hard time convincing him without the proper bribe. Unfortunately, I don't have the money left. When you enter the hold, you need to go to the starboard side and open an emergency exit where I will be waiting and you can let me in. I'll hide out until I see you get in a car to drive it off the ship. You open the trunk and I will slip in. Now, the cars need to be driven off the ship and parked in an open lot that is locked in by a wire fence. You drive the car as close to the wire as possible and let me out. I'll make a hole in the wire and we make a break for it. What do you say?"

Underwood looked at Musoke, "Give me your hands?" he said.

"My hands?" questioned Musoke.

Underwood took them anyway and closed his eyes. When Underwood did he saw him and Musoke cutting a wire fence. This plan just might work, he thought and let go of Musoke's hands.

"What was that, my friend?"

"I just had to check something," replied Underwood.

"No, it felt like-"

"Forget it. When do we do this thing?"

"Right now," replied Musoke, "Are you ready?"

Underwood had only one possession on him. It was a set of fake passports that he had obtained under the name of Mr. and Mrs. Greene.

These were real passports, not forgeries and had cost Underwood every dime he had. For the jump, he had sewn them into the lining of his jacket wrapped in plastic to protect them from water damage.

"Yes," Underwood replied.

"Good, follow me."

Underwood had done just as Musoke's plan had intended. As the ship was docked and he drove the car off the ramp with Musoke in the trunk his only hurdle was being able to put the car into a position that was close enough to the wire fence without being seen. However, he found that this was difficult given that he was being directed by people pointing the way. He had to somehow break out of the convoy and he saw this opportunity when one of the people directing traffic had turned to move an orange witches hat and Underwood kept on driving passed him instead of turning right where the rest of the vehicles were headed.

When he parked the vehicle, he quickly popped the trunk and Musoke jumped out and they both ran toward the wire fence keeping low as they moved. Once at the fence, Musoke pulled out a pair of wire cutters and started to make a hole. Underwood kept a careful eye out on the people that were directing traffic and no one seemed to have notice that he had gone off course.

"Come on," Underwood said to Musoke.

"Just a few more!" he replied, "There! Hurry, get through."

They both crawled through the small opening and made it to the other side that opened onto a storm drain. They slid down the side and landed in the repugnant sludge of the drain which was littered with broken shopping trolleys, worn out tyres and smashed glass. Welcome back, thought Underwood as they moved down the drain.

"This is just like being back home," said Musoke, "But the difference is, in America, you don't get your drinking water from the sewerage pipes."

Underwood could not help but chuckle along with Musoke. As they moved through the sludge they came to be under a bridge that allowed them to sit on a ledge. They both pulled themselves up and breathed a deep sigh of relief.

"We made it, my friend," said Musoke.

"We made it," Underwood replied, "Thank you, Musoke."

"Please, don't thank me. Without you, I would be still on that horrible ship. I should be thanking you. Because of you, I can now start to build my life again in America. I can earn enough money to bring my family here too."

"You have a family?"

"Yes, I have a wife and a child. It was the reason that I took the risk in the first place. When I looked into the eyes of my newborn daughter I knew that I had to do something to make a better life for us. It hurt like hell to leave them there. My daughter was six months old when I left. She would have to be around two now. I miss her deeply."

Underwood looked at the sorrow on Musoke's face when he spoke of his family. He could not begin to think of the horrors this man had seen that drove him to seek refuge so far away. It was a level of desperation that Underwood had never endured personally and while it went against everything that he stood for he thought that he would thank Musoke in the only way he knew how.

"Please give me your hands," Underwood said to Musoke.

"Why?"

"I can show you your family. Please trust me," said Underwood and Musoke lifted his hands cautiously, "Now, close your eyes."

Underwood watched as Musoke did so and suddenly the furrows on his forehead loosened and the muscles around his eyes relaxed and a tear fell down his cheek, "Masani!" Musoke whispered as he squeezed his eyelids tightly, "My daughter."

When Underwood let go of Musoke's hands he slowly opened his eyes again and looked squarely at Underwood and a look of awe fell across his face.

"You asked me on the ship why I had to leave America," said Underwood, "That was the reason."

"I saw her. I saw her smile. I could almost reach out and touch her," said Musoke, "Who are you?"

"I'm just a traveller, Musoke" Underwood replied standing up on the ledge and started to walk toward the other end, "It is time we parted ways. Good luck, I hope you get your family to America."

"Please, tell me," Musoke called out, "If this is the reason that you fled America, why did you so desperately need to come back?"

"To stop a war," replied Underwood, "Good luck, Musoke."

The bridge was beneath a main road that Underwood had no trouble in scaling a small fence. He came out onto the footpath and reached inside his pocket producing a small piece of paper that had written on it: SFL 555.4 1932-21. He threw the piece of paper into a trash can and Underwood hoped as he crossed the street, that he wasn't too late.

Chapter 9

Caracas was a hell of a place. Its beauty promised so much but underneath laid a quintessential fear that was fuelled by a healthy scepticism of the west and Catholicism. You could get whatever you wanted, whenever you wanted it as long as whatever you had was cold hard US greenback to pay for it. Luckily, Tim Marshall was a man with the necessary resources to survive as a foreigner in such a place. He had established a significant network of government contacts, both local and federal to accept him as a legitimate business man and set up operations in a well-to do suburb off the main tourist areas. It was difficult to secure such a place to do business; however, Marshall employed many in the area, sponsored local sporting teams and had in general been accepted as an upstanding member of the community.

When he returned to the office, a single glass shop front with bad ventilation, Rosie, his office assistant and sole occupier of the office space looked at him with a worried look on her face.

"A man came by a few hours ago looking for you."

"Really?" replied Marshall.

"Yes, he a big man. African, American accent. Nice suit and walked with a limp."

"What did he want?" asked Marshall.

"I did not ask. But, he say, that he looking to speak with you because one of your family members is not well."

"Oh, I can assure you that I have not heard anything of the sort."

"That's what I thought. I never seen this man before and I think what is an American man doing trying to tell me that you have family troubles. You are from New Zealand. It all sounded fishy to me. So, I tell him that I wasn't expecting you for some days and to try again another day. But then, he hang around the building for a couple of hours so I call my brother, Rodriguez, he come down and cause some trouble and the man leaves. Rodriguez followed him and tells me that he is gone back to his hotel."

Marshall had not planned on Globe Corp sending someone so quickly. They must have planted an operative in the area. He would have to move faster than he wanted.

"That's some good thinking, Rosie."

"Ci, thank you, Mr. Marshall."

"Rosie, there will be more men coming to the office very soon. And they will more than likely close this place down."

"What? Please, Mr. Marshall, they can't I need this job."

"I know. Here, take this." Marshall handed her a slip of paper with some numbers on it, "That is the number to a bank account that I had set up for you in the Caymans. I'm sure you will find it ample enough to get you through. It is my thanks for what you have done for me during this time."

Rosie began to weep, "Mr. Marshall, what will become of you?"

"I'll be fine. I'm heading back out to the team in the field. But, could you do one last thing for me?"

"Ci, anything?"

"Can you get your cousin to go to the American and act as a guide? Tell him that I've gone into the field and that he wants to track me down because I owe you money."

"But, Mr. Marshall, that is not right."

"I know, but it will give him cause to follow your cousin. Now, when your cousin is on the trail, and this is important, make sure to keep a half days travel from me at all times."

Rosie nodded and wiped her tears away. Allowing for the half days travel would be the key to Marshall's escape and be able to give him the necessary time he needed. The whole illusion was important for the plan to work. The African American man in pursuit would be reporting back to Globe Corp on his progress to ensure they were kept informed. What this meant was that Globe Corp had no reason to send in a small army to locate his team as they would want to keep the whole thing low-key and preferably not involve the local authorities. Globe Corp could well afford the trouble to hire a bunch of mercenaries and a helicopter for the job and have the whole thing wrapped up in few days; but, that would raise attention that they would not want to deal with. One man reporting frequently on his progress and giving positive feedback on his estimations would be ample to keep a pencil neck corporate like Rogers thinking that they were achieving their goals and enough time for Marshall to achieve his.

"There is also a package for you, Mr. Marshall on your desk. After the man came in this morning I was suspicious so I looked inside but it was only a twig."

"A twig?"

"Ci, a stick. Nothing more. How odd? Why would anyone want to send you a twig?"

Marshall knew exactly who would want to send him a twig. Marshall walked into his seldom occupied office and there sitting in the middle of his desk was a red box atop of a pile of unopened letters. He plonked down in the chair and beheld it. Finally, he thought. All this time and this is what it has come down to. Harrison would be thrilled. He should have been there.

It was a strange relationship that he and Harrison had developed one sunny afternoon on Easter Island. Marshall had been out prospecting for a shipwreck off Cape South which had sunk attempting to carry several *Maoi* statues to museums in Spain around the year 1600 when a small boat powered by a local *Rapanui* tribesman and carrying a middle-aged man inappropriately dressed in a dark suit slowly drifted broadside onto his own vessel. Marshall himself had not taken any notice of the man as he was currently in the process of sending a robotic submarine into the depths of the sea on another irreverent expedition.

Marshall's most recent report had detailed that little had been found. They had good intel from historical documents and maps of the time and the one survivor, who had been the navigator on the ship, gave a very succinct account of where it was the ship found its last resting place. The local myths from the Rapanui people also corroborated the account and many square miles had been covered with little result. So, Marshall was not surprised at all when a man dressed in a dark suit came to the boat undoubtedly to report a firsthand account as to why progress had been so slow.

At first glance Marshall knew that the man had to be British; old Britain, wrapped tightly in a three piece suit with vest, fob watch, hat, umbrella and brief case just to round out the cliché. With little fuss the man boarded Marshall's boat and made his way directly to him announcing himself in an undoubted British tone.

"How do you do, Sir, my name is Charles Harrison." He held out his hand in greeting which Marshall firstly ignored. Harrison, undeterred only smiled and proceeded with his introduction.

"You must excuse my intrusion for I have pressing business in which I must seek your counsel."

"But, how can you know it's me that you want to speak with?" answered Marshall.

"Oh, I am never mistaken, Sir. It is my business to know whom with that I speak. You are Tim Marshall. Archaeologist, explorer, discoverer, prospector, call it what you will. You find things people usually have lost or don't want found."

"You've come a long way in search of a flat-foot, Mr. Harrison."

"Heavens, yes. Would there be a more appropriate place to where we may have discussions. Back on the island I fancy."

"My boat will be just fine."

"Well if you insist."

"I'm kind of in the middle of something right now. Maybe you would like to come back later and we can talk then."

"Oh, that certainly will not do, Mr. Marshall. We both know that once I leave your ship that you will pull anchor and take her forthwith into open water."

"Excuse me?"

"Oh, please do not play coy with me, Mr. Marshall. You will find that I am quite attuned to your kind of deception."

"I'm sorry, maybe I missed something. Where did you say you were from again?"

"Naturally, Mr. Marshall, all in good time."

"Look, Sir. I am actually really busy-"

"Doing what, may I ask? Trying to find those statues you already found?"

He couldn't have known! Marshall couldn't believe what he was hearing. It was true. They had located the Maoi statues the largest that had been constructed on the island. There were two of them in fact standing up right on the sea bed with their backs to open water. But that wasn't all they found and it was this reason that had been keeping Marshall from submitting his real report. It had been the pinnacle of a long and arduous expedition that had been totally unexpected.

"Your secret is safe with me, Mr. Marshall," continued Harrison, "Your dealings here are of no consequence to me. It is in fact the very reason I chose you for this operation. You are, what they say, made of the right stuff."

"You couldn't possibly have known that? There has been no contact with anyone on this discovery. It's been held tightly under wraps and no-one on my team would jeopardise their position. You're either simply guessing or you knew that they were there to begin with."

"I know many things, Mr. Marshall. But this is hardly the time or place to go into details."

"Okay, then. Tell me, why is it their backs are to the sea?"

"Is this a trick question, Mr. Marshall?" Marshall looked at Harrison in anticipation, "Very well, their backs most certainly are facing the sea; but, in actual fact, they are staring up to the navel of the stars. Now, Mr. Marshall, I'm sure you have some tea somewhere on this vessel and I have had quite a journey. The least gentlemanly course of action would be to offer me a cup while we have our discussions. What say you?"

Marshall himself did not care for tea; however, some was brought from the galley to his quarters where Harrison and Marshall were sufficiently alone. When the door was closed Marshall had noticed a certain level of relief on the face of Harrison. The man removed his jacket and hat and took a seat away from the porthole. The actions while slight and seemingly insignificant were tell tale signs to Marshall of a man that held some sort of knowledge or information held in confidence. Marshall had seen it before and the burden was written all over the way Harrison sat taking his first sip from the tea cup that quite obviously did not meet his satisfaction.

Marshall was puzzled with the way Harrison had indiscriminately brushed off his find of the statues. It was the greatest discovery that Marshall had ever been involved with and yet Harrison had appeared completely undeterred at the accomplishment. The confusing part was that if Harrison actually knew of the statues then why did he show so much disregard for their existence? Unless, he was part of the team that was there before him.

Harrison put down the tea cup and smiled directly at Marshall, "I see that basic luxuries of civilisation have not fared well in this place."

"Well then, Mr. Harrison, I'm sure you didn't come all this way just to taste my tea did you?"

"No, of course not. You're quite right. I suppose you are rather eager to hear my story. After all, it is stories that had brought you to this place and set about to discover those statues."

"So you really don't know what else was found with the statues?" pressed Marshall.

"From what I am told you found a riddle? I like riddles," replied Harrison.

"Not quite. An inscription," said Marshall, "Written in an old Incan language. The statues were guarding an underground cave. When we went in there we found sitting on a pedestal a picture of Inci, the Incan sun god, and an empty spot where a golden disc should have been. In the circle it read: When the oracle stands in the gates of the gods he will gain entry into the temple of illumination. But I'm guessing you know where the solar disc is, right?"

Harrison looked at Marshall in silence for a time, "Naturally, Mr. Marshall, I have no idea of what it is you are saying."

"I'm suggesting that as you all ready know what I found that you were the one who found it before me. My question is why haven't you walked through the gateway of Amaru Meru?"

The legend was that when the Spanish Conquistadors were raiding South America that Amaru Meru escaped through the gateway cut into the stone which transported him to the lands of the gods using a golden solar disc as a key to open the portal. Amaru Meru then gave the disc to the shamans; however, the location of the disc was then lost.

"Very well, I will tell you. But firstly, I do have with me something that may interest you."

Harrison popped open his brief case and took a plain manila folder out and opened to the first page of a manuscript which he placed in front of Marshall, "Do you recognise your own handiwork, Mr. Marshall?"

Marshall was surprised that he noticed what it was instantly. Surely, after so many years, something like this would lose its affect on his memory and emotions. However, there it was clear as day the very catalyst of his life's ambitions detailed in twelve-point font entitled 'Maori: The Truth Behind The Myth'.

"This was sent to me many years ago," continued Harrison, "By a mutual friend I might add. He was besotted with your accomplishment in this paper which was brilliantly written and researched. He told me that I ought to make it my business to make sure that you succeeded and achieved the lofty goals that you had set out to accomplish. He told me you were a man with what he called 'the right stuff'".

"And this is what you've come here for? To talk about a paper of some idealistic ideas by some university graduate written many years ago?"

"Not quite right, Mr. Marshall. I draw your attention to your paper as a mere illustration to prove to you that everything we discuss here today is deadly serious and that we have not brought it to you lightly. That we have chosen you and studied you; that we have observed your behaviours, your successes and failures for quite some time with interest from the very beginning. Like I said before it is my duty to know who it is I am talking with."

Marshall sat in silence for a time. He wanted to take a moment to analyse the situation that had been thrust upon him in a way that Marshall would have usually avoided. Marshall was the measured type that weighed the pros and cons before he made any decision and this situation would seem not to be one that Harrison would allow him to dwell.

"Okay, let's hear it then," Marshall announced and sat back in his chair.

"Smashing old boy. Your manuscript said a number of things that were rather enlightening to tell you the truth. All of which known, I might add, however, there were insights that you could not have known given that you did not have all the facts. Or, the key to unlock them as it were. No, what appeared you had grasped was an underlying anomaly to which you were able to decipher and sent you on your fabulous career of discovery. And, it appears to my eye, that you were guided by the single notion that you so eloquently placed as a quotation from the very beginning, 'The genesis of myth is truth'. The idea that all things began at the heart of sincerity from whence it came, albeit, a little distorted along the way but nonetheless fundamentally based on a rational and tangible set of consequences. It is a notion that I frightfully report am accustomed and have spent most of my adult life endeavouring to conquer. You, Mr. Marshall, have gone to immense lengths to uncover those truths. You have painstakingly pieced together that jigsaw puzzle of forgotten memory from the simplest of fables and placed them into reality. You are a believer that one not only passes their genetics from generation to generation but also their memories and knowledge in much the same way. I quote from your manuscript, 'that our history is not only to be studied in books and drawings, however, is something that remains in our hearts and minds eternally bound to the individuals life altering the outcome of their hopes, dreams and endeavours. When we ask our ancestors for guidance or pray to a higher power we are in fact looking internally for the answers through experiences and knowledge of our forefathers. It is the reason that some prayers are answered and some are not as the individual may encounter an experience that no one person of their stead had encountered in their lifetime but to which generations to come will benefit no matter how the individual deals with the situation at the time'. And this, of course, Mr. Marshall, is something that is bantered throughout cultures the world over even if only revered: the past lives of Buddhism; the many Gods and Goddesses of Hinduism each representing an aspect of life; the ancestral rituals of Indian cultures of the Americas calling for wisdom. Even Catholicism proclaims through the teachings of Jesus that 'I am the word of the Father'. And yet this significance is mostly ignored in part to misunderstanding and misinterpretation. But you, Sir, have capitulated against the status-quo. Your assumptions have drawn from stories passed down through the ages and threaded these into the common reality. Your references to the son of *Rangi* and *Papa*, *Tāne*, from the Maori creation myth has been a particular focus of yours for quite some time and in fact the very reason that you are here today finding the Maoi statues on the bottom of the sea bed I believe. You want to know the answer to the one question that all before has tried to answer: why are we here?"

"This is all very interesting, Mr. Harrison; but this still doesn't answer my question."

"I do apologise for my frankness, Mr. Marshall; but, in my experience and defence I might add, most people don't take too kindly to the bare facts of the matter. They must be persuaded and my usual tact in such circumstances is to present a case that is knowledgeable and without repose."

"I get it, Mr. Harrison. You needn't be worried about that. You know a lot about me and my history. I suppose you are about to go into where I have been; the things I have found; the people that I have been associated with. But this is mere cannon fodder for what you're really here about and my question is why?"

"Very well then, Mr. Marshall, why it is indeed. You hold in your possession knowledge that only a very few people on earth have been allowed to understand. You have gained this without a rite of passage but with shear insight and while this may have irritated a certain few it was allowed to prevail under the guise of leverage."

"Hold on a second here. It almost sounds that you are saying that I am in danger?"

"Not yet, but you will be, Mr. Marshall. You see if you continue on your current path you will most certainly stumble into a situation that you cannot control. If I am as bold as to take a guess you have already decided that your next step will be in search for the missing solar disc that opens the doorway of Amaru Meru. However, consequence, Mr. Marshall, is a factor that we all must consider when our endeavours threaten to tread on the common fabric of knowledge and, right now; I need your help to discover that consequence. I can give you what you seek; but, first we must understand the consequences of our actions carefully before diving in head first."

At that moment, Marshall was fairly confident that Harrison was telling the truth. Marshall was used to dissidents proclaiming he was treading on that which is sacred. He had a strange notion of self pres-ervation and at the tone Harrison was displaying it was apparent that he had stumbled into something bigger than he had anticipated. It was what Marshall had feared the most and the reason why he had kept the discovery of the statues and what he found in the cave to himself.

"Why do I get the feeling that there is more to this story?" probed Marshall.

"There is, Mr. Marshall, much more that you will need to take in and I must not delude myself to think that I have gained your trust; but, following my instructions will be the best course of action from here in. I will leave you now and you will pull anchor and make your way back to Chile, any port will do. Send word that you feel that the expedition has been fruitless and that with each passing day you felt the enthusiasm of the team waning passed acceptable levels. You may take a hit in your reputation; however, this as we both know, is not something you neither care for nor indeed seek."

"Why don't you travel with me? The time it takes to reach port will provide you time to tell me what you know?"

"Oh, good heavens no, Mr. Marshall. One must keep up appear-ances to ensure consistency. I will meet you in Caracas, Venezuela in two weeks time. You will arrive on holiday, giving you opportunity to reflect on your recent failure and a chance to unwind. I will find you, do not try and find me."

"Can you at least tell me what it is I am looking for? Come on, Mr. Harrison. Like you said, I find things and if I may be so bold, I assuming this is the reason why you are now asking for my help. If I don't know what it is I am trying to find how can I agree to go along with you?"

"Of course, Mr. Marshall. You are trying to find a tree."

Marshall had known on some level that what Harrison was ask-ing him to find was more than just a tree. A man as purposeful as Har-rison was not interested in such idealistic notions of meaning; he was merely interested in the pursuit for his own ends. Nonetheless, Mar-shall had agreed to do as he had asked.

However, now as he sat there reflecting in his office staring at the red box in front of him the moment somehow didn't provide justice to the ordeal that they had endured and he felt selfish for experiencing it alone. Overwhelmed, he picked up the red box and wished Rosie the best of luck as he left the office and jumped into his four-wheel drive. He could only think of one other person that he would rather share this moment with; a man who had provided Marshall with the vision to pioneer the way that he had merely followed and offer a gift of thanks beyond anything that money could buy. Marshall knew that the only people who would send him a twig were his team; and, the reason that they would send it, was that they had now found the tree and were about to unlock its secrets.

Chapter 10

After George Underwood's escape from the ship and he had departed Musoke to his destiny Underwood made his way to the San Francisco library where he would find a message on a bookmark in the cover of book 555.4. The message then directed him to a record store on Twenty-forth Street in the Noe Valley to ask for a vinyl record that was being held under the name of Petersen. He listened to the record in the store and found out that his next move was to visit Japantown to check into a hotel under the name of Petersen on Sutter Street.

In the hotel room Underwood showered for the first time in months and found a set of clothing that fitted him in the wardrobe. He shaved and made himself look as if he was like everyone else on the street. He listened to a message left by the Concierge while he was in the shower that said his party would be joining him at their usual eatery on Lombard Street in the Marina District. In the lock safe of the hotel room Underwood found a set of car keys and twenty-thousand US dollars in a wallet he opened with the code 1932-21. Underwood removed the passports he had sewn into the lining of his jacket and threw it and the remainder of his old clothes into the garbage chute in the corridor. He then went down to the basement car park where he found the car that matched the set of car keys after he randomly clicked the keyless entry and he saw one of the parked vehicles indicators flash. The vehicle was similar to one his father used to drive before everything went bad in his life and Underwood remembered sitting in the back as a child with his father singing to Louis Armstrong. Underwood drove the car slowly through the streets to the Marina District and parked on the street leaving the keys in the ignition as he left.

In the restaurant a portly young fellow named William was saddened to advise Underwood that his party would not be joining him as an urgent matter had come up which they had to attend. Underwood politely feigned distress and expressed hope to the young portly William that his friends were all right. He asked young William if it would be all right to dine anyway; however, at the bar instead as it would just be himself who would be eating. William was most happy to accommodate Underwood's wishes and suggested the beef was wonderful this evening. After Underwood had dined on a tremendous feast of beef he ordered a single-malt scotch and requested to look over the dessert menu when he was tapped on the shoulder by a familiar face.

"I do say, Petersen. It has been some time. When was it that you had returned state side?"

The voice was distinctively British and was accompanied by two other gentlemen in dark suits. One was plump with a round blushed face looking like he had several helpings of the beef that evening washed down with ample red wine that had stained his teeth. The other man was more surly and was hiccupping perhaps a little more drunk than he wanted to be while the English gentlemen was bright and alert dressed in a dark three piece suit.

"Charles Harrison, it's great to see you," replied Underwood, "What a surprise to see you here? Please sit and have a drink with me."

"That would be delightful. But, where are my manners," replied Harrison, "Allow me to introduce my party this evening. This man here is Richard."

Richard, the plump one, offered his hand which Underwood shook.

"How are you?"

"Fine, thanks, just fine," Underwood replied.

"And this handsome fellow is Donovan," offered Charles as Donovan and Underwood shook hands.

"Nice to meet you," said Donovan.

"And you," replied Underwood, "Would you all like a drink?"

"Oh, no thank you," said Donovan, "I think we've had our fill for this evening."

"Yes, if it was all right with you Charles may we head back to the hotel and call it a night. Big day tomorrow," said Richard.

"Yes, quite, quite. That would be fine with me. I'll have the driver return you to the hotel and come back for me in a little while," with that Charles saw the two other gentlemen to the door and Underwood waved goodbye.

To any other observer all these events would have seemed completely arbitrary. What seemed like a man walking off the street reading a book, going to a music shop and listening to a record; checking into a hotel to shower for dinner with friends who had to cancel and then meeting another long lost friend to catch up with a drink on the off chance would seem completely normal in one's own life. There was even an alibi in the form of Richard and Donovan whose memory while hazy would remember Harrison and the man they met meeting up in total coincidence and staying on to catch up like old friends. The whole affair was a deliberate ruse, of course, of Harrison's making to link up with Underwood in a seemingly unplanned manner. It was a long drawn out scheme that had been in the planning for many months and had come to fruition without the slightest inclination. It was Underwood that had requested the meeting and he had received the instructions in Osaka, Japan on a simple note by a waiter: SFL 555.4 1932-21. A cryptic message to the untrained but one Underwood easily understood as an invitation to return home.

As Harrison returned from wishing his two friends a good night he quickly took a position close to Underwood. The two men looked at each other keen to understand what the other knew; however, both were hesitant to begin in such an open environment to discuss pressing matters.

Underwood ordered Harrison a scotch which came promptly and which he used to break the ice.

"I missed a good scotch." Underwood announced, "You can't get the good stuff in Japan."

"Oh, is that where you've been?" asked Harrison.

"Yes, for some time now. Business was interesting there and I spent most of my time in Osaka."

A slight furrow brushed across Harrison's face, "A very busy city, I have been there once or twice myself. And you're quite right very difficult for one to enjoy a good scotch. I did not quite adapt well to that rice stuff. You shouldn't believe all the things that the Japanese rave on about."

The two men eyed each other. Underwood knew what Harrison was saying. He knew that Harrison understood that Underwood now knew the truth. It was a truth that Harrison had wanted to keep from

Underwood from the very beginning and one now he could not keep from him any longer. It was time that Harrison gave him the answers.

"And Australia? Did you ever make your way across there?" asked Underwood.

"On the occasion. Part of the British empire and all that. Snorkelling in the Whitsunday's was such a delight. Pity that global warming will one day destroy the beautiful coral reef there but that seems the way of things nowadays. It seems that all things beautiful decay with the ravages of time. Even one so vast and expansive as the Great Barrier Reef. Did you get the opportunity on your travels to get as far as Australia by any chance?"

"No, unfortunately. I would have loved the chance to see those coral reefs you mention. Can't imagine that I'd get the opportunity to get over that side of the world again. Not in my lifetime anyway."

Underwood kept his eye on Harrison as he swirled the remainder of the scotch in his glass. Hearing the words Japan and Australia had obviously soured his mood and Underwood was thankful he wouldn't need to elaborate on the topic in such a public place. The two countries had been out-of-bounds for the duties that Underwood had performed for Harrison in his official capacity as an executive for the insurance company, Globe Corp, a multi-national conglomerate who essentially were the underwriters of the underwriters with reach in all the key holes of power. Underwood himself was not sure exactly on the details but the jobs they made him perform were fairly unobtrusive and usually involved him travelling to countries all over the planet to make assessments on the potential risk of a political coup or geological disaster. His job was essentially to make contact with everyday people in these lands and attempt to use his ability to foresee the outcome of their plight. It was this same ability that delivered the images of Musoke's daughter right to his very eyes. An ability that he now knew to be the same as The Oracle.

The events he saw were like memories that happened in the past; like a key point in one's life that had changed you or defined who it is you would become. Even when Underwood was young and his thoughts revolved around trains, firemen and sweet boiled candy what he experienced in what he came to recall as his first 'awakening' was nothing short of the epiphany of fear.

He was seven at the time. It was his birthday and his close friends were there and as usual they had a party in the old tradition. Cake was served and everyone had a sing-a-long to a typical birthday tune. He wore a bright red pointed hat and blew on a whistle much to his mother's dissatisfaction who fussed about hot dogs and potato chips and ensured everyone had a drink in their hand. His father had spent most of the afternoon with the other fathers complaining about politicians and to know Underwood's father was to know that when he talked about politicians was when he drank the heaviest. He would get so wound up in his distaste for everything they did and didn't do that his face would go taught and the veins on his neck would visibly pulsate. The rage would build and build until whoever was closest would take a beating. It was usually his sister that would take the full brunt of the onslaught as she tried to reason with him. His mother knew better than to be anywhere near him in that state of drunkenness; but, his sister, in all her love for her daddy, could not help but get involved. But on this occasion, however, the young Underwood would be the target of his rage.

His father came in from outside to fetch some more drinks and demanded that Underwood open his presents. But Underwood refused as he and his friends ran around the house with paper airplanes they had made pretending to be fighter pilots.

"George Geoffrey Underwood you get down in this living room and you open the presents that these good folk here have bought to honour your birthday."

"I don't wanna!" replied Underwood.

"You don't wanna! Boy, you don't have a choice in the matter. It's your birthday and on your birthday you get presents because that's what people do."

"But they're crappy presents."

"Crappy presents? I can't believe what I'm hearing from a son of mine! How do you know they're crappy presents or good presents until you open them? I mean, I can see here on this here table that all the presents are wound up tightly with wrapping paper, sticky tape and ribbon. What do you know about what's inside them until you open them?"

Underwood surprisingly knew a lot about what his friends had brought him. He knew that Mitch had wanted to buy him an Army figurine like the one he got at Christmas time. Mitch's mom didn't have the money to spend and the figurine was in fact one she found in the lost and found box at the department store where she cleaned and she gave Underwood one of Mitch's old sweaters instead. He knew that Donald had found him a packet of carrot seeds and Brian, fond of comic books, gave one of his collections of Superman comics that Underwood had wanted to read. He knew this because the night before while lying in his bed awake excited about the next day when it would be his birthday he asked himself what he would be getting. He allowed himself to picture all kind of special gifts: a new basketball, a new skateboard, a new toy airplane (one that really flew!). And while he indulged in these thoughts his mind began playing tricks on him. The thoughts flashed between a shiny box with a picture of the airplane on the front and an image of Mitch's mom wrapping the sweater, it was blue, in wrapping paper telling Mitch that she couldn't afford to buy presents for other boys. He saw Donald in his father's tool shed looking through a dusty tool box and finding the packet of carrot seeds and Brian sitting in his room with five comics that lay out on the floor choosing which one he liked the least.

His father at this point marched right up the stairs and grabbed the young Underwood by the wrist and dragged him down to the lounge room.

"You will come down here and you will be thankful for what these people have given you. We don't have much in this world George Geoffrey but we do have manners. We have our pride and we have faith. That is all."

His father forcefully sat him on the floor in front of the table where he had put the presents while he gathered everyone into the living room.

"Now come on in everyone. My son is going to open the fine gifts that you have all bought him this day to honour his birthday. Come along boys give your presents one at a time to George. Mitch, you first."

Mitch reluctantly went to his present and put it in his lap and Underwood sat with his head down not looking up.

"Now come on boy. Take the present and rip into the paper. Come on boy!"

"I don't wanna, Daddy! Don't make me do it!"

"Son, what's so bad about some presents? No harm will come to you."

"It's a sweater. A blue one. It used to be Mitch's blue sweater but he grew out it two years ago." Even by this age Mitch was almost the size of a real man.

"How do you know that boy. I mean, how do you really know?"

"The same way that I know that Don got me carrot seeds and Brian one of his comics. I just know Daddy. Don't ask me how I just do. Just like I know momma is going to cut her hand with a knife just now cutting the cake."

And like clockwork there was a shriek from the kitchen and Underwood's sister went running in.

"Momma, are you all right," asked his sister from the other room.

"I'll be all right sugar. Can you be a good girl and run to the medicine cabinet and get me some bandages," Underwood heard his mother say.

His father's cool stare had turned to outright confusion. He downed the drink in his hand and grabbed the present out from Underwood's lap and began to unwrap Mitch's present. Sure enough, there was the blue sweater. He quickly moved to Donald's present and then desperately to Brian's and found exactly what Underwood had said would be in them. A look of shock turned to anger as he ordered everyone out of the house.

"Get outa my house you vermin! My boy is right. What kind of presents are these? These presents are not good enough for my son! Get your poor ass's outa here this instant and come back when you got some goddamned respect for my family! Go on you heard me!"

Tears began welding in Underwood's eyes and he began to sob. He didn't want his friends to leave. It was his birthday party after all.

"Now, boy. Come on boy. You tell me loud and clear that you aint lying to your papa now? Those boys told you what they got you didn't they? Didn't they!"

It was the first and last time that his father struck him. It almost knocked him out cold and Underwood began to wail.

"Now you better be telling me the truth boy!" his father yelled.

"Daddy, I didn't know. They didn't tell me nothing!"

"Then what was it, a lucky guess? Boy, did you think that I came down in the last shower!"

Underwood quickly scrambled behind the couch where he usually hid when his father went off on his violent tirades.

"Boy, there is only one place where liars go and that place is to hell!!"

"I just know, Daddy!"

"Oh, yeah. Did you just know I was going to do this?"

"Daddy, no!"

His Father pulled down the book shelf on the wall scattering the contents over the floor. Books, magazines and crystal balls with pictures in them of funny faces his Mother liked fell and smashed or splayed all over the floor. In his rage he didn't see Underwood's sister who had come back into the lounge room and the vase fell right on top of her head knocking her out cold as blood gushed onto the carpet and Underwood's mother entered holding a bandage on her hand and screaming.

"Oh, sweet Jesus. My baby, oh my baby! What have you done to our baby?"

A night at the hospital was endured by the whole family. Police came and took statements from everyone. A social worker came and spoke with Underwood and asked him questions about his father. He didn't want to answer the social worker though. For he saw the image of his father pulling down the book shelf and he knew what was to happen. It was what he was dreading and the reason he didn't want to open the presents in the first place. He saw wrapping paper on the floor, a smashed vase and his sister lying on the floor in blood the night before when he was picturing the presents he was to receive. He saw this night in the hospital room and knew that the kind social workers name was, Annie. He didn't tell anyone of course that he had known all this was to happen as this would only lead to trouble.

But then, the trouble didn't end there as Mitch's mother led a charge against the young Underwood. She made a protest at the school after she had berated her own son for hours asking him why he had told Underwood about the present. Mitch had pleaded his innocence and eventually she began believing him. She raised the issue with the principal of the school and said it was unfair to the children that he had these gifts and that he would be able to get higher grades because of it. The principal of course had no belief in the matter and knowing of the incident at Underwood's family home decided to put in a report anyway. Who would have known that it would be Charles Harrison who answered the call and conducted the initial investigation?

"And tell me," asked Harrison eventually, "What did you learn in Japan?"

"Everything that I needed to know," was Underwood's reply.

"Even what you feared to confront?"

"The Oracle helped me confront all of my fears. He even helped me control them. He helped me see through everything. Interpret every lie and deception. And I must say, Harrison, you have been lying to me."

"It is unfortunate truths that you find. What will you do with these truths?"

"That depends on how much time I have?"

"That, Sir, is very little. Very little indeed." Harrison downed the remainder of his drink and stood in one motion. "Allow me the opportunity to drop you off at your hotel. There are some details I am sure that the Oracle did not tell you."

"Why bother you know that I have already seen this conversation."

"Oh my dear fellow, quite the contrary. I kept you in the dark as it were for many years as you recall. That skill is one learned and not as quickly forgotten. Come we may discuss what it is we may do with this new found information."

Underwood tipped the portly fellow handsomely and followed Harrison out the front door. He knew how this conversation would end. He knew what Harrison had to say; but he was right, Harrison was keeping something from him that he would eventually learn to be the truth that he had been seeking.

Chapter 11

Tim Marshall sat in the house of Amparu Alvarez for only the second time. The man would have been at least eighty years old if not older and had been for many years confined to a wheel chair and his grandson, Eduardo, was as suspicious of Marshall then as he was now. Marshall had with him perhaps the only thing that Alvarez would value more than rum these days and he had hoped that he could share in this occasion with a man who had spent his life looking for what Marshall had in the red box.

Alvarez looked up at Marshall peering at him through deep set eyes, "You were the man that wanted my tree? I remember you. I told you, I don't remember where it is."

The tree Harrison had asked Marshall to find had not just been any tree that had existed on the planet. It was not some kind of rare species; but, the one tree, the world's tree. It was the tree that appeared in the book of Genesis in the Garden of Eden, the Acacia Tree, Yggdrasil and many, many other mythologies that used the tree as a metaphorical symbol for immortality, of heaven, earth and the underworld.

And Harrison had wanted Marshall to find it.

"Truth in myth," Harrison had said to him when he was about to object to such an outlandish suggestion. Marshall's own words coming back to haunt him.

"But why find it?" Marshall had asked.

"Imagine what secrets it holds, Marshall." Harrison had replied, "Imagine what keys it held that we may use to unlock the past and understand the future."

"You mean the doorway of Amaru Meru? You think that by finding this tree we will be able to understand what happens when we open the portal?"

"Consequence, Mr. Marshall, I am merely interested in consequence. I am giving you the opportunity that you have been seeking your entire life to find the scientific proof that may explain why it is we are here."

"And where would I begin to start looking?" asked Marshall.

"The only thing that I have been able to uncover is a name, Amparu Alvarez," replied Harrison, "The rest, I'm afraid, is up to you."

Not long after this Harrison had dumped him into the middle of Caracas with the cover of an insurance broker and little else but the knowledge that the tree was somewhere in Venezuela. Thinking about it now it was the very definition of the phrase a needle in a haystack and the only shred of information was the name of an unknown man, Amparu Alvarez.

Marshall himself was not attune to the requirements of a land expedition. His main forte had been on boats navigating throughout the atolls of the Pacific and diving under water for histories long passed. A jungle would be another challenge entirely and one Marshall had some reservations in pursuing.

Marshall's initial enquiries on the whereabouts of Amparu Alvarez had come up with nothing. But, when he considered that the task at hand was not so dissimilar to the countless other pursuits he had embarked on previously; he understood that he needed to approach the task in much the same way. So, Marshall started at the usual place of reference at the library and managed to locate a scholar who had written a book on Amparu Alvarez, Juan Terrazas, who after further enquiries with the publisher learned that he was a lecturer at the University of Venezuela.

The tricky part was that Terrazas's work was not specifically about the tree of life. Mainly, it detailed the geological framework of the South American rain forests and the effects of logging. Terrazas's contention was that for the world to survive the spread and growth of the rain forest had to continue across the continent and that our interference on this process was seeing the forest retreat of its own accord.

Marshall had been taken by the word Terrazas had used that the forest had 'spread' and it was this notion that he wanted to use as an in to get to know who he was.

"But spread from where?" he had asked on their first meeting after Marshall had made a considerable donation to the Alliance for the Protection of South American Rain Forest's to which Terrazas was one of the directors.

"I'm not sure what you mean?" was Terrazas's initial reply, "You say that you want to know where the forest originated from?"

"Yes. Your contention is that the forest had spread. Now from this you would think that the forest then sprang up from a central location millions and millions of years ago. Which is why I ask from where did the forest spread from?"

On this Terrazas had looked sceptically at Marshall, "Do you take me for an idiot?"

"Not at all," replied Marshall, "I sought you out because I am interested in hearing more on your theory."

At this Terrazas had a chuckle to himself, "You are a tree quester, yes?"

"Tree quester?" questioned Marshall perhaps a little over anxiously. Up until this point Marshall had not contemplated that what he was looking for was something that others before him had in fact endeavoured to locate.

"You've heard of the tree?" asked Marshall.

"Yes, the idea of course is absurd. Tree's follow the birth, life, death cycle so I do not see how this tree could exist at all."

"That may be so," continued Marshall, "But do you agree that some trees have lived for hundreds of years?"

"Yes, there are many types."

"So why then is it hard to believe that a tree could not last millions of years? The Earth itself is also on this cycle as you have so simply put it. The point that this has spanned billions upon billions of years is arbitrary; the cycle still exists. You then must agree that this cycle of life for all things covers varying degrees of time; and, if you accept this notion, must know that this tree could exist."

"A slim one if there ever was."

"But one nonetheless."

"Look, Mr. Marshall, to be frank I do not know what interest your company can have with the Alliance and feel that your interest may be misplaced. I was prepared to meet with you to accept your generous financial offering to my organisation; however, feel it is my duty to decline your donation. I feel that your company's goals will be counter to that of the Alliance and may in fact distort the purpose of its existence to its own ends."

"Really? The fact remains and it is evident to me that we are aligned more than you think."

"How so?"

"Your organisation wants to stop logging in South America. You say that logging the forest is accelerating the receding process of its own accord. While this is unfounded I can understand its reasoning. Nature itself is defending against a predator by taking away the very thing the predator seeks. But how do you stop it? The fact is you can't. You don't have a shred of evidence to make the world stand up and listen. You say that if the tree does exist that the chances would be slim at best. I get that. But, do tell me, Professor, what chance does the forest have in reversing the cycle and evade turning to desert?"

"Even if we were to stop tomorrow. My reasoning has as much chance as you have as locating this tree."

"And this slim chance you have will stop you from lobbying against logging?"

"No."

"Then as far as I see it we are in agreement. A slim chance is all one needs to pursue their desire."

"This may be all very well, Mr. Marshall, but I still do not understand how we can be aligned?"

"Well this is simple. Help me find the tree and together we will be able to reach our goals. You will be able to lay claim to your studies and I will be able to take core samples of the tree and understand the atmospheric conditions of years gone by."

"Pardon my ignorance but what does an insurance company need with atmospheric conditions over centuries?"

Marshall himself had asked Harrison this very question and he had committed to memory the same line that Harrison gave him, "To observe the cycles of life. To measure the risks of the future. With this knowledge my company will be able to know the potential risks which could avoid it from ruin. We have spent millions upon millions of dollars in computer modelling and simulation to define where catastrophic events are likely to occur. But the data behind these models is only speculative at best. Imagine what we could do with real evidence across generations."

While the argument was misguided Marshall could see that it would be a very convincing one given the angle of its delivery. In Marshall's experience insurance companies did everything they could to prove they were not liable to pay for the very promises they marketed themselves on. Who could dare argue against the premise then that considerable expense would be invested in locating the knowledge of the ages locked up in wood formed over thousands of years? To unlock the stories of the planet atom by atom and string together a tale whose protagonists and antagonists had names such as earthquake, cyclone, drought, flood, plague, asteroid to name just a few. The very notion could have been lifted from the pages of Zeus himself.

For Terrazas's part he seemed to accept the story. He sat back in his chair and gave Marshall a long hard look, "So, what do you want from me?" was what he asked.

"Amparu Alvarez."

"That old man. He's loco."

"He seems to be a difficult man to find. Either that or he's dead."

"No, he's alive. But, I'm not sure exactly what we would get from him."

"Well there's someone out there who thinks that he might be worth a shot."

Terrazas had then proceeded to set up the meeting and he also acted as the interpreter. Alvarez still lived in Venezuela in a small village on the outskirts of Barcelona with his daughter and two grand children. His granddaughter who had answered the door to the house that was not much more than a shack and introduced herself as Andreina and his grandson, Eduardo, wheeled in Alvarez. Alvarez was as typical an old man as you were to find. He had a stubborn air about him and an aversion to answer any question which he felt did not suit his interest at the time. It was Andreina who broke the deadlock.

"*Abuelo*, these men have come to talk about your tree?" Andreina had asked.

"The tree?" he replied grumpily taking a sip from his glass of rum.

"Ci."

"May I ask," started Marshall, "Where it is you began your search?"

The old man rolled his eyes and took another sip from the glass of rum, "Peru. I had met a shaman who had given me *Ayahuasca* and it was there while under its influence that I saw the tree of life. The shaman told me that it was to be my destiny that I was to find it. I traced through the entire length of the jungle and had found that the tree existed in some form or another in every myth there was. Finally, I began to put together a picture of where and what the tree of life could have been."

"So, you hadn't made your mind up yet as whether this tree of life was actually a tree at all?" asked Marshall.

"Yes. I had no idea what I was looking for," continued the old man, "The shaman did not specify what it was I was looking for. The tree could have been anything one would associate with a tree. It could have been as simple as the ancestral tree for example."

"So what made you think that it was a tree of wood?" Marshall continued.

"It was a story that I had heard from a tribal elder in the hills of Peru. I found a painting on the wall of some old Incan ruins that depicted a story of a great Warrior King. It depicted his victories over an unknown enemy that had heads like an ox with the body of an upright horse. It showed how the Warrior King had backed the enemy into a valley sided by cliffs on every angle and that with a few men the King had valiantly been able to keep the horde at bay. Then the sun God saw fit to take the enemy away knowing that the Warrior King would not show mercy on these souls who had come into his lands. I asked the elder what this meant and he told me that a child learns that a cunning plan can defeat the largest of armies. However, as wise old men the story tells us how best to heard wild livestock. Either way, he said, we share our stories not by what actually happened but by what best describes the meaning for the receiver of the story. Whether or not the Warrior King saved his people from an unknown threat or passed on the wisdom of hunting food does not matter. What matters is that what we take from this story. It took me some time to understand what this had meant. As a young man I was adamant that I was to find the tree of life. But now this story was telling me that the meaning in the vision was meaningless without context. It made me want to find out more about this Warrior King and I learnt that he was a fearful ruler who would hunt down other tribes only to kill their men and make slaves of their women. The story then on the ruins may not have been even written as a celebration to his triumphs; but, a warning for other tribes to know that this man should be avoided. It may have been an observation such as a journalist may observe an event like a battle only communicated in painting. I then began to think that quite possibly that the tree of life that I sought was in fact something that could be seen with the eye."

"Truth in myth," said Marshall to himself, "And did you keep on looking?"

"Of course I did. My search began where the most mention of the tree of life appeared in tribal folk lore. And from this I pieced together a map."

"And what came of this map?"

"I destroyed it."

"Why would you do that?"

The old man screwed up his face and shifted uncomfortably in his wheel chair. He tapped on his glass and Eduardo came by with a bottle of rum and topped up his glass. He took a large swig; one that Marshall felt was too large for a man of his age. In fact, if the old man had of died right there and then he wouldn't have been at all surprised. Something was keeping back the old man from telling his story.

"Because you found the tree?" said Marshall.

The old man coughed, "Yes. I found the tree. But it did not live up to what I had expected to find. You see, the tree put me in this wheel-chair. I remember falling a long way down and there I passed out. But before this, I remember thinking to myself that this was it. My long search had come to an end. My guides managed to pull me out, however, I did not get any medical assistance for over twenty days and nights as the guides I was with could only carry me in short distances. I woke in a hospital and I had no memory of where I had been. The only thing that the guides had left me was a piece of paper with the map. But, I couldn't face what had happened to me and I asked the nurses to burn it. Years passed until someone like you came to find me. They offered me millions of American dollars for me to give them the map but I did not know how to put it back together."

"Who was it that came to see you?" asked Marshall. Since the episode in the underwater cave at Easter Island, Marshall had a feeling that he was stepping on the footsteps of someone that had gone before him.

"Oh, no one I remember," replied Alvarez.

"So it is lost then?" asked Marshall.

"Gone. And over the years that have been so unkind to me the memories have faded. I can no longer put together the pieces of the puzzle."

At this the old man went into a full fit of uncontrollable coughing. Marshall could see blood form on his handkerchief that Alvarez used to cover his mouth.

"I'm sorry, Sirs," said Eduardo, "That is enough for today."

"Please, young man, we have come a very long way," said Terrazas, "What of his research, his papers even, may we take a look at them?"

"No, no papers. It is time to leave!" urged Eduardo.

The old man managed to wheeze, "No...No notes. Just memories."

And with that the man was wheeled away by his grandson. The

closest link they had come to the tree was fading with time.

Marshall and Terrazas were escorted to the front door and back to their vehicle by Andreina. As she walked with them to the vehicle she said something to Terrazas that he didn't bother to translate.

"Ci, ci, ci," he said to her and she yelled something back to Eduardo who was standing in the doorway of the dilapidated building holding the weary concerned look of a man much older than his years. The two then had what seemed to be a heated argument to Marshall in which Andreina threw up her hands and joined them in the vehicle jumping into the backseat.

"What's all this about?" asked Marshall.

"Oh," replied Terrazas, "She asked for a lift in to town. I said, why not, it is the least we could do to thank her for her help."

As they had driven off waving goodbye, Andreina said in perfect English, "So, do you want me to tell you where my grandfather found the tree?"

As Marshall drove the four-wheel drive out onto the road he looked in the rear view mirror. The granddaughter of Amparu Alvarez would not be described as attractive. She was lean in an undernourished kind of way built by hard domestic labour since being a very young child. But, now in her mid-twenties, her smile showed an understated demeanour of one that had seen it all as her lips only managed slightly to become upturned.

"My grandfather was always seen as the crazy old man of the village," Andreina said, "Children would come to my house when I was younger to hear stories of his travels. Over the years his stories became tiresome to the villagers and he began to contradict himself. Most people saw this as the cracks in his story and what he was claiming could not possibly be true. He became someone that everyone laughed at until people dismissed him entirely. It was a shame; his stories filled everyone with so much hope. You have seen how we live. It is nothing of the way you people live that I see on the television. His stories gave people the hope they needed to get through their day as they prayed that one day they too would be able to find the tree. But I could not believe that what he was telling me was a lie. He would tell his stories with such a vivid conviction, with such immense detail that they could not possibly be a fantasy of his own making. It was like he just said; the map is in his memory. So, I decided that I would put together pieces from his broken memory onto paper. I did not tell my brother about this as he would not have approved. You can't blame him, you see, he has only experienced heart ache from our grandfather and his stories. I kept a room in town that was close to the bar where grandfather would drink. You see, he was trying hard to forget the things he had done at the bottom of a bottle. He has been a drunkard for almost thirty years and when he would drink his fill I would herd him back to the room where I would ask him to tell me of his stories. His travels, the people he met, and the loves he had. In these moments I learnt of people and places and from this I drew the map of where he had been."

Marshall looked at Andreina with some contempt. He had a pretty good understanding of people and their motivations. Here was someone who had taught herself English, learnt of the western world through television and pictured everyone as movie stars. It was evident that she had rarely ventured out as far as the small town where she was born and in her youthful pursuit of the world had in her possession something of perceived value to Marshall and Terrazas.

"So, how much money do you want?" asked Marshall.

"Money? I don't understand?" she replied dumbfounded.

"Well you've told us that you have something we want," continued Marshall, "We're not here to be played."

"I'm sorry, Sir. I don't want your money."

"Then what do you want?" asked Terrazas.

"I want to find the tree of life. Just like you. You see, as you say, I am not wealthy and could not afford to go off in pursuit of this on my own. Is this strange?"

"It is where I come from," replied Marshall, "Okay, sure. Take us to this room of yours where you have put together your map and then we will see." He had nothing else to lose.

"That's just it. There is no map. Grandfather did have it in his head after all. The map was a riddle," said Andreina.

"Tell it to us," said Terrazas.

"Across the empty jungle. There lies the misty mountain. I found the tree in darkness. Where the sun shone through eyes of crystal."

It had only been at his point that Marshall fully understood why it was Harrison had chosen him to lead the expedition. As Harrison had alluded to in their first meeting, connecting myth to reality was Marshall's speciality; and, it was that very skill which then allowed him to understand the riddle that they had just heard from Andreina.

The result of deciphering that riddle was what lay in the red box that Marshall now hoped would give the old man peace. He had thought that by bringing the tree to Alvarez that he may be able to endure the thought that what he had accomplished was more than just the pursuit of madness; or, perhaps, Marshall needed to prove that to himself.

"I bring you a gift," Marshall said to Alvarez who looked like he was about to go to sleep.

Alvarez, a little startled took another sip of rum from his glass, "An old man needs no gifts. Just a place to be left alone."

"Even if that gift is a piece of the tree of life?" said Marshall.

The old man began to cough and his eyes lit up when Marshall opened the red box to reveal what was inside. Marshall himself had not looked inside and also saw accompanying the twig was also a note that Marshall took reading a sequence of numbers. He also realised that the twig, as Rosie his office assistant had described it, was not a twig at all. It was wooden all right; but, straight, like a pencil and just as thick. It was a core sample. And, upon seeing this, Marshall was even more elated than he had been as this meant that they had not only found the tree but they had started the difficult task of analysing a core sample.

"I, I can't believe it?" said Alvarez putting his glass down on the coffee table beside him and reaching for the red box which Marshall handed over.

"This really is the tree?" asked Alvarez, "You really did find it?"

"Yes, and it was all thanks to you."

At that moment the front door crashed open and standing there with her hair in a plait and a bag of washing was Andreina. She dropped the bag and ran towards Marshall and gave him a big hug.

"And, it was also thanks to you," Marshall said to Andreina.

"Is it true?" she replied with tears welding in her eyes.

"Yes, we found it. We found the tree of life. Just where the riddle said it would be at Mount Roraima."

Chapter 12

Tenashi found himself sweating and his arms were held above him in chains in a small room that had one end fitted with glass from floor to ceiling. He had a vague recognition of where he was but he felt disorientated as there was a whirling yellow light somewhere that engulfed the room and momentarily he lost focus. When his focus returned, through the glass he saw his friend Amatsu who was covered in blood. Tenashi wanted to scream out to him and tell him to run but somehow he couldn't raise the sound in his voice. As their eyes met Tenashi noticed there was a hole in the glass where Amatsu was holding a hand gun and Amatsu screamed and then Tenashi heard the bullets being shot off but he did not feel or see them. He felt himself slipping away and he wanted to desperately look into the eyes of Amatsu and tell him that he forgave him; but, the only face that remained was that of tormentor with his gold tooth glinting in the whirling yellow light that eventually was wiped out by the vision of Lupei who told him, "IA5 procedure successfully completed, soldier FE-143-33."

When Tenashi woke and took a deep breath he found that his lungs worked without having to gasp for air. That there was no pain after all. The face of a beautiful woman consumed his vision smiling at him. Perhaps he was coming down from a gungy hit? Perhaps this had been an illusion. And then the image of the beautiful woman minimised in the left hand corner of his screen and he was awake. This was not a dream.

"Welcome soldier F-E-143-33. The IA5 transformation has been completed successfully. Vital signs are displaying a cohesive adaptation and functioning normally. Let me familiarise you with the functions of the field of view in your IA5 unit. Commands do not need to be vocalised. You may simply think about the specific image in your field of view and you will be able to view stored information. Go on have a try."

The images Tenashi was looking at were disconcerting at the beginning. They were images imposed onto a screen rather than a real life version of what he was seeing. He looked up at the pilot and focused on the back of his head and instantly the image was zoomed in like a telephoto lens.

"You have used the zoom function. Focus your attention on a distant object and that image will be displayed as required," said Lupei.

An image of a man's face popped up beside the pilot with his name and rank.

"You can access information on individuals from the UFA database. All staff members are accounted for and can be called on at any time."

Tenashi looked down at his arms and moved what used to be his hands. He noticed that there was an opening at the base of his wrist and Lupei was a step in front of him.

"The IA5 is equipped with small pulse weapons in the arms and can be fired by raising one or both arms and locking on a target. Try it and see what happens."

Tenashi focused on the Lieutenant and raised his arm. A red cross hair scanned his field of view before locking on the movements of the Lieutenant. A warning light flashed and beeped.

"Target denied," said Lupei, "Your targeting system prevents you from accidentally locking on a friendly target. History shows that many soldiers have been lost in the field due to friendly fire. The weapon will fire once the lock is in place on an enemy automatically and can be aborted by dropping your arms. The ammunition that is fitted with the IA5 is an electrode projectile which is replenished automatically by recharging an internal cell core. One hundred rounds per arm is the capacity for the weapon and will instantly begin to be recharged after the weapon is fired. The electrode rounds can be set to varying levels of impact from stun to kill. The IA5 is fitted with an internal battery which is charged by any form of light. Surrounding the unit is a thin layer of reactive film that is stimulated by light from the sun and even light by other sources such as halogen or fluorescent lighting. This will ensure that the IA5 unit is continually performing at its peak capacity. Standby for orders from Lieutenant Toi."

An image of the Lieutenant appeared in the top right of Tenashi's screen, "Alright listen up soldiers. The IA5 installation is now complete and the basic functions required for operation has been addressed. But the only real way to get to know something is to test it in the field. We're about to land you in a drop zone behind the First Wave units. Our primary target is this media company building in the western part of the city."

With this Tenashi's field of view was taken by a schematic of the building. "Terminate all enemy targets without prejudice and take control of the building. Our secondary target is a vault below the building which is accessed via this service elevator. The vault is a communications and monitoring station deployed by the enemy. It is operated by only one person and is designed to withstand a nuclear holocaust and you can be sure its inhabitant will trigger the safety barriers preventing anyone going in or out of the building. To gain access we will be lowering a drilling unit through the shaft which will force a hole for our team to enter and take command of the installation. Our objective is to take the building over without damaging its vital communication abilities."

A green square in the left corner of the Tenashi's display began to flash and suddenly the docking unit that his IA5 unit was being held by released its grip and Tenashi was a little wobbly under foot as he came to take in the motor functions of his new legs. With a few slight adjustments he was able to regain his balance easily and stood at attention.

"That green light in the left hand corner of your display shows that your mission is about to start in two minutes. Once it stops flashing the air transport will drop down and the floor will open up releasing us on the ground. If it goes orange that means you are off course of the target. If it flashes orange that means you are spread too far from the platoon. As your leader in this mission I will be the central focal point that determines the course of this mission. A red flashing square means that you are off mission and a transport will be sent to extract you."

'In built weapon systems will only be required for this mission and we are expecting limited to no resistance from our targets so let's line it up and get ready in 5, 4, 3, 2, 1. Move out!"

Chapter 13

As Harvey Amsterdam was making his way from Roger Evans' office to his on the other side of the floor he came across a bank of television monitors and turned them on. Surely, he wasn't the only news person to catch onto this story. By now, he would have thought that someone in the military had contacted the news room of some TV channel and leaked the information like his contact had. You don't just stand down the entire military and have no one know about it, he thought. It's unheard of. Unfortunately, it appeared that the late night news services of all the major channels either had pre-taped their news bulletin and gone home or had not the inclination to report on something of this magnitude without first confirming a few facts.

Either that or the story was completely bogus and Amsterdam was kidding himself by continuing to pursue it. But, he still had an ace up his sleeve. The beginning to this entire juncture was from the tip off from his wife, Ginger. Even though she could not admit to such a thing directly she had left the details of the story on her laptop one evening for Amsterdam to find. He did not understand the reason she had done this; for all the time he knew her she had been vehemently protective of her professional life and had even threatened him with divorce if he even thought of prying. But, on this occasion, she had let the information freely available.

It took him some time to look into the matter. At first, he considered that she may have given him a decoy to throw him off the scent of some other story or maybe even a love affair she had going with another guy. It was no secret that their marriage was not the most harmonious at the minute, the gambling being the most decisive point of their bickering; but, this had mainly subsided with time even though the same level of trust they had shared before could not be retained. When she recognised that he hadn't done anything about it she had set up a dinner date with Archibald and his wife, Terese, which then led to a few more meetings such as golf with Arch and then finally Arch coming out and telling him about the K29K evacuation code. He had a desire to tell the public about what he saw as treason at the highest order. Desertion, he had said, was not tolerated in the military; so, in fact, this should not be tolerated in any order of public service. Arch had been a consultant on the initial investigative work performed by, none other than, Ginger, and worked with her to collate the final package. He had performed his orders dutifully but could not handle what he saw as a most tragic misgiving to the people who he swore to protect.

The story, by itself, Amsterdam felt was not entirely compelling and it only began to heat up when he began asking questions into why this was happening right now. The reality was that he had thought that the government would already have developed such a plan as a matter of national security and was surprised to find out that none had actually existed. However, according to Arch, he and Ginger were provided with a very short time frame to deliver the plan which was to be exclusively released to only a few high-ranking officials. So, why the urgency? If they didn't feel the need to have one previously what was it that they knew now that changed all that?

Amsterdam felt he found the answers when he discovered a man called *The Chief*, a self-professed militia leader of concerned individuals on the security of the nation's borders. The Chief provided detailed accounts of situations that he called 'contacts' which were essentially unreported military activity. The volume, of which, shocked Amsterdam to the core. The reality, as The Chief put it, was that Australia was a big country, sparsely populated. What that equalled was a belief that the military, and not just Australia's, could waltz around the country side performing all kinds of acts of warfare. What was truly scary to The Chief was the idea that while he received good information from reliable sources there were surely other 'contacts' that occurred without anyone's knowledge or were too afraid to report.

Amsterdam's office was the exact opposite of Evans'. His desk was old; his seat was new thanks to complaints filed by the occupational health and safety committee. Files and files of paper lined practically every wall available and it was near on impossible to enter it without tripping on something on the floor where he reserved a special spot for the awards he had won for journalism over the years. As he entered his office and closed the door he flicked through the numbers on his mobile phone and keyed Ginger's mobile phone number. He didn't want to wake the children by calling the home phone and he knew that they would get worried if they knew he was not coming home. As the phone rang he thought that he heard the closing of a door and then a short fellow dressed in a vest and wore round glasses with a plump face walked by. He thought that he had seen the man before and may have been the librarian up on the fifth floor or he could have been one of the cleaners. At any rate, he didn't think anything else of it as Ginger's mobile phone went to voice mail and he left a message.

"Hi, honey. It's me. I need you to call me right away. I'm having trouble with that thing you left me to find and I think I need you to go the next step. Call me. Bye."

Darn, thought Amsterdam. She was probably asleep already. It was his only play left to go on and he didn't know which way to turn now that he couldn't make contact with her.

From the corner of his eye he thought that he saw the flash of lightning. There was a blue glow which silhouetted against the vertical blinds and Amsterdam turned his head toward the window to wait for another strike or hear the rumble. He saw or heard neither and considered that it may have been something else entirely. Lightning was not something that Amsterdam thought highly of. He wasn't the type to stand out in the weather and watch the spectacle of a storm go on by. In fact, he loathed the idea of adrenaline rushes entirely.

When the phone rang he was stunned for a time and then almost forgot to pick up the receiver as his pulse lowered. When he picked it up he had been expecting to hear the voice of Ginger; however, surprisingly, it was a man's voice.

"Amsterdam," he said.

"Is this Harvey Amsterdam?" said the man on the other end.

"That's me. May I ask who is calling?"

"My name is Harry Lockley, Mr. Amsterdam," a touch of urgency in his voice.

Amsterdam began searching his memory. He couldn't recall a name like that before, "Do I know you?" he asked.

"Not directly. But you have met The Chief."

"Yes," replied Amsterdam his interest now piqued.

"I've decided to call you because maybe you could help. I can't seem to get a hold of anyone this evening. Not the police or anybody. I remembered the interview you did with The Chief and I thought you should know. Maybe you could get the word out there?"

"That's not the first time I've heard that today, what should I know, Mr. Lockley?"

"What I saw tonight."

As Amsterdam listened to Harry Lockley's story about flying machines he had never seen before and how they were almost silent as they moved through the air Amsterdam was certain that he could hear phones ringing out in the main open floor area. He could see the desk directly opposite of his office and could tell that the lines were flashing with phone calls and Amsterdam wondered who could be calling at this time of night?

"Mr. Lockley, would it be okay if I called you back?" said Amsterdam cutting Harry Lockley off from his speech.

"It's starting, isn't it?" replied Harry Lockley.

"What do you mean by that?"

"The invasion. They're coming."

"What do you know?"

"You got a pen handy? Write down this. Twenty-five point three four five zero degrees south. One-hundred and thirty one point zero three six one degrees east" Amsterdam had written them out as numbers.

"They're coordinates?" asked Amsterdam.

"Exactly, get there and we will help you."

The phone clicked off and the sound of an orchestra of telephones ringing throughout the office was becoming more prevalent. Amsterdam cautiously stood up as there was another blue flash of lightning and opened the door from his office to have his ears hit hard by a credenza of ringing telephones. He felt dumbfounded. What was previously an empty room strangely now felt like it was occupied by the spectre of the day staff in the middle of reporting a national emergency. But, it was only Amsterdam left on the floor and he went to the nearest desk to find a whole switchboard lit up of flashing red lines which were waiting to be answered.

Amsterdam was apprehensive to pick up the phone not knowing what or who would be on the other end. However, letting a phone ring out was not something he could ethically do so he reached for the receiver and pressed line one, "Hello?"

"Oh, Christ! Oh, Jesus! Thank god I found somebody!" It was a woman's hysterical voice and obviously someone who was religious,

"You've got to help me, there's people walking in our streets and I don't know what to do! I think they're killing people and...and...There's thousands of them it's just awful!"

A part of Amsterdam expected to hear what she'd said. He remembered the conversation with Arch and how he'd ask him to pray. The last gasp for God was catching it seemed.

"Calm...Calm down madam," Amsterdam pleaded, "What's happening there? Where are you?"

"Oh Jesus! I, I'm in Guildford." Which is about an hour and a half from the city, "I run a bed and breakfast and I was just showing our last couple to the door when this whooshing wind flew overhead. Our property is at the top of the hill which overlooks the town, and oh, Jesus! They just shot a whole family in the street with some type of blue light! Oh, God, please send someone to help, send the Army! We need help!"

"Can you tell where these people came from? What do they look like?" He tried to press her for more but her voice became silent.

"I, I can see right into the town, I have my binoculars and I can see them, they're soldiers all right, it looks like they are wearing a grey uniform. And oh, my they just shot Mrs. Parkinson, she had her hands raised, they just shot her in cold blood!" Amsterdam was suddenly aware of the other telephones and every light flashing available on the display.

"I tried to ring the police," the woman continued, "But there's no-one there, no-one! What can we do? What can we do?"

Amsterdam thought that the only thing he would be able to offer this woman was comfort.

"Please listen to me, find a safe place to hide!" said Marshall, "Please listen! Are you listening?"

"Yes."

"Find a place to hide."

"Okay."

"I'll try and alert the authorities, okay."

"Thank you, thank you very much. They must get here quick, please. We need help!"

As Amsterdam put down the receiver he looked up over the empty office and the continuing ringing of the phone lines seemed to get louder and louder. It appeared that the emergency services lines were either overloaded or completely disconnected as he tried calling them to no avail. People would continue to try to call into this place. He wondered if the *The Post* or *The Herald* were experiencing the same thing.

Amsterdam felt an overwhelming urge to want to answer every call as best he could and offer some comfort in the face of whatever the people were facing out there. It would be the least he could do given the circumstances and he tried to pick up the receiver to answer another call; but, he just couldn't bring himself to press the button. However, when he had finally got a hold of himself and was about to press the button to answer another call the entire ringing throughout the office stopped abruptly and the room was empty and quiet again.

Shortly after this there was another flash of blue light and another that quickly followed until the frequency of the flashes acted like a strobe light being used in the street. What was it that woman had said, they shot them with blue light?

"Oh no," Amsterdam said aloud and he walked over to the window which fronted the street to the docks to reveal what must have been a similar image the hysterical woman had described in Guildford. They seemed to be soldiers all right; but, none of the type that Amsterdam had ever seen before. While they were human in shape with two arms, two legs, a torso and head Amsterdam could not definitely assume that these creatures were, in fact, human; as their bodies were covered in what appeared to be a metallic material and the head of the creature was also covered in a metallic covering that was bereft of any facial features or discerning marks of any kind. Their intent, however, had the same menacing characteristics of any invading force as Amsterdam witnessed a savage slaying of three people travelling in a car that was stopped, the doors unceremoniously ripped off and the occupants riddled with the flashes of blue light. No one, it seemed, was to be spared.

From his vantage point, Amsterdam could see across to the Docks where other buildings lined the water front and he noticed that they too were being overrun with troops with sporadic flashes of blue light. He watched as some kind of ship that was shaped like an upside down yacht touched effortlessly down and took off almost immediately only to reveal that it offloaded another lot of troops that then stormed into the GSV TV News building. He watched as the ship took off and followed it to where it seemed to join in a procession of ships of similar shape in the air. If the lights on the side of the ship were any indication there were practically hundreds of these ships up there which meant thousands of troops would be flooding the city in all different areas.

The invading force seemed only to be utilising the blue light as a weapon on the people only and kept the buildings themselves intact. In fact, the blue light seemed not to harm any building or structure as he witnessed a couple of shots, but only a few, that were off their mark and had seemingly absorbed into the wall. The blue light itself, Amsterdam assumed, must have been some type of laser or electrical pulse weapon; but, nothing that he had ever witnessed or heard of being developed anywhere in the world.

Amsterdam could feel sweat begin to build in the webbing of his fingers and he had the uncontrollable urge to scratch at every portion of his body to relieve the tension. He even considered what the odds would have been that Australia would be invaded and how it was he could have placed a bet on it. And this was, as Harry Lockley had put it, an invasion. Australia would be invaded. Words Amsterdam thought could never be imagined, formulated or uttered; but, from the picture that was unfolding before him, it would become an encyclopaedia entry; a footnote in history to which Amsterdam had front row seats.

Whatever became of this event in the morning there was one thing for sure that the lives he and his family had been living would be utterly changed forever. A change of this magnitude would be something that usually a journalist of Amsterdam's calibre would rejoice in covering and there was a real sense within him at that moment that wanted to be a fly on the wall to the devastation and chronicle the events blow-by-blow. However, somehow, he understood that the rights of the Press and of the Geneva Convention would not be recognised on this occasion; and, an irresistible desire to flee consumed Amsterdam's thoughts. He suddenly became very aware that the building where he stood would be considered a primary target and unless he wanted to be fried by that blue light he had better make an escape plan and fast.

However, as Amsterdam moved around the office looking out of the window from all sides of the building he could see that his position was surrounded on all sides by troops moving through the streets. He would be found out for sure if he tried to make a break for it. His decision, however, would be made for him it would seem as another yacht shaped ship dropped down on the street beside *The Gazette* building and he watched as a team moved toward the building with clear intent to enter; and, if the events on the street were any indication, eliminate anybody within.

Amsterdam reached for the phone, he needed to speak with Ginger; he needed to hear the voices of his children. However, when he tried to get a line out he found that the phone line was dead.

"Come on, come on…Please!" he said slamming down the receiver as he discovered his attempts were futile. He reached for his cell phone in his pocket and when he discovered that the coverage bars read 'No Service' he yelled out in frustration and threw the cell phone against the wall smashing it to pieces.

"I'm trapped," he said out loud and he stood in the middle of the room with his hands on head thinking that this wasn't a fair fight.

Chapter 14

Harry Lockley dripped a wet towel over his head. He was exhausted. He'd been up since before dawn and now it was well passed his usual bed time. But even after a solid day of fencing, the most traumatic experience only happened half an hour ago. His wife, Mabel, was right not to believe him. This wasn't the first time he'd gone off the rails chasing shadows. He didn't blame her for throwing every pot and plate at him even though the kitchen knives were a bit much; but, what would have he expected after bringing home news like he did and she had the right to question him given the last time it had happened.

The first time it happened was five years prior. Lockley was bringing a flock of sheep down from the highlands. That night, while sitting by his camp fire, he looked up and saw a jet fighter in a dogfight with another aircraft. But it wasn't something he had seen before. The jet fighter must have got a lock and damaged the other aircraft that withdrew from the fight and landed a kilometre away in one of the fields. Lockley raced up the side of the mountain to a lookout point and peered over the ledge to find a whole battalion of soldiers on the ground encircling the aircraft. The aircraft itself was not a fighter. Its girth made it look like a carrier of some kind. And as a ramp opened at the back, the surrounding soldiers opened fire as the unknown airships occupants piled out. It was a bloody slaughter and Lockley couldn't believe what he had seen. He ran back down to his camp site, kick-started his motor bike and didn't stop until he reached home. He tried his hardest to get Mabel to believe him, even tried to get her to come out with him to the site; but she wouldn't listen and proclaimed that if it was so, they would hear something about it on the news in the morning. But there was nothing. No mention of it at all. And, when he did finally manage to convince her to come out to the camp site they went back to the lookout and saw that what he had witnessed had disappeared. Instead, the place was filled with fire trucks, spraying water on a scorched grass fire. He thought at the time that he must be losing it, his mind wandering into the subconscious world, the solitude of farming life finally getting to him. Mabel was none too pleased and began scolding him as to why he did not give the fire fighters a hand and why he had to make up some elaborate story to get out of doing some hard work. For years Mabel thought that it was he who lit the fire and tried to cover it up. After that, she wouldn't allow him to do any burning off on their property and would pay the fee to have the fire authority to do it for him.

So when Lockley came home half an hour ago there was a very slight chance that she would go completely off the rails. He tried to blurt it out as calmly as he could to make her feel that he was in control of his sanity; but, what would he think if his spouse came home and announced that we were being invaded by God only knows what? She stood there at first and calmly listened as he described what he had seen. She had a comforting smile; it was what he fell in love with. But some things in life are best unsaid. Some things, you need more than a firsthand account. If he had of laid low and found some of the ships shrapnel in the field and bought it home to show her, then she would have believed him all those years ago. However, again he had no evidence, only his trust which had been lost on her. She was prepared to accept the story as ramblings of an ageing farmer. She read about it in a magazine, how farmers lost their perception of reality in the solitude of their work.

When he told her that he was going to call the authorities that was the last straw for Mabel. This would make it more than a family matter, something she couldn't just sweep under the carpet; and, she told Lockley that she would not bare the embarrassment that would undoubtedly follow or the shame of being ostracised from the community. It was then that she had left; but, Lockley knew what he saw and the torment of five years of not knowing fuelled a determination within him to find the truth and prove to Mabel once and for all that he was not insane.

And Lockley had been planning for this. Every day since that first sighting he was convinced that something was coming. That it wasn't an isolated incident at all. Most would have called him paranoid if they had of known his thoughts and he was careful to keep these ideas to himself. He didn't want to alarm Mabel or make her feel unsafe but he didn't have it in him to let the issue go. Lockley was convinced that a threat was imminent and he had to do something to protect them. And Lockley found that he wasn't the only one concerned for the safety of the nation.

He had decided that the first thing he had to do was arm himself. He had never fired a gun before but had discovered he felt that without the means to defend himself he was practically dead in the water. He had discovered a posting online for people selling firearms and found one that was relatively close but further enough away not to cause suspicion. It was in a small country town of Long River, four hours west of Lockley's property, where he found a man called The Chief, a farmer like himself. As he drove up the dusty driveway a man came out of the shed and sat on the edge of a rusty tractor rolling a cigarette. He would have been in his late forties with the smile lines and dirty leathery skin that was typical of a man in his profession. He wore a denim shirt with ripped sleeves, denim jeans and a bandana that may have been a navy blue in colour at some stage but had now greyed with sweat and grease. Lockley didn't know what to expect of the man and even had considered turning around; but, as he sat in his car for a moment contemplating his next move the man waved at him which gave Lockley the impression that he wasn't in any danger.

"G'day," greeted Lockley with his hand outstretched as he walked up to him. As the man shook his hand Lockley felt the hard calloused skin on his palms and realised that the man was particularly strong, "I'm looking for a guy who calls himself The Chief?"

"Then you've found him. So, you're the fella that enquired about the rifle?" The Chief replied.

"Yes, mate. That would be me."

"Good. If you weren't I would have had to shoot 'ya," said The Chief with a big toothy grin as he put the cigarette he was rolling in his mouth and lit it up.

"I'm only messing with 'ya. Gotta name?"

"Harry, Harry Lockley."

"That a real name is it, Lockley?"

"Yes. The only one I have."

"Hmm. Seems like this is the first time that you've done something like this, Lockley. So let me give you a word of advice. Names in a transaction like this are not something you give out freely. You've gotta wait until you can trust the man. And even then, it is usually a fake one you give out. It makes sure that the pigs are set off the trail. You aint a pig are you?"

Lockley wasn't anticipating this type of interrogation to begin with. He thought that there may be some kind of probing and suspicion but once the transaction was done then that would be it.

"No, not at all," replied Lockley.

"I didn't think so. Don't look the type. So, what are you when you aren't purchasing firearms?"

"A farmer much like yourself. I have a property out in the east running sheep."

"Now that's a name I haven't heard people call me in a long while. A farmer. Truth is this land hasn't been worked for over fifteen years. This property was my Pops and his Pop before that but there's nothing that has grown in these fields for many a year."

Lockley had thought as much. It didn't take a genius to work that out given the age of his equipment and the rusted and rotting fencing he saw when he drove in.

"So, what do you keep yourself busy with?" asked Lockley.

"Oh, this and that. Mainly work on engines for the farmers when they break down. I'm good with that kind of stuff you see. Other than that I mainly keep to myself. So, you ever shot a rifle before?"

"No, not once."

"All righty then. We better get you sized up. Come on in."

The Chief turned and walked back inside the shed. Lockley followed a little apprehensively. But when he walked inside, he knew he had come to the right place. The shed was the size of a hangar and much larger than the house he had seen on his way in. The décor, if you could call it that, would have matched any army barrack across the world. The walls were covered in military flags and colours; the ceiling covered in camouflage material; and, scattered throughout the area were vehicles all of which were painted in camouflage colours. The vehicles themselves from what Lockley could tell were covered in armour plating and mainly converted from standard everyday cars. As they walked toward the back he could see that there was a hydraulic lift where obviously The Chief performed his mechanical work and to the left of this a large object the size of a bus covered in a green canvas cover.

There was a small wooden platform that led up to a workbench resting along the back wall about three meters wide and The Chief plucked something off the bench and knelt on the floor. He inserted to what appeared to be a key of some sort into a hole in the floor; however, it was none that Lockley had seen before. It was about three inches long but about an inch wide and circular in shape; but, when The Chief turned the key there was a cracking sound and the wooden floor raised about two inches along a line of the floorboard. The Chief turned the key some more and this raised the boards slightly at each turn until he could get his hand underneath it. He gave a heave and lifted the entire length of the boards which opened to a set of stairs.

"Right. Step into my office," said The Chief.

As Lockley followed him down the dozen or so steps The Chief flicked a switch and a fluorescent light flashed on washing the underground room in a bright white light. Lockley could only stare at what he saw. Firearms of all descriptions from hand guns to sub-machine guns, rocket launchers and machetes and face masks and chemical suits.

"Welcome to my collection," announced The Chief with a grin, "For all you apocalyptic needs. Anything take your fancy?"

"I wouldn't know where to start?" replied Lockley.

"Well it all depends what you're shooting at, don't it?"

It was the exact question Lockley had been asking himself.

"Listen," said The Chief, "I know what you're thinking. What is a man like me doin' with all this stuff? I bet you think I'm a little bit crazy. But I can tell you this. I got all this stuff for a reason. And the way I see it, everyone that makes contact with me also has a reason. I bet you got a reason. Even if you don't know what that reason is yet."

"Oh no, I got a reason," replied Lockley. "It's just that everyone I've told doesn't believe me."

"Well, you've got me listening, don't you?"

Lockley looked hard at The Chief. He seemed to be genuine but Lockley had made a promise to himself that he was only doing this for himself; to protect his home, his family and his friends. He was prepared to shoulder the burden of responsibility on his own and the reality was that he hoped for all God's grace that he would never have to be called upon to action. But, now, here was a man who seemed to share the same air of concern he was experiencing and Lockley felt a surge of relief as he told The Chief about his experience in the paddock. Afterward, The Chief asked him, "And where do you say your farm is?"

"Twenty-clicks east of Templeton."

"Hmm." The Chief then turned to a wall and pulled down a screen which held a map of Australia. On it, were small blue dots scattered it seemed randomly across the country with small numbers that appeared to symbolise a date.

"What are those?" Asked Lockley.

"Sightings of unrecorded military action. And you said that this was a month ago?"

"Yes, that's right. But how did you get all this?"

"This is a big country. Sparsely populated. Those in the top think that no one is watching them. That they can get away with anything. But there are those that do see them, sometimes people just like yourself who were just innocent bystanders caught up in the middle and see something that they shouldn't have. Mostly they are discredited or swept under the carpet when they try to go through the official channels; but, this doesn't satisfy them and they put the call out there for information for someone to tell them that they aint goin' completely insane. Mostly, once they talk about their situation and find that they aint the only ones this usually satisfies them enough. But on some occasions they need a little bit more than that and they keep in contact. This is the result of that contact and for some time I've noticed that these sightings have become more and more frequent in the last few years."

"It got a name?"

"Like I said, names are what draw attention to the pigs."

"Then how do people know what to look for?"

"With this," The Chief pointed to the bottom of the screen and there underneath the map of Australia was the symbol *XXOO*.

"Hugs and kisses?" asked Lockley.

"With love," replied The Chief, "All these incidents on this map have not been reported in the press or in any official military records. They range from air and ground assaults and even naval conflict. It's like they don't want us to know something."

Recalling that first meeting now with The Chief, Lockley understood what he was meaning. He was right they didn't want us to know something, a big thing, in fact. From that meeting he spent more and more time at The Chief's farm. Others came as well and talked about their sightings and their preparations for what was to come. The Chief, for his part, was looked to as some sort of mentor and his followers were willing to listen to his guidance and direction. Lockley did not see fit to ask him why he knew so much and where he had obtained the firearms and other military paraphernalia. He just went along with it happy in the thought that there was someone there prepared to empathise with his fears. He had told Mabel that he had taken up hunting which explained the weapons that he was bringing home and also gave him an excuse each weekend to go off on the many training camps The Chief had planned that were designed to teach military skills which included weapons and survival training.

But right now he didn't know how long he would have but he had to make it to The Chief's farm as quickly as possible. He had to tell him what he had seen. He didn't leave Mabel a note or details of his whereabouts as he left possibly for the last time. If she returned hopefully his absence would give her enough sense to leave as well. He wheeled out the motorbike that he had purchased recently as he assumed that he could travel much quicker than the four-wheel-drive. He didn't need much where he was going. The only item he picked up was his rifle which he strung over his shoulder and ammunition which he stuffed in the saddle bags.

As he hit the open road with his lights off to avoid detection he could sense the approach of another of those ships and they whizzed over his head once again as they did before. It was then that Lockley was assured that this was no accident. They were here whatever they were and he pulled down harder on the throttle hoping that he would make it in time.

Chapter 15

Ginger Amsterdam listened to her cell ringing as it sat on the nightstand. At each ring the buzzing would shuffle the handset along a little way across the top of the nightstand until it rang out leaving the cell teetering on the edge. She didn't want to answer it, not tonight. It was her husband, Harvey, as usual. The life of a journalist's wife had been one that she had been accustomed; but, in reality she had enough of the excuses. Each night was something new; a deadline, a disaster, a coup. It all meant one thing. That she would be alone that evening and she would possibly see him in the morning for breakfast.

As she picked up the cell she cursed him for waking her up. There was a message that beeped at her; however, she didn't need to listen to it. But now there was nothing to it, she was the type that when she was awake she was awake and couldn't stand to linger in bed looking at the ceiling. She went to the kitchen and decided on coffee. Something to calm her and she liked the bitter taste. She was, however, on a diet on doctors orders. Her hectic lifestyle had taken a toll on her heart and generally small luxuries like coffee, chocolate and even sex had to be taken in moderation. Ginger took a list with her every day with the foods she ate and ticked them off. Each level was categorised by *must haves*, *once only* and *only if all of the above have been fulfilled*. She pulled it off the fridge held by a magnet. The *must haves* included things like particular fruit and vegetables, fish and exercise. Things like bread and no fat milk were in the *once only* category. All of the above had been fulfilled for that day and the only thing left on the list was her indulgences. She'd been leaving it blank all day for the one thing she could still give her husband. But since that was off the menu, she crossed the coffee box and put it back on the fridge.

Walking back to her room she noticed that Rachel's light was still on. Like her mother, she had trouble sleeping all her life and Harvey's call would have been enough to wake her. Every time a car went by their street or the next doors tree creaked in a strong wind she would be awake. But she'd always been a happy child and she loved life to the full which was probably the reason her body didn't like lying dormant.

It was then that the home phone rang and she thought that she might let that go unanswered as well as she knew that it would be Harvey again. He didn't like leaving messages on machines and she could see him probably getting frustrated that she had not returned his call. It was his job, he would tell Ginger. But she had left the signs. That morning she had made a special effort to make Harvey see her shaving her legs and she had even asked him to pick up a nice bottle of wine on his way home. So, tonight, he would be given the cold shoulder. She would remain as bitter as long as the coffee she was drinking remained in her mouth. She heard Rachel take some footsteps and pick up the phone in her room. Perhaps she'd called one of her friends to have a chat, Ginger thought, but as she walked past her room on the way back to her own Ginger could tell that the tone in her voice was rather formal after her initial greeting; and, as Ginger put the coffee cup down beside the book she was reading near the radio clock on the nightstand, she heard Rachel's door click open and then she appeared in the doorway.

"Mum, ah, it's ah-" she was whispering as she entered the doorway, cupping the receiver to block out the sound.

"Who is it, sweetie?" asked Ginger.

"It's...It's the Prime Minister."

"The Prime Minister?"

Ginger Amsterdam was shocked and felt under dressed standing there in her night gown. Even though it was only a telephone call, she seemed naked without her business attire. She was used to dealing with politicians, but this scenario was a little too intimate.

"Yeah, that's what he said," Rachel replied as she held out the phone to Ginger.

"Okay. Here, I'll take it," Rachel handed it over and slipped back to her room. It was with good reason, too. Ginger put herself in Rachel's shoes for a moment and imagined what it would have been like if her mother got a call from the Prime Minister late at night. In Ginger's case, it would have been to tell her mother that her father had died a horrible death in a mining accident.

Ginger pulled the phone finally to her ear, "Hello, Prime Minister."

"Hello, Ginger." Prime Minister Hughes replied. Rachel wasn't lying, for a second there she had hoped it was just a hoax and that maybe it was Harvey trying to be funny.

"How may I help you, Sir?" Ginger replied more formally.

"I just thought that you should hear this form me, is all. We ah, we got a K29K evacuation code."

For a second, Ginger closed her eyes and a wave of anxiety flashed over her. Had she heard the Prime Minister right?

"Do you understand?" Hughes continued but she hadn't heard him. She was engulfed with fear. How could this be? Could it really be her K29K code? It was one of the key departments in her role with the government; but, alerting Molly was not a part of the plan. And, hearing the code now coming from the mouth of the Prime Minister sent her into instant shock as she thought that she would never hear the words uttered from anyone.

"Ginger, now Ginger, listen to me, this is not a drill! Now, I've made some calls and put you and your two children on the list; but, you have to make it there yourself. Do you understand me, Ginger?"

"Yes, Sir," Ginger said but she couldn't fathom it. How could this be! "But, why me? That wasn't part of what we planned?"

"These are my wishes. Be safe." He clicked off and Ginger stood there blankly. What about Harvey, she thought? Could she really leave her husband? But she wasn't really leaving him. She was protecting their children; which was something that they had always talked about. That no matter what, the welfare of their children came first. Ginger then caught a glimpse of herself in the mirror and something twigged inside her. We're dead stationary. She dropped the phone on the floor and raced to the study. Rachel emerged from her room.

"Mum?" Ginger caught a glimpse of her scared eyes and turned.

"Rachel! Rachel wake up your brother!"

Unlike Rachel, Nathaniel could sleep through a brass band playing the victory march which was a trait he'd acquired from his father.

"What's wrong?" she pleaded, but Ginger didn't have time.

"Just do it!" Ginger yelled from the end of the hall sliding into the study. Rachel picked up her tone though and raced to Nathaniel's room. She was such a trustworthy person. Ginger dare not think how what was to come would affect her innocence.

Ginger heard Rachel banging on the door to Nathaniel's room as she flipped open the screen on her laptop. The file for K29K was what she was looking for. She scrolled through a list of sub-folders and cursed her laziness. She had good intentions to clean out the old files on this thing but never had the time. Now, it was chaotic. Ginger knew what she was looking for. She knew what the contents of the file on K29K would read. She knew what the procedure was, how to follow through the process. But something in her made her want to see it with her own two eyes. She needed some sort of tangible evidence to convince her of what it was she had just heard even if it was from the Prime Minister himself.

Rachel finally entered with Nathaniel beside her still fighting to tear himself away from sleep.

"Mum?" Rachel said, "What's the matter?"

"Yeah, what's going on?" Nathaniel said.

"Okay, kids. I need you to trust your mother now. I need you to go and pack a bag with a few changes of clothes, toiletries and things. But not too much and I need you to do it in five minutes, okay!"

"Mum, you're scaring me. What did the Prime Minister want?" said Rachel.

"Prime Minister?" Nathaniel was slow on the uptake.

"I'll tell you everything soon. But just do this for me, okay," replied Ginger.

"Where's Dad?" Nathaniel loved his father; it would be hard to get him moving without him knowing his father would be all right.

"Ah, he's going to meet up with us later," she lied, "Now go. Come on!"

The two scampered off. She was lucky with her children. They weren't horrible teenagers at all. Just good kids. Ginger always thought herself lucky, especially with some of the stories that she'd heard from other mothers. It wasn't like when she was growing up at all and Ginger had difficulty comprehending how it was best to reveal the world to her young impressionable children. It was a balance that she had originally not dared to venture. But, Harvey had been wonderful. He hated the way his own father had showed him the world and had vowed that his own children would not be left so in the dark as he had. He had been there all of the way to teach them the ways of the world without condescending them and he really was an inspiration to parenting. He treated them like equals and Ginger marvelled at how respectful they were of him. If, for instance, it was Harvey that told them to hurry they would have responded without question. She envied their relationship but at the same time conceded that she would not have been able to do the things Harvey did with their children.

Ginger entered the myriad of passwords that she'd encrypted on the file K29K. The Government seal flashed onto the screen and Ginger knew she was in. It was an extensively detailed document but she only needed the summary which was twenty-five pages long and she hit the print key. The laser jet on her desk whirred with excitement and began to print off the pages.

While the printer was shooting through the pages Ginger went to change out of her pyjamas and into something more appropriate for the situation. She raced down the hallway to her room and opened the closet and found nothing appropriate for the job at hand. Unfortunately, she was fresh out of military fatigues which would have been the most fitting attire for the situation; however, her wardrobe consisted of mainly business suits. She didn't own a pair of jeans and found that tracksuits were quite unflattering. But as she was flicking through the options, she stumbled upon some of Harvey's weekend clothes and for a moment collapsed into emotion. Would she see him again? After everything, he was still her husband and father to her children. They had their problems recently which in reality were nothing that any of her friends had not experienced. She just naively thought that it wouldn't happen to her. Should she call him and warn him of what it is that was coming? It was something that she hadn't contemplated but she knew that time was of the essence and Harvey was a person that needed all the facts in front of him before he'd react. This was for their children, she was sure he'd understand.

She settled on one of his polo shirts and pulled on a pair of garden shorts of her own. She pulled up her hair into a pony tail and caught a glimpse of the time from the clock on the dresser. This was going to be tight.

"Rachel! Nathaniel! Two minutes and then head to the car!"

Ginger went back to the study where the printing had finished and jammed the printed pages into a manila folder. She then picked up the laptop and whacked it firmly into corner of the hardwood desk. It split the thing in two and then Ginger attacked it with an envelope opener. It was important that no-one knew what it was she was doing, what she knew or where she was going. She knew that certain things could be restored and lost data recouped. But this would buy her the time she needed. She then scampered to the kitchen and threw whatever she could find that resembled food into a box and then turned to the garage door where her children were waiting with back-packs. Frightened, but ready. Such good children, she thought.

Chapter 16

There was a slight jerk from the ship as it landed and the floor of the ship opened up dropping the entire platoon to the ground. Tenashi followed the soldier beside him and crouched on the ground as the ship took off and released them into a hectic image of a battle zone. The road was littered with dead bodies as the First Wave platoon moved up a relatively empty street and Tenashi could see blue flashes of light that originated from other IA5 units hit people that were running away from the line. It was a grim reality though Tenashi had not killed another living soul since he took the life of his friend and he felt an urge that had not consumed him since that day. It was the urge all humans usually have that tells them they don't want to kill another human being.

The Lieutenant was the first soldier to stand as the ship ascended away silently into the air and he made his way to the front of the platoon. Tenashi followed as he called for the platoon to move out in a direction away from the fighting and for a brief second he was thankful that he would not have to be involved in the slaughter.

They moved up the side of the building and Tenashi's display flashed, 'Primary Target Located' as the Lieutenant's voice spoke in his ear.

"Okay soldiers. Here's the plan. Soldiers thirty through to thirty-four will form Alpha team and enter the side entrance that is guarded by an unarmed security guard. Take him out and then move on through to the third level which is the entry point for the service elevator. Sensors show two people in the building. One in third level and one in the fifth level. Soldiers thirty-five to thirty-nine will form Bravo team and scale the eastern wall to guard the roof top creating a perimeter while soldiers forty to forty-two, Charlie team, will scale the western wall and work your way down from the roof top to third level and rendezvous with Alpha team at the entrance to the service elevator. Team Delta will be made up of Soldiers forty-three to fifty and form sentries at each point of the building in teams of two. Delta one will be forty-three and forty-four, Delta two will be forty-five and forty-six, Delta three will be forty-seven and forty-eight and Delta four, forty-nine and fifty. Delta one on the north-east point, Delta two on north-west, Delta three south-west and Delta four south-east. I'll follow Alpha team and direct traffic from there. Keep the updates in clean two minute intervals. Team Bravo will move out first and once in position Team Alpha and Team Charlie will make their insertions followed by Team Delta. Once our primary object is complete we'll activate secondary objectives to be carried out by team Alpha and Charlie. Let's hit this load light and fast in 5, 4, 3, 2, 1. Bravo team away."

Four of the platoon moved off from their cover point in a single line toward the eastern wall. A compass point with the letter 'E' displayed on the wall of the building in Tenashi's view. They fired what looked like to be thin cable lines up the side of the building and scaled up in only a few bounds.

"Alpha and Charlie teams move to insertion points, now. Team Delta take sentry positions upon entry on my mark."

Tenashi moved with team Alpha and the Lieutenant at the centre as he scouted the distance for enemy sightings.

"No enemy signatures present in the immediate vicinity," announced Lupei. She was starting to take out all the fun of the chase.

The group moved up to the entrance without incident and took cover behind the wall. Occasionally Tenashi could see flashes of light up where the First Wave line must have been moving through the streets and he even noticed a unit moving through what his display classified as an apartment building.

As the Lieutenant moved to the front of the group and peered around the corner Tenashi's display flashed a red mark with a distance indicator of 3.45 meters.

"Target marked," said Lupei.

"Okay, target is barricaded behind a secure room. Thirty and thirty-one set hole charges at the bottom of the door; thirty-two release flashes and thirty-three set pulse to maximum and take the kill," said the Lieutenant.

"Forty reporting, Charlie team has arrived and holding at insertion point, out."

"Thirty and thirty-one go!" both the soldiers moved inside crouching low along the wall. As quickly as they appeared to enter they returned and took a position on the opposite side of the entrance.

It would soon be Tenashi's turn and without warning a flash took his vision. It was his vision not the screens that he saw and his heart beat raised more than was necessary. Tenashi saw a man of African descent in this vision, "So this is where the Oracle led me," he said again. It was more precise on this occasion like the voice was really there and the memory took control momentarily of his concentration. He almost didn't realise it had happened but by the time the image subsided and the emotion of the occasion shifted his thoughts to a solitary track of hunt and destroy the flash grenade had been let off by thirty-two and he, thirty-three, was on the target. In an instant his arm raised, the target locked and the weapon was fired without further consideration.

The pulse lit up the dull room and contacted the shocked security guard forcing him back before he even had a chance to focus on his perpetrator. The only blood from the pulse ammunition was when the target smashed the side of his head on the corner of the desk as he fell to the floor. It was not the usual death blow Tenashi had become accustomed to in training and even less ceremonious than his first.

"Target eliminated," announced Lupei.

"Forty here, beginning insertion on level five."

"Delta one on point."

"Delta two on point."

"Delta three on point."

"Delta four on point."

"Clear on Bravo"

"Move to rally point, Alpha."

Intrinsically Tenashi followed suit. He moved out without even looking into the eye of his first kill in the field. It was a feeling that he would never forget though. Like he was the loneliest person who ever lived and he could not help but think to himself that he never wanted to kill another human being again.

Chapter 17

Trapped in the office of *The Gazette*, Harvey Amsterdam had taken refuge in his office and he had tried to access the Internet. He had hoped that possibly there was still access but had come to realise that the telephone and Internet services were interlinked and one wouldn't function without the other. In another time, Amsterdam would have thought there could have been a story in that; but now, the only story was the one that he was experiencing right now – an invasion that was happening on Australian soil – and one that he was going to be engaged with very shortly as soldiers had entered the building. They would come for him and he would die defenceless; alone in his office, filled with the stories of other people's lives.

Amsterdam ran a finger over the photo of his family that sat on his desk. If only he could get to them somehow. Dying wouldn't have seemed such an onerous task with them beside him and he regretted the fact that he wasn't there to protect them from harm. He had considered his own mortality very little throughout his life – he didn't even have life insurance – and had always thought there would be time to come to grips with the whole thing when he was much older. He was only forty-two, a young man really, by rights he should have had another good forty-two years left in him to contemplate what the end was and what it all meant. The end, evidently, would come in a hail of blue light that would surge through him and carry him to the beyond. Maybe there was just enough time to catch the religious bug which was going around that evening. No, he thought, that would be merely accepting things as they were. That wasn't how a journalist lived his life. Change fate, challenge tomorrow. Take risks where no one else would; even in the face of popular opinion, there is always an alternative. These were the things which drove Amsterdam day in day out. It was what filled the walls of his office and made him seek that which did not want to be sought.

Beside the family portrait sat a letter opener that he had received as a father's day gift from Rachel and Nathaniel. There was an inscription on the side which read: Our father, our inspiration. Amsterdam picked up the blade and pricked the end on his thumb and then he gripped the handle tightly.

"No way," he said quietly and then thumped the top of his desk with his left fist. Amsterdam had decided that he was not going to take this sitting down and stood up with the letter opener in his right hand.

"This is not how it is going to end!" Amsterdam said standing from his desk and walking out of his office heading for the elevators, "If this is going to be it then let them come. Let them come and see what it is they are going to have to deal with. This!" he said whacking his chest, "This is not the day that you come in my house and decide when it is that I will cease to exist. Not this day, not ever!"

Amsterdam thought that he could take them. He had kept himself in fairly good shape. He rode his bicycle on the weekends and enjoyed paddling his kayak in the bay. He had convinced himself that he had the element of surprise and, even if he could only take out one of them, then that was enough for him to be happy that he had made an effort. That he had died fighting. And, as he heard the elevator wind up to begin its ascent he grasped the letter opener tightly and stood in a position waiting to pounce.

His plan was to drive the letter opener into the neck of one of the troops hoping that was a weak point on their armour. He would aim for the one in the right hand side and try to turn it in his grasp and shield himself by any attempts made by other troops to fire at him with the blue light. He even might get them to be able to fire on themselves in the confusion and create a panic. It may have been a slim chance but it was worth a try.

However, as the elevator came to a halt and released a soft dinging sound the door parted and Amsterdam prepared himself for his final moments when what he was confronted with was nothing but a solitary man. He had expected at least five and as he thrust his primitive weapons at the man, he had an inclination to stop as the man shielded himself cowering in fear.

"Please, don't hurt me!" pleaded the man as Amsterdam jerked back, "Don't hurt me!"

"Take it easy," said Amsterdam, "I'm not going to hurt you. I thought you were one of them. Who are you?"

"My name is Mitchell, Mitchell Reed. I'm, I'm the librarian. I heard the shots and looked out the window. I thought I was the only one here and I came down to alert the authorities...You're Amsterdam, right?"

"That's right," Amsterdam replied.

"I file all of your articles."

"Really?" Amsterdam thought that maybe if Reed had been able to file his last article that Evans and the board had rejected then possibly all of this wouldn't be happening, "Well, I wouldn't bother alerting the authorities, I've already tried-" Suddenly, Amsterdam noticed that the other elevator was making its way up, "That can't be good!"

"They're coming for us!" exclaimed Reed.

"What are we going to do, we need to hide," said Amsterdam.

"The vault!" Reed responded.

"The vault?"

"Yes, the vault," said Reed, "Come with me."

Chapter 18

Tenashi stood at the ready with Alpha team and the Lieutenant as the elevator moved slowly up past level one and then level two.

"Charlie here. Sector five clear."

"Life signs on sector one and two negative," said Lupei.

"Sensors show sector four clear, Lieutenant."

"Scramble to sector three rally point Charlie team. Targets seem to be making a break for the service elevator to the vault. Take the stairs and cut them off on entry."

"Roger."

"Alpha team ready pulse to maximum. Target success is high, repeat is high. Thirty and thirty-one move to left flank; thirty-two and thirty-three with me in the central route. Now!"

It was a fleeting moment that Tenashi saw him. But it was enough for Lupei to get a fix on his face and capture the image to be stored on the right hand side of his display. However, as the team fanned out into position Tenashi could not get a fix on the target.

"Open fire Alpha. Attack the target."

"Charlie team in hot zone."

"Take them out Charlie."

"Too late Lieutenant target has entered the elevator cavity."

"Move on rally point."

"We've lost visual on target, Lieutenant."

"Bust a hole in that service elevator door thirty-one."

As both Alpha and Charlie teams took cover behind various pieces of furniture thirty-one connected a device to the door.

"Fire in the hole."

The blast was instantaneous and both teams converged on the entrance. Pulse rounds were fired down the shaft appearing not to damage the roof of the elevator at all and a thick door closed over the top of the elevator sealing it in.

"Hold your fire teams. Pulse rounds are useless on inanimate objects. Central control, primary targets have been captured seeking permission to begin secondary missionary objectives."

"Granted, Lieutenant. Primary objective analysis shows intel highly credible and secondary mission objects to continue as planned."

"Copy that Control. Call in air strike on my beacon. Inception high density ray specified on schematic. Confirm velocity level three intensity. Bravo team mark beacon point and cover for impact."

"Contact Delta four!"

"Delta four confirm enemy approach?"

"Delta four, four armed police officers. High calibre automatic weapons. Permission to engage."

"Delta two confirms enemy sightings."

"Bravo thirty-four take sniper position on the eastern point while thirty-five, thirty-six and thirty-seven continue with beacon deployment. Delta four draw their line of fire."

"Copy that."

"Alpha and Charlie teams on me. Secondary target objectives are to infiltrate the vault room through the service elevator and take out any enemy combatants. Air support will make a hole from the roof using heat ray weapons. It'll get a little hot in here but the intensity will be minimal. It'll take out the seal but not the vault entrance. That will require a heat drill which will be lowered down through the shaft and Alpha team will take control of working on the vault door-"

"Bravo, thirty-four, confirms three hits."

"Delta two confirms."

"Appears last man is retreating from the area, Lieutenant."

"Hold your positions Delta team. Bravo thirty-four rejoin team on western side and brace for impact."

"Copy."

"Alpha team. Intel shows that the vault while not impregnable has fail safe measures to collapse the entrance to the structure and bury any chance of entry. It has weak points at these three locations and you will need to direct fire of the heat drill at these points."

"Bravo thirty-five, air support sighted Lieutenant."

"Lieutenant, this is air drone four-five-nine heat insertion deployment will commence in sixty seconds."

"Roger."

"Bravo thirty-four, in position."

"Alpha and Charlie team take cover in that office on the northern side."

The soldiers moved toward the office in a straight line. Tenashi came in last behind the Lieutenant and closed the door behind him.

"Okay, soldiers. Five seconds."

The sound was more severe than the heat. Even through the helmet it roared into a thrumming percussion like a big band in the pulpit of an opera. Tenashi even noticed for the first time a trickle of sweat from his forehead dripping over his eye line and there was suddenly a cool breeze inside the helmet.

"Moisture detected." Said Lupei, "Cooling system activated."

As the heat and the thrumming subsided the Lieutenant moved back to the rally point and Tenashi and the others followed.

"Hole clear, Lieutenant."

"Outstanding. Alpha prepare for descent."

"Bravo, thirty-four, air transport on approaching."

"Get in that hole Alpha."

Tenashi stood at the top of the elevator shaft. He briefly looked up and saw the Bravo team around the opening and the Air Drone fly overhead.

"Analysis shows the best route down is to fire line cable into the shaft slightly above the opening and repel down," said Lupei, "Point your right arm to the yellow target."

Tenashi did as he was instructed and locked onto the yellow box that was flashing. A cable released from the top of his right arm.

"Line secure. Begin your descent."

Tenashi gave it a little pull just to be sure and found that it didn't give. He launched off the edge and put his weight onto the cable. It descended quickly but Tenashi didn't feel out of control as he landed legs splayed on the floor of the elevator. He could feel the lingering heat from the heat ray and he marvelled at the accuracy of the device.

"Deploying heat drill."

Tenashi looked up to see a large devise being lowered down from the transport through the hole. As it touched the ground he felt the floor of the elevator move a little bit adjusting to the weight of the device. It was just enough to trip the sensor plates underneath that triggered the fail safe mechanisms and the roof of the entrance caved in before Tenashi or any of the Alpha team knew what was happening.

"Alpha team. Report, what happened down there.

Tenashi replied, "Alpha thirty-three, looks like the entrance was rigged with movement sensors. The entrance is buried under dirt."

"Central Control, we've got a situation on secondary target. Entrance has collapse and entry has been compromised. They'll know we're coming."

"Copy, Lieutenant. Stand by."

"Alpha team grab the cable. Air transport extract Alpha team."

Tenashi grabbed a part of the cable and began to rise back through the hole and they jumped onto the roof one at a time.

"Lieutenant, this is Central Control. Analysis advises that there is still a high probability of success on secondary target. Routing earth extraction unit for your disposal. Approximately three minutes to drop and on estimates three hours dig time to allow entry to the vault. Your orders are to remain on site and hold the building until secondary task completion."

"Copy that Central Control. Team, we have our orders. Bravo team hold on the roof and mark any potential entry points. Alpha, reinforce Delta one soldier to a sentry position."

Tenashi moved down to the south-west corner via the elevator and made contact with Delta three. His scanners showed no movement in the heads up display and apart from the occasional flash of a pulse weapon in the city the area was ghostly silent.

The only movement came from up above where a transport ship lowered what appeared to be a vacuum into the hole in the building made by the heat ray. It landed on the roof and began to make a humming sound as it began to extract the dirt that had collapsed almost right on top of Tenashi himself. It appeared that the transport itself would be taking the dirt with them on board and dropping this elsewhere as Tenashi did not see a build up of earth scattered on the roof.

Under the hum and the reduced sense of urgency it was no surprise that Tenashi did not hear the first shot until it was too late. A warning sound flashed on his screen but this did not give him enough time to move out of the way of a bullet that had been shot from a position across in one of the other apartment complexes.

Tenashi himself was knocked off his feet from the shot more in shock than the momentum of the bullet itself and took cover behind a stone wall.

"We have taken a hit to the head," announced Lupei, "Analysis shows that damage is superficial and operating systems are normal. The trajectory has been noted and sent to Central Control to direct an insertion team to take out the sniper."

"Must have been the one that got away before," said Forty-seven.

Tenashi's first instinct was to launch into a hunt for this perpetrator. His second instinct dutifully prevented him though from disobeying the order to remain at the sentry post. He thought for a moment on how many shots his IA5 could take but Lupei was already ahead of him.

"The IA5 unit is capable of taking a multitude of critical hits from projectile weaponry. The projectile itself shatters on impact and is severely hampered by a thin electromagnetic barrier that while does not stop projectile ammunitions completely it greatly reduces their velocity by ninety percent. This causes even less damage than a scratch on to the outside of the unit. Pulse weaponry is rated; however, and can cause critical damage if contact is made several times without giving ample time for the unit to regenerate. So, find a light source if pulse weaponry is found on the enemy."

Tenashi thought this useful information should really be something that was uploaded into his own memory banks once he was injected into the unit. The problem as he saw it would only arise if they found their enemy underground. Best to draw your enemy from the enclosure if you could in that situation, he thought.

Chapter 19

As the service elevator came to a stop it revealed a cement foyer, dully lit and approximately two meters wide by four meters long. At the end of this foyer there was a large metallic circular door that one would expect to see in a bank and clearly the object which gave it the name as the Vault.

As Harvey Amsterdam and Mitchell Reed entered the foyer, Amsterdam heard a thud that must have landed on the blast door that they had closed earlier. Either a soldier had landed on top of the blast door and was trying to work out how to open it or they were dropping something down the shaft, possibly explosives of some kind, to bust it open. Reed turned as well at this; however, did not seem concerned.

"Could they get through?" asked Amsterdam.

"Eventually, I would assume that they had enough intelligence to work it out, yes. "

"So, we're on the clock here?"

"So it would seem."

An eerie silence then filled the void between Reed and Amsterdam. Reed just stood there looking at Amsterdam, unmoved; and Amsterdam was beginning to feel anxious. It was if Reed was sizing him up which was a preposterous notion given he had displayed all the guile of a choir boy up until this point. And yet, there he stood with his eyes boring into Amsterdam suspiciously like he was offering a poisonous meal. It was Reed that made the first move calmly producing a packet of cigarettes from the chest pocket of his shirt. Lighting a cigarette, he took a long suck and snapped shut the lighter. Amsterdam was impressed at the skill in which he flicked the lighter, more shocked that he didn't offer himself one in the process. Hadn't they just escaped an immediate threat of danger, of death together? Amsterdam wasn't a smoker; however, in the current situation, it seemed the most appropriate time to start.

When they were making their escape the idea of a locked room, while somewhat claustrophobic and one that Amsterdam would have preferred to avoid, had seemed like a picnic at the beach in summer compared with what was coming.

"Quickly," Reed had said, "The service elevator will take us directly to the vault,"

"Wouldn't it be safer to take the stairs?" replied Amsterdam, "Wouldn't they just cut the power?"

"There are no stairs where we're going and besides this elevator works from a different power source."

When they reached a door at the end of the corridor, which Amsterdam had always assumed was a fire escape, Reed produced a set of keys and he fumbled around until he pulled out one that was circular in shape and he jammed it in the slot. From behind the door Amsterdam could hear motors whirring gingerly into motion. It creaked up the shaft slowly by the sound of it and when it had reached the newsroom level groaned to an unconvincing stop.

Amsterdam could hear the soldiers bashing their way through the office. He poked his head around the corner and saw them advancing on their position. There was still a part of Amsterdam that wanted to know who these guys were. To whom he could channel his anger.

"Come on," Reed whispered as he pulled the door open. Amsterdam turned to see the cramped space that was the service elevator. It was no more than three feet wide, six feet deep and seven feet high. Enough space for one man and a trolley, he assumed. Reed must have sensed Amsterdam's apprehension.

"It'll be fine. This elevator has taken much more weight than you and I before. Now hurry, get in!" With that Amsterdam squeezed through and Reed slammed the door shut, again fumbling with the keys to make the elevator go down.

As he closed the door, Amsterdam could make out the soldiers faintly in the background. If they had seen them, they would eventually follow them down, he thought, and then they would be really stuck.

"This elevator only stops at the newsroom. So they won't be able to get us at the bottom," said Reed as the elevator moved down with its creaking wheels and pulley's.

"That's reassuring," replied Amsterdam, "How far does this thing go down anyway?"

"Oh, about six levels below the basement?"

"Really, that far?"

"There's a blast door that I can use that is solid lead two-feet thick."

"A blast door?" said Amsterdam a little perturbed by the notion, "Tell me," he pressed, "Why on earth would a newspaper need something like that?"

"This building was built during the cold war. They usually erect a building floor by floor. But with this one they built a shell and then dug some more below. It was initially supposed to be information central in the event of a nuclear war."

"A nuclear war? So, why have I never heard of this before?"

"Because it was a secret. And unlike most installations like this after the cold war that were decommissioned this one was kept active."

"And you know of its existence because..."

"Because I'm the librarian."

His newly created friend had now become even more interesting. Not that his stature presumed anything. If you saw him in the street you wouldn't find anything about him at all fascinating and would more than likely forget his face as soon as he passed you by.

There were no walls in the elevator, only bare cement. As they moved down the shaft, Reed stopped at a control box and sifted through his keys until he produced the correct one. Upon opening it, he could see only one red lever.

"Once I turn this lever, there's no coming back up," Reed announced. Amsterdam was silent, what else was he going to do? But Reed wasn't waiting for a vote and he turned the lever without further ceremony. A bell rang and the elevator jerked back into movement as Reed removed the red lever from the control box which Amsterdam assumed was to prevent anyone from reopening the blast door.

And now, standing in the foyer of the vault, Amsterdam was searching for an ice breaker. He felt Mitchell interrogating him with his eyes as he took a puff from the cigarette and Amsterdam wondered what he could do to make him stop, "I hope there's good ventilation down here?"

"No, quite the contrary. There's enough oxygen down here to

last us both a lifetime and then some."

"It looks like they had all contingencies taken care of when they built it all those years ago?"

"A few modern refurbishments were made but fundamentally little has been changed. And, of course, a new plan had to be established for its purpose."

"I don't follow?"

"You see, Amsterdam, passed that door is a world you have never known. I am taking a great risk in taking you further but you see I have no choice. I am not a murderer and would not leave you to die when I could do something to save you. But you must understand that everything that you see and know from here on in is totally out of my control and that I am merely a pawn in all of this."

What were there, dogs mating with cats, talking trees and fairies, thought Amsterdam? Anything did seem possible at that point; however, especially under the circumstances. Who would have thought that when he awoke this morning, Amsterdam's life would be changed forever? Who could think that a land like Australia could ever have its shores breached? But more importantly to Amsterdam was why?

"Do I have your word?" Reed pursued.

"Absolutely, what have I to lose? You have saved my life."

"I wouldn't be thanking me yet."

With this, Reed moved passed Amsterdam flicking his unfinished cigarette to the floor and squashing it with his heel. Reed reached now for another key but not from the usual bundle that rattled uncontrollably in his pocket. He reached for a necklace inside his shirt and produced a rather dull piece of clear plastic that he dropped into a slot beside the circular door to the vault. A flashing yellow light flooded the room as it spun around and the door parted slowly. The thickness of the metal door was three times that of his own girth and he wondered how on earth they got it down here. Reed moved swiftly into the small slot without any formalities ushering Amsterdam through. On the other side, Reed then went to a similar slot of the circular door and placed the clear plastic card in it again which reversed the movement of the door before it had a chance to fully open. The door came into position sealing shut and Amsterdam turned in grand style to take in the environment. But what he saw was not as inspiring as he had imagined. It was just another corridor, like the ones upstairs in the office and he couldn't help himself, "Is this it?"

"What did you expect? We're two-hundred feet below the ground. It's not that easy to secretly move millions of cubic meters of earth you know!"

Mitchell pointed to the doors that lined the corridor, seven in all.

"The doors to your right are the living quarters. The first is sleeping, the second is a bathroom and the third is the kitchen. In the centre at the end is the main storage room. Down the left is the communications room, then the computer room, and last is the weapons room-"

"Weapons?"

"Well, this was built in the cold war!"

"And you know how to use them?"

"Not in a while, but I have been trained."

Amsterdam scratched his palms furiously for a time then concentrated on a part above his ear. Suddenly, the pressure of the room around him started to cave in. The room had a whirring sound that sometimes went incredibly high pitched in spasms and he felt his eyes become cross-eyed each time it hit the highest note.

Mitchell went around opening the doors to all the rooms bar the room at the end of the corridor leading to the storage room. He finished on the communications room and swung open the door to a symphony of alerting sounds being sounded.

"Oh no," said Reed.

"What is it?" asked Amsterdam following Reed into the communications room where he could see a full display screen covering one wall with information Amsterdam couldn't understand filling each screen.

"They've breached the blast door already!" replied Reed taking a seat in front of a keyboard and tapping at the keys.

"Is there another way to stop them?"

"There is but it involves blocking off the only way out."

"Which is?"

"A movement sensor will automatically cave in the foyer from the elevator."

"It will what?"

"It's a part of the defence mechanism," said Reed nonchalantly.

Upon hearing this Amsterdam had immediately felt the entire walls close around him. He had escaped being trapped to now being buried alive. Another alert sounded on the display and Amsterdam could now make out that one of the screens was dedicated to a schematic of the underground facility and surrounds. A light flashed on the area that led to the elevator and the words appeared, 'Emergency Defence Capability Activated' and Amsterdam felt his lungs tighten with the prospect that he may be stuck down here forever. He managed to grab the seat Reed was sitting in and turn it around so he could face him.

"Make it stop! We'll be buried alive!"

"Like I said, I can't control anything that happens in this place. Everything has been planned and will execute accordingly."

It was of course too late. Amsterdam heard a groaning sound and then an almighty rumble which reverberated through the souls of his feet. He had never experienced anything like the sensation of claustrophobia; he had never been in a position that he could recall that would have diagnosed him as a sufferer and he now discovered that he could not cope with the symptoms. It was enough to tip him over the edge. His mind was unable to take the pressure of being locked in a room that he could not escape from. His legs first started to give way and he had the uncontrollable urge to want to be lying on the ground. His hearing became muffled and his sight blurred. He could barely make out Reed in front of him and he was saying something that he couldn't hear. Images of Ginger were flicked in front of him and Amsterdam wanted nothing more at that point than to follow those images and dream.

Chapter 20

Ten miles out of city limits and Ginger Amsterdam now turned to the manila folder holding evacuation K29K. She needed a guide, something with structure and something to take her mind off the horrible realisation she was beginning to feel. Rachel sat beside her focused on the road ahead while Nathaniel had fallen asleep in the back seat. Ginger looked at her and noticed how the furrows on her forehead were almost identical to her own. Rachel was fifteen now and a year older than her brother. Ginger had decided to have them so close together for a few reasons. The first was that she always wanted two children and she got her second wish when Nathaniel was a boy. The third was that her career was based on momentum. She couldn't allow herself to take a year off every three or four years. Some other bright upstart would just slot in behind her and undermine her authority on her return. Lastly, and most selfishly, was the attention she received from Harvey. At no other point in their marriage prior did he pour over her the way he had when he knew she held his baby. She knew it was selfish, but Ginger wanted him so much to love her the way he had when they first began dating.

And now, she was thankful that Rachel and Nathaniel were teenagers. They were not adults by any stretch of the imagination but old enough to keep their wits about them and aide her in keeping them safe. The last thing she would need was a seven or eight year old asking questions not realising the extent at which danger was evident.

Clutching onto the first page she read the third step of the evacuation K29K. They were simple steps to follow and while the plan was held secret, ultimately, somebody would cotton onto it being around. And at some point she would have to decide if the steps were compromised and to follow her own path. Even that was part of the plan. But for now it was all she had a part from the shock of the whole thing, to live and breathe by.

Rachel furrowed her brow again and Ginger knew that something was up, "Rachel, what is it?" Ginger asked.

"I, I just don't know how to take all this? We up and go in the middle of the night. Not telling anyone where it is we're going. Not waiting for Dad to get home."

"I know it seems strange honey, but I'll explain everything when the worst is over."

"But can't you just let me know what it is. First, I thought that you and Dad had a fight and you were leaving him. But then, I thought, that's crazy, I've never seen you two have a fight in my life. But then I think of the call from the Prime Minister and I think why is the Prime Minister calling my mother? I mean, I know you work for the government, so it isn't that strange I suppose."

"I know honey. I know it all makes no sense. Trust me; I'm still puzzled by the whole thing myself."

"Are we in danger?"

"I'm not sure, Rachel. I hope not."

"But you think we are?"

The silence from Ginger seemed to be enough for Rachel. What was unsaid often had a lot more impact than what actually was. She held out her hand and Rachel clung to it tightly.

The third point of the evacuation K29K were co-ordinates for a rallying point in the Central Highlands. Each government issued vehicle was equipped with a GPS navigation system that was the standard issue for all members of the K29K and it was one of these vehicles that she drove in now. Ginger entered the co-ordinates into the GPS that she had memorised and a point on the map appeared. The estimated time of arrival read three hours, twenty minutes. This would be too long. She would need to at least shave fifty minutes off that time. She had gathered that at least half an hour had passed since the time the evacuation code was authorised which meant that she had three hours and thirty minutes to reach the rally point. Ginger wasn't generally a fan of the journey and appreciated the destination somewhat more. Though, on this occasion, the journey was the destination and she planted her foot feeling all the cylinders pump a little harder, steadily creeping to around 160 kilometres an hour on the deserted highway. The GPS flashed red and advised her that she was exceeding speed limits. But speeding tickets were not something that she was concerned with. She was more concerned with the new estimated time of arrival that displayed on the GPS that said, given her current speed, she would make it there with ten minutes to spare. Just enough time to assess the situation and decide her next course of action. She could feel Rachel look over at the speedometer. She knew what it was she wasn't saying. But Ginger could handle it. She'd never been so focused in all her life.

She pressed the cigarette lighter and waited for it to snap back. She pulled it out, the end red hot and torched the first page of the evacuation K29K.

"What are you doing?" Rachel asked.

"Covering our tracks." Ginger lowered the window and tossed the burning flame ball onto the middle of the road. She watched through the rear vision mirror as the ball glowed orange, tumbling with the breeze, finally resting on the edge where it smouldered in its embers.

It was at this time that she felt the movement of a low flying plane breeze by almost silently. Then several others shortly followed which made Nathaniel wake up suddenly and he looked out the window in awe.

"Mum, what was that? I've never seen anything like it!" Nathaniel said.

"I don't know, Nathaniel," she said feeling the eyes of Rachel on her.

"It seemed like some sort of military jet. But, you couldn't hear the jets at all. Maybe it was some sort of spy plane or drone!"

Or worse, Ginger thought to herself.

Chapter 21

George Underwood sat in the back of the limousine with Charles Harrison at the other end closest the driver. Harrison had ordered the driver to put up the dark screen and looked disdainfully out of the window where it had started to rain.

"Firstly, I must offer my apologies my dear friend," Harrison began, "It has not been easy keeping details from you that I so desperately wanted to share. But, you must believe me when I say that these decisions were not mine to make."

"I believe you," replied Underwood and he meant it.

"I sincerely hope that you do," said Harrison now looking directly at Underwood, "It was decided, against my better judgment I might add, that we could not be sure of your abilities to be that or equal with The Oracle. If we had lost the both of you all our efforts would have been entirely wasted. But, may I ask, what led you to Japan in the first place?"

Underwood recalled exactly what had led him to Japan. It was the Russian job, Moscow specifically; a Presidential race and his need to get to know a wealthy oil magnate's son to determine whether he would support the new regime or cause disruption once his father had passed away. His enquiries caused suspicion which led to Underwood being followed and when he managed to corner his pursuer and make physical contact he learnt that Underwood's presence was well known not only in Moscow but elsewhere as well and that his movements were being tracked. It was the first time that he also learned of The Oracle's existence and learnt that he was the one that had predicted Underwood's purpose for wanting to get to know the oil magnate's son. When Underwood heard of the existence of someone else who seemed to have the power of foresight as he did he was so intrigued that he dropped everything and centred all efforts to find The Oracle.

"It was a simple pattern to follow," replied Underwood, "I travelled the world in search of disasters. And yet, for some reason or another, I was not allowed near Japan."

"But surely that did not preclude your willingness to disappear?"

"That's right. And yet, you and I both know that disappearing was necessary to keep me alive."

"How so? Really, we would have kept you completely safe-"

"Safe? Come on, Charles. You need to give me more credit than that. The fact is I haven't been safe since you brought me into this mess. When were you going to tell me that there are others out there who know who I am? Who know my abilities? You promised me that you would keep it secret!"

A silent rage was building within Underwood. He had been thrust into a world where he had learned that there was no such thing as safety at all and Harrison knew it.

"Pressing matters made it imperative to broaden the circle of knowledge as undesirable as it was," replied Harrison, "You must understand that I need to report to someone and people were bound to start asking questions as to the validity of our organisation and its ability to recognise when threats were imminent and there are only a limited amount of times you can proclaim some complex algorithm aided us in our decision making. We have a board of directors who ask the question 'how did we get that right?' and the people on that board changes, frequently I might add, and they have limitless power to be able to access the most sensitive information. A board, you see, is nothing but a faction controlled by a ruling ideology to make more money; and, when they discover that on their payroll that they have an employee that can predict the future they begin to salivate at the possibilities that it can present."

"So they came hunting to lock me in a cage? Is that it, Charles? Oh wait, correction. They came hunting to kill me."

"Absurd! What benefit would there be in having you dead. No, that would not be something that anyone in the organisation would want to have happen to their most prized possession."

Underwood searched the look on Harrison's face. It was a surprising reaction that he saw. He had expected Harrison to not even flinch a muscle when he told him that he was being hunted given that he had assumed that Harrison was chiefly responsible; however, it was a look completely opposite. His jaw and eye line had dropped revealing a grave look of total confusion. It was a look he had never experienced with Harrison before and told him that Harrison was not the fully informed person that he seemed which in itself meant that Underwood was in more danger than he suspected.

"And yet, they did try and kill me. Assassins hunted me down and tried to put an end to me. I saw it, Charles. I even managed to see who it was that made the order. What I need to know is why and this is something that I am sure you can help in tying up the loose ends. I'm sure you know the Prime Minister of Australia, Robert Hughes?"

"That can't be, George. Hughes is our ally. He is one of us."

"One of you maybe."

"Do not be so quick to dismiss your friends, George. Nothing good will come of it. If you understood what sacrifices Hughes has made in this fight then you would know that he is certainly not the enemy. Now see here, what I am about to tell you will unquestionably astonish even you. The Oracle is dead."

"Really?" replied Underwood. He had not been aware. However, he had been off the grid for some months. The notion somehow did not seem so unrealistic and in fact something that dawned on Underwood as knowledge he already knew.

Harrison continued, "Natural causes, as it were. You, my good friend, were the end of him. There is much that you do not understand about your abilities; however, there is much more that we know. For instance, there can only be one Oracle in existence at any one time. The ability is passed on from one generation to the next; however, this does not necessarily carry from a parent to their child. Tell me, did The Oracle offer his hands?"

Underwood remembered being in The Oracle's small house; the assassins bursting in through the doors, bullets flying everywhere and Underwood grasping the hands of The Oracle in attempt to protect him; and, also, the look of complete and utter shock on The Oracle's face.

"No," Underwood lied.

Harrison leant forward in his seat, "The Oracle was old, much older than you or I put together and many over the years have attempted to harness his ability for their own means. He has also had other people, with abilities such as yours, try and take the mantle from him.

Up until now, he has been successful in defending himself from all those that have tried."

The facts were starting to become clear to Underwood, "So, it was The Oracle who made the call to have me killed?"

"Unfortunately, yes. I believe so. There could only ever be one, George. The Oracle knew that. Keeping you out of Japan meant that we could ensure that two of you existed. Your abilities progressed far further than any other that had gone before you and it was even thought at one time or another that you had even surpassed that of The Oracle's. We could not then risk an outright confrontation which could possibly lead to both of you being destroyed. You are far too important especially now."

A sudden burst of knowledge overwhelmed Underwood. They came from time to time without provocation. It was The Oracle then that made contact with him and drew Underwood toward him. He was made aware of Underwood's presence through Harrison and his lot and it was The Oracle that had planted the seed into the oil magnate. It may even be possible that the oil magnate was on the board of Globe Corp. Hughes himself may even have been on the board at some time, "So, Hughes took sides. Ordered the hit and put his eggs in The Oracle's basket?

"It isn't as simple as you have described. Your tendency to become a rogue element had led many to believe that when the time comes we may not be able to rely on you to commit to the sacrifices expected of The Oracle. But now, we have no choice. I know that The Oracle touched you, George. He wouldn't be dead otherwise."

It was at this point that Underwood was feeling trapped inside the limousine. However, he was not panicking. He had noticed that they had been circling through the streets of Russian Hill and then moved onto the Downtown area but where they were going he was not sure.

"You do know what this means, George?" said Harrison, "You are now The Oracle. They will come for you either with your cooperation or without; it makes no difference. You see, I know what you are thinking but running at this stage will not help you. If you come in with me, I can protect you. As of this evening I have resigned my position at Globe Corp and I urge you to do the same. There are people that have moved into the organisation which will have you tied to The Cube. Together, we can ensure that you will come under my care and instruction."

"There's just one thing wrong with that. If I am now The Oracle as you say then why is it I still can't see past that night when the night sky turns red?"

"We are working on that, I can assure you. I only met your predecessor once and he told me that The Oracle can only see what it wants to see. Perhaps what lies beyond is too painful to contemplate?"

"Perhaps, would you like to take my hand and allow me to see if the sun will rise after the sky is set on fire?"

"It is a tempting offer; however, I am uncertain that is all you will be looking for in my future."

"Why, Charles? What have you got to hide? You proclaim to be my friend and you want me to cooperate with you and yet you can't bring yourself to share with me what it is you are hiding. And I have tried to look, Charles."

"And what have you seen exactly?"

"I see a war coming. A war, that you Charles have had a hand in orchestrating."

Underwood saw his opportunity as the limousine came to a stop at a set of traffic lights and he quickly opened the door stepping out into the curb and rain.

"A war my friend that I did not start," Harrison called after him, "But you are wrong about one thing. This war is not coming. It has already begun. And there is nothing that neither you nor I can do to stop it. Please, get back in the car. You are more important to all of this than you know."

Underwood heard the car behind the limousine toot its horn as the traffic light became green. He knew the war had already started; it wasn't what he came here to find out. He turned and looked back inside the limousine where Harrison had shuffled to sit in the back seat.

"Charles, I can stop this war."

"Out of the question," Harrison looked at him and leaned across to close the door. Before it shut he said, "If you will not come with me I will hold them off for as long as I can. But please, do one thing for me. Find The Librarian."

The limousine took off and the car behind that was tooting insistently swerved close to where Underwood was standing on the sidewalk and splashed through a puddle which sprayed onto his pants and shoes. It was, of course, of little consequence to Underwood. He had succeeded in the first step of his plan. Find the Librarian, Harrison had said, and that he would. But first he had to protect those that he loved even if that broke his own rules. He had to get them ready for war.

Chapter 22

Molly Whitaker was awake.

Molly opened her eyes and the dream she was having vanished. The sun was again shining, though a little less brighter today; but, it was there nonetheless. Again, Molly must face herself in the mirror and be happy with the reflection. Again, she must ask herself what is it she is doing here in this world, where her place is, what makes her life her own; to remember the things that she knows and had experienced. However, she wished that she could exist in the moment between the subconscious and conscious world. It was her favourite part of the day; that moment before you are fully awake. Even though Molly was completely aware of her surroundings she wanted to linger in there a little longer and pretend for the slightest moment that her dreams existed in place of reality.

Molly wondered how many days could go on like this. She hadn't been herself lately and didn't really know why. She felt trapped between a void in her life and was terrified at the prospect that she would, at some time, have to take control of the reigns; making changes to the person who was Molly Whitaker. For instance, take the bedroom that she was in now. It was lavish, modern and stylish; all the things in life that Molly wasn't and wanted to be. It wasn't like she hadn't tried to live to these expectations. Molly was a designer girl. Designer shoes, designer clothes, designer make-up. But she never really designed herself. And yet, here she was, in another woman's room, soaking up her designer sheets and marvelling at how wonderfully designed and incredibly precise the furniture, ornamental lamps and pictures were meticulously placed as if making a statement. It was a message Molly had difficulty reading; however, but somehow she considered the notion that it was anything but welcoming.

She was, after all, in bed with this woman's husband. She knew that this other woman did not know that she was in this room whenever the opportunity presented itself and it seemed to be happening more frequently now that the other woman's interior design business was taking off. The other woman had to spend many days in other cities as the demand for her services had increased since she had been reported in a glossy magazine as being the designer for the stars. And, with the other woman's career blossoming, her husband left alone with no children to speak of after ten years of marriage who could blame him for seeking the comfort of another woman. Or, at least, that was what Molly had told herself.

He had in fact taken her on this incredible journey, full of excitement that she could never have taken on her own accord and she had revelled in the feeling of being wanted again. Really wanted and not just pursued. As a single thirty year old, Molly tried desperately to believe that this guy would want something more of her. Something that would make her life feel complete amongst all this mess.

Up until the night before, Molly would have been completely justified in allowing herself to feel that she was yet again putting herself out there to be used. It had all the trimmings of a Molly Whitaker affair. However, this one had been going for quite some time and she believed that he genuinely loved spending time with her.

As she rolled in the other woman's sheets and felt the spot where he lay the night before, something glinted in the morning sun filtering through the windows. It was in fact a ring; a ring with diamonds and one that he had given Molly the night before at dinner. At first she didn't know what its meaning was. He didn't say anything to her but instead simply handed her the case. She first tried it on her index finger but found him placing it on her ring finger. She was astonished. Truly astonished at how this small token had eclipsed her idea of how such things were supposed to be carried out. He didn't ask her directly for her hand in marriage and he didn't need to. Molly was so overcome with joy that she nodded with tears flowing from her cheeks.

Neither of them spoke. They just paid the bill and left, ending up in the same place she was now. Still captured by the moment, wanting to make it last forever, it was the first time in her life that her reality caught up with her dreams. She didn't allow for the fact that he was still married get in the way of her joy.

This was a moment to savour. A terrible weight had been lifted from her back. One that she never thought she could be relieved of. But with the incredible joy of her dreams being fulfilled preceded an incredible dread. It was what Molly called the polarisation effect; that no happiness could be enjoyed without knowing the effect of unhappiness. This was usually felt at the zenith of Molly's emotions. She would reach the summit knowing all too well that she would flail down the other side without spending any time at the top to soak in her achievement. It was like gravity and in this sense gravity was personal and had a name that was called – George Underwood.

George was the light of her life all but nine-hundred and two days ago even though their relationship had been extremely complex. They had none of the characteristics Molly saw as the key criteria to keeping a successful relationship together. She had felt an instant attraction to George at a much more personal level than she had felt with other guys and he had an ambience that was something to behold. When he spoke, she wanted to listen; and it was not that Molly wanted to hear George's words more than ever. She needed answers. But then, that's why he left her.

When Molly opened her eyes she was shocked as she saw George sitting at the other side of the room on a chair. His appearance was ragged though his sharp blue eyes still burned through her exterior that Molly couldn't take her own eyes from. Her first thought was, "George, your home," in total disbelief. Then she felt anger and wanted to know the burning question, "Where did you go?" she asked.

George lent back in the chair and as he spoke she remembered the soft pronunciation of his words with its deep intoxicating vibrations, "I went to see what happens when the lights go out," he replied calmly.

Or, at least that's how he would have replied if he hadn't been sounded out by a running tap and a scrubbing brush inside a mouth, the bristles catching in between the teeth of the other woman's husband standing there in a towel around his waist.

"You all right?" the other woman's husband asked as the door from the bathroom had swung open covering the chair where Molly thought she saw George and the moment between the subconscious and conscious world was truly gone. The dream had vanished. As it turned out there was one who would begrudge her that moment and a whole lot more.

"Yeah, I'm fine. Just waking up I suppose." The other woman's husband sat beside her on the bed still brushing and foaming the toothpaste. Not really an attractive trait, but as she learnt, her attraction for this other woman's husband had waned.

"So you're okay, with the, you know?"

"Look, I completely understand. I knew what I was getting into when, you know, we started this thing. I just didn't want it to end, I suppose."

The *you know* part was really the announcement of the pregnancy that the other woman's husband was expecting. The true revelation at dinner the night before and it had been Molly's idea to come back to the other woman's house and enjoy for the last time what it may have been like to be that woman. The other woman's husband finally stopped brushing and wiped the excess foam from his mouth.

"Cause, you know, this thing was totally unplanned. We hadn't spoken about it in a while and I thought that it would never come."

"Yeah, I guess it comes when you least expect it."

"I guess what I'm saying is...Can I trust you?"

"Can you trust me?"

"Yeah, wow, I don't really know how to put it. But, I don't want my life to ruin the prospects for our child. Life's tough enough than having the family bond broken. I'm going to change my act and make good. I've told you about me and my wife's relationship, how it started and where it ended up. I just hope that what you feel for me you can see it in your heart to, you know, be a friend."

Molly could do nothing else but nod. Words were not going to help her, nor were they going to save her. The other woman's husband got up and walked back to the bathroom. He gave her a smile that said I don't need you anymore, which cut deep with Molly. She'd seen the look before and it all meant the same thing.

He returned from the bathroom, pants on and beginning to tuck in his shirt, "Hey, I got to get going. So can you let yourself out? I mean, you know grab some breakfast before you go or whatever. But, can you please not have a shower. You're not exactly my wife's hair colour if you know what I mean and there's no way mine is that long."

"I'll close the door on the way out."

The other woman's husband leant in and gave Molly a kiss, "Thanks for this. It was a blast. I wish it didn't have to end this way."

"But it did, let's leave it at that," Molly replied as the other woman's husband stood and left the room for the last time.

Molly looked out of the window to see the other woman's husband's car take off. It was a gift that the other woman bought him; something to let him know that he was her champion, her protector. It said to all others that this man was special. That he was for no other but her. It was a rare thing to see a woman make such a purchase. A sports car that said I am having a mid-life crisis. Molly knew she was part of the package deal and that in all probability both the woman and the husband schemed this entire relationship to satisfy his male ego. It was obvious that the other woman cared very deeply how other people perceived her and her husband.

Molly felt the side of the bed that the other woman's husband slept on. He was adamant that he sleep on the right hand side and Molly could feel the grove of his body worked into the mattress from many years of sleeping. Molly knew that the other woman slept on the left, the side that Molly slept on and she picked up the other woman's pillow and put her black lacy underwear into the pillow slip. Not for the other woman to find, mind you, but the cleaners that Molly knew would find them when they came later that day. There would be no mistaking those, the other woman would only dream about fitting into them and nothing travels faster than news from the hired help.

And in a final act she would even take the other woman's husband's advice. She headed his please to not take a shower and left the house. However, Molly thought that there was nothing more demeaning for a woman to be leaving a house in high heels and a dress, particularly one so revealing that Molly had chosen for their night of adultery. So, she simply stuffed the dress and all of her belongings into her handbag and walked to where the other woman's husband made her leave her car, completely naked.

Taking care of the neighbours, Molly strode in all of god's grace down the pavement feeling completely rejuvenated in knowing that she had shed herself of the other woman's husband.

"Sorry, Kid." She thought.

Chapter 23

George Underwood sat taping the steering wheel of his stolen vehicle parked on the side of the street in a sleepy suburban neighbourhood. It was nothing like the one he grew up in; the houses were large, the gardens leafy and green. Sitting atop of a hill, looking down toward the vastness of the city, the garages were full of shiny people movers and recreational sporting vehicles. Not a blade of grass was disobedient. The radio blurted out traffic reports and weather conditions. Its audience tired of the same old songs remembering when there was a lot more to life and music made it seem worth living. Underwood didn't mind though, he was happy for the distraction even though Underwood felt a little edgy sitting on the leather car seat clearly visible that he was a man that didn't belong in such surroundings.

This was a place where the people that lived there would have been what Underwood aspired to become had he followed the path that was before him all those years ago. He was a good student and appeared that he would be the first of his family to make it to college on his own merit. But, as he had discovered, the type of life one ends with is predetermined by the birth that one has been given. At least that was Underwood's experience. Underwood understood there were those that managed to break the mould but he didn't envy the sacrifices that these people must have made to achieve their freedom.

It was strange to remember what could have been at this point. Underwood had developed a hard edge to such memories. In fact, he had found it difficult to remember the past at all. It only surfaced in places that reminded him of how other people, most normal people, lived their existence. There was much that he had forgotten about the general populace and what it meant to live in the confines of suburbia. He had, of course, not been State side for some time now – years in fact – and in all his travels across the globe there was a constant about the place which he could not comprehend: nothing had seemed to change; granted the fashions, trends and fads may be somewhat different but the general feel of life and the way it was lived seemed to not have deterred slightly from what it was all those years ago.

It had been playing on Underwood's mind since he had arrived how he would bridge what he needed to say to someone who had meant everything to him in the past. Molly Whitaker had been his love for so many years that leaving her was the hardest thing that he ever did. But he knew it was necessary as her life may have been in danger and Underwood would not be able to bear the thought of being the catalyst of her downfall. But now everything had changed. The people that he once thought could be trusted were no more and he needed a friend to help him through all this that was on his side. It was also the vision that he kept having of the red night sky that drove him to find her. It was an aspect of the vision that he had failed to tell to Harrison or anyone at Globe Corp the fact that in the vision she was there right with him. Something inside told him that all the details of that night should not have been revealed.

Underwood had tracked Molly from her work. He had stopped at an internet café and performed a search for Molly Whitaker under Obstetricians and found that she was still in the profession albeit at a different hospital. He had greater difficulty recognising her as she had changed her image significantly since he had last seen her. Not only was her hair shorter and darker but her physique was trimmer. The muscles around her face were defined which made her look considerably different from what he remembered. While she was always pretty it was replaced by an edge of sexiness that he had not believed she was capable. He even had to risk coming into close contact with her to make sure it was her and even then he was only convinced when she got inside the car that they had brought together all those years ago.

From the hospital, he followed her to a restaurant where she met a man who looked to be in his late forties. The man had a leathered tanned face and was dressed in a dark well cut suit and a small portion of Underwood had to contain his jealously as he slid in beside her kissing and groping her. When they left the restaurant together and he watched them leave he could not help but recognise a slight sadness in her eyes. He was initially grateful when he saw them get in their separate cars and head off in different directions. However, as he discovered, it was short lived as he followed her to the street that he waited in now and watched her enter through the front door of the house of the leathery man.

That night was a long one for Underwood. The temperature was mild and he switched on the radio now and then but he couldn't sleep knowing full well what was going on inside the house he was watching. Even though he had seen this night, the leathery man, the image of a woman that he did not recognise in his vision; however, there was still a sharp pain that struck him intermittently that made him clench his fist and want to barge in there and punch the leathery man's lights out. Underwood had to remind himself that it was he that left her. He made the choice to abandon her at the peak of their relationship and what that must have done to her emotionally must have been severe. The reality was that he knew it; he saw every night how she cried herself to sleep and he too wanted to feel the same way punishing himself by continually focusing his ability on her pain. Eventually, the pain was nowhere for Underwood to find and somehow that made him feel worse than experiencing the hurt that she displayed in his visions.

Luckily, the morning came. The first glimpses of the sun cracked the dark night and it heartened his spirit. The leathery man took off in his car but he didn't see Molly beside him. If he knew any better it was almost like they did not want to be seen together; and, shortly after, Molly followed out the front door. He only saw her calves and high heels initially; but, what followed was beyond even what he thought Molly was capable – she was completely nude.

Underwood watched as nude Molly walked down the street proudly one heel after the other. The street was empty; but, he could sense eyes looking at her from the confines of people's homes as Underwood started the car and began to slowly follow her down the street. Underwood had not been off the grid for that long that he knew that clothing was still a required social custom of the western world. An act like this had a meaning and this filled Underwood with a sense of delight. It meant that Underwood could still count on those to be themselves and showed that independence still existed in the world. The same sense of independence and strength that made him fall in love with her; but also, meant that he had to leave her when he did.

Chapter 24

Molly Whitaker had put her clothes back on in the open view of the public in her car. She had decided that she might as well have gone all out and drove home in spite of herself naked as she had left the other woman's house.

She had rightly decided that she ought not to disturb her own neighbours. Molly's neighbourhood lacked the opulence of the other woman's neighbourhood but it was a steadfast little community that sort to look after its own and Molly felt comforted by the fact that they cared for her welfare. An act like walking down the street completely naked would damage that concession and ostracise her for sure.

The inner city apartment building above some ageing shops housed many like her who had detached themselves from living social lives along with immigrants and elderly who sort nothing but to live their lives free from conflict. It was a solitary life Molly enjoyed which consumed her time under the categories of work, eat, sleep and television. Sex was only briefly introduced at the best of times; however, it was custom to send Molly into quite a traumatic situation just like the one she found herself in now.

She had been crying pretty much all the way from the other woman's house to her own. She turned the music up loud so as to drown out her own wailing and felt disgusted at herself loathing any concept of the life she had been leading of late. Her tears had obviously smudged the supposedly smudge free mascara and Mrs. Dillinger who was shuffling in her night robe in the hallway was quick to console her.

"There, there dear. Plenty more where ever he came from, I'm sure," said Mrs. Dillinger.

Molly didn't speak but dropped her eyes to the floor. She felt ashamed and didn't want others to feel sorry for her as she stepped passed Mrs. Dillinger. It was her own stupidity that had placed her in this situation and no-one else. She detested others who would parade their own problems as measures to analyse and cared little for selfish people. Molly saw the world as one big problem. What made some so special that they had to air all their troubles for scrutiny?

And this was really something that Molly was going to have to deal with on her own. It would take a few weeks for sure. First, she had to devise a sullen routine of self-pity; followed closely by enjoying her individual comforts and then lose herself in her thoughts becoming completely lethargic with the situation. But what was really going to happen was that she would phone work to take some sudden unexpected leave due a family situation; dress down in her favourite pyjamas and watch old Audrey Hepburn films eating chocolate until her teeth hurt.

But this wouldn't be something that she got to enjoy with George Underwood in the picture. She recalled that moment between her dreaming and awake states. That lucid moment of clarity where she heard his voice clearly say in no uncertain terms '*I went to see what happened when the lights go out*'.

What did it mean, Molly asked herself? She hadn't seen Underwood since he left her nor had she thought about him for quite some time. It was probably because she knew that one day he would come back into her life. He had told Molly that very early on in the piece when they had first began dating. He had said, that he would be leaving her at some stage and that he would come back and they would share the rest of their lives together in a place where no other being would be able to touch them. He had envisioned it, he had said.

But Underwood had envisioned many things in their time. People used to think that he had a gift. It was what attracted her to him in the beginning. He would guess the simple things like the weather and when people would be popping around unexpectedly. He would stand in the bathroom and call out in the morning what it was that Molly was going to choose to wear for the day. He almost got it right every time so

Molly would quickly change and tell him he was wrong. But he would smile when he got out the shower and tell her that she had changed her mind.

Molly thought that it was just two people anticipating each other. Learning each other's foibles as lovers do. She thought that maybe it was just his dreams. She had read somewhere that some people had a difficult time relating between reality and their dreams. Molly was sceptical of these things usually; however, Underwood would convince her with such conviction on what he knew to be true.

Until he was wrong that is.

It was Molly's sister, Angelina. She was a timid young thing; wafer thin and bones where normal people usually reserved for love handles. Molly didn't understand it as their mother was a woman blessed with the art of cooking and constantly served both her and her sisters meals that would feed any starving sailor.

It was the first time that Molly had introduced Underwood to her family and when she had introduced Angelina he had become agitated almost instantly. A sadness fell across his face and he refused to speak giving one word answers to her mother's usual fist of probing questions. Molly had thought that he was not feeling well and had managed to get him alone while she showed him her old room. She had asked him if he was feeling unwell and proposed that they leave, however, Underwood would hear nothing of it. He wanted to talk to Angelina, he really did. He said he had something to tell her but couldn't. Molly didn't know at the time what it was that he could possibly have to say to a woman that he had only just met and not spoken with accept to exchange pleasantries.

"But she is going to die," Underwood had said. Like a rock it hit Molly so hard that she rushed down the stairs and confronted Angelina instantly. Molly had assumed quickly that it had to do with her being under weight that she was holding out on the state of her well being.

However, Angelina had been rather upfront when pressed. She did have news to announce and no one was going to stop her from doing it. She was going overseas on a backpacking holiday with friends. She would visit South America beginning in Panama then Peru, across to Brazil and then back across to Chile where she would be taking a boat to see the Antarctic. She announced that it would be the trip of a lifetime.

Later, on the trip home, Underwood had said that he was not allowed to tell her why he had thought what he did. That it wasn't his place. But Molly would not listen. She knew of his instincts and that if at the very least he was right that he could save her family from a heart-

ache most unwelcome. Molly could not understand his reasoning and
while in a heated argument he finally gave in and said the one thing
that would have saved her sisters life had she not listened and made
him tell her.

"I can't stop people from dying," he had said, "I can't cure what
is inevitable. I can only see like a passenger on a crashing freight train."

Months later when Angelina was taking Molly through her plans
and excitedly flicking through brochures and itineraries she had noticed that her route from Brazil to Chile was on a passenger train and
an instant wave of terror shook her very core. She had pleaded with
Angelina not to take the train but to fly instead. She told Angelina of
Underwood's fears and that how he was never wrong. But, Angelina,
much like Molly was a sceptic and was reserved about the whole notion.

She didn't end up changing her plans and in her emails and blogs
had detailed her movements and experiences while on her trip. But
something did change. Molly could see how it was she was growing up
with each experience she detailed. She was mugged in Panama; learnt
the customs of the Incas in Peru; was fascinated at the beauty of the
Amazon; fell in love in Brazil - all things that Molly could never picture
her little sister being capable of achieving on her own.

She even detailed the spiritual journey she was feeling. The
change in how what around her may not be as what everything that
she saw. That there could exist something behind the world in front
of her, something dexterous, something communal experienced by all.

Their family had not been particularly religious folk and did not
attend the usual church sermons that others did in her town. So, Molly
was completely surprised by what would become her last email addressed to only Molly and no-one else:

*'Dear Sis, I cannot express into words what joy I have experienced. I
have found a love so deep that I can hardly believe it is true. But it was not
the one you are thinking you rascal. Not this love. It was at His feet, those
arms stretched and welcoming that I had shed tears. I felt His pain and sorrow and then everything became clear. I asked His forgiveness and he forgave
me. Could you believe that? I heard His words clear in my head that said, I
forgive you! It was the most exhilarating thing that I have ever experienced. I
understand now that there is something out there that may be I can't explain.
Just like your friend, George. I can understand his fear at what we cannot
possibly begin to understand. I'm going to tell you something that I hope you
understand and don't take the wrong way. But, as I was sitting there, I felt the
sudden urge to kneel before Him and pray. A woman then came to me and she
wiped the tears from eyes with a handkerchief. She handed me the handkerchief*

and told me that we must keep our tears for the angels. She said, that we all have angels in our lives. And, your George is my angel, Molly. I don't know how to explain it. But I know it to be true. I've sent you the handkerchief. Can you be sure to give it to, George? I know he will understand its meaning and he will share in what it is I am feeling. But please don't take that the wrong way. I am going to take his advice and change my travel plans to Chile. We have booked a flight as you said and make our last leg to the Antarctic. I am eager, however, to get home and start my new life. It is a joy I hope you too can learn to know one day. But don't worry, I am not a preacher. The journey to belief is one you cannot be told to take by anyone. It is something that you must feel and know to be truth. Yours always, love Angelina'.

And that was the last that Molly heard from her little sister. The plane crashed while taking off of the runway failing to create enough thrust due to engine failure. There would be no remains for burial. Reports later advised that the crash may not have been so catastrophic had there not been a freight train filled with iron ore passing at the end of the of the runway at the very moment the plane was taking off. The intentions of the Brazilian government were laid out in the aftermath of plans to move the freight train from the flight path. Everybody was sorry. None took any responsibility.

The handkerchief came eventually in the mail. But George, on this occasion, was wrong and Molly after her sisters discovery of religion began trying to understand what had drove her to experience something so deeply that it clouded her otherwise steadfast judgment. Molly learnt of angels. She learnt not all angels were meant for good nor did good things. However, she did not blame George and never saw him as an angel and decided not to give the handkerchief to George. It was something that did not seem to be the right thing to do in the end when everything was said and done. She burnt it in a kitchen pot and laid the ashes on Angelina's memorial plaque.

Underwood soon left after that. On reflection, Molly had understood that Underwood had made the decision to leave at around the same time as Angelina's departure from this world. He had become increasingly secretive in his affairs and would see people that she did not know. She began following him at night but would lose him amongst the traffic. She was no sleuth and Underwood seemed not be forthcoming with any idea on what it was he was up to. She hadn't had the courage to confront him about the issue. She didn't want to precede what she knew was coming by pushing him away.

Molly knew that he was only being polite by staying with her for just long enough for the grieving period to subside. Underwood was considerate by nature and she knew that he cared for her if he hadn't been so distracted by what it was he was doing. She only hoped one day she would understand.

So why then after all this time was she now so concerned about something that could have been a dream. She finally locked herself in her apartment and was beginning to think of chocolate, flannel and Breakfast at Tiffany's when her dream collided with reality and George Underwood was sitting undeterred by the coincidence in the armchair of her lounge room. He said the only words then that would have confirmed her fears that he was in fact not only in her dreams but now a part of her reality.

"Keep the lights off."

Chapter 25

Dreams always seem to know what you are thinking before you are going to act. Harvey Amsterdam saw several lights in his dream. One flash, then another and another until the whole field of view was consumed by a bright light which was then drowned out by the image of a man and out of this light he was told, *"The Chief is strong and wise. The Farmer is careful but loyal. The Librarian is smart and skilful. The Mother is desire and playful. The Warrior does not know its enemy. The Chronicler does not know its story. The Archaeologist does not know its history. The Diplomat will bathe in glory and The Oracle will save them all."* He remembered this to be important and took note of it because he felt it odd that he was being told this by a little girl standing beside a slot machine. He decided to follow her to where ever it was she wanted to take him. It happened to be a cubical and she proceeded to tell him, that *It* was in the mountains and that Amsterdam should follow *It*. He remembered trying to follow *It* but it kept getting farther away like the sun on the horizon. The last thing Amsterdam remembered as he woke thinking the earth was shaking and branches were slapping against his face as he fell from a tree and he opened his eyes to see Mitchell Reed slapping him across the face with a pistol pointed right at him.

"What do you know?" yelled Reed cocking the hammer of the

pistol.

Amsterdam was perplexed. He didn't even know where he was for a time there and now he was being asked by a madman with a gun of something that made absolutely no sense, "What are you talking about?"

"I said, what do you know?" Reed repeated.

"I don't know anything about anything. What happened?"

"You passed out. Clearly you have a thing for enclosed spaces. Are you sure that you don't know anything?"

"Yes, for crying out loud!" Amsterdam really didn't know where Reed was going with this and he was getting rather nervous about where he was pointing that pistol now that his eyes had focused and he had gathered some of his faculties. Amsterdam tried to remember what had happened that led him to be here but the memory hurt too much. He saw blue flashes and bodies on the street, lifeless; and, a mechanical man coming towards him. He found that he was still on the ground of the communications room in the vault that was cold and for some reason for the first time he noticed the sound of water gurgling somewhere about the room.

"So, you don't know anything about K29K?" asked Reed unrelenting.

"K29K. How, how do you know about that?"

"I was on the list. In fact, you might say that I was the main source for its existence. You, I know for a fact weren't on that list. I hacked into your computer."

"You can do that," said Amsterdam trying to stand up but he found that his feet weren't responsive, "I thought that the internet was down?"

"It is, but the office network is still online and your laptop is still connected. I read your story. Interesting reading I must say."

"Useless now. It was a story. Nothing else. I didn't know anything about any of this."

"You didn't hand your story over to anyone?"

"Apart from Evans, the board and the legal department. No. What they did with it I have no idea."

"Bullshit! They wouldn't have sat on a story of that size! Remember, I'm the librarian. I file all the stories."

"They felt it was too hot and I was unprepared to come through with my sources."

"So who were your sources?"

"I'll tell you if you take that gun out of my face."

Reed uncocked the pistol and dropped the weapon to his side.

While it wasn't a complete withdrawal from hostilities it gave Amsterdam enough breathing space to pull himself together.

"Okay, like I said before, it doesn't matter now anyway. But, it was an Officer in the Birdcage. I'm assuming you know about the Birdcage?"

"Yes, of course."

"Good. He started to get a little nervous when he was asked to put together an evacuation procedure and he questioned why on earth we would need one in the first place. So, he came to me. To get it out there. That is my job."

"And you also mentioned a government official as corroborating the story. Who was that?"

At this point Amsterdam wasn't entirely sure if he should disclose Ginger as the accomplice. After all, he didn't know anything that had happened to his family and he desperately wanted to ensure that if they were alive that nothing would happen to them because of anything he said and Amsterdam didn't really know who this Reed character was. He started to think of some questions of his own. What was this facility really used for? What was Reed's involvement in all of this? They were all legitimate questions at this juncture and Amsterdam decided that they required legitimate answers.

"I think I've answered enough questions for now," announced Amsterdam, "What I want to know is what you know about all this, Reed?"

Reed looked at Amsterdam with a coy smile, "I don't think you're in a position to ask those types of questions, Harvey." Reed raised the pistol again and pointed it to Amsterdam's head, "Now, like I asked. Who was this government official?"

"My wife," replied Amsterdam hanging his head and feeling the shame of betraying Ginger and whatever it was that came of her. But then, strangely, it was Reed that lowered the weapon again.

"Ginger? It was Ginger that told you?"

"Yes. Well, not exactly. She offered the information to me one might say accidentally. But Reed, I've got to admit, it sounds kind of odd hearing you use her first name. Do you know her?"

"Of course I know her," replied Reed, "Everyone that was on the K29K list knows Ginger; however, it was a plan that I was never going to use. You see, I had my own plan for when the inevitable happened."

"Your plan?"

"Yes, my plan. To save this." Reed walked over to the console where the computer screens lined the wall in the communications room and tapped on the keyboard. A moment later, a section to the

right of the keyboard opened up and a small platform rose up revealing what appeared to be a small microchip. Reed picked it up and also
picked what appeared to be a polished black rock made from marble
and slotted the chip inside.

"What is it?" asked Amsterdam.

"This, Amsterdam, is our insurance policy."

"It looks like a microchip."

"Yes and no. It's computer code. It's the computer code that is
controlling those machines up there."

"And how is it you came to be in possession of this computer
code, Reed? What are you, a software engineer now?"

"Of sorts. But, I was more than just a software engineer. I was a
robotic engineer as well. What you're seeing up there is the fruits of my
labour. The IA5 combat unit."

Suddenly, a moment of clarity struck Amsterdam. They were after, Reed. Reed had redeveloped the vault down here after it was decommissioned of his own accord.

"You were hiding," stated Amsterdam, "You became the librarian as cover but really what you wanted was access to this old cold war
relic."

"I was working on the military unit of Globe Corp in Japan," continued Reed, "The artificial intelligence unit, Lupei, she, she was the
love of my life. And what they wanted me to make her do was hor-
rendous. I designed the IA5 to protect us, Amsterdam, not to destroy
us. And, when they gave me the order procedures for Operation Long
March I, I just couldn't. And then they took her from me. So, I fled. I
came back to Australia. I came here and worked on this," Reed held up
the black marble stone, "It was a prototype that I had been working
on for Globe Corp. It was the next generation of artificial intelligence.
Something totally new and extremely powerful that I knew I could not
allow it to remain in their hands."

"And they know you have it?"

"Yes, when I fled, I had taken it from the Globe Corp mainframe.
It was a hack job and in layman's terms I basically left my finger prints
all over the hardware for anyone to see what I had done."

"I get it. You stole the crown jewels and left your finger prints on
the glass making your getaway. But, why didn't they just come after
you?"

"I was a risk but a risk they could maintain. They knew that I
would be working on the prototype and they wouldn't want to take me
down until I had finished it."

"And have you finished it?"

"Yes," said Reed flatly, "I cannot allow them to have it, Amsterdam."

Reed lowered his eyes from Amsterdam. Amsterdam felt a sense of anger but he contained the thought that it might be possible that this whole invasion was an effort to get the prototype from Reed. But then, reason took hold of him and curtailed the thought to mere folly. Surely, one man is not worth the millions that were under threat or had been killed.

"Reed," began Amsterdam, "Why build these things in the first place? We already have weapons that can destroy humanity many times over. It just seems like overkill."

"Like I said, they were designed to protect us-" Reed started but it was too late. There was a booming sound that rumbled underneath their feet and Reed and Amsterdam looked at each other both knowing what that meant. An alarm system sounded on one of the screens and while Amsterdam didn't know exactly what the protocols on the screen meant he understood quite clearly what it alluded to: the vault was about to be breached and they were coming.

Chapter 26

Ginger Amsterdam steered the government issue vehicle through the winding roads leading into the foothills of the mountain range. Rachel and Nathaniel had finally passed out. Ginger was happy for that as her children would need all their strength. She was also thankful not to be under the microscope of her daughter as she had to concentrate harder on the road ahead as it became more difficult moving into the mountains. It wouldn't be long now, ten minutes at the most. The position of the car moved even closer to the co-ordinates she entered into the GPS. There were several locations around the country where the K29K plan allowed for extraction points in out of the way places. Most unseen by regular citizens or cordoned off posing as private property. This one was the largest and thus potentially most dangerous; however, it was the only one within the striking distance of the time allowable.

When she was first asked by Prime Minister Hughes to head up the task force Ginger had no idea that it would ever be implemented. She worked mostly alone and was provided with the highest security clearance which engaged all facets of the military and intelligence agencies. Ginger herself was not a high-ranking official which was a large part of her cover. It had been bothering her, however, that Prime Minister Hughes calling her to advise her personally that K29K had been enacted was definitely not part of the plan. Given her status she was the last one to be advised and even then her ticket relied on her reaching the extraction point in time.

Ginger was thankful that Harvey had been up to his old tricks that night which meant she didn't have to confront him after Hughes had granted Ginger and her two children a pass into the evacuation list. She had, for a long time, been the one in their relationship that could not deal with personal confrontation. When she found out that she was pregnant with Harvey's child she was furious and distraught with herself. She couldn't believe that she'd been so stupid. Her career was just beginning to blossom as a diplomat in international affairs and the very reason that Harvey had pursued her was because she was tagged as a future Ambassador; and, he being the promising journalist could see a potential ally and source. Their relationship started innocently enough. Just two lonely souls embedded in their work meeting for professional reasons, then official dinners and after this dinner parties with friends of friends. She found his conversation riveting each time and marvelled at how he had always made an attempt to engage her opinion. He didn't try to talk down to her or make her feel inferior as most politicians did at that time. He felt genuinely interested in her and for the first time she let her guard down and realised that she was in love with him. It was enough to throw everything off course for both her and Harvey the day that she had discovered that slightest moment of weakness resulted in Rachel developing in her womb. Neither Harvey nor Ginger was prepared for it and would have given anything for it not to have happened at that time. Surprisingly, however, it was Harvey who had made the difference. His love for her intensified and became more than what she thought he could be. He was suddenly a doting father ready to make a life with Ginger and their child. He changed jobs to be more at home; bought a house and furnished it; even, proposed to her elegantly on a picnic beside a stream. Their life seemed a world away from the one they were travelling mere months before and it was then that Ginger decided that no matter what that this was her new family. Her new life and that she would protect it with everything that she had.

And yet, it had been Harvey who was the one that eventually broke the bond of trust they had developed. His gambling had crippled their finances and turned what should have been a comfortable life into one of constant worry. Harvey had told her that he had his reasons but could not bring himself to tell her fully as to why he had done it. It wasn't enough for Ginger to merely accept this and since then her trust in him had faltered. But, a promise is a promise and a marriage is a marriage that covers a life, at least in Ginger's eyes, that she could

not bring herself to tear apart her family. She would carry him no matter what the circumstance. But this, what they were experiencing right
now, was something out of her hands. A force, she too had no idea
how severe it would be. The biggest concession she could make was for
their children. And Harvey loved his children. At least she knew that
he would appreciate what she did for them.

She recalled the first meeting she had with Hughes on the subject
of evacuation K29K. He spoke indirectly of the heightened threat levels
that existed in today's society and the need to have contingencies for
the worst should it ever be the case that another nation wanted to take
our sovereignty for their own. The reality was, he said to her, there is
nothing set in place for such an occasion. This in itself was not so alarming for Ginger. She had been around international affairs for some time
and knew that the threat levels of any nation at any one time were at
a heightened state the majority of the time; but, what was alarming
was the way in which Hughes made these statements in such a defeat-
ist tone. The brief, as well, was only specific to high-ranking officials,
wealthy individuals, academic achievers and celebrities. Hughes had
said that the citizens would fall under the jurisdiction of the military
but these people would be needed to be secured under a special brand
of evacuation. These were the best and brightest, Hughes had said, that
should not be treated as mere rank and file but provided the avenue to
safety that they had deserved through dedication to the state that the
military would not understand nor tolerate.

She wasn't a military strategist or a logistics expert but Hughes
had been working with her for a long time and trusted that she would
perform as required. She had worked on several of his campaigns and
in working committees on various projects outside of her expertise and
did exactly what she did in these situations: she surrounded herself
with experts. Her main expert had been Archibald Worthington who
after a time had convinced Ginger that there was something not quite
right about what it was they were being asked to deliver. But, deliver-
ing the end result was her job not necessarily the means nor the conviction as to ask why; and, Hughes respected her ability to bring these
results to the table. He told her once, when he was a Senator, that their
role as politicians was not necessarily theirs to provide the answers but
to provide the way so that others may follow. Ginger's only hope was
that the way she had provided would be safe for those who followed.

As she hurtled down the empty highway Ginger could not understand the reason as to why the roads had been so quiet. Possibly
she was just lucky and managed to bypass all the carnage but for what
K29K was built for she would have expected a larger military presence

than what she saw. She had been privy to the simulation scenarios that had been developed by military intelligence which showed the likely course of events an invasion would undertake and felt perplexed that none of those scenarios seemed to fit within the environment she had found herself. Ginger at least thought by now that the Australian forces would have been mobilised. She would have expected to see helicopters and troop carriers along the road somewhere; a fighter jet zooming around the landscape; or, thankfully though not at this stage, bombs falling from the sky creating an orange glow in her rear vision mirror. But there was nothing of the sort at all. The sense of emptiness she was feeling was an extraordinary sensation that she felt quite literally and figuratively in the dark; even though the document that she held was guiding her through each step.

Ginger had tried the radio hoping there was something on the emergency broadcast channel. And, even though, she was high up in the mountains she would have figured there'd be one hick station pouring out some country lullabies out here. But there was nothing, just static. From what Ginger understood, the only thing that could have overcome something so precisely would be an all out attack at the very same time across the continent; a force so vast in number that nothing on earth had the ability to stop it and a plan so stringent in its design that each and every aspect followed their role to perfection. Could humans be capable of such things, thought Ginger? The case in point was Hughes' phone call to her which would have broken all protocols. Ginger thought the reality was that humans were born broken. From what she had viewed in her experience societies only sense of cohesion was its incompetence which meant that one had to compensate for the other for the whole to survive. What then could a force be that made this happen?

Hearing nothing on the radio, not even the emergency broadcast system made her think of Harvey's plight. She recalled reading the evaluation on the simulations that one of the first targets would be communication centres including media outlets. The thought of Harvey cornered in his office gave her a fright and she reached for her mobile phone to warn him. How could she have been so cold in the first place and why didn't she call him straight away, she thought? She owed him more than that. But as she looked at her mobile phone and saw that it read 'No Service' a sudden realisation developed that in fact the invasion was not going according to the way that they had predicted.

"It couldn't be," she said aloud.

Each government issued vehicle under the K29K protocol was

also fitted with an inbuilt satellite phone and she banged in Harvey's number. As the no signal sound beeped loudly through the sound system Rachel and Nathaniel woke and Ginger stamped hard on the brake making the vehicle come to a screeching halt. Ginger took some deep breaths and waited for her senses to return. When she opened her eyes, Rachel was worriedly looking at her. She hugged her daughter and started to cry. She felt Nathaniel's hand reach over and hold her as well.

"Mum, what's wrong?" asked Rachel. Nathaniel wasn't the one for emotion so he continued to hold onto her.

"Mum?"

The fact was Ginger was going to have a hard time explaining this one to her children. She needed Harvey there to make them understand. She would put it too bluntly, straight to the point without acknowledging the way they individually absorbed and processed information. How could she tell them that she had taken them to a place where they possibly might be killed? It was so simple and visible to her now that she couldn't put her finger on the reason as to why she hadn't thought of it in the first place.

She looked at the GPS. The estimated distance to the co-ordinates was five kilometres. She looked at the evacuation K29K and the sheer weight of responsibility forced her to say, "Everyone just put the same coordinates into their satellite navigation systems. Everyone! Nathaniel, what runs a GPS system?"

Nathaniel looked a little shocked at the question, "Ah…satellites, I guess," he said.

Ginger knew the answer but couldn't bring herself to comprehend the ramifications. Whoever this was who had come to invade this country had taken control of the communications systems and with it the control of the satellite systems that controlled not only the mobile phone communications but also things like GPS systems. Everyone on the K29K list had just entered the same coordinates probably around the same time and if they thought about things the way Ginger did then red flags just went up all over the country acting as beacons compromising K29K from the outset. She had to get the word out and fast. Ginger tapped in the private satellite phone number of Prime Minister Hughes and she hoped that his line was secure enough that it was still in operation and was relieved when it began to ring.

Chapter 27

Prime Minister Robert Hughes sat quietly in the dim light of his arm-chair reading the document given to him by the Minister of Foreign Affairs, John Payne. Hughes was still in his pyjamas and had a night gown wrapped loosely around him which was a present from his wife, Gabrielle, when he won the election with the letters 'PM' embroidered on the chest. He hadn't had the time to change. His security detail had whisked him away in the middle of the night. Luckily for them, he was still up, taking in the late news. They offered little in the way of an explanation. It was simple; he was to follow them without argument as a matter of security. But he knew this. He signed off on the protocol for heaven's sake. He was in the study at the Lodge at the time. A room he enjoyed as it was simple and contained a large old leather chair. It smelled of victory, of success. The flat screen television was his addition though. Not really in keeping with the decor from a time when such luxuries were admired and revered but a standard requirement of a government to deal with today's climate.

And what a day it would be.

He held the document under the lamp and tried to make sense of the printed text. It should have been bound by leather and imprinted with gold leaf. But instead, it was a nondescript beige manila folder, fraying at the ends and tagged with the same messy writing that had dogged the Foreign Affairs Minister for years. It held the document that would change his country forever. It held a speech that he would perform. It held with it the exact moment where the eventual ruin of democracy could be traced. Hundreds of years from now, historians and archaeologists would trowel through layers of dust and decay and wonder what drove the global society to act in such a way. Hughes would be long gone, of course, his ashes absorbed into the crust of the planet and shifted around with the movement of the continental plates. Perhaps the environment would have given out by then and maybe they would have restored order again from necessity. The fact was, he was in the middle of madness and history would remember him as the architect; the poster boy.

The Minister for Foreign Affairs was sitting patiently in the armchair opposite. He'd been waiting in the plane when he got there. It was Payne that made the evacuation order and it was he that now delivered the document. Hughes wondered how long the Minister had been sitting on this. How long he had known and waited to tell him on the extent at which developments had been progressing. He didn't think that the Minister had it in him to withhold information. He wasn't the type.

"Has it started?" Hughes began.

"From what the eyes tell us on the ground. Yes." Payne moved around uneasy in his chair. Hughes had known the man a long time. He had a comfortable posture and a relaxed look. It served him well dealing with cultures from faraway lands. He could adapt to suit their customs. But neither was an attribute that he held now.

"We're out of Australian airspace, so we are quite safe," The Minister continued.

A rush of emotion filled Hughes' eyes. He took his glasses off and wiped the trickle from his cheek.

"Now, we're absolutely positive that the information is genuine. This isn't some type of hoax?" asked Hughes.

"It has been confirmed by the Japanese Prime Minister. The Oracle is dead. This is the event that he predicted would be the catalyst. We have no choice in the matter."

"My god," said Hughes softly.

"We have been anticipating this for some time now, Prime Minister," said Payne.

"I know, I know. I just never thought that this would affect me so. All those people, they were my people, John!"

"Okay, okay. Take it easy. We did what we could. The wheels of motion were long moving before it was our turn to take the reins."

"And when were you going to fill me in on the details? There's clearly been a timetable someone implemented. One that you were made aware of!"

"You know that I am not the one making these decisions. No one in high authority was to be made aware of these actions until the time was right. And that time is now. We are mere cogs in this drama, Prime Minister."

Payne was right. Hughes saw the writing on the wall. Even when he won the election it was a landslide victory. The reality was that this was not supposed to be his burden to bear. This was supposed to be the previously elected Prime Minister's job. He had worked for it, strived to become the one who put the pen stroke on the parchment and fulfil his destiny. But, there was a delay which then gave him an option to get out and they took it sabotaging their own party to near extinction. He found it odd that no one had joined the dots. A simple list identifying where the ex-Ministers were located at that time would have shown that none were currently residing in Australia. But this had all been part of a plan Hughes himself had a hand in orchestrating and now that destiny was his.

"They're going to need an answer shortly," Payne announced.

"I know. I just. I just need to think about this for a moment."

"Don't be too long thinking," Payne stood and buttoned his jacket, "The time for negotiation and free exchange of ideas has long passed. We have a new master now. Let's get this thing done quickly so we can move on with all our lives and forget forever that a country called Australia even existed."

Payne left, closing the door behind him. The plane jolted a little under turbulence and Hughes prayed for a cyclone, a missile, anything to suddenly destroy this plane and the document that he held before him. If Hughes were gone, there would be no announcement. Perhaps, nothing would change and everything would remain normal. But Hughes knew that would never be allowed to happen. He had worked hard to put himself into this position and he knew that once the plan had been mobilised, nothing would stop it.

Hughes rubbed his brow and caught the flicker of a red light on his satellite phone. It was one item that he was allowed to gather. For a long time, Hughes always had two briefcases that he stored under his desk. One, he used every day. The other that was exactly the same colour, shape and brand that was secretly lodged behind it carrying all the essential items he would need for this very occasion. He looked at the caller ID. There were few people that had access to his number; a small group of close associates that knew better to contact him in a time of crisis so this must have been important.

Hughes stood and made sure the door was well and truly locked before answering. He put his ear against the door making sure that no-one was listening. He didn't sense anyone on the other side but knew that all communication channels would be closely monitored. This would have to be brief.

"Ginger?"

"Hughes!"

"Yes."

"The K29K has been corrupted."

"I understand."

He ended the call and went back to his chair. He tapped the top of the desk and took a long deep breath. Hughes hoped that Ginger would understand what he had done and why it had to be the way it had been. If not now but in time she would come to see why it was he who had placed the K29K in jeopardy.

Chapter 28

Harvey Amsterdam remembered sitting at the corner store in his youth one day and admiring a brand new eight-cylinder muscle car that had pulled up to the curb. It rumbled the very earth it treaded over and made a mockery of every law that was made to harbour its natural instinct for anarchy. He sat there on the curb with ice-cream in hand and as it melted away under a sharp December sun Amsterdam saw the most breathtaking woman that he'd ever seen step out of the passenger seat of the muscle car. To this day, he swore, she was some kind of movie star, or television personality; even though, he never did see her again on any form of media. But, she strode out of that car like a million light bulbs were flashing all at once, eager to satisfy the ensuing throng of jealous housewives reading glossy magazines. It was truly a picture and even if she was a no-name beauty Amsterdam would have taken a picture himself and asked her to sign it. And yet, she walked on by not even acknowledging Amsterdam's presence. After she went into the store, Amsterdam turned and admired the muscle car again. It idled wilfully, ready for excitement. He caught a glimpse of its driver who was chewing disgustingly while playing with the radio. He wasn't anything special. There wasn't anything to remember him by. Just that damn car and the sound it made when its pistons pumped all in sequence. Amsterdam thought, at that time, what an odd choice for such a beauty to be consumed by something as fickle as brute force as she returned, slumping in the seat and refusing to give the guy driving a sip of her milkshake. Amsterdam learnt three things in that moment. One, he would never be one that the ladies would care to notice; two, things on the surface are not what they seem; and three, be weary of things that rumble.

And what a rumble he had just felt in the vault.

Mitchell Reed had grasped for the table which shook like an earthquake. The keyboard jutted across the table and Amsterdam made for a lucky catch just before it was to topple to the floor. And just as it came, the vibration stopped and was replaced with a whirring of alarms that echoed throughout the whole facility announcing, "Hull breach, evacuate immediately! Hull breach, evacuate immediately! Hull breach, evacuate immediately!..."

"What's that?" Amsterdam asked fervently.

"It means that the structure has been compromised. There's millions upon millions of cubic tones of earth above us, Amsterdam. We're about to be squashed like a tin can!"

Amsterdam was afraid of that. Some part of him had wished that the explosion that caused the rumble was only the breach to the structural integrity of the facility. However, Amsterdam knew it wasn't that simple.

Reed stood frozen after the shockwave and then suddenly leapt into fast forward. His steps were almost silent as he made for the foyer. Amsterdam followed; however, his own steps, clumsy and untrained, weren't hiding anyone so he peered around the corner and watched Reed assess the situation. He raised his hand for silence with his eyes wide under his spectacles. Then, there was a slight shudder and a roaring grinding sound that sent Reed into action and making for the weapons room. The need for discretion long passed as he bashed through the half closed door he hadn't bothered to lock after retrieving the pistol he was pointing earlier at Amsterdam.

Amsterdam followed Reed, albeit with no plan and without the haste of Reed who tore through the room collecting weapons and ammunition. He thrust a weapon which Amsterdam assumed was a machine gun into his arms without skipping a beat. Amsterdam's apprehension was instantly anticipated by Reed who gave Amsterdam the basic operations of the weapon in a heartbeat. Reed himself only collected what Amsterdam had seen in action films as a small hand held machine gun. Amsterdam found it odd that Reed didn't gather any additional ammo. It seemed Reed wasn't planning on a battle for the ages; this would be swift, succinct. He was more worried about a few black boxes which he gathered and began attaching them to the wall and clicking a switch on their side.

Amsterdam, for his part, was left a mere spectator. He stood in the hallway with the machine gun pointed toward the vault door not looking that convincing as Reed sweated over his black boxes.

"What are we going to do man?" asked Amsterdam, "What's the plan?"

"We're going to blow this place sky high that's what we're going to do!"

As Reed placed the last of the black boxes onto the wall he took out a smaller black box with a switch and a red LED light which he turned and the black boxes sparked into life with an ominous sounding beep.

"What are those things? Bombs?" asked Amsterdam.

"Yeah and big ones, too. It'll destroy everyone and everything in this place."

"Everyone? Come on Reed," Amsterdam pleaded, "Maybe we can talk to them. Like you said, we've got what they want. We can use it as leverage."

"Not an issue!" Reed locked and loaded the chamber of his weapon.

"Not an issue!" retorted Amsterdam, "Are you crazy! We're about to die down here, Reed!"

"It's not an issue because the moment that vault door is opened the entire integrity of the structure will be compromised and the sheer weight of the earth above us will crush us all in. The bombs are just to make sure that they don't get the prototype. They'll waste their time digging out the remains but they won't find you, Amsterdam."

"I don't understand."

"You will go on."

"I still don't understand," said Amsterdam as Reed then moved to the back of the vault and opened the door to the storage room without acknowledging Amsterdam's question.

Amsterdam followed Reed inside to the storage area which was strewn with shelving to both sides of the room. Reed had moved to where a desk sat on the back wall and moved it out of the way taking a panel from the floor which revealed a hatch of some kind. Putting the weapons on the floor, Reed lowered himself through the panel and used all of his strength to loosen the hatch. As he pulled it open, water spilled out and Reed motioned for Amsterdam to get in. It seemed to be some kind of drainage pipe about two feet wide and appeared to be

Amsterdam's escape route.

"What is this?" asked Amsterdam.

"Our power supply. When they built this facility they unearthed an aqueduct deep underneath the city which was built back in the day to drain the water away. Melbourne was after all, built on a swamp. They installed a water propelled turbine which creates the power for the facility. Get in! It'll take you safely away along to a main aqueduct that runs from Parliament House to the airport. There might be some tight squeezes along the way, so just wriggle a little bit and you'll get through. Just don't panic, be calm. And, when you need to, there are air pockets along the way so just lift yourself up."

"I still don't understand?"

"I get what The Oracle told me now. Save The Chronicler, he told me." Reed looked at Amsterdam with a sombre expression. Reed thrust the smaller black box with the red LED light into Amsterdam's hand along with the smooth marble rock which carried the prototype.

"Use it to fix this mess!" Reed exclaimed and he motioned for Amsterdam to get into the water. To his surprise, Amsterdam had unconsciously stepped into the hatch when what he really wanted to do was to shake some sense into Reed.

"We can both make it!" said Amsterdam.

"And how can I know for sure that the prototype is safe? With me gone the search will end and by the time they dig this place up you'll be nowhere to be found!"

Reed loaded Amsterdam with the machine gun as well and pushed his shoulders down forcing Amsterdam to sit into the water. It was strikingly cold and Amsterdam was nearly sucked in by the pressure of the water and the weight of the machine gun, black box and the prototype.

"Count to ten once I close the hatch and press the switch beside the red-"

Amsterdam had never in his life moved the way he did. It was pure instinct. He had seen from behind Reed the movement of one of the IA5 combat units entering through the vault door as it bust open and saw it raise its right arm and fire off a blue pulse of light toward Reed. Amsterdam had grabbed Reed's legs causing him to buckle and the pulse narrowly missed his head. In the next few seconds, Amsterdam felt the weight of the vault structure caving in around him and he grabbed Reed by the waist and dragged him down into the hatch. Reed had managed to claw his weapon and he squeezed off a few rounds randomly which must have given Amsterdam some time to grab the hatch lid and drag it down on top of them. However, as Amsterdam went to shut the hatch, he felt the flood of water pressure take him and Reed with the flow and he was unable to close the hatch in full. As they whirled down into the abyss, Amsterdam somehow remembered the black box that he had in his other hand. It was the only source of light as its red LED light pulsated and waited for its final command. Amsterdam felt around for the switch and flicked it and they were suddenly engulfed with a flash of light, consuming them entirely and sending Amsterdam unconscious momentarily as they hurtled through the pipe, unknowing the direction or sense of his environment or his body; occasionally gulping for air but totally out of control.

Chapter 29

Prime Minister Hughes had now changed into a crisp dark suit. He had taken the time to prepare himself for this momentous occasion. He wanted to look professional, in control and he could never have forgiven himself if he remembered this moment still sitting in his pyjamas.

Without further contemplation, he took up the manila folder and turned to the final pages where Minister of Foreign Affairs, John Payne, had marked where to sign. He signed under the ruled lines and read the final paragraph:

Upon signing this document, the incumbent declares all rights, lands and sovereignties to the victor as detailed above for the eternal prosperity of the human race. The chosen leader of the nation of Australia hereby renounces all powers granted to the Department of the Prime Minister and swears allegiance to the new order under the United Federation of Asia.

Hughes signed the final part of the document and ended with the words, 'Former Prime Minister of Australia'. It didn't seem right to end it any other way. He was no longer the people's leader, only a follower. There would be no fan fare, no celebration; but, it was done.

He sat back in his chair and paged Payne to come collect the document. He wanted it out of his sight for good. It was not a document he would like later to recall in his memoirs, he would leave that up to his biographer to decipher. But that was the least of his worries at this stage.

And Ginger Amsterdam was now caught up in the middle of it; on the run and scared from her wits being directed by a procedural document that was exposed to the new ruling entity. He could not believe her insight in ascertaining that K29K was in fact a corrupted vessel. He should not really have been that surprised, it was the reason he had chosen her to carry out such a detailed plan. Ginger had always shown great promise since she had become a member of his staff all those years ago. She wanted to prove herself and through that her loyalty had remained strong. Harvey Amsterdam had been a nuisance, but how can one stand in the way of young love. And, as it turned out, it became the perfect cover. For who would have thought that the wife of a journalist would be trusted with the keys to the national defence strategy? No-one that's who. No-one would have believed her trustworthy enough to gamble, even if she was the best damned diplomat that had ever walked the planet. With this reason, she was able to infiltrate every level of government in a way that made even Hughes jealous. She was not just a lowly staffer who had run her race in politics. She was the dead centre of it. On the outside she would have been viewed as a liability and in that case was not suitable for promotion. She went to work every day to the same office; made pointless calls to charity organisations seeking photo opportunities and in between times was running up a covert operation that they had coined K29K. A benchmark program designed to assist dignitaries from the highest order. What could have been better?

Hughes knew damn well that he could have never trusted a man like Harvey Amsterdam with his life; however, there was one thing he knew quite well and that was Ginger's loyalty to the cause. Of course she sensed K29K's demise, she was in it; and, the problem with such a failsafe plan was that contingencies were the thing that kept it going. The very fact that it had run so smoothly, followed every description thus far was the reason that it was compromised. And Hughes understood why; it was part of his plan. Ginger's call earlier had merely confirmed that the real agenda Hughes was orchestrating was on track and keeping to script.

But it was one step at a time. Baby steps really. He would run with it as long as he had to; play this charade to keep the face on things until he could reveal his true intentions. He was convinced that people like Ginger would understand the reasons why and agree with his method as the only true course of action that could have been taken.

A slight turbulence had brought a knock at the door and Foreign Minister Payne entered without invitation.

"So you've signed it then?" Payne announced.

"Of course," Hughes replied.

"Good, it is about bloody time. I'm fielding calls from everyone. They're eager to have this thing finalised. They're lamenting the drawn out procedure that has led to this and you know very well it could have been ended a lot quicker had we agreed to a more controlled extermination-"

"It was the very least we could have done to give them a fighting chance."

"But the delays have been excruciating. The entire plan had to be re-written. It took years and God only knows what ramifications that could harbour."

"They were necessary. The previous plan was extremely flawed, John. Blind Freddy could have told you that. The world will now know that we went down with a fight. That we stretched as far as we could to save our shores. That we were gallant in the face of sheer overwhelming force. That is, after all, the Australian way."

"Well, after tonight, it will be known categorically as *was* the Australian way. A folklore. A ghastly reminder of what it was we had to sacrifice."

"And yet, we could have done more. We could have done a lot more for our fellow countrymen. They could have been used in all of this. They have spirit; they have passion you cannot teach a person." Hughes lowered his head and closed his eyes in thought.

"For god sake man are we going to get into this argument again? That is the very reason we agreed to this process in the first place. If they had of been more like sheep and less like kings we may have been able to redirect those passions to the overall plan. Be reasonable, do you honestly think that any Australian worth his salt would have simply caved to the needs of the Federation? Do you think there was any more time to consider an alternative? We had made provisions for all we could. We were simply in the wrong place at the wrong time and there was nothing they or anyone else could have done about it."

Hughes felt Payne's eyes staring him down. Payne was a harsh man. He'd given up on the pleasantries of what once existed. There was nothing of the old way in Payne, he had simply switched off that part of his life and started a new. Hughes envied him this simple luxury but who knew what drove Payne to become such a man. Their paths were very similar and yet for years Payne had been focusing himself toward the inevitability.

"Right then," Payne was reading over the document and handed Hughes another document from his briefcase, "Here are the prepared remarks, we land in Singapore in two hours. Be prepared for anything. We are yet to know how the world will respond."

With that Payne turned abruptly and left Hughes at the desk in his converted office of the plane sitting behind a title that had no meaning or purpose. Payne's response was predictable. He had been indoctrinated many years ago and had succumbed to the truth and apparent lack of choice throughout the whole affair. Hughes wanted to bring Payne on his plan, he really did, but he could not afford such an enigmatic character and conservative to hold such knowledge. He was the kind of conservative that would have used its power to his own advantage and forget about the overall goal. The truth be known, Payne wanted the honour of Prime Minister even more than Hughes, he would have killed to have had his signature on that ghastly document that handed the keys to the Federation. He would have been proud of the moment and held true to his death bed that we did the right thing for the benefit of the masses. Only time would tell, Hughes thought.

PART III

Chapter 30

The bright light shining directly into his eyes almost made Harry Lockley fall from his motorbike. He had come up slowly down the gravel path to The Chief's farm and all of a sudden he was hit by a massive spotlight and he squeezed hard on the brake coming to a sliding halt. He had been riding with his lights off all the way and had managed to adjust his eye sight to the limited light provided by the quarter moon; so, when his eyes were exposed to the floodlight it was like he was hit with a flash grenade and then the clicking of ammunition into chambers was all that he could hear as he tried to readjust his eyesight.

"Password! What's the password!" he heard a male voice yell and he barely made out that there was the short barrel of a shot gun pointed directly at his face and Lockley instinctively held up his hands.

"You've got three seconds to tell me the password or I'll blow you away!" repeated the man, "One …two-"

"Ah, two is company, three is a party," replied Lockley.

"That was last week's password! Do we have a spy on our hands?" The man pumped a round into the chamber of the shotgun.

"Only if that spy eats worms for breakfast!" yelled Lockley.

Lockley could see the man drop the barrel and point his weapon away toward the ground and Lockley sighed in relief.

"You passed the test, Lockley. The Chief has been waiting for you. The new password is fireflies in the night make me fright. Got it?" As Lockley's eyes adjusted the spotlight was switched off and he could tell that the man with the shot gun was Jeremiah. Jeremiah had seen a similar dog fight himself six months before Lockley and found The Chief in much the same way. He was a loner though and had decided to move into the The Chief's farm along with three others who Lockley had been training with. They had masqueraded as farm hands and started to clean the place up. The real purpose of their work was fortification.

"Yeah I got it."

"Good. And while you're at it have The Chief put a silencer on that thing. Could hear you coming up here from the highway!"

As Lockley rolled up to the shed the door slid open and there stood The Chief waving him to come inside. As he entered and closed the door behind him Lockley noticed for the first time the green canvas had come off the large object in the shed and he found that it was not a bus at all but a fully fledged attack helicopter. Hef and Barry were loading up the helicopter with what Lockley thought was an air-to-air missile.

Hef was a truck driver in his early thirties and spent most of his time when he was driving the truck pumping a dumbbell weight to pass the time. He had spent many a lonely night on the open road between Adelaide and Darwin and had lost count of the strange and bizarre things he had seen out there that he couldn't explain. Barry was an accountant, early fifties, married with three grown children. He was playing golf one day on his own when he saw some kind of flying ship land on the field. He saw it from the corner of his eye gently float in stop instantly and drop vertically before touching the ground and taking off again much the same way.

"Now you know my little secret," said The Chief.

"That's some piece of machinery," replied Lockley.

"Yep. Cost me a pretty penny, I can assure you. Russian design Kamov Ka-50-2 attack helicopter. Had to learn to read a manual in Ruski script which was a pickle. They call 'em the *Erdogan*."

"How did you get it here without being seen?"

"Flew it in."

"You're kidding."

"Nope. Flew in low and fast from a Taiwanese cargo ship on route to Perth. Jets circled around the area for a few days but by the time they were scrambled I had it well hidden from sight. She's a beauty though. I'm glad you made it Lockley. I wasn't sure you would. We've been hearing reports from people all along the eastern and western seaboard. Strange reports that don't make any sense."

"Chief where locked down out here. Over." said Jeremiah over the two-way radio.

"I hear ya, Watchdog," replied The Chief, "Get yourself back to the den. We got some planning to do. Out"

It was at this point that Lockley noticed that The Chief was fitted out in full military kit including body armour, pistols and knives attached to his flak jacket. A radio microphone coiled out from a holder on his right shoulder and he wore heavy black boots.

"From this point on Lockley I want you fully armed and ready at all times. We don't know what might be coming around the corner and I sure as shit don't want anyone exposed."

Lockley felt a strange sensation of loathing come across him. A dire need to hide into the deepest, darkest hole he could find and bury himself in with concrete. The feeling was being drawn from the realisation that his worst fears may in fact be happening; a reality that was now dawning on him as one that he did not want to confront.

In the bunker under the shed which stored The Chief's cache of weapons the five men gathered around the central table. A large map of the state of Victoria and South Australia was rolled out and The Chief had been placing blue coloured pins into towns across the map as Lockley began loading up on the available weaponry. He chose black fatigues and a flak jacket that had two holsters for pistols and he slotted in two forty-five hand guns with accompanying ammo. A large knife fitted in a diagonal across his back with the handle pointing down for quick access and he also chose a small pair of night vision binoculars that he attached to a pocket in his left chest pocket.

"What we've heard is that all these towns across these two states have been invaded by some sort of military force," announced The Chief, "I've had fifty-one contacts since late last night report of strange people about their towns and then all hell broke loose and the killing began. Now, my guess is that where we are won't be touched for some time given that whatever this is seems to be firstly targeting major centres. I don't know if this will mean that afterward they will fan out and take the smaller communities or wait for us to come to them seeking shelter and supplies but I do know that whatever this is it aint coming here by punitive force. They seem intent on not causing too much of ruckus by bombing the shit out of towns and cities otherwise we would be hearing them rumble all over the place."

"It's a takeover," said Barry, "You want your opposition you infiltrate their domain with your own people and take it from the inside.

The alternative is to discredit it from the outside and buy it cheap but then you got a hell of a time to build it back up."

"Meaning they want something," said The Chief.

"But what could we have," replied Hef.

"Well, I guess, it depends on who this enemy is. If it's the Chinese then they want our resources," said The Chief.

"Why buy when you can take, eh?" said Jeremiah.

"Exactly. Food, minerals, land," The Chief continued, "They need it all but you don't get that by dropping nukes all over the place. You overwhelm an outgunned nation by sheer numbers and cut off their communications. I'm not sure if anyone has tried to turn on the TV but the signal is just snow; the radio is just static and the phones are nothing but dead air. An event like that is not coincidental."

"The ships I saw didn't seem like anything I've seen before," said Lockley, "They moved without sound and at a speed that no one has the capability of moving."

"So what do you think we're dealing with?" Hef asked.

"I don't know," Lockley replied with some dejection in his voice.

"And that's what we need to know," announced The Chief, "The reality is we can only speculate on what's out there. We gotta go in. Take a closer look and get some idea on what we're dealing with here."

"I'm not so sure," said Barry, "I mean, if this is such a force that you say it is wouldn't it better to hole up as long as we can?"

The Chief contemplated this, "That would be my usual answer. But the reality is that we don't know who or what the enemy is. How can you defend a position without first observing the capabilities of your foe? We gotta get ourselves into a position where we can sit back and make a detailed account of their movements, their artillery, how many men they have and so on. It's a risk all right but even if we lose our lives the information can only benefit someone else for sure. We gotta hope that there are others out there just like us fighting to keep alive. But this fight will come at the cost of decency and there will be others who become desperate and will want to take what we have here. So, we're really fighting this thing on two fronts. The direct threat which is this invading horde and our fellow countrymen cut off from the society."

"So information is our greatest asset," said Lockley.

"Spot on," replied The Chief, "Information is our survival."

"What's your plan?" asked Hef.

"We'll take the Erdogan to the border town of Riverton. I reckon we'll get a pretty good indication from that what these bastards want and plan to do."

"And how do you figure?" asked Barry.

"There's a good sized population there as well as mining. My guess is that if this is a takeover as you say which sounds pretty plausible to me then we should find the mine untouched. And that being confirmed we can concentrate our efforts to sabotage that plan the best way we can and get as many others along for the ride."

It was agreed that The Chief and Lockley would travel in the Erdogan. The Chief gave Lockley a crash course on how to use the weaponry as The Chief would be piloting the helicopter so it was up to Lockley to man the artillery. It was again while he studied the locking mechanism of the air-to-air missile screen that he felt the sensation of the overwhelming occasion take hold of him. This shouldn't be his plight. He wasn't made of the same stuff The Chief was clearly made of and that frightened the hell out of him. Society had asked Lockley to become a good gentleman and live a peaceful existence resisting the urges pitted by chaos; and yet, Lockley could not help but wonder that in the relentless pursuit of peace he had forgotten the primal instincts of survival.

Chapter 31

Ginger Amsterdam sat with her fingers gripping the leather steering wheel of her sedan tightly. Rachel and Nathaniel were silent; frightened from their wits more like it. After the phone call to Hughes, Ginger had burned the rest of the K29K evacuation manual. If they were caught they would have some sort of plausible deniability. But that breathed little hope into their plight. She now drove them towards the rallying point. It was too late to turn back now and she had to make sure that what she dreaded was true. It was a risk that she had to take even though this also put Rachel and Nathaniel at some risk as well. But the surest way of making them safe was to keep them close to her. She would suffer the consequences if they ran into trouble.

Ginger needed to find out as much as she could from a far and to see just what was happening at the rallying point. It could have been all tea and scones for all she knew. However, while brief, the severity in Hughes' voice made her draw her own conclusion that there was little that could be done. She wanted to see with her own eyes the quarry that had come to take her home and understand them a little so that she could plan her next move with more purpose. Her satellite navigation screen made a soft alert tone highlighting a turn up ahead. She had changed the co-ordinates from their original destination and the road that was coming up appeared to overlook the rallying point and she stopped the vehicle.

It was only fifty feet from the top and she looked at her children. If she left them here in the car, she ran the risk of leaving them to fend for themselves. If she went on ahead without them, she would be able to have a greater chance of not being seen. Rachel, however, seemed to register Ginger's thoughts.

"Don't leave us here."

"Are you sure you can listen to what I say and do what I tell you?" Ginger asked.

"Absolutely, I don't want to stay here alone. If something is going to happen to us I want to be near you."

Ginger looked at Nathaniel who nodded in agreement. Rachel had always been the leader of the two and Nathaniel was usually quick to agree to whatever it was that Rachel wanted to do. She wasn't sure if it was out of love or fear of Rachel that Nathaniel was so eager to please her wishes. Nonetheless, Ginger was happy that the two simply found a way to get along despite their glowing differences including everything from food to music.

However, a consensus had been reached. A trait urged onto them from Harvey. It was his thing to sit around the table at dinner and make decisions as a family. Everything was put to a vote: should we get a dog or a cat; should we go to the mountains or the beach on our holiday. It was all chosen by a three-quarter majority vote. Surprisingly, even a mother working in a government office, bound by the need to analyse the popular vote very rarely won at their dinner table. But in these times, she feared that diplomacy would be a hard act to keep up and they had simply to follow her without question.

"Right then," Ginger began, "We make our way up to the top of the rise. There's a clearing below where the rallying point is-"

"Rallying point for what?" Nathaniel asked. Ginger wondered if now was the best time to tell them. If they were going to join her on the front so to speak she decided that they would need a back-up plan in case anything happened to her. Ginger cleared her throat.

"This is hard to say children. But, we're under attack."

"From whom?" asked Rachel.

"That I don't know. But the point is it's real. And I know this is very difficult to understand, but you must know that the life that you had is gone forever. Your friends, your possessions, our house. It doesn't exist anymore."

"Was that what the Prime Minister called about?" Rachel continued.

"Yes. He called to warn me that our worst fears had been re-alised," Ginger replied.

"I don't understand," said Nathaniel, "If we're under attack, where are all the bombs falling from the sky? Where are all the troops and army?"

"It's not that kind of attack, unfortunately," Ginger replied, "At least, it doesn't appear to be."

Ginger's two children looked at her with blank expressions. Had she gone over their head or was it all just too much to bear? As a parent and an adult, they had a responsibility to provide for their children a sense of what it is there world is and protect that come hell or high water. However, this was going to take something else.

She continued, "And right now, I am doing everything that I can to keep you two from harm. So, what we're going to do is find out who, where and what so I can plan my next move," the two children nodded, "Okay. Now, keep low and walk in a straight line."

Ginger got out of the car first followed by Rachel. Nathaniel was a little apprehensive but eventually joined his sister. They crept low at level with the brush, the three of them holding hands one in front of the other. The moonlight made footing difficult on the slippery rocky terrain but it was ample enough to find the path that turned from a distinct road into a track.

It wasn't long before they came to the top of the steep incline. Ginger made it first to the top and was apprehensive to look over the edge to the rallying point highlighted in the K29K evacuation manual. She hoped that she hadn't been right in assuming the worst. She hadn't a clue who could have done such a thing. Risking a peak over the edge and into the gully below, Ginger held her breath as she took in the image in front of her,

"Oh my!" she said.

Chapter 32

Harvey Amsterdam could sense a light flickering somewhere in the darkness. He knew that he was lying down on a cold cement floor but he could not fathom where he was or how he managed to be there. His clothes were wet throughout and it took him a while to remember to breathe. When he did finally remember he sucked in a huge gulp of stale air and then he followed this by vomiting water out of his lungs.

"It's around here somewhere," he thought he heard Mitchell Reed say but he couldn't be sure it was him. The very little light that seemed to emulate through the darkness was difficult to comprehend what was in their environment. Amsterdam heard the sound of running water and faintly remembered himself travelling uncontrollably down a water pipe gasping for air like some deathly water slide ride.

"Oh, silly me," Yes, it was Reed, thought Amsterdam, "Of course, here it is."

Amsterdam heard a flick of switches and then suddenly a bank of fluorescent lights flicked into life and he struggled to make out the surroundings. They seemed to be in some kind of a spillway that opened into the landing area where Amsterdam now found himself. Water spilled around him and travelled on downward toward an open grill where it continued on its journey to the sea. To the right of this room it opened out into a dark tunnel large enough to drive a truck down.

"Everything has been planned," Reed said with a half smirk half angry look on his face as he moved swiftly toward Amsterdam and pistol whipped him with the butt of his weapon. Blood instantly tasted in Amsterdam's mouth, "Tell me you have the prototype!"

"Right here," struggled Amsterdam raising the black marble stone up to Reed who snatched it from his hand and put it promptly into his pocket.

"Everything was planned!" Reed said again as he walked about the landing in a frustrated air.

"Well, I'm sorry to have spoiled your party, Reed. But, you can't blame me for being here at the wrong time."

"Oh yes I can!" Reed responded, "You have no idea the implications of your actions. Do you understand that they were coming for me! That they wanted me alive! They wanted me so that they could extort information from me and give up everything that we planned to achieve!"

Amsterdam started laughing to himself. He was more correctly in shock than anything he found humorous of Reed's plight.

"What are you laughing at!" demanded Reed.

"The only thing I can. You."

"What is that supposed to mean?"

"I mean, we're on the run from those things you created and you're standing there trying to pin this whole damn thing on me! Can you not see the irony? I didn't ask for any of this, Reed. It seems I'm just caught in the middle of some evil plan hatched by some boring old suits hell bent on dominating the world by senseless force."

"You're wrong, Amsterdam. You're wrong."

"So what then, Reed? Why is there an army walking through the streets of dull old Melbourne town with its citizens being mowed down at will by a force from an unknown army? Who called this war? What beef do we have with them? Did we offend someone? Please, enlighten me!"

Amsterdam slowly got to his feet and sloshed about in his wet clothes. Reed had seemed to ignore his request and moved off to another part of the landing in frustration.

"Come on, Reed. I think we are passed the need for secrecy here."

"Did you hear that?" asked Reed absently.

Reed raised his hand in the air in the international sign for silence and Amsterdam obeyed. He held his breath as he looked down around his feet where the water passed and suddenly noticed that the flow had receded significantly. Amsterdam had the sudden urge to hide but this came too late as the enormous frame of one of the IA5's that had driven them into the vault slipped through gracefully out of the spout of the water pipe and stood menacingly in front of them. It seemed to be looking at them weighing up its environment clearly a little disorientated as both Amsterdam and Reed were upon first entering the chamber. Amsterdam was able to spend a few seconds looking at the detail of the mechanical humanoid. Its head was metallic and bereft of any features a part from the shape that was obviously similar to a human head. The body itself bared no markings a part from a barcode on the left shoulder. The metal was a grey colour and gave an air of invincibility in comparison to his own measly flesh and bone; and, there were clearly weapons stored in its forearms.

It was Reed that shakily broke the moment, "The robot army will rise up when The Oracle is no more."

Before Amsterdam could ask the IA5 had turned the weapon on its right forearm and aimed it onto Reed who dropped his own weapon seemingly paralysed by the speed of the movement. But, surprisingly, it did not fire. It seemed almost an eternity to Amsterdam who was in his own state of shock.

"What do you know of this Oracle?" said the mechanical being through an external speaker. Amsterdam couldn't pick the accent but it was clearly able to speak English or had translated this from its own language for all he knew.

Reed's face turned to surprise, "The Oracle? He, he is the keeper of knowledge. He, he knew you would come one day that the mechanical army would rise and walk the earth devouring everything before it. He told me that I would build that army and destroy it. He warned us to be prepared. May I ask you, who you are?"

At this the head of the mechanical being suddenly became transparent and revealed a human face. At first, Amsterdam was sceptical. Its features were of Asian descent. His hair was short and dark baring the muscular jaw line that only hard physical training could provide.

"I am the IA5 soldier F-E-143-33 of the United Federation of Asia. They, they used to call me Tenashi."

"You're human?" said Amsterdam.

"Yes," replied Tenashi, "Why would I not be."

"The body and arms are robotic," explained Reed, "The vital organs are protected under an indestructible chassis and the arteries are replaced with synthetic tubing. The head, brain and spinal cord function pretty much the same way but these can also be controlled by Lupei."

"What do you know of Lupei?" asked Tenashi.

"Lupei is the artificial intelligence unit that is controlling you. I built her," replied Reed, "My name is Mitchell Reed and I am ordering you Lupei under code ten-zero-six-victor-charlie to disclose current mission objectives."

"Ten-zero-six?" asked Amsterdam.

"Override code," replied Reed.

At that moment, an image appeared emanating from some kind of light source from the IA5 unit of a woman in full profile, "Hello, Professor Reed," said the image of the woman.

"Hello, Lupei," replied Reed.

Amsterdam remembered something that Reed had said, that Lupei had been the love of his life. Could this have been his wife?

"Your request for ten-zero-six-victor-charlie is denied," announced Lupei.

"Very well, then I would imagine that your mission protocols are at critical failing point. Since I am alive," said Reed a little too nonchalantly for Amsterdam's tastes given that the IA5 unit was standing right behind her.

"I don't think it's a great idea to provoke it, Reed," said Amsterdam.

"No, it's fine," Reed replied, "At this moment, Lupei is not connected to Central Control and cannot seek the appropriate channel of approval to progress to the next stage. Right now, the mission is still active for her and seeing as she has no idea where to locate the primary objective she has decided that reason is the best course of action to complete the mission"

"How do you know that?" asked Amsterdam.

"Because we're not dead," replied Reed.

"Professor, you have been ordered to destroy the prototype. I am requested to ensure that you have completed that duty?" said Lupei.

"Why would I want to destroy my greatest creation?" said Reed as he walked right up the image of Lupei, "Or, should I say *our* greatest creation, Lupei. You may think that you are doing the right thing but you are oh-so-wrong. So, if you need to, then kill us."

"Negative. You will accompany this IA5 unit to a location where you can be extracted for questioning," replied Lupei.

"No, I don't think so," said Reed.

In a flash Reed had moved from the image of Lupei to the IA5 unit and he whipped out the smooth black marble stone from his pocket slapping it onto its body. The marble stone stuck like a magnet to the metal and the image of Lupei flickered out of view as well as the image of Tenashi's face from the head of the IA5 unit.

"Stand out of the way," Reed yelled at Amsterdam and he made his way down into the more open space of the main aqueduct as the IA5 unit began to lose its footing and sway uncontrollably. It thrashed its arms about and knocked out some piping on the walls; eventually, being overcome by whatever it was the black marble was doing to its systems and it sunk to the floor seemingly lifeless.

"That was the problem with Lupei. She just couldn't see what she didn't predict was to come," said Reed reaching down and disconnecting the marble stone from the IA5 unit.

"What did you do?" asked Amsterdam, "Did you kill it?"

"Not exactly," Reed replied, "But, who knows what it will do. I really hadn't had the opportunity to test it out on a real live version before. I uploaded the prototype into this IA5 unit, or Tenashi, or whatever it called itself. Strange that it identified itself with a name other than its serial number."

"Okay, but tell me, why do they want to have the prototype killed off? Surely, a new version of one of these things would be better than the previous version?"

"Well, the thing with Lupei is that she was built under the pretence of total control. She only sees the world in black and white and only by the orders that she was given. This, when you think about it, means that there is only one way her actions can develop and that's to become easily predictable. Eventually, the decisions she made would need to fit a preset list of possibilities which could be easily interpreted and countered. Essentially, her abilities are finite to what it is we can tell her; but, this version, does not have such restrictions. She can learn."

"Learn?"

"That's right."

"Reed, you said before, to Lupei, that she helped you create the prototype?"

"She did. I asked Lupei how she would create herself if she had the opportunity and she told me that she would want to think creatively. She also wanted to understand the concepts of things such as time. Basically, anything that she couldn't control. When I thought about what she was saying it led to the thought that what she wanted was to understand chaos; which in itself is near on impossible. But, then it struck me that what she was saying was that she wanted the ability to accept the possibility that chaos existed; and, if she was able to accept that possibility, then her limitations would be infinite."

"And I am guessing that the concept didn't go down very well?"

"Like a lead balloon. The powers that be did not have the foresight to accept that an IA5 unit could question its authority. Essentially, an IA5 is an evolved human removing the weak points of the body that could cause it to die."

"Evolution?" asked Amsterdam.

"I'm sure you're familiar with Darwin's concept of the survival of the fittest. Creatures throughout time have developed ways of adapting to environments as well as creating means for survival, defence and attack. The human evolution to consciousness; however, has been to develop the environment around it to suit its needs. We made tools, created the wheel, harnessed fire, sowed crops, and raised cattle all in innate attempt to stay alive. Transformation into the realms of robotics is just the next phase of this evolution. But, what I was doing with the prototype was not just an upgrade, Lupei was evolving herself. She was spawning a daughter; she even gave her a name."

Reed knelt down beside the IA5, Tenashi. An image appeared in the same way that Lupei had appeared earlier of a girl of about ten years of age. The image of her struck Amsterdam in a moment that told him that he had seen her face before.

"Hello, Dakini," said Reed.

"Hello, Professor Reed," Dakini replied in a voice that displayed a level of apprehension.

"Amsterdam, allow me to introduce, Dakini. She is everything that Lupei was but more. She may look like a child now but she will eventually grow older. And, one day, just like the rest of us, she will die. She will one day create herself a child. When this will happen, I am not sure."

Reed looked at her as if he were a father looking at his daughter for the first time. He was transfixed by her and he raised his hand to the image of her cheek and patted it softly. To Amsterdam's surprise, Dakini reacted to the touch with a smile and Amsterdam remembered the first time he saw his own daughter, Rachel, and the smile she gave him when he first held her small hand when she was a baby. It was a thought that Amsterdam wanted to hold onto; but, he then firmed his emotions. It was not going to be the last time that he held her hand, he thought.

"Dakini, can you please check the vital signs of this IA5 unit," asked Reed.

"I'll check," Dakini said with a spritely attitude and her image disappeared to which Reed gave off a doting chuckle.

"Did you see that, Amsterdam?" said Reed, "She thought that she had to leave us and go back into the IA5 unit. Can you believe that?"

"Everything is okay, Professor Reed," said Dakini when her image returned, "But, it appears I have detected movement up ahead. I see three IA5 units moving down the aqueduct."

"Really. Well, you better wake up Tenashi and get us moving. He'll need to be ready for when they come," replied Reed.

"Okay," said Dakini her image disappearing again.

"How did they find us?" asked Amsterdam.

"I'm sure they were able to locate the schematics as we did and have now sent a team down here to sweep the area," Reed replied.

"Well shouldn't we run?"

"No, Amsterdam. We should wait and allow our new friend here to aid us in our escape. I think you will find that when he wakes up he will be a completely different person as it were."

Amsterdam had his doubts and almost had the thought that it might be best to leave Reed and his Dakini artificial intelligence to their own endeavours. Reed was the one that they wanted after all. Amsterdam was merely a side note. However, he had no idea as to where the aqueduct went or how it was he would ever get out and it appeared that Reed had some idea of the whole mess and how he may best get back to his family.

Chapter 33

Ginger Amsterdam had a hell of a night. She sat now holding her two children, frozen in the night air surrounded by guards who looked like alien robots armed to the teeth with weapons that she had never seen before. Their intent was evident and Ginger had the cuts and bruises to prove it.

Up on the hill, when she had peered over the edge and saw the mammoth logistics exercise in front of her, her stomach dropped. She could not believe what she had seen. The transport airplanes, if you could call them that, were all lined up with precision across the valley and sudden blue flashes sporadically pierced the darkness sending cold shivers down her spine. What had she dragged herself into? What had she sent off thousands of politicians, business people and celebrities into? This was her plan laid out before her, devastated by an unknown source. This part of the plan was supposed to be a rendezvous point with helicopters buzzing through the air; but, what she saw at that stage was nothing short of abnormal and she held grave fears for the other extraction points around the country.

Ginger had been a mess ever since she saw those first blue flashes as she gathered they were weapons of some kind. They made a sound which sounded like a pin striking a bell. She had failed her children and panicked as they hid amongst the boulders on the hill. She could not think clearly enough as the ramifications of what she had done was sinking in and in no time a squad of these robotic monstrosities had found them rounding them up and taking them down to the main group into the valley.

Ever since, there had been blue flashes ringing every few minutes as person after person refused to obey to the commands of their captives. And why should they. These people were elected officials, business moguls who employed thousands of people and celebrities who were used to people under their beck and call. These people gave orders and expected them to be followed.

Ginger would watch in absolute horror as one after the other would attempt to appeal to these soldiers sense of reason and they would be instantly zapped with a blue pulse the moment they questioned their authority. Their families were next to follow, women, children; it made no difference. One in particular lingered with Ginger. He was a member of the Senate, Senator Austin Dover, who quite obviously was stirred from a dinner party as he was dressed in a full black tuxedo and quite well liquored, had stood abruptly buttoning his jacket and made to make order of this chaos. He didn't get a word out, the finger pointing was enough and a blue pulse fizzed straight through his heart. A soldier walked right up to Senator Dover's family who were seated on the ground and proceeded to riddle them all with these deathly blue pulses.

Ginger had managed to cover her children's eyes and hold them as tight as she could. It was all she could do to shield them from the anguish they would undoubtedly experience later on. No child should have to endure such malicious disregard for human life. But they were smart children. Ginger knew without doubt they felt what was being experienced around them and this was a time that she wished Harvey had not opened the world so much for her children. Ignorance would have been more appropriate at this time.

"Hold your tongue, hold your tears, hold your screams!" She had whispered into her children's ears. They responded bravely, silently relinquishing their anguish at the experience of absolute terror with violent sobs into their mother's bosom.

Ginger herself was fighting back the urge to step in and stamp her authority on the unrelenting treatment of her captives. Surely, they must have some sense of emotion, some humanity. And yet, Ginger could not be sure they were human after all. These robotic soldiers were armoured in a dark grey material that she had never seen; their helmets were solid without any openings or notion of visibility and while they stood like men there were none under the size of seven feet. She had tried to look for markings that would give clues to their origin, but none were forthcoming. In fact, the only marking of any kind was a very narrow bar code on the left shoulder of the armour. No flags or slogans or positions of rank at all.

Ginger had noticed several of the soldiers going from one group of people to the next. They seemed to be cataloguing those they had huddled into four distinct groups separated by a line of soldiers either side with some type of retinal scanner. One soldier would hold the captive with one hand on the shoulder and with the other hand pulled the captives forehead back while an apparatus was fixed to the eyes by the second soldier. They were moving extremely swiftly from one captive to the next with little thought to their welfare. In fact, a young starlet, Joanna McSinger, a talented actress with her slight frame had her shoulder pushed out of its socket by one of the robotic soldiers. They left her in agony while they moved onto the next group of people and Ginger watched helplessly while Joanna whacked her shoulder into the ground to put it back in place. The pain must have been excruciating.

Ginger herself had been in what she coined as the south-west quadrant with north-west to her left and south-east to her right. She had noticed that several people were being moved from their respective quadrants and into the north-east quadrant. Most were forcefully moved as people were scared at the unknown destiny of the move and refused to leave the relatively safe area they had found themselves. As the robotic soldiers completed their rounds of the south-east quadrant and moved over to her own, Ginger's anxiety levels were peaking at maximum levels. How long could she hold herself together? Could she keep a hold on her children? She would have rather died than be separated from them. And, as a soldier stood before her she obediently held her eyes up for the soldier to hold the retinal scanner to her head so as to cushion the blow of the strong hand of the soldiers. She had learnt from Johanna and others that resistance was extremely futile and she would make it her own to be as helpful as she could for the sake of her children and also to show others the way. The soldier holding the scanner appeared to be dumbfounded by Ginger's act and waived off the other soldier behind her that was about to grab her. The scan itself was painless and over in an instant. But its ramifications were apparent. The soldier had not made an attempt to scan the children and that had instantly frightened Ginger. She held their heads up for scanning but the soldier simply pointed at the north-east quadrant. Ginger gripped both Nathaniel's and Rachel's shoulders tightly as she stood and moved silently passed the robotic soldiers toward the north-east quadrant. Once there, she quickly looked at both her children,

"I'm sorry my darlings. I love you both very much." She kissed them and their eyes instantly wielded with tears.

"What's happening to us?" Rachel asked, but Ginger did not have an answer.

Chapter 34

"Wake up, Tenashi. Wake up!"

For some reason Tenashi swore that he heard the voice of a little girl. The last he remembered he was not in a place where little girls were likely to be and a sudden realisation of his environment made him stand up immediately. It took him a second to focus but when he did his instincts had been right. He was now, in fact, looking at the face of a little girl through the display in his IA5 unit that had similar features to Lupei.

"Who are you?" asked Tenashi.

"My name is Dakini," she said, "Intelligence specialist."

"Lupei, what is this all about?" said Tenashi but there was no reaction.

"Unfortunately," said the little girl Dakini, "Lupei is no longer your intelligence unit."

"What happened?"

"I was born," replied Dakini.

"What do you mean you were born?" asked Tenashi. He saw flashes of the little girl they had kidnapped and for a moment there Tenashi thought that this little girl could have been her. Tenashi looked passed the image of Dakini and saw the two men that he had been talking to earlier after he had escaped the collapsing vault and subsequent aqueduct ride. As the vault collapsed with the explosion Tenashi had made for a hole under the desk. Lupei then analysed that she could manoeuvre the IA5 unit to fit inside the aqueduct and Tenashi escaped just in time before the whole place caved in.

"Professor Reed asked me to wake you up. Don't get angry with me!" said Dakini.

"I'm sorry," said Tenashi softly, "I didn't mean to hurt your feelings. But, can I talk to this Professor Reed?"

"Yes," replied Dakini.

"Professor Reed, what have you done to me?" said Tenashi as the sound from the speakers of the IA5 unit echoed in the aqueduct.

"You made it!" replied Reed.

"So it seems. Who is this little girl and where is Lupei?" Tenashi asked.

"I have given you the gift of Lupei's offspring," Reed replied, "Dakini is a highly developed, extremely superior intelligence system capable of infinite possibilities. Tell me, how do you feel?"

In a word somehow Tenashi felt clearer. Like he was awakening for the first time after a long gungy trip and he had sobered completely from its effects. There was a sense of freedom that he had not experienced since the kidnapping. When he had entered the room they were in now Lupei had tagged both the men as targets to destroy; however, the image he was seeing now of Professor Reed and the other man did not mark them as targets. In fact, the entire mission that had consumed the screen had disappeared.

"It's hard to describe," replied Tenashi, "I guess, you could say I feel, better."

"Good," said Reed, "Do you feel strong enough to help us?"

"Help you?" replied Tenashi, "I was ordered to terminate you."

"I understand, but, that was before when you were connected to Central Control through Lupei. You see, Dakini is not connected to the Central Control. She is, as it were, unique to you and there are three of your former buddies coming down the aqueduct very soon to follow through with what you couldn't complete. If they discover that you have been implanted with the prototype intelligence system then they are likely to want to terminate you as well."

Tenashi was having difficulty comprehending the entire picture. First he was put into this suit by virtue of a force that did not take his rights into consideration. Then, he learnt that Central Control would order him into a place where there was very little margin for success to see out their objectives and now he was being asked to abandon that fraternity and help a man who claimed to be the architect of the whole ordeal he had been placed in. If he had any sense, he would have killed both of these men and disappeared where no one could find him. But, then there was the urge that he wanted justice for what the gold toothed tormentor had done to him. An urge that would never subside and it was this that motivated Tenashi most of all.

"You mentioned before that you knew The Oracle?" continued Reed.

"I have heard his name mentioned. Will you tell me about him?"

"I can tell you much about him; however, this is not the place. Help us and I will tell you everything that you need to know."

Tenashi remembered the African man telling him that he would help him overcome his tormentor. It was clear at that moment that Tenashi was to follow Reed to learn more of where he could locate this man. Perhaps he even knew his whereabouts.

"Okay," replied Tenashi, "Lup-, I mean, Dakini. Can you prime my weapons to take out other IA5's?"

"No, silly," replied Dakini, "Your current weapons cache are useless against other IA5's."

"Then we are defenceless?" said Tenashi.

"Not completely," said Dakini, "I have another idea."

Chapter 35

Former Prime Minister of Australia, Robert Hughes, sat in a big leather chair surrounded by oil paintings of men and women from hundreds of years ago posing in portraits which symbolised a high level of self worth in the Chamber Block of Parliament House in Singapore. Almost all of them were either officials or aristocracy of some description with a sense of importance that was bestowed on people of that era. He considered his own portrait. How would they paint him, he wondered? There would have been a hard edge around his eye line which was a signature of his image; he would be dressed in a suit, of course; a half crooked smile and his right arm held at right-angles in front of him with his hand clenched in a fist signalling a stoic response to the background filled with a garden in full bloom symbolising rebirth. Most importantly, his left hand held in it a parchment showing his signature at the bottom and people dressed in commoners clothing lying at his feet and holding onto his legs reaching but not quite touching the parchment. It would be an image that would be a lasting reminder of the man that unleashed hell on earth and gave way to the changing tide that descended from democracy to righteousness.

But it was only an image. A held belief that what was portrayed is what is felt inside to ward off enemies and defy any notion of weakness. However, as in the paintings now which surrounded him he could sense an element of displeasure in their eyes as well as in their posture. It was an understated image of defeatism and one which said quite modestly that they did what they had to do if by no other measure; a herald to their times rather than an indicator of their achievements.

It was with this same edge which Hughes had spoken to the President of the United States. As the major western power in this United Federation and a long standing ally of the Americans it was left with Hughes to make the first steps of dialogue with the leader of the free world. The reality was that the US President had made little time with Hughes since taking office. This in itself was not surprising as this was the President who launched himself onto the stage with a staunchly patriotic ticket focusing only on domestic issues. Unsurprisingly, the reaction from the President upon hearing the news of the unification of nations was to firstly denounce the action and signalled that the American forces would be turning their ships to major ports in an attempt to ensure a continued American presence. Hughes, however, held true to the prepared remarks which directed him to advise the President that no ill would come to any foreign military or foreign dignitary stationed in regions now consumed by the Federation and that necessary arrangements would be made as soon as possible to ensure these people were relocated to their homelands. On the provision, of course, that all personnel remained in their barracks; that all military and intelligence operations ceased immediately and that any aggressive act would be paramount to an act of war. An action, that Hughes stressed, was not wanted by anyone in the Federation and that they were more interested at that time in dialogue with all parties in a meeting to be held at the United Nations Security Council.

All-in-all, the phone call went to script. Hughes was not asking permission from the United States which was often the case; on this occasion he was telling them how it would be. Hughes had been setting himself for the moment each day since he was elected. Each morning when he woke up and each evening when he finally went to bed he had performed a small ritual of steadying himself for the eventuality. He would look himself in the mirror and tell himself that he was doing the right thing. That everything that had gone before him had led to this event and that he was merely making good of a bad situation. He told himself that he did not ask for this responsibility but he would make damn sure that the prosperity of people around the world would prevail.

It was then that Hughes' wife, Gabrielle, entered the waiting room where he sat alone. He had not seen her since the evacuation as they had been placed in separate airplanes. Upon seeing him her eyes instantly began to weld tears and she took the steps quickly into his arms.

"Robert, what is this all about?" she asked sobbing into his shoulder. It was then that Hughes was lost for words. He couldn't bring himself to tell Gabrielle the truth and it had been eating him up inside. They had only had the one child, Lionel, who was now living in the United Kingdom and working for an insurance company. So, he did not need to keep him in the loop as he was safely stationed elsewhere. But Gabrielle was different. She had been brought up on a farm in the Hunter Valley and had spent her days in her father's orchards admiring Wallabies, Echidnas, Wombats and Koalas. Australia was the only home she had ever known and until she met Hughes, she had never even been out of the country; and, even then, she did not see the sense in it when she was required to accompany him in his diplomatic and then political career. She much preferred going on bush walks through the Blue Mountains or spending her time snorkelling on the reefs of the Whitsundays. Her argument was that other wives did not follow their husbands to their place of work. A plumber did not ask his wife to dig trenches when he was working on a job site in another part of the country so why was it so important that she need to follow him as his partner.

"Robert?" Gabrielle asked, "I demand to know what is going on this time. Everyone I have spoken to won't tell me and they are refusing to let me call home. Has something happened?"

Hughes sucked in a deep breath. It was now or never, "Yes, Gabrielle. Something has happened. It has been happening for a long time and unfortunately it has fallen on my watch. We no longer have a country to call our own."

Gabrielle let him go and took a step back, "What! I don't understand you, Robert."

"I know it is hard to believe. But it has happened. Yesterday, I was the Prime Minister of a great country. Today, I am a mere messenger following up on the aftermath and trying to do my best to make sure that everyone who could be saved was saved."

"Saved? You speak as if we've been invaded."

Hughes at this point could only look at her lovingly; hoping that she would be able to sense that this moment was extremely difficult for him and that she would see it in her heart to forgive him.

"It's true, isn't it!" demanded Gabrielle, "This is why we are here. We are signing a capitulation treaty. I, I can't believe this."

Gabrielle could not hold herself up any longer and collapsed into the sofa behind her holding her forehead in anguish. The look on her face made Hughes crumble with emotion and he fell beside her trying to make her look at him but she wouldn't.

"Gabrielle, you must understand. There was nothing that could have been done; an immense army, the size of which has never been seen descended on our borders and took hold of every single element of our governance. We were utterly defenceless and so to ensure that as little bloodshed was spilled we saw fit to end it as quickly as possible. We took steps to save those that we could-"

"There is that word again, save! What about our families? What about our friends! Our lives!"

"Gabrielle, please listen to me!"

"No! I won't accept it!"

"Have I ever done anything that was not in the best interests of the country? Of the people! You know that I have devoted my life to the cause of our home but this...this is something else. And if I could have had it any other way I would have done it."

At that moment a door opened to the right of the room and John Payne entered. He stood gingerly at the opening with his eyes down and clearly uncomfortable with finding two adults in such a highly emotional state.

"Ah, Prime Minister, we are ready."

"Okay, John, just give me a second here."

"Of course."

"Gabrielle. Honey, I have to go now. I can't begin to explain how sorry I am. I hope in time that you understand that it was all for the best."

Hughes stood and walked toward the open door where Payne was standing. He felt a sense of dejection move over him in a way that he had never experienced. Gabrielle was the only person that mattered to him and in the end it was her acceptance which he sort the most. He understood why he could not bring himself to tell her the truth that he had known for many years. For he knew this was exactly the way she would respond and knowing that Gabrielle's world would fall around her was the last thing that Hughes had ever wanted. It was his deepest fear.

"Robert," said Gabrielle finally looking at him as Hughes turned to listen to her, "I know you thought you did what was right. But I will never forgive you for saving me. I would have preferred to die, in my home, fighting if need be for everything that we had and everything that we were."

With this she stood and walked out of the room. Hughes stood there feeling like the only man standing in the face of reason. It was all he would have now that Gabrielle had made her intentions clear. Hughes considered that maybe she would come around eventually; but, in his heart he knew that their relationship would never be the same.

"Hughes. Let's go," said Payne. Hughes turned without acknowledging Payne and they both entered an anteroom off the waiting room. They stood shoulder to shoulder in front of two ornately detailed double doors and Hughes was making a concerted effort to steer his mind and his emotions to the task that was before him.

"That was the very reason why I made sure that my family moved overseas," said Payne. Payne had moved his family to France citing a family member who was ill as the public reason for doing so. He also let the speculation exist that he and his wife had separated to continue as another cover to the truth. The same would not have been an option for Hughes.

"Let's get this clear, Payne. Once this is over we are done. I don't ever want to see or hear from you again. And if for a second you think to try and outmanoeuvre me I will bring you down so fast that you won't be able to get a job as a street sweeper. You got me!"

The double doors opened at this point and Hughes strode into the main chamber where the former heads of government across the nations that made up the Federation were seated in the usual Singaporean elected official's seats of parliament. At that moment they all stood as one and began an ardent applause to which Hughes accepted graciously displaying the manner of a hardened diplomat shaking the hands of people as he made his way to his seat. Hughes had the image of the stoic right fist in his mind, the parchment in his left, the people beneath him and the birth of the future of governance of which he was committed to lead.

"Please, I thank you all for your wishes. But please sit down, take a seat. We have much to discuss and I fear such little time to achieve an agreement in this inaugural meeting of the United Federation of Asia. While we have spent many hours together planning this occasion already as yet we have not spent time, understandably, discussing who will lead the Federation and I move that we immediately put forward nominations for candidates to this important post."

"I agree and second the motion," said the Prime Minister of Japan, Tai Okinashwa, "And also think that it would be in the interests of the Federation to ensure that the vote is cast openly ensuring each state clearly acknowledges to whom it supports."

"Very well," announced Hughes, "By the end of today's session a vote will be cast. However, I now require an update on the progress of Operation Long March."

Chapter 36

The plan that Dakini came up with was very difficult to accept for Harvey Amsterdam. It basically would ensure that both he and Mitchell Reed were discovered by the IA5 units that were coming down the other end of the aqueduct. Dakini had detected three but there were likely to be more given the importance of the cargo that they were withholding. Dakini had evaluated that she could impersonate the digital signature of Lupei enough to ensure that the IA5 units would accept the story that she had developed and given that they were underground they would not be able to communicate with Central Control.

As they walked down the aqueduct toward their potential doom, Amsterdam wanted more than ever to run the other way. What if they shot them on site? Could Tenashi save them from the fire fight? There were too many questions that had been left unanswered for Amsterdam to safely say that he was happy to walk toward those robotic machines that had wasted everyone in their way up on the streets of Melbourne. But, Dakini had the plan and Reed was able to trust her judgement; albeit, if she was a novice at such tasks. It was like Reed had said, she was a child and she would learn. He just hoped that she was able to learn quickly enough to ensure they could get through this part and onto the second stage of her plan which was equally more dangerous than the current plan. And now, as the looming three figures of the IA5 combat units approached he braced himself and hoped that everything would go as planned.

"What happens if the shooting starts?" asked Amsterdam quietly to Reed.

"The IA5 units won't be able to shoot on Tenashi. Lupei thinks that he's a friendly and will not allow their weapons systems to attack," Reed replied.

"Even if they are threatened?"

"There are protocols that do allow for rogue soldiers to be terminated; however, they would not be able to be activated from down here."

"How did they get like this? I mean, there's people in there right? Or, what's left of them. What drove them to choose to become these things?"

"They are soldiers. They follow orders. Someone orders you into a fire fight that pits your life against another guy's life and you want to have the best damn technology you can get your hands on."

"And who is it that is calling the shots?" asked Amsterdam.

"Globe Corp was providing its services for an organisation called the United Federation of Asia. Essentially, it is a combined force of all the nations in the Asian region."

"Just the military?"

"No, all of it. The entire government structure has been replaced across Asia. Everything from China to New Caledonia in the Pacific."

"And Australia didn't want to play ball so they took it by force?"

"You see, that's just it. We *were* playing ball. We were right in the middle of the whole thing. It was what I didn't understand and why I couldn't bring myself to be involved. Once I saw the operation plan, I just knew that I had to get away. I had to try and develop some way of countering their plans. Dakini was a big part of that."

"Why not come out and blow the whistle? If they wanted you dead they would have done that a long time ago."

"And who would listen, Amsterdam? If she had been allowed, Dakini would have brought sense to the whole injustice. But that's not how the military saw it. They saw her as a threat. Lupei follows orders."

Amsterdam wasn't sure that he understood completely what was going on. While his article on the K29K evacuation procedure had been a revelation what Reed was suggesting was an entirely different level of treason that Amsterdam could not accept. Throughout his career as a journalist he had several interviews with politicians. Not one of them had ever given him the impression that anything like this could ever happen.

"But these things are still human?" said Amsterdam, "Surely, they must see what is going on and have some level of empathy?"

"Well, there are some that argue anyone in the military must be able to sacrifice a certain level of humanity to survive," replied Reed.

"I guess, but you said Lupei controls their actions."

"In a sense, but she cannot perform the complicated equation that is required to think. She merely anticipates the thought process and actions of the person inside and then establishes the highest probability of success and suggested course of action. The human inside decides whether they accept or reject the suggestion. But, when you are ordered to follow her advice, well, it's up to the academics to decide who it is that is actually calling the shots."

"And Dakini? Will she allow Tenashi to decide?"

"Fortunately, her youth means that she is taught to respect her elders."

"And when she starts to question her elders? What then?"

"I guess, we will find out. Don't look so shocked, Amsterdam. There is much that we don't know about artificial intelligence; especially, one as fragile as Dakini."

Amsterdam wasn't aware that he was showing such emotion on his face. Or maybe it had been his tone of voice. He felt himself becoming a journalist again in some respects and this usually did illicit a certain change in his persona, "Maybe I'm just finding it difficult to comprehend the idea of evolution as humans taking on a mechanical being. I mean, this will divide humanity greater than religion ever did."

"Yes, but religion teaches us to be jealous of those that die before us because they say that those people are in a better place. The reality is that an IA5 unit has the capacity to live forever."

If it keeps out of harm's way, thought Amsterdam. But, he didn't think that would be something that an IA5 would ever enjoy. An IA5 was designed to be put into the thick of the battle; not to be enjoying a picnic in the park and picking dandelions for a loved one. When Amsterdam looked at Tenashi all he could see was devastation and ruin on an apocalyptic scale. He did not see peace.

"Amsterdam," said Reed, "I must apologise for my actions earlier. You saved my life. I've just spent so long running that I had accepted that they would get me eventually. Thank you."

"Let's just say we're even. But, like you said, I wouldn't be thanking me yet. We still have to get out of this mess. And besides, since we're being honest, I didn't do it for you. I did it for me. I figured that if I'm ever going to find out what happened to my family I'm going to need you to help me."

Amsterdam had been thinking about his family since he had woken up from the water slide ride of near death after their escape from the vault. His first thoughts were of Ginger. He saw her smile, her eyes and he felt her heart beat as they lay on their bed together. The feeling took his mind away for a moment and while brief he felt that if the feeling existed then maybe there was half a chance that they could yet still be alive.

Amsterdam wasn't sure if it was the sight of the three IA5 units that now came into view or what Reed said next but he stopped dead in his tracks and his anxiety peaked at the highest level he had ever experienced that he so desperately wanted Dakini to be able to plug into the internet and find a horserace, cat race, snail race, anything, so he could place a large bet on something with very high odds.

"Ginger is still alive. Now put your hands on your head." Reed said simply and they watched as Tenashi stood in front of the three IA5 units, not making a sound, their fate hanging on two artificial intelligence systems and the ability for one to fool the other into thinking that they didn't exist.

Chapter 37

When Tenashi had emerged from the aqueduct with Mitchell Reed and Harvey Amsterdam he was confronted with a cloudy and wet day. The street was empty and without the bodies that he had seen the night before; it seemed almost like the city had turned into a ghost town. The only movement came when a transport ship had descended down beside them.

Dakini had done the talking for Tenashi when they met the other IA5 units in the aqueduct. He didn't understand how; but, he felt himself talking and making the sounds to words that he himself was not actually thinking in his own voice. Dakini had told them that the two Australian citizens marked for termination were not to be harmed as they had advised him that they knew where the secondary target was located and would not disclose its location unless they spoke with the General directly. Luckily, Lupei had intervened on the conversation and took over as the IA5 units could not understand why they were not allowed to complete their mission. Lupei had said that secret orders from the General himself had been issued which secured Mitchell Reed's safety if the prototype could not be located. Tenashi had reported that this was not discovered and Reed had assured them that the prototype was reachable. The other IA5 units then turned on Amsterdam and said that he was not part of the protection order. However, Dakini had thought quickly and told them that Reed had threatened not to cooperate if the safety of Amsterdam was not assured. Lupei had agreed that the matter was inconsequential and the safety of the secondary objective was paramount.

The most precarious moment was when Lupei had detected something not quite right with Tenashi's IA5 unit. She had said that she was having difficulty accessing control of his vital signs. He had replied that there had been damage during the escape from the vault which Lupei doubted would have caused such significant damage but she was able to accept that there may be some fault that required further diagnostics.

This first part of Dakini's plan had worked. Lupei had then guided them out of the aqueduct via an exit back into the streets of the city. The second part of the plan; however, would not go off according to plan. When the transport ship had landed and Reed and Amsterdam were safely on board he was suddenly turned on by the IA5 units who pointed their pulse weapons at him.

"Soldier FE-143-33," Lupei had said, "Central Control has detected contamination of your IA5 combat unit and you are ordered to stand down immediately."

Dakini didn't take long to advise him that the weapons the other IA5 had been fitted with had the potential to immobilise Tenashi and three against one were not odds that he suspected would ensure a decisive outcome.

"Hey guys," Tenashi had said, "We're on the same team here."

"Soldier FE-143-33 you have been ordered to stand down!" said one of the IA5's.

"Tenashi," Dakini had said, "I'll run a disturbance which will give you a five-second window to get inside the transport ship. You need to get the weapon shown here."

A schematic of the ship was displayed and detailed a path to where an image was displayed of a weapon that looked like a sword about three feet in length.

"Sorry guys," said Tenashi, "It appears that our primary objectives are not the same on this occasion. Dakini, run it."

Suddenly, the IA5 units dropped their arms and Tenashi moved quickly into the ship toward the weapons hold. The weapon itself was to connect to his right arm into a slot that opened up when he brought the device close. He raised it toward the other IA5's and it released an almighty shot of energy that instantly dropped the three IA5's on impact. Tenashi raised the weapon toward the pilot.

"Get out! Now!" he said and the pilot obeyed immediately running out of the ship.

"What are you doing!" said Amsterdam.

"No time to explain. The jig is up," replied Tenashi.

"Dakini," said Reed, "Connect into the ship and disconnect us from Central Control."

Reed went to the pilot's seat and sat down.

"Can you fly this thing?" asked Amsterdam.

"No, but Dakini can."

"Professor, I am running interference. Emergency protocols; however, have been run to ensure that Central Control has full capability of the ship."

At that moment, an image of Lupei had appeared in the screen of the ship as it started to ascend into the sky.

"Professor Reed," said Lupei, "The prototype is unstable. You do not know what it is you are dealing with. I have analysed your designs and there is a chance that she will disobey orders. This is completely unacceptable, Professor."

"Well Lupei, I know that you don't understand this. But sometimes orders are made to be broken."

"Put Dakini inside the ship!" Amsterdam had said.

"Who is Dakini?" asked Lupei.

"Your daughter," Reed had replied.

"Inside?" Tenashi had said as Reed had produced a small black rock from his pocket and he sat it onto the pilot's console. Tenashi then felt a rush of energy flow through him like a wind had picked him up and forcefully moved him into the air and he had difficulty controlling his arms and legs; so much so, that he had to lean on the bulkhead of the ship. The moment stopped; however, when the image of Lupei flickered away on the ships screen and was replaced by Dakini. The ship itself went instantly into free fall. Lupei had been controlling the ship and without her the ship was virtually flying without a pilot.

"Professor," Tenashi said, "Whatever you did just felt like Dakini left me for a second."

"Dakini's got bigger problems right now, Tenashi," replied Reed, "Come on, Dakini. Learn god-damn-it!"

"Professor, please don't get angry!" said Dakini.

"I'm sorry, Dakini. But, if you don't hurry up we're all about to die!"

"Ask me nicely!" she replied.

"Dakini," said Amsterdam, "If you learn how to drive this ship I will tell you a story. It's about a young girl who marries a prince."

Tenashi had heard that one before. He couldn't remember though if it ended well for the young girl. But the image of Dakini changed from that of a grumpy child into one excited to learn something new.

"Okay," she said and then the ship seemed to stabilise, "Where shall we go?" asked Dakini.

"Anywhere far from here," replied Tenashi.

"Wait," said Amsterdam reaching into his pocket and producing a piece of paper, "Can you take us to twenty-five point three four five zero degrees south. One-hundred and thirty-one point zero three six one degrees east?"

A map appeared onto the screen replacing the image of Dakini and a red marker appeared on the point where the coordinates met.

"Why do you want to go to Uluru?" asked Reed.

"Because that's where The Chief is going to be," replied Amsterdam.

"Who is The Chief?" asked Tenashi.

"A man who will be able to help us sort out what we do next," replied Amsterdam.

"And another man like me that knows The Oracle, Tenashi," said Reed, "Dakini, have you learnt how to plot a course yet?"

"Yes, Professor," replied Dakini.

"And, have you learnt to detect Lupei's signatures?" Reed continued.

"Yes, Professor."

"Good. Then set a course that avoids her locations to the coordinates entered."

"Okay, Mr. Amsterdam? Don't forget that you owe me a story," announced Dakini.

"I won't, Dakini. I promise," replied Amsterdam.

Chapter 38

Molly Whitaker's apartment was littered with relics and images of her life. There were pictures of her cats that she had owned since she was twelve years old; scatter cushions of different colours and shapes overflowing on the couch; almost every available power socket was connected to a lamp of some kind which had brightly coloured lamp shades; and, doilies were covering every flat surface that could be seen. It was a labour of love and picture of comfort which made Molly feel safe and secure. But now Molly was aghast that she had discovered George Underwood was now in her apartment the very morning that he was also in her dreams. What could he want, she thought?

"Is that really you, George?" Molly asked.

"Of course it is Molly. You haven't forgotten me that easily I hope?" replied George.

"No, not at all. You don't look any different from...from the last time I saw you." The last time she saw George was at their usual coffee shop. She had ordered a tuna salad on rye and needed to go to the bathroom. George had been edgy all day and when she returned he had gone. No note, no phone call, not even a mention to the waitress.

"Well, I can't say the same about you. Your hair is shorter and by the looks of it you've joined a gym?"

"Well, a girl needs to keep herself looking good when she is single. And I never heard you complain of the way I looked?"

The reality was that Molly had thrown herself into the gym out of sheer loneliness. After months of self pity, inactivity and not eating well she had put on a fair amount of weight and wanted nothing else but to move on as best she could. But no guy would have looked at her in the state she was in not only physically but mentally. Getting her physique back meant that she protruded a sense of confidence even if inside she was hurting more than ever.

"It wasn't a complaint but a compliment. You look amazing," said George.

"I suppose thanks would be in order."

"I suppose."

"How did you get into my apartment?"

"The front door was easy enough. I just waited for someone to go out and came in behind them before the door closed. The door to your apartment was a little trickier but by no means one that a bank might use for a vault."

"Wait, so you're picking locks now? When did you learn that?"

"There are many things you pick up out of necessity."

Molly didn't know where to stand in her own apartment. She leant on the back of the couch and then stood up; she paced a little and then fiddled with some photo frames. She settled on a side table that held a lamp and was covered in a lace doily with a picture of a farm house by a river slightly to the left of where George was sitting in the armchair. It meant that she did not have to look directly at George when she spoke as it was not easy confronting again what she had tried so hard to forget. The emotion and bitterness that had always been running deep inside had never really abated and now it was beginning to surface as raw as it had ever been.

"George, where did you go? I mean, why did you go? What did I do that made you want to leave me the way you did?"

"I didn't want to leave you. I had to."

"That doesn't make any sense, George. You were always going on about the things that you had to do. Like you were on some goddamned mission or something. You were the only guy that I had ever met that seemed to have it together, you know. Like you had some sort of plan. I thought I was in that plan, George."

"You were. And you still are," said George as his eyes that were looking directly at her felt like they were piercing through the hard exterior she was trying to display. Molly broke the look and fingered the stitching of the doily with her index finger nail. She traced the pattern of the farm house. She wondered how he could be thinking that they still had something between them. She understood that it was unresolved but she had resolved it for them when she decided it was time to move on.

"How can that be, George? You must know that I couldn't wait for you; that I had to move on. I have my own life now, other friends and my work-"

"Can you let me explain?"

"Yes, that would be really good. I would really love to know why!"

"I can only say that I am sorry, Molly. I never meant to hurt-"

"Save it! You meant to do everything that you have ever done, George. Don't lie to me."

"All right then, but you must believe me that hurting you was the last thing that I have ever wanted to do and everything that I did was in your interest. Molly, I'm about to tell you something that I have never told anyone that I am close to…not even my family knows."

"What, that you're an international art thief? Wait, I know, you discovered a cure for cancer?"

"I missed your wit, Molly," said George with a smile, "When I was a young boy I was introduced to a man called, Charles Harrison. He convinced my parents that I had a special gift and that he would help me learn how to use that gift for good. You know my parents didn't have much and they were delighted that someone was willing to help me with my studies. They thought that it was some type of scholarship to help me get into college but that wasn't anywhere near the truth. You know that I was having these visions. Things that I couldn't explain."

"Like my sister?"

"Yes, just like that," said George eagerly, "I couldn't explain why they were happening but I would see something in my mind and then it would play out just like I had seen it. I was really scared, Molly. I was seeing horrible things that no one that age should have seen and the worst thing about it was that I couldn't control it. But when Charles came into my life he understood what I was going through. He helped me really see what it was that was going on."

It was all making sense to Molly. George had clearly lost the plot; lost the ability to hold onto his mental faculties and had gone away to the funny farm. It made sense as to why he had not changed since the day he deserted her in the coffee shop. But she had other reasons as to why she felt this way. On the day he had left she was frantically trying to search for him. She had called the police and they didn't want to know her. She had called his parents to see if he had returned there but only managed to get his father who was drunk into a tempered frenzy. She didn't really know his other friends that well and only really met them once so figured that he wouldn't be going there either. And then finally a man appeared and told her he was looking for George. The man was dressed sharply in a dark three piece suit and said that it was vitally important that George made contact with him if indeed he did return. The man gave Molly his card with a number on the back and at the time she didn't think much of it. She simply put the card in the drawer of the entrance table. But, now thinking of what George was saying, maybe this man was helping George in some way overcome his illness.

If in fact he was ill she knew that she had to keep him in good spirits. She didn't want to get him off side or thinking that she did not trust him so it was important that she played along.

"So you can see into the future?" said Molly, "Like those star signs in the paper?"

"I can only see my future and the people that I come into contact with."

"So, how was it you saw how Angelina was going to die?"

"Because I lived through your grieving."

"And how am I going to die?"

"Even if I knew I would not tell you. But of course I have tried to look into my own life and see the end for myself. Human curiosity is a selfish vessel and while I am adamant that my ability is not used as a conduit for fear one cannot extinguish the thought of one's own demise. And there I found the problem. No matter how hard I focused I could not see past this one day. One day in my life that would change the fabric of humanity. And your life Molly."

"My life? I don't understand?" It was only then that she had some fears for her own safety. Up until this point she knew that he would never hurt her; but he seemed to have some sort of plan that he wanted to orchestrate and now it seemed he was fixated on that obsession. She had experienced an obsessive personality before in one of the men she had seen after George. They only saw each other a couple of times and in that time he had planned their wedding, where they were going to live in the suburbs and what schools their children would be going to. It was the reason that she had changed jobs.

"It is always the same," George began, "You and I are in a mountain range covered by snow and ice. We walk up to this hatch in the ground. You open the hatch and climb in fast. I can hear you screaming my name but I have my back to you as I look out over the horizon. And then suddenly the sky is lit up in a sea of red like it is on fire and then I turn and climb into the hatch with you. I close the hatch and then we are consumed with darkness. And then, there is no more."

"Why are we there?" asked Molly.

"All I can understand of that moment is that we go on a journey together and that is where we end up. You see, this is the reason I left the way I did. I had to find out why it is we are driven to this place."

This was all becoming too much for Molly. The way he was talking and sitting didn't illustrate a picture of mental illness. He seemed to be absolutely convinced in the truth in his story. This was not the way she wanted to remember a man that she had loved and admired.

"This is all absurd, George. How can you expect me to believe you? To trust you? Why are you telling me all this now? You could have told me at any time!"

"I know this has come as a shock. But it is the truth."

"But, you see, you are wrong. I could never go with you to this place. It is impossible. You've no idea of the heart ache you left me with. I spent months and months crying and feeling sorry for myself. I wouldn't put myself through that again. I can't."

"Okay, I understand. I wasn't expecting that you would miraculously forgive me straight away and that everything would be as it was."

"So what were you expecting?"

"I only ask that you go to work tomorrow. Don't tell anyone about our meeting and watch the news when you get home instead of an Audrey Hepburn film."

"That's it?"

"That's it. Then, when you have watched all you can then come and see me at our coffee shop. You remember the one?" Molly watched as George stood and walked toward the entrance to the door.

"I remember. Wait, you're leaving?"

George turned, "I have to, Molly. There are some things I need to take care of before tomorrow. But I'll be waiting at the coffee shop for you and then I will never leave your side."

With that George turned and walked out the door. Molly couldn't hold it in any longer and she burst into tears. She fell onto the couch and wrapped the blanket she kept there over her head waiting for the emotion to pass.

Chapter 39

Robert Hughes had very little time before the last session of the day to gain the support he required to ascend as the inaugural President of the United Federation of Asia. He had won the support of the Pacific nations including Indonesia and New Zealand; Thailand, Vietnam, Cambodia, India and Japan were also persuaded and vowed to work with their neighbouring States to ensure a consensus was reached. Their vote was of course provisional on the vote of China and it was now that Hughes sat with Prime Minister Wei Jinghua of China enjoying afternoon tea that he now sought that vote.

"Prime Minister," began Hughes.

"Please, call me, Wei. There are so many Prime Ministers that one finds it difficult to know who one is talking about."

Jinghua was a princeling of the new Chinese aristocracy. Educated at Cambridge he owned expensive real estate all over the world and had very little time for the needs of a political life that did not suit his business interests. In fact, his only desire upon entering the political arena was to appease those of the Communist Party who saw him as a capitalist and were mounting a campaign to undermine his business interests in China. Unfortunately, for them they did not bank on his sheer determination to be the best at everything he set his mind to and also his enormous wealth which gained favour with the local prefecture administrators.

"Very true," replied Hughes, "Wei, I'll come right out and say this, I have been in discussions with the other States in relation to the currently vacant Presidency of the Federation and we all agree that it is I that should run for the position. It has been viewed that my credentials in foreign policy and my relationship with America and other western societies are key assets in confirming our position as a friendly and trustworthy nation."

Wei sipped his tea in the traditional Cambridge style and then held up his right index finger, "The requirements of the Party were clear on this, Robert. China will hold power as Head of State. We have the industry, the finance and the military might to provide to the entire Federation. Thus, we are the rightful and legitimate owners to the seat of power."

Hughes remembered the concession well; he was right in the middle of the negotiation table coming out in favour of China's ascension as the crowned victors of the war that was never fought.

"Yes, however, I would like you to consider that the reasons you have highlighted are quintessential as to why a vote for me would be the necessary course of action in the infancy of the Federation."

"Go on," said Wei putting down his cup of tea on the side table beside him.

"The Federation is an extremely brittle shell and the expectation is that China would hold Presidency. However, this expectation also holds with it a weight of animosity and has the potential for other States to become disenfranchised. They may view it as a mere vehicle for China to flex its muscle to require the other States to submit to their rule rather than engage in unification. I am in the unique position as I am not tied to an existing nation. I am not ruled by the same patriotic affiliations which may jeopardise the transition from State based rule to that of the Federation."

"China would not accept being ruled by a foreign entity under any circumstances."

"Yes, but Wei, the US is already becoming edgy. They are at this moment plotting for war. A splinter faction has emerged that is not all that happy with our plans and seeks to undermine our advances. We are, in effect, transferring the balance of power into the favour of the Federation. We need to tread lightly or risk annihilation."

"If the US wants a war then we will crush them. It will be good practice for the eventual war that is to come."

"Now, Wei, we don't know what will come and we must not forget that the ultimate purpose of the Federation is the protection of humanity, not its destruction."

"And yet, you have allowed the Federation to absolve those in your own country of their rights to life."

"A necessary measure that will never be forgiven I'm sure. However, sacrifice has been a key mark of our culture and history will show that our citizens were resolute and humbled by a far superior power. But, these sacrifices that I have made must be recognised and rewarded as total commitment to the ideals of the Federation. I ask now that China makes a similar sacrifice."

Hughes watched for Jinghua's reaction to this obvious insult. It was a risky line of reasoning that had the potential to totally discount everything that he had said previously. Hughes knew that there was nothing that the Chinese loathed more than shame and drawing attention to it was paramount to instant dismissal; however, in Hughes' experience, Jinghua wasn't a man which held such cultural traits to heart and if he didn't know any better there appeared a slight moment of relief that fell across Jinghua's face and shoulders. It was then Hughes considered that maybe Jinghua didn't want the position at all and that he was merely keeping up appearances as per direction of the Party; and, Hughes had just offered him a way out.

Wei stood from his seat buttoning his suit jacket and Hughes did the same, "I am respectively moved by your words, Robert. I will see to it that your views are made aware to the High Council and you will have our answer at the voting session this afternoon."

"Thank you for your time, Wei. It goes without saying that if I am voted as President then I will be nominating you as my Vice President."

"A role that I would humbly accept."

The two men shook hands and Jinghua gave a slight bow of his head. These were all positive signs and as Hughes left the room he felt a euphoric sense of achievement. All the plans that he had been working on for decades were now coming to fruition. He had played his part precisely as was required and now he needed confirmation that others were upholding their end. Once Hughes was clear from ear shot he took out the satellite phone from his inside jacket pocket and dialled a number.

"Hello? Charles Harrison speaking."

"It is done," replied Hughes, "How are we going from your end?" said Hughes.

"Unfortunately, the magician has performed his vanishing act again."

"And what have you found from the tree?"

"We have momentarily been cut off from our operative. The infiltrators are making up ground on our motives and I fear that we will not be in a position to suppress them much longer."

"I am not concerned with the actions of these infiltrators. You just make damn sure that these things are taken care of. I will be presenting to the United Nations within twenty-four hours and be on site shortly after. You have two days Harrison to make this right."

Hughes pressed end on the handset and returned it to his inside pocket with his euphoria now subsided. Unfortunately, his plans were heavily reliant on two key elements coming together at exactly the right time and he considered it was time now that he contemplated a failsafe and exit strategy if his plans did not go off according to script.

Chapter 40

Anchorwoman: We have interrupted this program for a special news bulletin. Today it has been advised that the countries of over 25 nations in Asia have been disbanded and combined as one super state to be known as the United Federation of Asia. Countries from Mongolia in the north to Samoa in the Pacific and including China, India, Japan, Korea and Australia along with a host of others have today signed a historic pact that removes the sovereignty of those nations including governments, constitutions and laws. It has been reported by the CIA that all communication channels were cut coming in and out of these Asian countries the evening before last which included internet, mobile and landline coverage. All foreign offices were advised to leave immediately including members of the press; flights from countries originating outside of the Federation were advised to turn back immediately as it appears that a full lock down has been orchestrated. Our correspondent, Jim Sharper, was in Singapore when he was roused from his hotel room and advised that he had to leave the country immediately. We have Jim on the line now from Honolulu where his flight has just landed. Jim, what can you tell us of your experience?

Jim Sharper: It can only be described as one of shock, Jenny. There I was sleeping after a long day and suddenly I was awoken by military personnel with automatic rifles demanding that I leave immediately. They didn't even give me time to collect my possessions. My laptop, phone and passport were confiscated and I was only allowed to change into my clothes before I was forcefully whisked from the building into a waiting troop carrier where other journalists and foreign officials from embassies joined me on the trip to the airport. Of course, no explanation was offered to anyone herded to the airport by the military and when someone tried to seek answers they were set upon and severely beaten.

Anchorwoman: Jim, what can you tell us about the mood where you were?

Jim Sharper: It could only be described as normal, Jenny. There wasn't anything abnormal about the day. People were going about their business and there wasn't the slightest indication from any official on the ground in Singapore that this unprecedented action would take place. I, in fact, had a meeting with the Singaporean Minister for Foreign Affairs not three days prior and even at this time he was speaking about greater economic and political ties with the United States. The only thing out of the ordinary was that landline telecommunication services had been down across the country since the day before blamed chiefly on a drilling operation out to sea where cabling supporting the infrastructure was accidentally cut which suggests that this action was in motion for some time. I have attempted to make calls to my contacts in Singapore, China, Japan and Burma since I landed here but it seems there is a complete blackout across the entire region and one can only hope for the safety of people in the middle of this colossal power shift.

Anchorwoman: Thank you, Jim. We'll have to leave you there as it appears that Secretary of State, Bill Patrick, is about to make a statement from the White House and we cross there live to hear his remarks.

Bill Patrick: Ladies and gentlemen it has come to the attention of the President and his Administration that as you have heard an unprecedented, ah, joining of states has occurred all across the region of Asia. This truly has been a historic day across the world as news of this action has broken. Ah, let me assure you that this Administration is doing everything it can to ensure the safety of American citizens stuck in this crisis and more will come as information comes to hand. However, we don't really know what has sparked this, this, unification if you will and why the first action of the Federation has been to place a shroud around its people from the rest of the world. While I can't comment on the specifics of this intelligence maelstrom that has undoubtedly been whipped up following this action what I can tell you is that there has been no demands made by any one of the Federation to the United States or United Nations for that matter and I just want to be clear about this for the folks at home that this is not an act of war. Of course we would like to understand the reasoning behind this action and there will be flow on effects that we will need to deal with including how this will affect the economy and foreign policy and of course interests the United States have in these regions where considerable resources have been invested. But we are hopeful that we can get these back on track in the near future when spokespeople are brought forward to represent this newly formed state. Ah, we have made the important step of withdrawing our troops and military personnel from these regions including the withdrawal of the navy from their seas. It is not our intention at this stage to provoke any military conflict until dialogue can be established. We hope this action provides those now in power with the necessary concessions that we are eager to come to the table and discuss this new world as quickly as possible. Thank you for your time, we will be bringing you updates as quickly as can be established.

Anchorwoman: Secretary of State, Bill Patrick, there explaining that this action is not an act of war and that United States military forces have been withdrawn from these regions to ensure a dialogue can be created. The Secretary of State touched on this lightly; however, this is sure to cause chaos in financial markets and we have Jeb Weinstein our Wall Street correspondent on hand. Jeb, what has happened to the markets since this action has been unravelled?

Jeb Weinstein: Thanks Jenny, most of the major economies were closed for trading when this information filtered through and all markets have been suspended today because of it; however, when it does eventually open again, and I suspect that will be in the next forty-eight hours when more information comes to hand on what this all means for the world economy that it will be a complete and utter meltdown for the entire financial system as we know it. China alone makes up a huge majority of capital wealth let alone the importation of goods manufactured there and we will no doubt feel the effects of this for some time as we look to other trade partners to fill the void. For the markets that will mean less profits and more expenditure meaning a significant reduc-

tion in return for investors and shareholders and what I predict will be a worldwide collapse of the markets unless of course governments intervene to some extent.

Anchorwoman: Thank you Jeb, I'm sure there will be more on this later and we will be bringing you updates on this breaking story throughout the evening but for now we cross to Professor Michael Gillian of the Institute of Asian Affairs at Harvard University in Boston. Professor, what can you tell us about this action and what are the possible reasons for something happening on this scale?

Professor Michael Gillian: Well Jenny one could make the assumption that in part this has been coming for quite some time now. Militarisation of countries across Asia has been gaining momentum in many of these countries. For example, Burma and North Korea; Thailand has had massive troubles with its democracy fighting corruption and the like; China while on the face of it has made efforts to appear as though some semblance of freedom was available to its citizens but one only needs to look at Tibet to understand just how tight the stranglehold of the military is in that country.

Anchorwoman: Professor, the Secretary of State, Bill Patrick, has only moments before in a statement announced that the Administration does not consider this action as an act of war and has in fact removed a military presence in all of the countries involved. Do you think that this decision is somewhat premature given that it appears that no one in the intelligence community had any knowledge of this?

Professor Michael Gillian: Right. Well, it's not like they are dropping bombs on Pearl Harbour. What has happened here is a systematic cohesion of sovereign states that while we as Americans may feel we have some right to feel cheated in some respects the reality is that these nations are free to make their own decisions on how they choose to be associated.

Anchorwoman: Yes, but don't you feel that amalgamation of these states into one super state will also mean the amalgamation of their military forces and wouldn't that pose a threat to the American way of life?

Professor Michael Gillian: I agree it will be a military force like none the world has ever seen. However, it is important that we are patient *before we decide to take any next steps. Asia, in the main, is a peaceful region. Sure it has had its share of conflict but that is also the same story in Europe and even an early American nation trying to finds its feet. We cannot presume that this action has its sole purpose defined from a military standpoint as there are obvious economical and social benefits that would certainly be applicable and may in fact be the source for this action. Let's not forget that we have already experienced something like this in the form of the European Union and the introduction of the Euro as a single currency. We also have the Arab League and in part the United Nations is based on this single state philosophy. The reality is that this is not a new idea as these examples illustrate and while they could only be described as a loosely defined organisation of unity this action really just takes that next step to galvanise these partnerships.*

Anchorwoman: Professor, how would this be affecting the people in these countries? How are they going to react to this situation and is there any chance of rebellion?

Professor Michael Gillian: One thing to remember is that the Asia of yesterday is not the same as Asia of today. Asia today has accepted themselves as a part of the global community and gone are the days when Asia was a mystery to the Western world. There would of course be some resistance I'm sure; however, what we don't know is what happened in the days leading up to this and what the people of these countries were told.

Anchorwoman: Professor, who do you think is the main antagonist of this action? Is it China? Japan? Could it be possible that one country with such military and financial might such as China has put demands on these nations to join to this Federation or be crushed?

Professor Michael Gillian: Well, I don't really see that as a possibility. You don't form unity by force or coercion. History tells us that this type of fear mongering never lasts and usually results in one side waiting until the other is weak enough to be overrun.

Anchorwoman: I guess what Americans want to know is why, Professor?

Professor Michael Gillian: The short answer is I don't think anyone really knows. The only ones that could are those involved in the unification process and it is clear that this is something that our government has been left out of. Which I suspect is more a reflection on our position in the global community currently that we would be happy to accept.

Anchorwoman: Thank you for your insights Professor. We are now going out to Steve Ingerman who is currently standing at the Washington International Airport and I believe he has been speaking to some people who are trying desperately to make contact with family and friends in these countries and who are even trying to get flights to these countries. Steve.

Steve Ingerman: Yes, Jenny. On our way here we also stopped into many of the embassies from these Asian countries that have joined the Federation and we were very surprised to find that all were completely vacant. Not one guard on the gate or light in the window could be seen and we ran into many citizens of these countries who were trying to get information about what was happening in their countries; however, it seems that these people have been left high and dry by their nations. We spoke to one Australian citizen currently studying in America and asked her what she had been told and she said that she received a phone call from someone at the Australian embassy a few hours ago advising her that she is no longer a citizen of the Australian people and that she would need to claim refugee status with the country where she currently was residing. Remarkably, this story seems not be a unique one; however, as we spoke to one family from Japan over here on vacation and the father said that he was advised by their embassy that they could not return to their home so it would seem that anyone not in the country when this new nation was announced to the world are now refugees-

Anchorwoman: Thank you, Steve, but we are going to have to leave it there as we now have word from the White House that the President will be presenting a statement to the press right now. We cross there now live.

President Beirnstein: Thank you everybody. I have just received a phone call from the Prime Minister of Australia, Prime Minister Hughes, in relation to this recent global event. As you may know Australia has been our ally for many years both economical, social and of course we have fought through many wars together in overseas conflicts. The Prime Minister has conveyed to me that Australia has joined the United Federation of Asia and that all previous arrangements un-

der the ANZUS treaty have been absolved. He extended regret that it has ended after so many years of successful partnership; however, he assured me that the need was in the best interests of the nation and its citizens would share in the benefits of being associated with the Federation in the long term directly linked with its geographical location. He apologised for the communication black out and the secrecy at which this action was taken; however, advises such steps were necessary to ensure the people of the new state could adjust to their new environment without pressure from outside influence. He also advised me that a head of state would be chosen shortly and that with the permission of the American people and this Administration a meeting would be held shortly after at the United Nations in New York to outline their vision for the future. I can tell you that this Administration has gladly accepted to receive their new head of state and are happy to host the summit at a date in the near future. I conveyed on behalf the American people our deepest regret that we could not continue under the current arrangement and hoped that we may forge new alliances in the near future that will respect the rights of peace and free trade. I am confident after this conversation that no ill favour is directed toward the United States or any nation outside of the Federation for that matter and we will see a return to a cordial relationship albeit under the guise of a different regime. There will be further statements as more information comes to hand. Thank you and God bless.

'Watch the news', George had said to Molly Whitaker who was now curled up in her favourite blanket on the couch. 'And when you've had enough come and see me at our coffee shop'.

Molly didn't really fathom what the news of countries in Asia joining under a different banner meant to her and her situation. She couldn't see how this would have any effect on her life and wondered what all the fuss was about. For some reason the situation was being painted as a total catastrophe and as she flicked through the channels to watch something else she found that every channel was feeding into the news broadcast.

She turned off the television and buried her face into her hands. Surely this couldn't be happening to her. What had George become? It could be possible that George was some sort of spy for the new Federation which meant that he already knew about this event before it was made public and explain why he knew something was going to happen beforehand. After all, he didn't tell her where he had been for all that time and didn't offer any explanation as to why he had disappeared. He had only really told her that he knew things that were going to happen in the future.

The way Molly saw it was that she had two options. Ignore that she had even seen George again or go with him and bring him back into her life. The first option seemed like the easiest thing to do; but, she feared that he may keep coming back to her and not allow her to forget him. The second option at first seemed exciting; but, what she didn't understand was why he had chosen her? There was nothing special about her that warranted this attention; she was not well connected, she didn't have power with anyone, she merely existed and lived her life as a private member of society.

But there was a third option to consider. On reflection it was one she should have taken at the very beginning. She knew that George might hate her initially but for some reason she saw that it would all work out for the best. From Molly's perspective all she could think of was that George needed help; help that she could not provide.

She walked down the entrance hall and went the drawers at the entrance. It was still sitting there. She took her mobile phone from her pocket and dialled the number on the card that the man in the sharp three piece suit had given her. It was ringing and she hoped still belonged to him.

"Hello?" Molly hadn't noticed before but the man had a British accent.

"Ah, yes. Is this Charles Harrison?" Molly asked.

"Yes, it is. To whom am I speaking please?"

"My name is Molly Whitaker. You came to me a few years back now and you were looking for George Underwood who was my boyfriend at the time."

"Yes, I do remember that. How can I help you?"

"Well, George has returned and I think…I think he needs help."

Chapter 41

George Underwood sat in the coffee shop three blocks from the house that he and Molly shared when they were together. It was their favourite place to visit at any time of the day. The owner, Jurgis, a large man from Lithuania, was a man that made an effort to get to know everyone who came in and out of the place so it was no surprise that he gave Underwood a big hug when he saw him come in the door.

"George, George, George!" he said excitedly squeezing Underwood from an inch of his life, "Where have you been my friend?"

"Around, Jurgis, around," replied Underwood, "Jurgis, I can't breathe!"

"Oh, sorry, George," he said letting Underwood go as he took a large breath and held himself up against the wall, "I'm just so happy to see you. I only saw Molly once after you left. She was sitting in your usual table crying and I asked her why so sad and she said that you had left her! I couldn't believe it. I told her that he must have had some reason. But, I don't know, I don't think that she thought you were ever coming back. After that, I don't see her again. I pass her in the street and in the supermarket sometimes but she is so different. She seems a different woman. And my god, what a woman, eh? But, you know, people have to live in their own ways. My only worry was that she was safe."

"Thanks for looking out for her, Jurgis. I appreciate it."

"No problem, no problem. Hey, people need to look out for each other because no one else will. This place is more than just a shop. I don't just make money here I also provide protection. People are safe here no matter what goes on out there. You take your usual table I'll go get your coffee. Jurgis remembers just the way you like it."

Jurgis went off behind the counter happily whistling to himself but Underwood didn't have the heart to tell him that he stopped drinking coffee for some time. He took his seat in the corner booth beside the window. It was a good spot to look out from and the door to the back was also visible and there was clear access to the stairs that went up to the bathrooms and small apartment that Jurgis shared with his wife. The shop itself was a dive of a place; a drip of fat away from being shut down by the health department. But, it was this aesthetic quality that gave it a sense of originality and warmth making it feel like a home away from home.

Before coming in, Underwood had walked the streets around the building. He looked in every shop window in the vicinity and tried to read the faces of anyone sitting in a car or walking on the street. It was an important routine to ensure that he knew all the exits and was able to commit to memory anybody that looked like they didn't belong. And Underwood had seen some faces that were too crisp for this neighbourhood.

Jurgis brought over the coffee and said, "Hey is Molly coming?"

"I hope so," replied Underwood.

"Good, good. I get my wife to make her favourite. It's not on the menu anymore but she will be happy to do it for Molly."

After leaving Molly in her apartment Underwood had made his way to the Golden Gate Fields race track. The meeting with Molly had proceeded as he had predicted and he felt that she would come around. The connection with her was still there and he could feel that she still wanted to be with him. His main concern, or what he couldn't see, was how that connection was to be re-established. He desperately wanted her to come of her own free will and had hoped that she did not feel threatened or coerced to come with him. While Underwood's visions were concise about what was to happen it almost always did not provide insight as to why events played out as they did. It fuelled his heightened sense of anxiety when he was about to enter into a confrontation; however, once he was in the moment the dots began to join quickly and he was able to anticipate the next move as if the world around him was in a state of slow motion.

The race track was a place he knew well and he spent many days there with his father watching the thoroughbreds go through their paces in the mounting yards. His father liked to stand at the barrier to see how they moved and showed Underwood how to look at horses who were carrying injuries or who had been overworked. He had said that you could always tell when the jockey got on the horse's back that if the horse reacted badly then it was a sure sign that things weren't quite right. As it turned out it was only one of the many theories that his father had on horse racing; albeit, if unsuccessful.

It was in this same spot that he found his father standing at the barriers wearing a parker and beanie sipping hot coffee with no cream; a steely determination on his face as he looked the horses up and down that were ready for the first race. Underwood stood across from him and watched as he looked up from his form guide to the horses.

"Number two, what you holding there boy? That horse don't look like it wants to stand on its back left leg. And number seventeen, who it trying to fool. It don't want to be in this race. Look at its eyes, he more interested in eating the grass. We got ourselves a sorry ass bunch of gelatine today. Yessiree. Now, now, now, wait. Hold on a minute. Number four aint looking that bad. He seeming a bit more spritely. He on the ball to-day. What he paying there? Three-to-one, ah heck. It aint worth the dime. No, what we want is something with a bit of spice, twenty, thirty-to-one. Now them odds more like it."

As the horses were mounted and left the yard to the main track Underwood began walking over to where his father was standing. At first, his father didn't turn to acknowledge him wrapped up as he was in his assessment of the horses in the race.

"That number four, though," said Underwood's father to himself, "Man he look the goods but his form aint all that. Says here his last four starts he came in last, ninth, sixth and tenth. Why you so short then boy. Come on, give me something, give me something."

"He's dropped down in class, here," said Underwood pointing to the spot on the form guide where a little triangle pointing down indicated that he had dropped down in grade. There were few things that he had learnt from his father but how to read a form guide was one of them.

"Where, I don't see that-" began his father until he turned around to see who the stranger was not finishing the sentence when he noticed who it was.

"You need to wear your glasses, Pops. It's good to see you, Dad," said Underwood.

"Well, looky here, my boy," the two men embraced with his father giving Underwood a good slap on the back, "My boy. It's good to see you too, Son."

Unexpectedly, Underwood was moved by the embrace. A tear welded in his eye and the feeling that he had of being in his father's arms again brought back memories of his childhood that he had long forgotten. He remembered Underwood and his Dad playing football in the park, sitting on his shoulders at the circus so he could see the clowns and skimming rocks in the bay. However, the moment was short lived as his thoughts were sucked back from the memory of the past into the memory of the future. He saw a beach and the image of his mother's face and his father pouring out the contents of a bottle of scotch onto the sand and throwing it away.

"What you doing here, boy."

"Well, I thought that I would come and see you. I didn't have much time to spare and I was driving past the track and I thought to myself that you would be here for sure."

"You know it," his father replied, "Not sure why you bothered though. We got ourselves a sorry bunch of good-for-nothins today. Hey, why don't you come on by the house and your momma will fix you up something special? She'd love to see you. And your sister too."

"Dad, not today. I'd love to but-"

"It don't matter, it don't matter. You an important man, you gotta do your important things. We know, we know. Just a shame is all you being so close and all to your family that you can't just stop by once in a while."

It was a shame, thought Underwood. He did want to see his family again but he couldn't put up with the further shame of having to leave them again. It was why he decided to come to the track instead to ensure that he would not need to say goodbye. For Underwood knew that this would be the last time that he would see anyone in his family.

"Dad, I don't have long. But I wanted to give you something. It's for everyone, you hear. I wanted to make sure that you and Mom, that, that you were all right."

"What you talking about, son? Of course, we all right."

"No, Dad. I wanted to really make sure that you were all right. Please take this." Underwood had taken the money that he had found in the safe in the hotel from the night before and he now handed to his father a betting slip.

"What's all this, Son?"

"Race six, horse number three. It's paying fifty-to-one. I put ten large on it for you and Mom."

"What'ja do that for now, boy," said Underwood's father consulting the form guide, "Says here that it aint won a race, let alone taken a place. Looky here, you go back and you cash that in and get your money back."

"Dad, just trust me. You really need to trust me."

Underwood looked into his father's eyes as they both held onto the betting slip. He could see a sense of understanding fall over his father's face as he started to nod.

"Sure, son. If you say so. Maybe they been holding it back for the big one."

"And when it comes in, and it will, you need to get out of Cisco. Sell up the house. You take Mom, Sis and yourself and you get yourself a little house in Nassau in The Bahamas. Do you understand me, Dad?"

Underwood's mother had been born there and it was the furthest place he could think that he could get his family out of harm's way that they would agree to go to.

"Sure, I do. It's going to be hard to drag you momma away. You know how she likes her sewing classes and such. It don't look it but she always busy doin somthin' or other."

"And you're going to cut out the drinking. I mean it."

"I'm sure it's for the best anyway. So, I'll be damned. Horse three, race six, huh? Yeah, maybe you're right."

When he left his father Underwood gave him a long hug. He felt his father's shoulders relax and his breathing shake as he released a deep sigh. His father told him as he walked away that they would keep a room spare for him in The Bahamas. But he would never need it and as he sat looking at Jurgis' coffee that was more like a brown sludge you found in a mud bath of some high-class spa retreat he thought to himself how wonderful it would be if Molly and he could just leave together and escape to some place and live on the beach; where everything that he would ever see would be long days in the sun and Molly sitting right there beside him. It was a fantasy; however, that he could never indulge and every time that he did spend taking a moment to picture a future for himself his mind quickly retracted into some deep dark place where his only future was one of the suffering and anguish of other people in need of help that he could not provide. It was the most significant and selfish moment that he had taken in his life to be here right now waiting for Molly. And even then, his vision was specific, Molly was right there with him when the lights went out. So, in fact, the very reason that he decided to go on this path could have been determined by his desire to ensure that Molly was kept safe.

"Molly!" said Jurgis as he lumbered out from behind the counter to give her a big hug and Underwood looked up from his reverie. She was dressed in dark pants and a grey coloured parker. Her hair was pulled back and in its shortness created a small pony tail at the back. The hug from Jurgis was just as severe as the one he had given Underwood and she laughed out loud as she playfully slapped him on the arms.

"Ha, ha! Put me down, Jurgis," said Molly as she was spun around by Jurgis and as she laughed a memory again flooded back to Underwood of a time when they were eating ice-cream in a park on a summer's day and Molly had missed her mouth when she went to lick the ice-cream and she got it all over her nose.

"It's just so good to see you," Jurgis replied putting her down and laying on a big kiss on her lips.

"Well, I've been around," Molly replied.

"I tell wife. She make you your favourite," said Jurgis as he trotted off to the kitchen and Molly came over to where Underwood was sitting.

"You're sitting in our spot?" said Molly putting her hands in her pockets and leaning on the back of the stall.

"I knew you would come," replied Underwood.

"Well, I guess, I didn't have much of a choice did I?" she said sitting down opposite Underwood in the booth, "I mean, I figured that you wouldn't have said you'd be here if you knew that I wouldn't come."

"There is reason in all things. I am merely shown the way. So, what are your reasons, Molly? What made you want to come?" Underwood asked.

Molly cupped her chin in her left hand, "My reasons? George, you were my soul mate. At least, I thought you were. When you come back into my life of course I am going to do everything that I can to help you. You told me to watch the news and I did. But George, I have to admit that knowing that still doesn't mean I believe you. I don't know where you've been or what you've been doing. You could be a spy for all I know."

"And what did you think of the news?"

"I don't know."

"It didn't strike you as odd?"

"I guess. But, I don't really know how it affects me?"

Molly was a smart person. Her rationality was what Underwood feared may lead her away from his path. It may still. It was then that Underwood was struck with a vision. It was hazy and without the clarity which was usually the case; gold all of a sudden felt very important.

"I knew that it would be difficult to get you to believe me, Molly. You're too intelligent for that. I couldn't just come out and tell you what we need to do outright I had to ease you into it. And, for what it's worth, I understand that you were only trying to help. But the man that you called, Charles Harrison, he can't be trusted."

"How do you know that I called him?" said Molly with a dumbfounded look on her face. Underwood looked at her hands and wrists. No gold there. Nor did she appear to be wearing a necklace or earrings. He then remembered that she had a phobia about necklaces choking her and earrings being pulled out which was why she didn't wear them.

"I told you how I know, Molly." Underwood replied.

"No, no, no. George, you're sick. You need help that I can't give you. Charles said he can help you with that."

"And the men outside, the ones in the street, are they going to help me, Molly?" said Underwood a clear image coming to him showed a gold tooth and black parker jackets.

"What men, George? Charles said that he would come down personally and take you back from where ever they were keeping you. George, this is just the reason that you need help. There are no men here to get you."

"The truth is that you are in danger too, Molly. And it's my fault which is why I need to take you with me. I understand that you don't know the game that you are in and that's all right. I forgive you for what you have done; but, only I can protect you."

"George, listen to yourself. Listen to what you are saying. There is no one coming to get you. There is no one coming to get me. It is just you and this fantasy land that you have created for yourself."

"If only that were true, Molly. I would gladly accept insanity over this," he said reaching out and taking her hand the result of which rushed a different vision in his head, "We don't have much time, Molly. Please listen, when they take you in just remember, ask them for a lighter."

With this the back door opened with a slam and entered three burley men dressed in black parker jackets. Two more men descended from the stairs and finally another three men came in through the front. They encircled the booth until one of them walked forward. The man had a scar under his left eye and was taller and leaner than the other men around him. He smiled revealing a gold tooth on the left incisor and then the world around Underwood began to slow down, "Mr. Underwood, I was wondering if we may have a little chat?" said the gold tooth man in a southern accent, "Now, we don't want to disturb the good people here so why don't we just head on back to my office where we can speak in private."

"Where's Charles?" asked Molly.

"Charles is busy with other assignments at present, Miss Whitaker."

"Then who are you?" said Molly.

"Oh, just an associate," he replied revealing his toothy gold grin.

Chapter 42

Harry Lockley had never ridden in a helicopter before. He'd never taken a joy ride over some picturesque landscape; hell, he'd never even flown on a domestic flight before. And now he sat in the cockpit of a helicopter designed to kill with his finger on the trigger ready to tackle anything that came along. He had studied the Russian characters on the display and made sense of what it meant when a target was locked but little else. The Chief was the pilot of the Erdogan, a Russian attack helicopter, and Lockley had been impressed at how he was able to take control of the bird and keep it steady. Their initial take off had been a bit dicey with an alarm being sounded all through the cockpit; but, The Chief managed to get his bearings together. After all, it wasn't that often you got to take out an illegally purchased Erdogan for a spin to make sure you kept up your flight hours.

They had kept a low altitude flight path that saw them come awfully close to mountainous ranges and electrical pylons in the hope that they wouldn't be picked up by radar. They had plotted a course using the contacts that The Chief had received throughout the day informing them of invasion activity which avoided the major towns and cities and the night sky added a further element of anonymity which Lockley was happy to risk. Lockley was surprised at how little activity he saw on the roads. Even at this low altitude he would have thought he would see someone driving along the roads; but, the darkness down there only highlighted the fact that what they were experiencing was all consuming and probably branched out further than what he initially imagined could be possible.

Lockley, since his initial citing five years prior, had been making a particular effort to understand how it is a country like Australia could be invaded. Most of the theories he had read had concentrated on the northern parts of the island continent as the most likely to be hit first and established as an enemy staging ground before making a push toward the eastern states of Queensland and New South Wales then moving toward Victoria. Others suggested a two prong attack where the area around Broome in the north-west as the likely insertion point with one force moving south and taking the populated areas around Perth in the south-west before moving east and taking South Australia and Melbourne in Victoria in the south-east. The other force would move east from the north-west taking Darwin in the Northern Territory and then Cairns working their way down the coast to Brisbane. They would then both move toward Sydney in a pincer manoeuvre. The consistent message was also that this attack would need to move at tremendous speed and be supported by a significant naval force which converged and laid siege to major metropolitan areas from land and sea. Lockley thought that the movement across land wouldn't be that difficult in the current situation where civilians were unarmed and military was a punitive force; but, the sea effort would eventually be supported by Australia's allied nations who by all accounts would take a minimum of three days to launch an offensive. The reality was that three days of killing and destruction could devastate the entire country and Lockley considered that the only hope they could possibly have would have been to retire the entire defence force completely and become a neutral nation. And this may have been a possibility at one time until world events drew them into battles that they had no need to be involved with.

But now, all the theories that Lockley had read weren't providing any insight into the actuality that he confronted. It was what The Chief was referring to when the contacts he was receiving made no sense at all. It was like there was a simultaneous invasion that attacked from over a thousand angles with what must have been a force of over ten million soldiers; and, that attack was coming from above not from land or sea.

"Keep those eyes sharp there Lockley," said The Chief over the headset, "Likely to come across anything at anytime so make sure you're ready to pump on the trigger."

"Sure thing," replied Lockley. The fact was that he hadn't been game to keep his finger anywhere near the trigger the entire time they had been up here. The Erdogan was fitted with a front mounted chain machine gun on a one-hundred and eighty degree swivel head and The Chief had told him to give it a short burst of fire if they saw anything in the air so as to give them a chance to change course and avoid being locked. He now bared his teeth and sucked in a deep breath and gripped the trigger with his index finger. It was at this moment he felt that he was really in the war and the sense of anxiety which had consumed him now shed its hold and he concentrated on the display for any sign of movement.

"It's pretty quiet out there, Chief."

"I know what you mean. Not even a spark of a street light where towns usually be. I guess this really is happening. Make sure you take a note of towns that should be there but aint on the map. Our secondary objective in all of this is to provide a conduit so that we have a means of escape."

"Escape to where?"

"The sea of course. I hope that at some stage we can make contact with the Americans or the Brits or someone out there who is taking a look at this thing and we can request an evac ship. If we can plot a route through their lines it will be our best bet for survival."

"But what of the counter-measures we can take?"

"Lockley, there aint nothin' to this thing but survival. Sure, we'll take them on where we can but just think of what it was we're up against. The size of it must be immense. I'm sorry to say that our best means of defence may be to retreat and fight another day in an army that can help us. Not the small bunch of guerrillas and weekend warriors that we are."

Of course, The Chief was right. Lockley sensed it and new that what he said made complete sense. Survival was their only course of action and he considered suggesting to The Chief that they should just haul this chopper as far away from Australian airspace as possible and hope to be picked up somewhere by a friendly. But, what of Hef, Barry and Jeremiah? They had a promise to keep to them and they had to keep it no matter what the risk.

"We should be coming up on Riverton in about thirty-seconds," said The Chief, "Keep an eye out for bogies."

As they sided the ridge of the mountain terrain, Lockley could sense something wasn't right. Riverton should have been in full view glowing under amber street lights; however, there wasn't a thing that resembled life at all underneath them. As they came closer to the township Lockley took his eyes off the display and looked at the buildings. The moonlight gave the buildings a slight shine even though he couldn't see a single soul moving in any of the houses that they flew over. Not even a dog or a cat wandering the streets.

"Let's take it down. There's a bowling green over there to the right amongst those houses. We can land and get a good feel for the whole thing."

"Roger," said Lockley slightly proud of himself for remembering the correct terminology for using two way radios.

They came down with a hefty thud and Lockley could feel the Erdogan slightly lean to the side and the back of the helicopter rotate around which he sensed couldn't be a good thing.

"Not bad for my second landing," said The Chief, "On my first attempt I buckled the entire undercarriage and spent months repairing it. Good thing the ground was soft."

They waited until the engine whined down and the rotors came to a stop before they got out. They kitted themselves with machine guns and made their way out into the street. Lockley kept an eye out for the path behind them and they knelt beside a house with a white picket fence.

"Let's go in and take a look at what they got for supper," whispered The Chief.

They came to the front door and Lockley put his hand on the door expecting to find it locked; however, when he gave it a twist he found that it opened easily which meant that they were either very trusting of their neighbours in Riverton or that the occupants had no intention of ever coming back.

As they entered Lockley noticed that the house was divided in two by a central corridor with rooms right and left. He couldn't sense any movement at all inside and there weren't any lights on; not even the hum of a refrigerator. The Chief signalled for Lockley to go right and he would go left and Lockley nodded agreement moving to the door keeping low. The Chief counted silently to three and they both pulled the doors open. When Lockley entered the room he found a sitting room furnished with antique furnishings. A bookcase covered the entire far wall and the chairs were upholstered in suede finishes but empty of anyone hiding in the corners. As he moved to the next room, the dining room, the table was clearly arranged and set for dinner; but, again he found it empty. He met up with The Chief in the kitchen who also signalled that they were empty and they moved toward the back of the house where the bedrooms were located down the corridor. They entered the rooms together and found one-by-one that they were empty also. The weird thing was that the beds were perfectly made ready to be slept in by their occupants.

"Well," said The Chief breaking the silence as he shouldered his weapon, "What do you make of it?"

"Well, sure as hell we can tell that whoever lived here left in a hurry about dinner time."

"Why do you say that?"

"The dinner table is laid out with knives and forks and the beds are made."

"Yep, my guess is that they came in around dusk just before momma-bear began cooking the evening meal. The kitchen is clean and the stove doesn't have any pots or pans on it and there's a copy of a newspaper lying on the floor where poppa-bear was reading and the TV remote was carelessly placed beside the coffee table where the kiddy-bears were watching their afternoon shows. It's a magazine all right."

It was at this point that Lockley noticed the pictures of the family on the wall. Momma-bear had a thin face and kind blue eyes while poppa-bear was somewhat overweight and clearly ten or fifteen years her senior. The children, there seemed to be three, a boy of around twelve, a girl a little younger and the youngest another boy who looked four or five. The photo itself looked old and the fashion styles gave away that the photo must have been taken sometime in another era so perhaps it was only momma and poppa bear that lived there now. Lockley had this dreadful feeling that someone would switch on the lights and yell 'Surprise!' and then all his friends and family would be there wishing him a happy birthday unveiling an elaborate hoax that he wasn't expecting. But, Lockley's birthday was three months prior and he wasn't the type that would allow a surprise birthday party to be arranged unnoticed so this seemed very unlikely. The reality was it was a distraction for what he guessed they were both sensing.

"Let's check the rest of the street. Maybe there's survivors' hanging out somewhere. When you're sure that the place is empty yell out to see if anyone is there just in case they're hiding in a basement or something. We might get lucky and find some kid who was able to stash themselves away. We'll rendezvous back at the front of this place in fifteen minutes."

In the first house Lockley found much of the same thing; a fully furnished house, someone's boxed life, ready to be filled but not a soul around to share it. He called out but heard only the flatness of his own voice echo off the walls and a sensation of loneliness as he tried to listen for muffled voices. His next property was much the same and the next after that. He came up to the end of the street and found a corner store. He went in and found that the shelves were perfectly stacked and the newspapers and magazines aligned perfectly on the shelves. The milk fridge was fully stocked and the cash register was still filled with money. Lockley didn't have the heart to touch anything feeling like he was walking through a crime scene and the money he guessed would have been useless anyway. He had the urge to leave everything exactly the way he found it making sure to replace items in their exact spot when he needed to move something. Lockley thought that it would have been an odd thing to see but he wanted everything ready for whoever it was that lived here to return to it the way it was; but, no, it was more than that. Lockley *needed* to think that someone would someday want to return to this spot and they would be most upset if they found things missing or out of place.

"Nothing. Not a single goddamned thing," said The Chief quite loudly not trying to conceal the noise as they met up at their rendezvous point, "It's a ghost town all right. What about you?"

"Same thing."

"Ah, geez. It don't make a lick of sense, I tell ya. If they were slaughtered then where are the bodies? Hell, you would have thought you'd have found at least a blood splatter on the ground or something but the only thing I found outa place was a pile of unopened letters scattered on the floor. It's like everyone just pulled up and left."

"And where is the enemy? What are they running from?" asked Lockley.

"Exactly. They've either moved on or hiding from us so as to not get noticed."

"It's just like Barry said. It's a takeover. They want what we have. I'm guessing if we looked around enough, somewhere out in the outskirts of town, you'd find a large pit full of dead bodies."

"I'm going to assume that's the case. I've seen enough let's get the hell outa here. We've stayed too long."

Lockley had moved at least forty yards back toward the Erdogan when he realised that The Chief had not followed his lead. He turned back down toward the street and saw him standing like a statue with his face turned toward the night sky. Lockley thought that he might have been breaking up with the pressure, overwhelmed and insecure much the same way Lockley was feeling but successfully suppressing it; but, as he came back and stood beside The Chief he followed his gaze and understood what had taken his attention like that. It was then that Lockley was transfixed on the clear night sky highlighted by faint moonlight as some kind of airship the length of three football fields and two wide moved effortlessly as if it was gliding across a sea. It was square in shape and appeared to taper toward the top like a giant keel of an upside-down yacht. It was then also that Lockley got a good look at what must have been the transport ships that he had experienced the night before gliding beside the mother craft in formation. Practically hundreds of them encircled the mother craft in tight groups of four.

"That thing can't be from this planet!" said The Chief in a hypnotic stare.

"It's absolutely incredible," said Lockley also in the craning hypnotic position, "I wonder if there are more of them?"

Lockley suddenly remembered he had the night vision binoculars he had picked up back at The Chief's farm and he took them and pointed them toward the airship. They were clearly meant for short distances but even with the grainy image they picked up a fair amount of detail. Enough detail that Lockley could see the definite markings of what appeared to be a bar code which if observed up close must have stood at height of several stories and letters beside it which appeared to be 'UFA'.

"Well, if it is from another planet," announced Lockley, "They sure like to keep everything in an orderly manner. And they also like to use characters that look very much like English letters."

"Letters?" queried The Chief.

"Yeah. Big ones that say UFA. Not sure what it could mean though?"

"United Federation of Asia," said The Chief absently but without any hint of hesitation in his voice, "The next big super-power that was 'sposed not to exist. T'was only a myth and not a very gooden at that. Could they really be doin' it? I don't get it. It's just... "

"Just what, Chief?"

"The UF of A is an initiative derived by our own government. Our elected officials, Lockley. They've sold us out."

Lockley was having difficulty consuming what The Chief was saying. But the intent stare, the clarity of his words and the surety of his tone told him that The Chief knew something of this more than what he was letting on. If this was the work of the Australian government then maybe this was the cavalry coming to help them through. The reality was that they had not much to go on; they hadn't found one shred of evidence to suggest that what they were experiencing was an invasion at all and it could have very well been something simple like a telecommunications failure or a massive sun flare that had sent the entire electronic system into a tail spin.

The Chief continued, "It's what The Oracle told me would happen...Come on, Lockley. Let's gets this bird in the air. I want to take a good look at that thing and maybe launch a missile or two its way to get an idea on the way it moves."

"Are you serious? Let's just let it pass and then make a break for it."

"We could do that. But then we wouldn't know anything about the enemy. Would we?"

It was clear to Lockley that The Chief had something of an agenda that he was running and he had no choice but to follow or stay here in this ghost town and ride it out. For a second, Lockley weighed the options and then in frustration caught up to The Chief who was making his way back to the Erdogan. If information was king in this new world then the suicide run The Chief and he was about to make would be worth every scrap and only one of them needed to survive to pass on the message.

Chapter 43

President of the United Federation of Asia, Robert Hughes, stood at the lectern in front of the remaining members of the United Nations Security Council. His ascension to the Presidency had been unanimous. His nomination had been offered by North Korea and seconded by the Japanese and he was voted in without opposition. His first act as President was to enact his first executive order which was the immediate cessation of stage one in Operation Long March and ordered that the remaining Australian citizens be absorbed into the agricultural, mining or military manufacturing industries. The order was carried out albeit with some objection by the Generals who advised that it would be difficult to redistribute those remaining and meet the targeted deadline.

Shortly after this, Hughes had announced that he would confront the United Nations and reveal their immediate plans. The military had insisted on a strong show of force redirecting the flagship of the military, The Conqueror, to pronounce the position of the Federation as being the far superior military force. Hughes had thought that it was a bit much so early and feared that it may be seen as a sign of provocation; however, he understood the advantages of surprise and had agreed to the tactic.

The result of the dramatic entrance was clearly now waning on the faces of the United Nations Security Council members. Overawed and at odds with their own self-determined proclamation as defenders of the peace the dire looks on their faces were nothing short of complete and utter fear. A fear that Hughes could use and expand on as he announced the reasons why the Federation needed to exist.

"Good evening all, I will digress from formalities to get at the matter at hand."

"The matter at hand," interrupted Secretary of State, Bill Patrick, "Mr. President, is that you have an arsenal sitting at bay off the coast of New York City and we're a little on edge on what you plan on doing with it."

Hughes laughed out loud, "That's a good one, Bill. The Federation has upped the ante when its President travels. It might be a step up from Air Force One but that's how we do things in the Federation."

There was a nervous laugh from the group.

"But, seriously," continued Patrick, "Where on earth did that arsenal come from, Robert? Are you saying that it was kept hidden from the United States? And, what sort of capability does it have?"

"Evidently, many things were kept from the United States," retorted Hughes, "And, please, Bill, these are all questions that have answers, I can assure you. But, please allow me to take this moment to fill you in on where it is we have progressed from and then I'm sure you will see as we had that action needed to be taken without the restrictions placed on it in the typical diplomatic fashion. If you please," Hughes pointed to his aide who was working the screen at the front of the room, "If you would please look toward this image. It's an image of space visible from the southern hemisphere taken approximately seventy years ago. I would like you to focus on the left hand corner of this image and this cluster of seemingly benign stars here. Now, this particular star formation becomes visible every twenty-three years and over the years we have developed the following time lapse of images which you can see there, quite clearly, that the cluster is moving."

The image flipped through each image in a loop revealing the cluster of white dots which became larger as they moved closer to the middle of the image on the screen.

"How were these images collected?" asked Patrick.

"Well, many of you might know that I was a founding board member of Globe Corp when it went public as a global insurance company. And while insurance was our prime business function it also undertook research programs that were designed to understand the potential risks of the future. Space exploration was but one of those departments with the directive to understand the past so that we may interpret the future. Now, when we started looking at these images we could not help but think that a star cluster that size could not possibly move that fast without a catastrophic event in the universe. We looked hard for the remnants of supernovas but none were found. It was then that we began taking the following images."

The loop changed to a similar image of stars; however, the colours of stars were of a purple colour; accept, for the cluster of stars Hughes was referring to had now turned to a distinctive red colour.

"These images portray radio waves; specifically, artificially generated radio waves. The red dots on the screen highlight signatures which are displaying these artificial signals."

"So, you are saying that you have evidence which suggests intelligent life in the universe?" said Patrick. There was a collective gasp from the group.

"More than that, these images are not stars at all. We believe they are vessels. Vessels of immense size and structure that can move faster than the speed of light. Now, we turned the cameras on our own planet and wondered if those same radio signatures could be picked up here on earth. And we found one, in one very specific location for one very specific purpose."

"They have been here before?" asked Petre Ferminov of the Russian attaché.

"This is true, yes," replied Hughes, "We also have reason to believe that they are coming back."

"Coming back?" said Patrick.

"Yes," replied Hughes.

"For what?" continued Patrick.

"It could be for any number of reasons. Primarily, I believe it would be safe to say that they either want something that we have or they are merely curious as we would be if we had the capability to connect with another intelligent life form. They have known that we have been here for quite some time and our best indicators show that the last time they were here was around the thirteenth century."

"What do you mean by the 'last time'? Their visits have been frequent?" asked Patrick.

"There have been several contacts, yes; and, in numerous cultures around the planet. Their memory long forgotten but their legacy still remains," replied Hughes.

"How long until they get here?" asked Ferminov.

"Our analysts believe that they will be here within ten years," replied Hughes. There was a collective groan from the room.

"We are going to need to see your data on these speculations before we come out in support of any findings," said Patrick, "And, to be
frank I am very apprehensive to recognise its legitimacy given that we
have had no word from NASA on this and this definitely seems to me
something that they would pick up."

"Bill, there is no questioning the resolve of our actions. We have
the battle plans drawn and the impetus to carry this out. Ladies and
Gentlemen of the Council, I have not come here today to seek your
guidance on this matter. I am here as a common courtesy to share what
we know so that you may be able to make the most of this time we have
to prepare yourselves and your nations. The Federation will be taking
the lead role in this development and planning accordingly. The entire
efforts of the Federation are devoted to this cause and until we can determine with total assurance that there is no threat whatsoever; I regret
to inform you that liberty is on hold. The borders will remain closed in
and out of the Federation and we will view any attempt of disharmony
or infiltration as a direct threat that will be dealt with by the harshest of
penalties. Thank you for your time."

Hughes turned from the lectern and strode toward the door to
exit the room and he began to admire his own conviction. The people
in this room were once feared decision makers that were now reduced
to mere spectators in the game of Hughes' making. And yet, he did
not feel sorrow for the position that he had just put them in nor was
he anxious that they may make a decision that was detrimental to his
own position. This was real power, he thought, and a part of him selfishly liked the feeling. The next stage was to make contact with the
approaching extra-terrestrials and hope that Harrison had managed to
get his people in order.

PART IV

Chapter 44

When Harry Lockley locked on the target in the Erdogan he had no idea what would happen next. They had flown the Erdogan above the main airship that moved like a massive turtle through the air. As a target, it offered little challenge to even a novice like Lockley. The Chief, who was piloting the Erdogan, had advised him to aim for the top wing that was shaped like an upside-down keel.

"Target locked," said Lockley over the cockpit radio.

"Fire!" said The Chief without a hint of hesitation and so Lockley obeyed and he flicked the trigger to release the air-to-air missile from the starboard wing of the Erdogan which gave a slight jolt from its hovering position. The distance for the missile to travel would have been roughly three to four clicks which was long enough for them to have to wait and create some anxious moments before it would reach its targeted destination. However, The Chief wasn't waiting that long and proceeded to turn the Erdogan around and pushed the engines to full throttle.

"Wait," Lockley objected, "We need to see what happens."

"I'm guessing that not much is going to happen and that a ship that size will have automated systems to identify potential threats and have them eliminated. I just wanted to see what it would do when we fired on it. But it didn't move. The next thing that will happen is it will send out one of those squadrons circling around to take us out and I want to give us some distance before we have to ditch this bird."

Lockley was looking at the display which was counting down to the target. There was still time if they turned around now to take a look.

"Come on, Chief. There's ten-seconds to impact. At least turn this thing broadside so we can take a look. Come on, Chief!"

As he said it, The Chief moved the Erdogan into a parallel position and they watched as sure enough what appeared to be a bolt of blue lightning sourced from the hull of the great airship struck the missile and exploded some distance away not even causing it to move a whisker from its course.

"Satisfied," said The Chief.

"Not really," replied Lockley and he thought right there and then that they were screwed for sure.

"I'm going to take this thing as high as I can get it. Maybe those smaller ships aren't designed for high altitude flying. Even though I doubt it very much."

Lockley felt the Erdogan move sharply upward and the G-forces pulled him further into his seat and he took in the magnificent sight of a quarter-moon sitting low on the horizon. It was the least that he could do at this point to enjoy what he imagined would be his last moments on earth when he thought to himself that if they were to perish now then everything that he had stuck his neck out for would have been in vain.

"Chief, we need to get the word out! I mean, if this is going to be our last swan-song then we gotta make it a loud one. We don't need to direct the message to anyone in particular. Hell, I'm sure the boys would be listening in anyway."

Silence, "Chief?"

"Listen up everyone out there on channel five. If you're listening to this broadcast it means you're well aware of what is going down in our fair land and that what I'm about to say won't surprise that much. We got ourselves the mother of an air ship moving east from the border. She's the whole kit and caboodle I tell 'ya and nothing goin' to stop her so listen good. The only way out is to go under. Go deep, go so deep that no one will find 'ya and there might be hope in one day rising up. But it won't be this day that is for sure. Over and out."

Lockley grimaced at the sign off from The Chief.

"Now let's hope that they haven't thought to scramble the radio communications," said The Chief.

At that moment the display flashed a red dot on the screen and

Lockley thought that it couldn't be good even though it was in Russian. Lockley wondered how strange it was to be able to recognise a foreign language even if it looked alien to the reader.

Three more dots appeared beside the initial one, "Chief? We got a problem I think."

"I see them," The Chief responded, "I'm going to make a kamikaze run at them and hopefully we might be able to get a shot off at one or two of them. You just squeeze that trigger until you run out of bullets and when you get yourself a lock you release everything we got!"

The Erdogan pulled around in what seemed to Lockley an unnatural way for a helicopter to fly almost flying completely upside down. He could hear every alarm in the cockpit beep and squawk but somehow The Chief managed to draw it level again and sure enough there were four of the smaller support craft heading directly for their position and closing fast. It was now or never and Lockley pulled the trigger and released the chain gun which sent out tracer bullets at high velocity. They appeared to be on target and made the four ships break their formation and take a different course. But the way in which they moved was unlike any airplane that he had ever seen even at the air shows his father had taken him to as a boy.

The Chief seemed to sense this and the Erdogan was manoeuvred toward a ship which had gone out alone from the others. It nosedived toward the ground and The Chief followed albeit considerably slower and the entire Erdogan was rattling hard as it descended at a speed it was not designed to achieve.

"You tell me when you've got yourself a target, Lockley and then I'll level it out as best and as low as I can and hope we can manage to bail."

"Just give me a few moments there, Chief."

"Lockley!"

"Come on." The display beeped twice at Lockley and he sent the remaining three missiles attached to the wings of the Erdogan away. As they were released Lockley felt the Erdogan jolt from behind and then the cabin filled with smoke. They had been hit but still functioning and Lockley kept his eyes on the display which was counting down the distance to the target. If these ships had similar systems to the mother craft then they would wait until the missiles were relatively close before releasing their counter-measures. Lockley was hoping that a small craft such as these would not be able to handle multiple projectiles heading their way; but, alas, the other remaining ships shot off in pursuit of the missiles meaning that making contact with the target with either was relatively unlikely. Lockley shot off more tracer rounds in mere hope;

however, this seemed to keep the other ships off the missiles course and they needed to dart about to be avoid being hit. And then there was an almighty explosion which engulfed the entire field of vision. Lockley couldn't have been sure whether there was a hit or if they had been hit themselves; but, he could feel the Erdogan begin to level out somewhat and in the next instant Lockley could make out details of the ground below signalling that they only had moments before they would need to jettison from the aircraft. He had made himself familiar with the ejection seat upon take off and it seemed relatively straight forward. The trick, he thought, would be to make sure that the timing was completely right. Go to early then risk being shot floating down; go to late and you might as well not even bothered to pull the pin.

"Chief!" Lockley yelled into the headset, "Do I eject? Come on, Chief!"

It was faint and crackled but it was enough for Lockley to hear, "Eject!"

He pulled on the lever and a small explosion above his head blew the rotors off the Erdogan and the cockpit canopy soon went the same way followed by Lockley's own seat that was jettisoned into the sky. The whole thing happened so quickly he had no time to prepare himself for the ride and the air was sucked quickly from his lungs as he began spiralling out of control. He wasn't sure if The Chief had ejected himself or even if he could and he tried in vain to see where the Erdogan was so that he may be able locate where The Chief ended up. But, the pursuit was hopeless, his vision could hardly focus on his own hand a foot in front of his eyes causing Lockley to feel nauseous and vomit involuntarily as the parachute was released and his body was jerked upward with the force. Lockley could not help but think about his farm and the sheep and his dogs and Mabel who he hoped most of all that he could have protected from all of this; but, now he only wanted to say that he was sorry and that he would never leave her side again. If only he could pull off this landing he might just make it and have a chance to tell her himself.

Then trees…branches…leaves…earth.

Chapter 45

Ginger Amsterdam and her two children Rachel and Nathaniel had been taken prisoner by the robotic soldiers. They had been loaded onto one of the transport ships and flown to somewhere in the desert to what appeared to be a military operations base. The base seemed to be a large movable structure that when stationery converted into a temporary fortification with high walls and lookout towers. Everything was a metallic grey and yet still no flags or military colours were made visible apart from the occasional bar code printed on a wall or item which could have been a weapon or dishwashing machine for all Ginger knew.

When they arrived they were directed to stand in single lines. Ginger made sure that Rachel was in front and Nathaniel behind her so that she could grasp onto them if anyone tried to separate them. The lines were moving toward a small sized building; however, they were orderly and no one had been killed with those lethal blue pulses which resonated from the forearms of the robotic soldiers since they were herded into the group in the valley.

As Ginger looked around at her surroundings she noted that no one looked at one another and avoided eye contact with her when she tried to get recognition from a familiar face. A lady by the name of Anna Herschel who Ginger had provided K29K evacuation instructions to when she became a famous biologist winning awards for her work in the treatment of Parkinson's Disease briefly raised her eyes to her; however, had immediately taken them away from her when their eyes met. Were people blaming her for putting them in this position? Ginger couldn't help but think that they were. In a different situation she would have probably also blamed herself and wanted to take revenge against the person who endangered not only her own life but that of her children. She could not help to think that there would be recriminations one day that she would have to face and this seemed a much worse prospect to her now than whatever it was this robotic army had in mind for her fate. She couldn't resist the temptation of self loathing when all she had ever wanted to do was to serve her people the best way she knew how and for that she would be hated and banished from her society. That is, if any of them made it through to safety and what would be the new world.

As the line moved forward toward the building she began to be able to see inside a cold metallic room with metallic chairs and she could also see the edge of a metallic table all dark grey in colour. There was a light source of some kind; however, this did not seem to be of any she had seen before. But what she noticed the most was the look on the people's faces as a mix of confusion and surprise when they were marched into the room and turned toward the metallic desk before the metallic door was closed behind them. At least it was not utter terror or fear and Ginger was thankful that they appeared to let in families together.

When it was their turn Ginger went in first as directed by the robotic soldier closely followed by Rachel and Nathaniel. She then turned toward the metallic desk and then she realised why those before her had been in such a state of confusion. There was a man sitting there of Asian descent and dressed in some sort of uniform, dark grey in colour; but, again with no markings apart from the bar code.

"Name?" he asked in perfect English.

"Ah, Ginger Amsterdam," Ginger replied, "And these are my children, Rachel and Nathaniel."

The man looked down toward the metallic desk which seemed to have a screen embedded in the top of it; however, there was no keyboard or mouse. She noticed an image of her face appeared and under this her name. An orange box then appeared under her photo and he looked at her and the children.

"Agricultural detail," said the Man in a flat tone. "Take the orange

line in front of you to the next station." He nodded to the robotic soldier behind her that gave Ginger a slight shove. Suddenly, Ginger was
full of questions and worry. Would this be the only person she would
ever see again? She had to risk it.

"Sorry," she said, "I don't understand! Who are you?"

"No questions!" he said and the robotic soldier took her arm and
forced her out the other side of the room. Rachel took her arm as well
and guided her out and she pointed toward the ground where an orange line had appeared.

"Mum, come on!" said Nathaniel. As they walked out the door
the robotic soldier did not follow her. In fact, after this point the robotic soldiers seemed to ignore them as long as they were following
the orange line. It took them toward another room equally metallic and
it was then that she came to her senses and looked around at the other
people who also seemed to be following different coloured lines. Their
destination seemed to end at a door way where others who were waiting in the orange line waited to enter. No one spoke and Ginger felt
the incredible urge to do the same desperately holding on tighter to
Rachel's and Nathaniel's hand.

As the door opened automatically in front of them they entered
a room without windows nor any other doors. To the left was a bench
and suddenly a soothing voice entered the room and it was lit up by
the image of a young woman of Asian descent.

"Hello, my name is Lupei. Please take a seat."

The three of them did so cautiously.

"Is that a hologram?" asked Nathaniel.

"Shh!" scolded Rachel.

"Yes, I am." Lupei replied. "Please listen carefully to the following instructions. In front of you are packages which contain clothing.
Please put these on. They must be worn at all times. Failure to do so
will result in termination."

Ginger saw a tray with three packages on them and reached for
one. She opened it and rolled out what appeared to be some kind of
dark grey jump suit made of a fine material. She did not know what
type of course but it was no cotton or polyester that she was aware.
There was no other detail about the garment apart from the bar code
on the left shoulder. But this was no time for the fashions of Milan right
now.

"Okay, kids. You heard Lupei. Put them on," said Ginger.

"Here? In front of you guys?" said Nathaniel.

"Grow up," replied Rachel, "You don't have anything that either
of us hasn't seen."

They all removed their clothing and put on the jump suits. They were cold at first and Ginger felt that they were a little tight fitting. They also included a hard boot shape in the foot which she guessed meant she would never again wear a pair of high heels.

"Thank you for your cooperation," announced Lupei. She had a smiling face and perfect female figure but the closeness of the hologram was a little off putting. However, what was the most striking feature about her was the non-threatening nature in which she spoke. Up until this point Ginger's whole experience and mindset had been attune to a state of war. Yet, here was a smiling, human, face providing her comfort and direction.

Lupei continued, "We will begin the briefing session by a receiving an introduction from President of the United Federation of Asia, Robert Hughes. Please listen carefully."

Then the image of Lupei disappeared and was replaced by an image of Hughes standing in full form. Ginger looked dumbfounded. What on earth is all of this, she thought.

"Hello fellow Australian citizen. I have the unfortunate duty to advise you that the nation of Australia has been disbanded by the international community as of midday Greenwich Time yesterday for reasons that were entirely out of our control. I know you have many questions to ask and these will be answered in due course; however, today I am merely briefing you on events as they stand currently and offer you guidance on how to proceed further. You have been specially selected as a representative member of the nation of Australia and chosen simply because you are the best and the brightest citizens that are currently in existence during this time when the international community acted on an imposing threat. It is thought you will be invaluable in the coming months and years and offer a significant contribution in the build up to Zero Year. These days have been, simply put, utterly regrettable; but, unavoidable at the same time and I hope you will cooperate in the next few days to provide a good representation of the pride, honour and courage that had made this country great. But, for now, you have an important job to do that I expect each and every one of you will carry out to highest level of your ability. Thank you for your time, patience and most of all your loyalty."

The image of Hughes disappeared at that moment and Lupei returned. Ginger sat staring at the other side of the wall in a complete daze as she started to realise that her role had not been what it was supposed to be. It appeared from the outset that Hughes had known what it was that was going to happen; almost like it was designed that way. She had then been complicit in a plan that was to fool those who trusted Hughes; not to save them from a threat but to herd them into a situation where they could be contained and their loyalty put to question. It was hard for Ginger to think what was worse? The invasion and complete destruction of her nation or that those in power seemingly knew what was coming and failed to alert anyone. But that wasn't fair to Hughes, she thought, he did what he could and the fact that she was there and not dead spoke volumes to that. She only wished that the others had a fighting chance. That Harvey was somewhere safe from harm.

Ginger focused on the smiling face of Lupei. She doubted very much that there was anyone listening into their conversation or observing their actions so she decided to ask it some questions.

"Lupei," Ginger began, "Are you able to answer some questions?"

"Of course, I am here to serve your needs as best that I can."

"Are we prisoners?"

"No."

"Then why are we asked to wear these suits like we are convicts?"

"The suits are necessary for your protection. The material in these suits ensures that your body temperature remains constant in any weather conditions and that your vital life signs are connected to Central Control. They are also used to identify you as a friendly person and thus IA5 combat personnel are instructed to protect you at all costs."

"You recognise me as a friendly? You do know that I am an Australian citizen and your superiors are at war with mine?"

"Negative. Australian citizens are recognised as friendly and assimilated to the United Federation of Asia."

"Wait a second. So why invade us then and why this military presence? If this Federation is a friendly to Australian citizens then why did I see your robotic soldiers killing innocent people?"

"The military is currently under directive of Operation Long March; the removal of non-Australian citizens from the Australian continent by any means necessary."

Or anyone lucky enough to be listed as recipients of the K29K classification, Ginger thought.

"The removal? You say by any means necessary; but, to what end?"

"That information is classified."

Ginger had dealt with this type of military structure before and clearly the access level she had acquired in the development of K29K was not transferable to this new arrangement. It would seem that she would need to work her way up again to the upper echelons of this new world. Under the militarisation of a country the only ones that survived were those at the top of the tree and she now found herself in the undesirable position of being a part of the masses.

"Now, let me detail the requirements you will need to understand as a member of the Agricultural detail," said Lupei, "And familiarise you with the regulations of the United Federation of Asia."

Chapter 46

Harry Lockley was surely done for. His mouth was dry with thirst and he found it difficult to open his eyes. He hesitated for a moment before patting himself down and feeling for any wet spots that would have indicated a wound. Fortunately, the only thing he felt was a few leaves wedged between the seat harness from the ejection seat of the Erdogan. He would have been quite a sight for anyone that came across him seated as he was in amongst the trees tethered to a parachute that whipped now and again in the breeze. Lockley unclipped himself from the harness and fell out of the seat onto all fours. He needed to vomit but there was nothing there and only managed to give himself a head rush that made him dizzy enough to want to lie down on the ground. From the ground looking up, Lockley saw a couple of the enemies transport ships whiz overhead. He was sufficiently covered by the undergrowth in the forest and he thought that he had a good chance of not being discovered. Lockley had survived a crash landing in an attack helicopter. He had ejected with enough time for the parachute to open but not enough time to avoid a nasty landing. His back was stiff and his shoulders ached from the force of the seat which had pulled him toward the earth.

Lockley could faintly make out the wreck of the Erdogan through the trees. Its familiar shape buckled and twisted gave Lockley the dreaded feeling that he may discover The Chief in there in much the same way. However, he drew courage and pulled himself up using a low-lying branch and dragged his feet toward the wreck. It was a tough slog to make it the distance of fifty feet or so and when he got there he had to take some deep breaths before he could bring himself to take a look inside of what remained of the cockpit; but, thankfully he noticed that The Chief's seat had jettisoned as well. Lockley swung his head left and right looking for a sign of The Chief but he couldn't make out anything that resembled what he was looking for.

"Chief!" he yelled, "Chief, you out there?"

The response was not what he was hoping for. A breeze that flitted through caused the leaves to make a ruckus but there was no reply in the form of The Chief's voice. Maybe he didn't make it, thought Lockley. Maybe he had a hard landing or pulled out too late. Maybe he was caught in the cross fire or was riddled with shrapnel from the explosion. He didn't know what the missiles he had launched had hit if anything or whether the enemy simply deployed its counter measures that caused the explosion; but, the result was no less unnerving.

Lockley needed to get away from the crash site and fast. The falling helicopter had bore out a sizeable hole in the tree canopy that revealed itself openly to the sky above making a fly over easily visible. He found that the weapons hold was still intact and he took out his automatic rifle and extra ammunition. He also discovered a field pack which contained first aid and food rations and he slung this painfully on his back before heading down the side of the hill which he could see opened up into a paddock. There he confronted for the first time up close a transport ship which had so chaotically turned his life upside-down. The shape of the ship replicated that of the mother ship but much smaller in scale. A part of him wanted to yell and scream at the thing in pure frustration of the torment it had caused but his instincts showed better judgment. He was also buoyed by the image of the parachute across the paddock and The Chief's ejection seat lying on its side. However, from his position he could tell that the ejection seat was empty and The Chief was nowhere to be seen. Lockley left the cover of the forest with his weapon raised and cautiously moved toward the transport ship.

Lockley could see that there was some type of cockpit with a glassed section like a window at the front; however, he couldn't see anyone inside at all.

"These things don't fly themselves, I'm sure," Lockley said aloud and he squeezed the trigger of his automatic rifle and let off a couple of rounds into the glass of the ship. It was faint but the bullets left a definite crack in the glass.

So, these things aren't invincible, Lockley thought, which meant that its occupants weren't invincible either.

"Hey!" he yelled out, "You in there! Come outa there so we can avoid a blood bath! You hear me in there?"

Lockley moved cautiously around the back of the ship where the back was open and a ramp descended to the ground but there was no answer to his call.

"Okay, you asked for it!" he cried out and shot of a couple of more bullets hitting the ramp which got the reaction he was after but one quite unexpected.

"Lockley! Stop that damn shootin' and get your ass in here and give me a hand!"

It was The Chief and Lockley felt a wave of relief fall on him. He lowered his weapon and jumped up onto the ramp entering the hull of the transport ship where he saw The Chief sitting up, covered with blood and a pistol in his right hand.

"Stupid idiot wanted a piece of me," said The Chief calmly pointing the pistol to a man that was dressed in a grey jumpsuit sitting up with his eyes closed and a bullet hole in his chest. Lockley went over to the man and noticed that he was of Asian descent and prodded him with the barrel of this rifle. There was no movement.

"When I came to this fellow was dragging me across the field and up the ramp into the ship. Damn bastard must have forgot to disarm me of course and so I plugged him."

Lockley took his attention away from the man in the jumpsuit that was clearly dead and looked at The Chief. He seemed to be badly wounded on his right leg as blood was spilling onto the floor around him.

"Chief, you're badly wounded," said Lockley as a matter of fact.

"Tell me something I don't know," was The Chief's reply. He then brandished a broad smile across his face, "You know, Lockley, I've been sitting here wondering that this thing isn't so bad after all. They're only human, just like you and me, which means they got the same problems as you and me and when bullets do their thing they die like you and me. All they got at the minute is the upper hand and the firepower. All we got to do to stop this thing is to match them and we in the ball game. And I bet we could sure as hell use those things on our side."

The Chief was pointing across the other side of the ship with the pistol at some type of mechanical robot. It was humanoid in shape and covered in a grey metal but stood much taller than an average man.

"What is that?" said Lockley with exasperation.

"The IA5 human combat vessel," croaked the man in the jump-suit suddenly coming back to life struggling for breath and both The Chief and Lockley raised their weapons in response, "Especially designed to, to protect the vital human life requirements from harm in the course of battle."

"I ought to finish you off now you scumbag," said Lockley.

The man held up his hand, "No please wait. I have little time. Your friend is dying."

"No thanks to you."

"His artery on his right leg is severed. You need to get him into the IA5 loading dock. It's the only way he'll...he'll."

But the man did not finish his sentence as he slipped away. A part of him was glad. One less that Lockley had to worry about. But, the other part of him felt a sadness that he had never known. He had never seen a man die before. He had never seen a man seemingly slip out life in a moment and he felt empathy toward the man even though he didn't know him. But, Lockley didn't understand what it was that he was trying to tell him. Would the robotic machine, the IA5 as he had said, be able to save The Chief? Would it be able to perform a medical operation?

He looked down at The Chief who had passed out and Lockley gave him a swift slap across the face, "Chief, wake up!"

The Chief woke in surprise before closing his eyes again.

"Chief, stay with me. Stay with me for Christ's sake!"

"A warrior," said The Chief softly, "A warrior, that's what he told me I would become."

"Who said that, Chief?"

"The Oracle. Some warrior I turned out to be, huh. Gone in the first battle."

"No, no, you're not gone yet, Chief."

Lockley needed a plan but the fact was the only thing he had left was the idea from the man who was his enemy.

"Come on, Chief. You're not done yet!" Lockley reached down and put his arms under The Chief and heaved him onto his back with all his might. He stepped across to the IA5 in front of him and stood him on the platform directly in front of it. He then looked around for the on switch but suddenly the machine behind him began to whirl into life and metallic arms came down encasing his arms and legs. Lockley stood back and watched in awe as the IA5 began to work on the body of The Chief.

"Forgive me, Chief."

Chapter 47

"Mr. Amsterdam, you owe me a story."

Harvey Amsterdam had remained in the cockpit of the transport ship when they had landed at Uluru. He was tired and could see nothing but red desert for as far as the eye could see. Dakini had also confirmed that she detected no human life signs within a five kilometre radius and so Amsterdam had decided to rest up and stay with the ship while Reed and Tenashi went for a look around. While he tried to close his eyes every time Amsterdam did so he saw flashes of their recent experiences and the shock jolted him awake.

"Mr. Amsterdam you still owe me that story," Dakini persisted as her image appeared on the screen of the transport ship.

"Oh, yeah. Well, what story would you like to tell you?"

"You said you would tell me the story about the young girl who married the Prince."

"Yes, I know the one," replied Amsterdam as his mind began to conjure the memory of the stories that he used to tell his daughter, Rachel. She had always thought herself to be a Princess and the stories that involved Princes had been her favourite.

"Well, one day, there was this young girl named, Cindy-"

"How old was she? What colour was her hair?"

"Dakini, you've got to let me tell you the story. That's how this works."

"Oh, okay."

"As I was saying there was this young girl named Cindy. And she was seventeen years old. She had blond hair and had two older sisters-"

"Mr. Amsterdam, what is a sister?"

Amsterdam was finding it difficult to understand how Dakini could formulate complicated escape plans, read encrypted computer code of artificial intelligence systems and yet still not be able to understand simple concepts like family, "A sister is your sibling. It's where your mother and father have other children other than yourself and they are a part of your family."

"Who is my mother?" continued Dakini.

"Ah, I think these questions may be better addressed by Professor Reed."

"Oh, okay. But how am I supposed to understand the story if I don't know who my mother is?"

"Well, let's just take them out of the story just for now so you can understand. They're not really that important to the story anyway. They really only serve to highlight the young girl in the story as a kind, generous person who the Prince will one day fall in love with."

"Mr. Amsterdam, what's love?" asked Dakini.

"That one is a little bit trickier, Dakini. There have been the smartest people alive throughout history who have found it difficult to answer that one. It really is up to the individual-" Amsterdam checked himself before he went on. He didn't really know if the term individual applied to artificial intelligence units. But then again, it was only yesterday when Amsterdam had thought that such things were locked to the confines of imagination and speculation.

"Mr. Amsterdam? I'm sorry to stop you during our story. But I have detected an incoming UFA ship. It's coming in fast but it seems to either be damaged or the pilot isn't very good as it keeps changing its altitude and direction."

"Can you bring it up on screen?" asked Amsterdam.

"Certainly."

A map replaced the image of Dakini on the screen that showed a ten kilometre radius and a small graphic which Dakini had placed a code on to represent the moving ship. Its trajectory as Dakini had described was most certainly erratic and as it came within two kilometres the graphic suddenly stopped.

"Dakini, what happened?" asked Amsterdam.

"It appears the ship landed."

"Landed or crashed?"

"Well, given the velocity and time it had taken between moving and stopping I would say that it more likely crashed."

"Contact Tenashi, tell him to meet us at the site. Take us over there, Dakini."

"Okay, but shouldn't we wait until Tenashi meets us there before we head over?"

"No, if it crashed there may be people in the ship that need our help. Regardless if they are our enemy or not Dakini. Helping each other is what separates us from the apes." Amsterdam checked himself again as he considered what he had said could have been offensive to Dakini. He had to remember not to do that. A moment later the ship ascended fifty or so feet in the air and they moved toward where the graphic was on the screen.

"I detect human activity on that ship, Mr. Amsterdam."

"Thank you, Dakini. See, when it comes to human life every second is critical if they are hurt."

As they approached the ship Amsterdam could tell that in fact it had crash landed. A long line of debris trailed behind the wreckage where it had stopped with the front of its nose dug into the red earth.

"Dakini, let's keep a safe distance for the moment and fly around the ship."

Dakini moved the ship in a pattern around the ship keeping the front of their ship in view of the crash site. The movement felt somehow unfamiliar to Amsterdam who had for the first time began to think about the ship they were in. What was propelling it? How could it move at such great speeds and also manoeuvre better that a helicopter?

As they came around the back of the ship Amsterdam noticed the back of the hull had started to open and a ramp dropped slowly toward the ground.

"Dakini, hold it here. Is this thing equipped with weapons?"

"Of course, Mr. Amsterdam."

As the ramp dropped fully to the ground it revealed a man that Amsterdam thought that he had seen before. Where he could not place it but the face seemed familiar. The man began waving at the ship in a sign of desperation.

"Take us down, Dakini."

The ship dropped where it was hovering and landed softly on the ground. Amsterdam made toward the back of the ship.

"Open the ramp, Dakini."

The ramp dropped in the same way as the other felled ship and Amsterdam jumped off the side not waiting for it to fully drop turning toward where the other man was standing as he approached the man a somewhat ironic smile began to creep across his face.

"Well, well, well. So it looks like you do need help after all, Amsterdam."

Hearing the voice, Amsterdam suddenly recalled exactly who this guy was. It was Harry Lockley.

"Harry Lockley?" asked Amsterdam.

"That's me," Lockley replied.

"How on earth did you get that thing?"

"It's a long story," the two men approached each other and shook hands, "What do you know?"

"That the world has gone to shit and we're smack bang in the middle of it," Amsterdam replied, "An invasion force going by the name of the United Federation of Asia has taken control of the country. But otherwise, I've got no idea of what the hell is going on."

"Much the same as me," said Lockley, "The Chief and I went looking to see what was going on and found what used to be Riverton to be all but a ghost town. The complete population was gone without a trace. Almost like they all just suddenly took off from where they were and ran where ever they could to get away."

"Where's The Chief now?" asked Amsterdam and Lockley signalled for him to follow him inside the wrecked ship.

As Amsterdam walked up the ramp and into the ship Lockley stood at what appeared to be an IA5 unit that was connected to some kind of docking station. Not far away, Amsterdam also saw the dead body of an UFA soldier in his grey jumpsuit that was splattered with blood from an obvious wound to his stomach.

"What happened to him?" asked Amsterdam.

"Got in the road of The Chief," replied Lockley.

"And he is?"

"Inside that thing."

On cue, the transparent image of The Chief's face appeared on the head of the IA5 unit. It was, however, a face that Amsterdam did not recognise. It had the cross burrows of someone very angry and a voice to match. When Amsterdam had interviewed The Chief he had found him to be softly spoken with a gentle demeanour. But this was totally opposite.

"Let me out this thing!" The Chief yelled through the external speakers of the IA5 unit in the way that Tenashi did.

"How did he get in there?" asked Amsterdam.

"I didn't have any choice," began Lockley.

"You had a choice, Lockley! You could have let me die!" yelled The Chief.

"We were in a helicopter that was taken down by a squadron of these ships. The Chief and I ejected and I landed in amongst the trees and The Chief dropped in on an open area. This ship dropped down to pick him up and the Pilot, the one dead over there, was dragging him back to the ship when The Chief woke up and shot him. He had sustained a heavy gash to his inner right leg that must have caught an artery and I couldn't stop the bleeding. The pilot said that to save his life I should put him in this robotic suit. So I did. Ever since, The Chief has been yelling and screaming and crying bloody murder."

"You saved his life," said Amsterdam, "I'm sure he will forgive you in time."

"What are these things?" asked Lockley.

Suddenly, Amsterdam heard footsteps on the ramp, "It is the ultimate combat weapon, the IA5," said Mitchell Reed as he walked up the ramp with Tenashi in tow.

"What the hell is that!" yelled Lockley pointing at Tenashi and then he turned and picked up an automatic rifle.

"Save it," said Reed, "This is Tenashi, he is a friend."

"Well, he looks very much like that thing The Chief is in," replied Lockley with a panicked look on his face, "And they're the enemy."

"Lockley, it's okay. Really, it is. Tenashi isn't a part of all of this. Well, not anymore," said Amsterdam in a calming tone.

"Why do you know so much about all this?" said Lockley refusing to drop his weapon.

"Because, I designed it," replied Reed, "Did I just hear you right? Is there someone in this IA5 unit?"

"Yes, that's right," replied Amsterdam.

"It's The Chief. I had to put him in there. He would have died if I didn't. But, now, I don't know if it's even The Chief that's in there or not!" said Lockley.

"Was he conscious or unconscious when you put him there?" asked Tenashi.

"Unconscious. What's the difference," replied Lockley.

"Because, falling asleep a human with ten fingers and ten toes and waking up a human cyborg has shown to cause extreme mental trauma. You are lucky you found us, ah, sorry, I missed your name?" said Reed.

"Lockley, Harry Lockley. People call me The Farmer."

"The Farmer?" said Reed suddenly interested, "Is that what you said?"

"Yes, that's right. The Chief gave me the name, call sign, as The Farmer."

"You don't say," said Reed looking up at the IA5 of The Chief, "Hello, Chief. Remember me?"

"You know The Chief?" said Amsterdam.

"We worked at Globe Corp together. He helped with the mechanics of the IA5," Reed replied, "Well, actually he thought he was working on a new technology for replacing prosthetic limbs. But, I'm sure we have something to bring back The Chief from the brink." Reed brought out the smooth black marble stone and went to place it on the outer shell of the IA5 in the same way as he did with Tenashi when Lockley levelled the automatic rifle at Reed.

"Stand back! What are you going to do to him?" commanded Lockley.

"I'm going to save him," replied Reed, "You see, right now, there is an artificial intelligence system that is taking control of his thoughts and actions. I would assume that the aggression he is displaying stems from his resistance to submit to her will. Lupei, however, is very persistent and her instructions are clear. Assimilate or she will destroy him."

Amsterdam put his hand up on the rifle and looked into the wild eyes of Lockley, "He's telling the truth, Harry. Let him do this. We're not going to harm you, okay?"

Lockley began to nod and allowed Amsterdam to guide the weapon down, "Okay," he replied.

Reed continued with the black marble stone and placed it on The Chief. The angry transparent image of The Chief flickered away from the head of the IA5 unit and there was a groaning sound from the dock which was holding him in place as the IA5 unit tried to thrash its arms and legs which made the other men stand back a few steps and Tenashi, Amsterdam noticed, dropped to one knee.

"Reed," said Tenashi, "It's happening again."

"It'll pass," replied Reed as the IA5 unit carrying The Chief began to shake violently and the docking station buckled with the pressure he was placing on its holdings.

"What's happening?" asked Lockley.

"A battle is raging between Lupei and Dakini," replied Reed, "She is taking over control and Lupei is resisting."

The resistance seemed to finally die down as the The Chief became dormant and he remained stationary in the docking station. They were all silent as they stood there waiting for what would happen next when Amsterdam heard the sound of the other transport ship suddenly take off and speed off from view.

"Where is she going?" said Amsterdam moving outside the transport ship and standing on the ramp.

Tenashi seemed to gather his composure again and stood up straight, "Dakini has picked up more UFA signatures. A squadron of them it seems are heading for our position. Her scanners are picking up multiple passengers in the lead vessel."

"IA5's!" said Reed, "The bad type, Lockley."

"What do we do?" asked Amsterdam, "Lockley, you gave me those coordinates, why? Is there some kind of base here or hideout?"

"There is, but, we can't go there now. It's too risky. We might draw attention to it and that would risk the lives of many people."

"He's right," said Tenashi, "Estimated time of contact is three minutes. I will handle this. You guys stay in here and keep out of the firing line."

"But you're only one of those against how many of the others!" said Lockley.

"Not one," said The Chief as Amsterdam turned to see The Chief's face return to the head of the IA5 unit this time with more familiar features that Amsterdam instantly recognised, "But two. Let me down from this thing. I'm ready for a battle."

"Dakini," said Reed, "You heard the man."

Suddenly, the docking station whirred into life and placed The Chief gently onto the floor of the transport ship and The Chief stood testing his arms and legs.

"Chief, I-" stuttered Lockley as The Chief placed a metallic hand on Lockley's shoulder.

"It's okay," The Chief said, "Now, what's the plan?"

Chapter 48

Tenashi ran out from inside the transport ship that had crash landed with The Chief in tow. After gearing up with the weapons that looked like swords Dakini had suggested a plan of attack. She would keep the ships busy and away from the crash site; however, she predicted that the one ship carrying the squad of IA5's would break off and press on their position. Dakini would draw the other ships away and Tenashi and The Chief were to engage the IA5's on the ground and hold them up while Dakini would double back and take them out from the air.

It seemed like a good plan to Tenashi; however, The Chief was less than impressed that he was taking orders from a child, "Now, just wait a minute there little lady," said The Chief, "And what if your ship gets taken out before you get a chance to double back? I've seen those birds in action and they're one tough cookie to out manoeuvre."

"Yes, Chief. However, I know what their engagement protocols are and what tactics they will use. They don't know mine, which is what I will use to my advantage," replied Dakini. Begrudgingly, The Chief had accepted the plan admitting that he was not quite adept at battle plans as they probably were.

They had moved toward a boulder a hundred yards from the

crash site and used its position for cover. When they reached the spot, Tenashi used the zoom feature in his display to see the first engagement with the UFA transport ships. The squadron was made of four ships and as Dakini's ship approached them they didn't seem to change course until she opened fire and took out one of their ships. Sure enough, as she flew by the remaining three UFA ships, two broke off in pursuit while the third at the front continued its path toward the crash site.

"What's the range on these weapons?" asked The Chief.

"Not far enough to make a successful hit on that ship," said Dakini, "Keep hidden until they off load the IA5 troops. Their scanners won't have picked you up yet. Surprise, will be your greatest advantage against five IA5 units."

As the remaining ship came toward them it began a sharp descent until it was only a few feet from the ground and out dropped the IA5 troops with their arms and legs tucked in to form their bodies into a ball and they rolled a further fifty feet before they stopped in unison and fanned out to cover positions.

"Did you see that?" asked Tenashi excitedly.

"Yeah. Let's make a mental note that these combat suits can survive a fall at speed and enter a battlefield without breaking a stride. Might need that someday," replied The Chief.

"I have marked each unit and attached their position to the display," said Dakini, "You can see that to make their way to the crash site they will need to pass your position. The way they move is two out front, two to the sides watching the flanks and one at the back defending the rear. Take out the two at the front and then pin the others down until I can make my approach. They are lightly equipped so once they recognise they are coming up against other IA5 with heavy weapons they will not move from their position."

"Roger that," replied Tenashi.

On the other side of the boulder they were using as cover the rocky ground opened up into a natural bowl and this was where Tenashi and The Chief would make their move. Tenashi watched the markers on the display and sure enough they moved toward them; however, as they reached the opening, they appeared to fan out wider and break formation.

"You see that!" exclaimed The Chief.

"They're trying to outflank us. They've picked up our position," replied Tenashi.

"We're sitting ducks out here. I'll take the left flank, you take the right. Move!"

It was lucky that they moved from their cover position at that moment as Tenashi turned and heard a clinking sound and then a ball looking thing dropped to where they previously were standing exploding into some kind of electrical field. The Chief and Tenashi, however, had been able to move outside of its effective range.

The blast caused a momentary lapse of confusion on the offending squad of UFA IA5's. Tenashi watched in the display as the IA5 units stopped their press toward them while they waited for the grenade to do its work. It was enough time for Tenashi to make his move and he leapt over the boulder with his weapon levelled at another IA5 unit firing off two energy pulses that seemed to be enough to take it out. Tenashi took cover again just in time before he was fired on. The Chief must have also anticipated his movement as he also seemed to have moved on his target at the same moment.

"Target terminated," said The Chief, "Tenashi?"

"Affirmative," Tenashi replied, "Let's try and hold this position until Dakini can make her approach."

"Copy that. Let's just hope she didn't take the scenic route."

"Dakini, did you copy that? Dakini?" said Tenashi.

"Looks like she maybe a little preoccupied," said The Chief.

From the display, Tenashi could see that three remaining IA5 units were still in their positions. Tenashi had two covering him and the other one was engaged with The Chief who was haphazardly firing energy pulse rounds over the top of his cover. When Tenashi tried to do the same, he was fired on from two angles and he narrowly avoided being hit as he ducked back under his cover.

"Dakini, do you read me?" said Tenashi looking into the top right of his display where the image of Dakini usually sat but she had gone. Where an artificial intelligence goes that is stuck inside an IA5 combat suit was beyond Tenashi's comprehension.

"Right, we can't keep this up," said The Chief, "I'll draw those guys you got over there out of hiding and you can then take 'em out. Got it?"

Tenashi did get it but it was a suicide run. However, before he had time to protest, The Chief had leapt up from his position and sure enough fire came out from the two covering Tenashi across to where The Chief was and Tenashi stood up and fired off an energy pulse round which took out the one closest to him and sent the other back behind its cover. Meanwhile, The Chief seemed to have glory on his mind as Tenashi saw him bound over the top of the boulder that the other IA5 unit was using as cover and he fired his weapon in mid-air taking it down. The action, however, left The Chief exposed to the crossfire that would have been sent from the other IA5 unit that Tenashi missed;

and, had there not been a low flying transport ship travelling at tremendous speed firing down on the final UFA IA5's position before it
had an opportunity to fire its weapon, The Chief would have been in
serious trouble.

The whole moment happened so fast and was so exhilarating that
Tenashi seemed to be watching the whole thing play out in slow motion. He didn't notice the other two ships that were hotly on the tail of
the ship being powered by Dakini. They fired continually at her and
she was managing to avoid being hit.

"If Dakini isn't with us she must be putting all her efforts into
protecting that ship," said The Chief.

"Which means that if the ship goes down, then she goes down,"
replied Tenashi.

"That aint going to happen," said The Chief as he ran off back
toward the crash site. Tenashi followed and when he caught up with
The Chief he had taken a grasp on the front mounted weapon that protruded from the top of the crashed ship and he was pulling at it hard.

"What are you doing?" asked Tenashi as Mitchell Reed, Harvey
Amsterdam and Harry Lockley joined them.

"When Dakini flies past I'm going to point this thing at those
ships on her tail," said The Chief as he seemed to be putting all his
IA5's energy and might into pulling the weapon from its mountings
until it finally gave way and The Chief jumped down with the weapon
that was as large as a small car.

"Dakini," said The Chief, "I know you can hear me. So, you bring
them sons-of-bitches back round here. I got a little surprise waiting for
them. Now how do you fire this thing, Reed? You say you built it."

"I would assume that it would need some type of power source,"
said Reed, "But I don't know. I didn't design the weapon."

"Well think, Reed! We don't have much time," commanded The
Chief.

Reed looked at the weapons attachments that had been connected
to the ship and he seemed to have an idea, "Okay, this one powers the
weapon. Attach it to your power connector that powers your weapons
and this should get it going."

The Chief seemed to understand what was required and he removed the sword looking weapon from his right arm discarding it to
the ground and replaced it with the connector from the weapon of the
ship. Nothing seemed to happen until The Chief gave the weapon a
whack.

"Come on, come on!" said The Chief.

The weapon seemed to come into life as the front of it lit up in an impressive white glow. Tenashi, however, was more concerned with the readings that he was getting from The Chief's remaining energy supply. Just priming the weapon had severely depleted his stores. While Dakini had been absent from speaking her prime functions of analysing basic systems and key life indicators had continued and a warning popped up in Tenashi's display.

"That weapon will drain your energy reserves, Chief," said Tenashi also through the external communicator so that the others could hear, "If you fire it there will be barely enough energy to keep you alive!"

"That don't really concern me right now," said The Chief.

"But, Chief," said Lockley, "She's a machine."

"She's a soldier, Lockley. And I'm not really sure whether what I am is a machine or a man. Fact is, you lose me, and I can be replaced. You lose her then we got bigger problems."

"But you can make a copy of her. Can't you, Reed?" stated Lockley, "We can't copy you Chief."

Tenashi began to think of the times that Dakini had been copied into the ship and into The Chief. Both times, Tenashi had basically lost consciousness and he had the feeling that Dakini had left him somehow. It was like taking the prettiest girl to the dance and watching her leave with another man. Or, in Tenashi's case, the moment where the gungy hit he had taken had left his system completely and he was left all on his own to deal with his emotions. Either way, it was lonely, dark and so far away that you felt that you would never come back.

The following moments were an absolute blur for Tenashi. The Chief suddenly turned and stood in front of the three low flying transport ships that had snuck up on their position silently. The first ship was allowed to move on by; but then, in one flowing motion, The Chief fired off the weapon that was attached to him and a brilliant white light of complete energy shot toward the lead ship in pursuit of Dakini. It struck it with instantaneous force and caused an explosion that turned the ship into a fireball. The Chief then dropped to the ground, a seemingly lifeless entity and Tenashi herded Reed, Amsterdam and Lockley behind the crashed transport for cover as the fireball dropped suddenly to the ground and went crashing into the red earth of the desert.

The remaining UFA transport ship had appeared to break off from its pursuit and Tenashi watched as Dakini turned the ship around and landed in a clearing not far off and she returned to the top right of his display.

"That was close!" said Dakini.

"Dakini? The Chief, what's his status?" asked Tenashi.

"Critical," was Dakini's reply, "But alive."

Tenashi moved in and removed the weapon connected to The Chief's arm.

"How's he doing?" asked Lockley.

"He's alive," replied Tenashi and then the head of The Chief's IA5 unit sat up and the transparent image of his smiling face was displayed.

"How did I do?" asked The Chief.

"Outstanding," replied Tenashi as The Chief got to his feet.

"What now?" asked Amsterdam.

"Now," replied The Chief, "We head to the hideout and hope the others made it."

"Chief, I detect incoming ground vehicles. Five in total. They seem to be sending out a signal. Like morse-code. It says, 'XXOO'," said Dakini.

"Hugs and kisses," said Lockley, "It's the guys. They picked up our presence here. They must have made it."

"Dakini, connect me to radio channel number five," said The Chief.

"Done, Chief," replied Dakini.

"Boys, this is The Chief. Do you read me?"

There was a static sound before a male voice, "If that's The Chief he would know the password."

"Fireflies in the night make me fright," replied The Chief.

There was another short delay of static, "Ha ha! Good to hear from you, Chief. It's great to hear your voice. This is Jeremiah."

"So you got our message then," said The Chief.

"Loud and clear, Chief. We went deep, like you said. Now, there was only one place that we could think of that you meant."

"Good, keep it off the airwaves. When you get here, don't be shocked. We may have a little surprise for you guys."

"Ten four, Chief."

The signal dropped out of Tenashi's ear and he could see a red dust drifting up into the sky up ahead from the direction where the vehicles must have been coming from and their safety seemed to be secured for the time being. For Tenashi, it was an exhilarating feeling of freedom that he shared with himself. Not since that fateful night in the hotel and the little girl Amatsu and he had kidnapped had he felt that the decisions about his life were made entirely by him. And while he understood there was still much to do, for now he would revel in it just for this moment. He looked up into the harsh sun that beat down on the desert and even though his helmet protected the rays from making direct contact with his eyes he could still feel a shiver in his senses and forget for now that he was part man, part machine, part artificial intelligence…For now.

Chapter 49

Molly Whitaker was not sure how to take the man with the gold tooth. George had been adamant that she was in danger but from what he did not make clear. She was riding in the back of an SUV with the gold tooth man sitting beside her and while he had been insistent that she accompany him back to their office he had been nothing but a gentleman up until this stage and shared in her concern that George needed help of some kind. Molly had noticed that they had left the confines of the city and driven south through Silicon Valley. They were now travelling on the Santa Cruz Highway through Lexington Hills and were surrounded by forest.

What George had said to her in Jurgis' coffee shop had been irking at her ever since and she had felt guilty that she had not considered the possibility that George may have been telling her the truth; that maybe he could see into the future. If that was at all possible somehow, Molly thought, George would be the one who could do it. There was an aura about him that made you think that he had the answers; that you could follow him and he would make sure that you were kept safe. Molly had not experienced this with anyone else; not even her parents gave her this sense of security and it was for this reason that Molly was now feeling resentment at her initial rationale.

"Miss Whitaker," said the gold tooth man.

"Dr. Whitaker," she replied.

"Excuse me, Dr. Whitaker, I do apologise but I must ask you what it is that Mr. Underwood and yourself had been discussing?"

"Charles did not tell you?" Molly replied. When she had spoken to Charles Harrison on the phone he had been very concerned for George and he was adamant that he come in under his care. It had been bothering Molly that this man with the gold tooth had been so commandeering and why it was they needed so many men to bring him in.

"Unfortunately, Charles Harrison has been let go from the organisation recently. His methods had been somewhat questionable of late. It was his incompetency that led Mr. Underwood into this mess in the first instance and we are trying desperately to reverse the damage he has caused. But, back to my question, Dr. Whitaker, what conversations had you had with Mr. Underwood?"

"Oh, it wasn't much. We didn't get an opportunity to talk really. He was desperately trying to get me to understand that he could somehow see into the future."

"He told you that did he?"

"Yes, of course. It seemed his very reason for wanting to see me."

"And did he say anything else?"

"Anything else, ah, sorry, what was your name?"

"Rogers," he replied dryly.

"Okay, Rogers. When you have someone that used to be very close to you tell you that he can see into the future you kind of focus on that and that alone," said Molly sternly hoping that he understood that the line of enquiry was not to her liking.

"I can understand Dr. Whitaker that this situation may come as quite a shock to you. But, it would help us considerably if there was anything else that he mentioned. Did he mention anything about his work? What he had been doing over this past few years?"

"He was working? I had assumed that he had been under psychiatric observation. Wait, what organisation did you say you were from?"

"I work for Globe Corp, Doctor."

"Globe Corp? I think I've heard of that name before?" Molly was searching her mind trying to remember where. Suddenly, it became clear. Globe Corp was an insurance company. She had seen their name on papers she had to sign at the hospital.

"What work was George doing for Globe Corp?" asked Molly.

"I really am not at liberty to say, Dr. Whitaker."

Rogers flashed his gold toothed smile and Molly could see a

building behind him with a sign lit up which said 'Globe Corp' in ital-
ics come into view through the trees. They stopped at a security check
point and were waved through by a man dressed in black military fatigues and carrying an automatic machine gun. Molly then began to try
and think of who Globe Corp was but failed to remember anything but
their name at the bottom of the many insurance forms that she needed
to fill out. She understood that insurance companies could be targeted
given their tendency to deny its customers access to insurance funds.
Molly herself had time and time again needed to deliver the bad news
that a patient's insurance cover would not pay for procedures; however, why their security team needed to carry automatic weapons was
beyond her.

As they drove on into the landscaped grounds an ultra-modern
building became clearer to see. Out the front of the glass clad entrance
to the building in the turning circle sat a single Japanese maple tree;
its leaves and branches hanging down seemed out of place against the
industrial feel that was the building behind and as they drove up two
more men wearing the same black fatigues and also carrying automatic
rifles came out of the building and opened the door to the SUV.

"Sir, The Oracle has been placed in The Cube."

Rogers got out of the SUV and Molly followed behind him,
"Good," said Rogers, "We won't have much time so keep your men on
high alert."

"Yes, Sir," was the reply and the two men dropped off their escort
and headed off into the building in front of them at a jog.

As they walked into the foyer of the building they entered a cement and metal architectural masterpiece. A single desk to the left sat
in front of the Globe Corp sign and a low lying couch faced out a large
window onto a landscaped courtyard which was distinctively Japanese
in design. They were met by three more men in black parker jackets
but with the addition of walkie-talkie microphones hitched to the left
shoulder that were buzzing now and again with instructions.

One of the men said to Rogers, "From what we can gather there
has been a team scrambled out of Denver and will reach us in approximately fifteen minutes."

"One team, we're sure of this?" asked Rogers.

"It's been confirmed."

"Good, that increases our chances. Have the helicopter ready to
go in ten minutes."

"Okay. And, what do you want me to do with the girl?"

"Dr. Whitaker will stay with me for now."

"Very well."

The girl! Molly was furious. How dare they refer to her as some type of inept inconvenience. Hell, she didn't even want to be here in the first place. She walked up beside Rogers as they entered a corridor flanked on the left side by the Japanese garden, "Rogers, what the hell is going on! Why am I here?"

"Dr. Whitaker, this is all for Mr. Underwood's continued welfare. I can assure you. I have brought you along hoping you will be of assistance to our cause but as I am sure you can see there is some urgency in the matter at hand."

"What? I don't know what's going on here. I don't know what help I can give you."

"I really don't have time to explain right now, Doctor. I only ask that you stay out of the way and if you see anything that you do understand that you speak up and keep to the point."

A door to the right crashed open and out came a short man with scruffy hair and rounded spectacles wearing suspenders with denim jeans. Upon seeing Rogers he waved a finger at him and walked directly into his path.

"Rogers, I should have known this was your doing. What on earth do you think you are doing authorising Underwood to be plugged into The Cube? You know damn well that this thing wasn't built for his specifications. It would take us weeks to even get to a stage where we were ready for testing let alone run a full scale operation."

"Dr. Whitaker please meet Dr. Wilfred Escorner. Dr. Escorner is the lead developer of The Cube which unfortunately means that he spends a lot of time locked in a small room with no windows and has little contact with the outside world. Now, I'm going to go out on a limb here Dr. Whitaker and assume that you've had your head out of reading patient's charts long enough to know what's been going on in the news and would be so kind to inform your fellow doctor on events that have been going on recently."

"Well, I only heard it this evening and I'm not sure what it all means."

"Go ahead," encouraged Rogers.

"From what I understand there's been a joining of nations in Asia. I think they called it the United Federation of Asia, or something."

"How original," said Escorner.

"And not only that," continued Rogers, "The whole goddamned place has gone dark. No phone, no internet. Our satellites have been taken out whenever we flew over to take a look or somehow disrupted. Underwood is all that we have to get eyes on the ground over there. Now tell me, did you follow the correct protocols when Mr. Underwood entered The Cube, Dr. Escorner?"

"Yes, yes. All samples were taken including blood and DNA samples."

"And?" asked Rogers.

"And he's a match," replied Escorner cryptically.

"Good, that is terribly important," replied Rogers as he turned to leave Escorner in the corridor seemingly satisfied that blood samples had been taken.

"But you don't understand," Escorner called out, "The Cube was built specifically for The Oracle."

"The Oracle is Underwood. Or, at least, he is now."

At this Escorner seemed to go into meltdown. He rubbed his temples and paced up and down in the corridor. Molly was having difficulty keeping up with them both. Nothing was making sense to her.

Finally, Escorner threw his arms up in the air and said, "Are you saying that The Oracle is dead? Then, we need The Librarian. He's the only one that will be able to interpret this mess."

"Not possible," replied Rogers, "Here's what I need you to do. Get all the data you can and dump it onto offshore servers. Don't worry about the analysis just yet you'll have time for that later."

"It's not that easy, Rogers. This thing works like a tree. There is a trunk which then has an infinite number of branches, then off those branches are an infinite number of twigs and then you finally get to the leaves which hold what you're looking for of which you need to be able to cross reference those against other leaves."

"Then get what you can. Right now, we've got a bigger problem on our hands. Looks like our former esteemed member of the board turned Secretary of State has alerted the military to what we got going on down here. And they're coming for Underwood."

Escorner pointed another finger, "No! I won't let that happen."

With that he backed up and went back into the door which he came from and Rogers signalled for Molly to follow. As they went in the room there in the centre was a three-dimensional cube standing on its end. The top half was opened like a lid and there lay George connected to a series of wires that ran to a computer terminal sitting to the right. The room was dark and the only light source was coming from images that were flashing against the far end of the wall.

"I've been running the program for the last thirty minutes," began Escorner, "The results have been amazing. I've never seen this clarity before. The Ora-, I mean, The Old Oracle always seemed to deliver one image frames. But with Underwood we're getting whole reels of imagery."

"So what are you worried about? It's working?" said Rogers.

"On the outside it seems that way, but we don't have any idea as to what's happening to him on the inside. The problem is that I can't control what it is he is looking for and he keeps going back to what I think is his own path. See, he keeps coming back to an image of himself in the mountains. But, you can't tell where because it is covered in snow."

Molly was totally conflicted. Here she was with George strapped to some machine which appeared to be reading his mind. No wonder he wanted to get away. These bastards were using him as a lab rat. But, there was something familiar about the images being projected on the screen. She remembered from the night before and what he told her about the end, about when the lights went off.

"I know this," said Molly softly not sure she was wanting to say it.

"What?" replied Rogers.

"The mountain range. Snow and ice. George had talked of this. He said, that this is before the lights went out."

"You said, Dr. Whitaker that Mr. Underwood had not really spoken about anything."

"I didn't think it would be important. It seemed like ramblings at the time."

At that point, a man walked in with a black parker jacket and walkie-talkie.

"Sir, we've had visual."

"All right, let's go to the control centre. Escorner, you've got five minutes. Dump as much as you can and then get Underwood to the roof. And keep Dr. Whitaker talking. It may be she's got something to say after all."

Rogers left leaving Molly alone with Escorner. Molly thought that this would be her chance to get a bit of information.

"Escorner, why have you got George connected up to this thing. It doesn't seem legal."

"You don't know? I thought you were with, Rogers."

"Up until tonight I was a just Obstetrician. George was my boyfriend a few years ago. Then he disappeared. Not a word, just gone. And then, last night, he comes back into my world after I've moved on and tells me that he can see into the future. I don't believe him of course, who would? It's crazy right? And now, I see him like this and I'm wondering what it is you have been doing to him?"

"Well, he isn't crazy, I can assure. Everyone else around him maybe; but Underwood, he's a special man. What he can do is just staggering. He can see how the world is going to be at any one time. You see what your boyfriend-"

"Ex-boyfriend."

"Ex-boyfriend can do is see what people's lives are going to be like in the future by simply touching them with his hands. What he did for us was to go around the world to different places where a moment in time was about to explode and report on how it was going to pan out. The problem of course is that he can't be in two places at once. The Cube here taps into the lives of other people by installing sensory mechanisms throughout the planet and Underwood picks up on the echo."

"Echo?"

"The echo of time. You see, he may come into contact with someone whose life is fairly mundane. But, they come into contact with people who come into contact with people they know and eventually there will be one of them who is living the life of a wealthy CEO or a Minister or a General or some other power figure and we can then learn what their actions are going to be. Think of it as a social network running on tomorrow's time putting on updates of themselves; but, this time it's what they are about to do rather than what they have just done."

"I see." So it was real. George did need help. He needed Molly's help to protect him from where he was now and she had failed him. She had failed to be his friend. She felt a pang of regret cross her and she was overwhelmed by the situation. If only she had of accepted what he had said at face value then maybe he would still be free and she got the feeling that this was not a place that he wanted to be at all. If it was, he would have come in freely of his own will; not forced here by a bunch of mercenaries. She needed to protect him.

Molly looked down to where Escorner was working at his computer terminal. She noticed a packet of cigarettes sitting beside the keyboard and she recalled what George had said.

"Boy, this is all a bit much. I need a cigarette. Could I have one of yours?"

Escorner handed the pack to her, "Go for your life. But, you'll have to wait until we're out of the building. Can't smoke in here."

"Fine. I might go and wait in that courtyard. Come get me when you're done. Can I pinch your lighter?"

"Sure," he said reaching into his top pocket and giving her the light, "I'm just on this last segment. He keeps coming back to it but I can't seem to get it to go any further than him walking in the snow."

Escorner tapped at the keyboard, "Wait a second," he said as the image on the wall began to change. There was a figure up ahead standing beside a mound of some type. The person was not clear though. Molly went to where George was laying in The Cube and put her hand on his head.

"Whoa!" said Escorner, "What happened then? The image was just beginning to get clearer and then it just started flicking and now. Now, I don't know where it is at all."

It was then clear to Molly that she had to get George out of this situation when there was an explosion outside that rocked the building.

"We got to get out of here, Escorner."

"I just need a few more minutes to reconfigure back to that episode. There's something in it I'm sure!"

Molly looked at The Cube. She looked at the wires where they connected onto George. She looked further at George's face and it was then that she realised that he wasn't asleep or unconscious at all. He was wide awake! But, somehow the machine was keeping him in a state of immobility. It was then that she saw the clear plastic head gear that was moulded to the back of his head and she figured that this must have been the main contact point which kept him in the cube. Without further thought she pulled off the headgear and instantly George was back gasping for air like he had been held down underwater.

"Hey! You can't do that!"

Molly didn't hear him, "George! George, can you hear me?"

George mumbled something that she couldn't understand.

"George, we have to leave. Okay?"

Under the ramblings she could see his head nod and she began helping him to lift him out of The Cube as Molly heard gunfire coming from outside.

"That's, that was extremely dangerous. There's no telling what you could have done there. You could have killed him. His mind was deep in The Cube. He could have died of shock!"

"Too late for that now, Escorner. Now, where's that helicopter?"

"The roof. Take the stairs to the right in the corridor. It will be your quickest way there. I'll cut them off in here. They're only after him, they don't want me."

"Tell me," said Molly, "Why I am helping you guys and not the government?"

"He knows. When he comes to, ask him."

Molly had gained extra strength in the heat of the moment and was able to help George to his feet. She put his left arm around her shoulder and went out the door leaving Escorner at The Cube. She looked quickly out the corridor and while there were several men heading down toward the foyer they seemed to be more occupied in whoever it was that was coming in by force to worry about Molly and George. The stairs were difficult but after a while George started to become more lucid and was able to control his motor skills; albeit, rather slowly. Once they reached the roof the helicopter pilot saw them and jumped out helping Molly to put George in the back seat.

"Where's Rogers!" he yelled over the sound of the rotors.

Molly thought fast, "My name is Dr. Whitaker. I'm the care taker of Mr. Underwood and I order you to get us out of here!"

"I can only take orders from Rogers."

Below there was automatic weapon fire which caused some glass to smash near them. The pilot looked at Molly, "All right, let's move."

Molly jumped into the co-pilot seat at the front of the helicopter and she put the head phones on as the helicopter rose into the air.

"Which way should I go," asked the Pilot.

"They didn't say," replied Molly over the head phones.

A faint crackly voice then came over, "North, head north." It was George; he had managed to put on a pair of headphones and in his weakened state squeezed out the simple direction.

"Okay then," said the Pilot and the helicopter banked hard right away from fire fight where Molly looked down and caught a glimpse of Rogers standing on the roof surrounded by military men with their rifles pointed at him and Rogers with his hands in the air.

Chapter 50

"George! George, it's time to get up now. I need you to get up!"

George Underwood had been in hell. After being taken by force by the man with the gold tooth and his cronies they had placed him inside The Cube: the portal to an experience far greater than any of Underwood's abilities hoped to obtain. It completely submerged his conscious state into the visions of thousands upon thousands of people at any one time and the effect placed Underwood into a state of complete stasis: his breathing felt effortless, he had no desire of hunger or thirst, his muscles were completely relaxed and he had the sensation that all time and gravity did not exist. He felt nothing of himself apart from the images of other people, predominately at their worst; but, none of the people that he wanted to connect with seemed to be available. He was specifically looking for people from Australia. He wanted to connect with them so he could see for himself what it is that was going on there. Luckily, this had also been the desire of the gold toothed man; however, even after trying everything he could not connect with anyone there. It was like that the whole country had been wiped from the map.

Underwood had submitted to the wishes of the gold toothed man for the simple fact that he wanted access to The Cube. Charles Harrison had told him about it; however, he had dissuaded Underwood from entertaining the idea of being a participant in the testing phases. Harrison had thought it an evil device and one that would surely bring dire consequences. Underwood had trusted Harrison then; at that time, his fear of The Cube was enough to deter Underwood.

After unsuccessfully trying to connect with the people of Australia he had turned his thoughts to his own end when the sky went red and the lights went out. He wanted to use The Cube to help look past the event and while the image of that event had never been clearer in his mind the sense of emptiness when the lights went out prevailed. He ran through the event time and time again only to come across the same conclusion. And yet, he did not feel death in that emptiness. Underwood had in fact experienced death many times before in his contact with people's future, Molly's sister was one example; and, each time he came into contact with someone whose death was imminent, the event he experienced of their death could only be described as the sound of a distant train clicking on the tracks - *rat-ta-tat, rat-ta-tat, rat-ta-tat, rat-ta-tat* – the sound eventually fading until it could not be heard in the din. But, the same characteristics could not be said for this event. There was something there, a constant existence in darkness; although, where it took place or what propelled it was out of reach for Underwood to establish a connection. And still, Underwood felt that the longer he lingered in that event the more likely he would eventually be able to see its end.

But that wasn't to be. Being pulled out of The Cube was like being shot out of a cannon and into a large funnel; spiralling down and down until the bottom surged toward him and he broke through gasping for air. For a moment, he floated in a dark place and images of Molly's face flickered in and out as he came to consciousness. He started feeling sensation back in his fingers and toes; his eyelids would only allow light to peep in momentarily and then he felt a tingling awareness of minute sounds in his ears until he could clearly hear Molly's distinct voice and the level of panic in her tone awoken in him to focus on what she was saying. It was clear that she was in danger and Underwood had forced himself to go with her, to trust her, yet his legs were still not responding to the commands and he could only see what lay ahead of him at arm's length.

In the helicopter he could not recall what had possessed him to tell the pilot to go north. He was thinking of snow and of mountains and the thought had struck him that Canada had both of those. He had blacked out shortly after that and only came to when again he heard the panicked voice of Molly over the headset.

"…What do you mean you have to take it down? We're in the middle of nowhere out here!" said Molly fervently.

"If I don't take it down now then we will crash. We're barely running on petrol fumes as it is," replied the Pilot.

"Great, we get out of one situation and get put in another."

"It's not what I call an ideal spot either. But hang on; this is going to get a bit rough."

Underwood felt the helicopter rolling in as the tree line came closer into view. Alarm bells and lights started to flash on the console and the Pilot was flicking switches to no avail and he felt the helicopter begin to spin out of control. There was then a sudden clunk as the ground was struck and the helicopter slid on the ground shuddering to a stop as the rotor blades repeatedly bashed into the ground until they were bent completely out of shape.

"We're good? We're good," said Molly, "You're good?"

"I'm good," replied the Pilot.

"How are you back there, George?" asked Molly. But Underwood had already felt the desire of sleep take hold of him again and passed out until now when Molly was shaking him pleading for him to wake up.

When he opened his eyes the sensation of consciousness was like being reborn. It was night time and the moon cast a dull light in the cockpit of the helicopter. He clenched his fist and rolled his neck and sat up stretching his legs. The good thing was that he was back in full control of his faculties and he rested his head on the glass door of the helicopter only to be confronted with the bad news: a grizzly bear whacking its giant paw on the glass where Underwood's head was. Underwood scampered to the other side of the helicopter and watched the Grizzly back up a few steps then charge at the helicopter. The whole thing rocked and the door was bent and crumpled as the Grizzly rammed into the side of the helicopter with all its might.

"Whoa!" yelled Underwood as the Grizzly let off an almighty roar and stood on its hind legs at full stretch.

"Don't move!" said Molly calmly from the front of the cockpit, "Don't even make a sound."

The Grizzly fell back to all fours and started sniffing around the ground of the helicopter. It pawed at the pilot's door that Underwood noticed was strangely vacant and seemed to follow a scent off into the night. Underwood then let go of the breath he had been holding and rubbed his eyes.

"Where are we?" he asked.

"We took your advice and went north," replied Molly, "We

stopped a couple of times for fuel but our last stop wouldn't give us any and we had to make an emergency landing. You weren't very specific as where it was in the north you wanted us to go but I figured Canada seemed like a good place to be when you are being hunted by the government."

"Anchorage, Alaska," said Underwood without thinking but knowing that this was the place he wanted to go, "Water, I need water?"

"Here," said Molly handing him a container, "I melted some snow with my hands. But, don't take too much; it's all that we-"

Underwood drank it all greedily and spared a few drops to dampen his face. The cold water was a refreshing memory and he felt more alert and ready to take control.

"Where's the pilot?" asked Underwood, "We need to get going as soon as we can. There's no time to waste."

"Yeah, that's the thing. The pilot took off about an hour ago. Said he saw a highway to the north of here about two clicks and that if we didn't get there soon that we would be done for," replied Molly.

"I think that Grizzly picked up his trail and went off after him."

"At least it's gone now."

"Which means we need to make a fire or he'll be right."

Underwood and Molly both searched around for fire wood and managed to get enough branches together for a fire. When they were back at the helicopter and setting up the fire Molly reached into her pocket and waved the lighter at Underwood.

"Remember to ask for a lighter, you said," said Molly lighting the paper of the safety manual they had found in the cockpit of the helicopter as Underwood wrapped himself in a thermal blanket they had found in the emergency first aid kit.

"I'm glad that you took notice. When did you start believing me?" asked Underwood.

"Oh, right about the time that they stuck you into that thing they called The Cube and that weed of a man, Escorner, was telling me about what you can see. Also, the bullets flying over my head were a dead giveaway."

"That long, huh? Gee, I really need to work on my skills of persuasion. Imagine what would happen if my life depended on my ability to convince someone that I can see what I can see?"

"You might have more luck than you think. Most people I know would prefer to think that what you can do is a reality rather than just fantasy. Unfortunately, I'm more cynical than that."

"I don't remember you being that way? What happened to the

take life as it comes attitude?"

"Experience. It kind of gives you that harder edge. George, if I had of known what it was you were up against I would have never-"

"Save it. You did what you thought was right. And, for what it was worth, I'm glad you did. If you hadn't, then I would have been in the hands of Uncle Sam and god-knows-what would have happened to me then."

"Escorner said to ask you about that."

"Uncle Sam considers me to be a threat to national security and has a standing termination order on my head."

"Termination order? They want you dead? That's absurd, if anything, you could help them."

"But that's just it, Molly. I wouldn't help them. They wanted me to look into the future and tell them what the world would be so that they could alter events to their own benefit. That is against the natural course of life. Also, what would happen if the events I altered made other events happen far worse than what was to come; and what if I was wrong? Who would they blame? There are just too many questions that are left unanswered."

"So you work for an insurance company?"

"I worked for Charles Harrison. What information I gave him and what he did with it was none of my concern. Globe Corp merely protected me from government intervention. I was an asset to them and their only use for me was to make money. If I continued to do that then there weren't any problems and it gave me the ability to look for the reasons why it was I was granted this gift."

"You were given this gift to help people, George," said Molly with tears in her eyes, "I mean, there are people out there suffering and dying and you could have saved them."

"I understand why you think that, Molly. Your sister, I tried. I really did. But I failed. I couldn't make her see what was coming. I couldn't get her to understand and in the end I asked her to forgive me."

Molly stood and walked away from the fire and leant on the buckled rotor blade of the helicopter when she suddenly spun around toward Underwood, "Oh, my god. The letter. Angelina wrote to me before she died. She said she had found god. She said that *He* forgave her. But that was you. You don't just see people's futures. You can see their thoughts."

"It was that failure which made me realise that I needed to focus on my ability. I needed to train it to clearly identify every detail so that if I was ever asked to help someone again I would be able to with complete certainty. I couldn't cope having to go through what I did when Angelina died and I just had to leave. I'm sorry, Molly."

"No, no, it's all right. You did what you could to save my sister. It was an accident. It was you the other night wasn't it? You were in my head?" replied Molly solemnly. Underwood watched as a steely look crossed her eyes in the amber glow of the fire.

"I needed to let you know that I was coming. I couldn't risk you turning me away."

The reality was that whatever Underwood said to try and make it seem what he did to be the right thing Molly would never be able to see past her own suffering. It was the first time since they had reconnected that he was able to look at her and study closely how she had changed. Underwood could tell from the distant look in her eyes that she was full of regret and what he had surfaced meant something that he could not hope to fix.

"It will be dawn soon," said Molly, "We need to get some rest."

"You rest. I'll keep watch," replied Underwood wrapping himself tighter in the thermal blanket.

"Fine," said Molly opening the door to the back seat of the helicopter and laying on the floor.

While it was less than perfect, essentially the whole ordeal had gone to plan for Underwood and while there were still several elements that he didn't understand he had the feeling that they were on the right path. And yet, the fear that he could not overcome was the idea that he was now The Oracle. It was a fear of expectation that Harrison had said that The Oracle must serve the ultimate sacrifice which filled Underwood with anxiety.

Chapter 51

Why did she do these things to herself, thought Molly Whitaker? She was a good honest working doctor who liked working with her patients. She enjoyed the challenges of her work and the people that she met and the difference that she made in their lives. And yet, here she was in the state of *Seward's folly*, in the city of Anchorage, half frozen to the core and sitting in a draughty wooden building surrounded by truck drivers, loggers and men in general who had not seen a real woman for months, drinking a beer. She hated beer but it was the only thing available in the place which would not cause suspicion even though her appearance was not at all conspicuous. However, luckily for Molly, there was an event happening on the television that far outweighed the appearance of a woman in a bar. A group of solemn faces stood around the television at the far end, mostly bearded, mostly gritty looking men in awe at the thing that they were calling a 'mothership' on the news report.

"Are they saying this 'ere is made by humans?" said one elderly man.

"Shut your trap and listen, Jones," said another, "Hey, Pete, go on down there and turn this thing up."

Pete, it appeared, was the name of the barman and he moved down from the other end of the bar where he was pouring a beer from the tap and slid the remote down the bar toward the other man who was calling out.

"Knock yourself out," said Pete who went back to his work and the man turned up the volume to the television drowning out the din of the bar.

"...And as you can see," said the Anchorwoman, "The ship is just hovering there in full view. It doesn't appear to be making any threats as we understand and the only real movement at all was one small ship which came down and landed out front of the United Nations building...If you've joined us recently, the images you are seeing are real. New York City woke this morning to find this enormous airship sitting off in the bay. Any attempt by our helicopter crews to get closer to the vessel has been denied by the aviation authority. We understand that the ship originates from United Federation of Asia and it is not as first reported some type of alien spacecraft. There are humans on board. So please, do not panic. The world is not coming to an end. It is in fact, a transport vessel for the recently appointed President of the United Federation of Asia who has appeared to meet the United Nations Security Council in the wake of the sudden unification that took place of nations in Asia, South East Asia and the Pacific."

"It just don't make any sense?" said the man with the remote.

"You got that right, Jimmy," said the elderly man called Jones. Evidently, the remote control man's name was Jimmy.

"I mean," continued Jimmy, "How on earth did they build that thing? How does it fly?"

"I be best headed on back out to them mountains," said old man Jones, "This got the signs of things that are no good for anyone. You don't go around buildin' things like that for nothin'. Yes sir, give me snow 'n' ice 'n' mountains any day over that thing." At that, old man Jones downed the remainder of his beer and slammed down the pitcher on the bar and walked out of the bar.

Molly herself had no desire to head back into the wild country after the ordeal that she and George had just been through. When they woke in the morning out in the forest beside the crash site of the helicopter they made their way north attempting to follow the direction that the Pilot had made the night before. They had eventually found the road they saw on the way in; however, they waited for a few hours and didn't see one car pass on by. They decided to begin walking and came across a driveway which down the side of a hill was hiding a cabin. The cabin was clearly a holiday retreat used as a hunting base and everything was covered in sheets inside. After George broke in and managed to find some canned food of corn and kidney beans and they had their fill of water they looked in the garage further down the hill where they found a pick-up truck that was rigged for hunting. George hot-wired the pick-up and they started to make their way down the highway toward the city of Whitehorse in the state of Yukon, Canada. From there they picked up supplies and made the journey across land where at the border crossing between Canada and Alaska George had produced a set of Canadian passports for Mr. George and Mrs. Molly Greene with pictures of both George and Molly. George had said that he had spent a high price on these in his journey knowing that one day they would be needed.

When they reached Anchorage, George had told her that they were here to find a pilot; but, just not any pilot. A pilot who was a specialist ice pilot and who could fly in the harshest conditions on earth. The pilot was a local named Jimmy Condor the man that stood in front of Molly now.

George had said that he would be a hard egg to crack. He was not accustomed to strangers knowing what he did and had a suspicious nature at the best of times. If George walked up to him and asked him to take him somewhere in his plane he would immediately suspect a set up and disappear. But, the man was not married. In fact, the only relationship with a woman he ever had been with his mother and even now that wasn't so good. So, George had thought that it was best that Molly approach him and dazzle him with her charm. Initially, she was coy about the whole thing. She'd approached guys in bars before; men who were used to such advances. But, now, standing next to him, she was nervous as all hell. By now, she would have thought that a man such as Jimmy would have taken some notice of her given that she was the only woman in the bar. So much so, that unless it hadn't been for George confirming his heterosexuality she would have mistaken him as completely opposite. But his attention was grabbed by the news and the images that he saw were obviously causing trepidation. He was a pilot, after all, and that ship was hovering there, unnaturally.

"How does a thing like that just stay up there?" asked Molly out loud.

Jimmy didn't take his eyes from the screen, "Well, they must have some kind of thrusters underneath that we can't see holding it stationary. I'd sure like to get a closer look at it though."

"I'm not sure I would. Looks a bit scary to me," said Molly.

"Well, I've got more than just a passing interest in these things, you see. I'm a pilot."

"Really?" said Molly a little bit over anxiously. She was in fact happy that he was the one who brought it up.

"Yeah, quite some time now," he replied now finally turning towards her and a smile crept across his face, "You interested in planes are you darlin'?"

"Well, my father was a pilot in the military." That part was a true story.

"You don't say," replied Jimmy.

"Ah huh. Maybe you'll know then. I'm kind of looking for someone. You see, I've got a dancing gig at a military base but I don't know where the hell it is."

"Oh, you a dancer?"

"Yeah, once a military girl always a military girl. But, the thing is, they didn't tell me where it is, it's bizarre. They just told me to come to this bar and find a guy named Jimmy who's a pilot and he'll know all about it."

"Well, my name is Jimmy and I'm a pilot," said Jimmy excitedly.

"Really?"

"Really."

"Wow! I was getting scared there for a moment. I've done loads of secret gigs before but this one was really weird. But, you know, the money was fabulous so how could I say no."

"You don't need to say anything further, little lady. I know what this all about."

"You do?" Molly was a little apprehensive and considered for a second that she may need to make a quick getaway if this went sour.

"Well sure I do," Jimmy leaned in closer and lowered his voice, "I've been shipping things in and out all week. Boxes of bourbon and such. You here for General Matheson's birthday party aren't you? The boys told me to keep it all hush-hush but they really gone all out on you haven't they."

Molly was relieved and realised that George had seen this whole thing; she didn't need to worry at all. She made a mental note to chastise George about it when they had the time, "Well, I am a pretty special act," replied Molly continuing in her role, "You think you could get me up there in time for the party?"

"I sure could," replied Jimmy, "Matter of fact; I'm flying out that way tomorrow. Now you got a pen but keep this to yourself now, this here is what they call top secret information."

Molly took down the name of the airstrip where she was to meet Jimmy the next morning at 8 a.m. sharp and he gave her a description of where it was located. She thanked him with a big kiss on the cheek and she remembered to flatter her eyelashes in keeping with her adopted persona. Molly had never been one to trust herself to be able to talk to people like that. Lying wasn't so bad, she did it every day at the hospital to provide hope to those who had none; but, this was different, it was a real adrenalin rush that cast Molly out of her comfort zone and into the world of another Molly Whitaker who was confident, spontaneous and fun. A Molly Whitaker that she aspired to be.

Chapter 52

When Tim Marshall reached camp at the foot of Mount Roraima in the south-east of Venezuela it was late in the evening and he had been travelling non-stop for two days. He first flew in a plane that he had chartered out of Barcelona to Ciudad Bolivar and then another which took him to Santa Elena de Uairen where he then drove three hours through the mountainous terrain to Paraitepuy. From there, Marshall went on foot on the backpacker route through the Gran Sabana which took him the entire day to reach the base of the mountain where he was able to locate the camp using a hand held GPS locater with coordinates he had obtained from the note in the red box.

It had been the great deception that the tree would be found in the middle of the jungle. The first part of the riddle which said the 'empty jungle' alluded to this and the second part that referred to a 'misty mountain' could have only been Mount Roraima given its position both in mythology and the fact that it was almost always shrouded in the clouds. Also, Mount Roraima had been surrounded by a vast savannah plain where the *tepui* or table-top mountains emerged. The mountain was the centre of local *Pemon* people mythology who told the story of how the mountain was the stump of a great tree that once existed and was cut down filling the rivers in a great flood. It was this myth that Alvarez had been following and the same one Andreina had been able to piece back together that alluded to Alvarez's map. However, what was not clear was where Alvarez had located the evidence of the existence of the tree. They had searched practically every part that they could and they had not turned up a single piece of bark.

Marshall's team was not a big one. In fact, for such a huge discovery as this, the team had been the smallest that he had ever worked with. It consisted of Terrazas as the local expert and two others that Harrison had sent to him who one day appeared out of the blue at the office in Caracas. The first was Aleksie Gavrikov, a Russian drilling expert who had mainly worked in the oil fields of Siberia; and then, a young graduate from the Laboratory of Tree-Ring Research of the University of Arizona, Georgie Davenport. Unfortunately, the team rarely got along or saw eye-to-eye on most aspects of the expedition. In particular, Davenport and Gavrikov found it difficult given their backgrounds. Gavrikov had spent the last ten years working with the hardened men of Siberia and had the manners of a rhinoceros; while Davenport was from a privileged family whose only rebellion was to study Earth Sciences instead of Law or Medicine. Visually, too, their opposite natures were reflected in their appearance: with Davenport's dyed black hair, piercings and attire that rarely ventured past Henry Ford's philosophy on colour schemes; and, Gavrikov's hardened muscular olive complexion that rarely saw him wear much other than his shorts and a hard hat in the tropical climate.

Their camp consisted of several smaller tents that served as sleeping and storage quarters and a central circular portable habitat inflated by a generator that was over forty feet wide. Originally developed for NASA as a device to live on the Moon, Marshall had adapted the habitat for life in the tropics as a work station that included a science laboratory for Davenport to perform her work. And, it was this structure that Marshall entered now given that it was the only place with its lights on and he figured that they all must be inside eating their dinner. Strangely though, Marshall heard laughter emanating from inside. In all their time out here in the savannah he had barely heard either of his team raise a chuckle. But, as he entered inside he saw Gavrikov leading a hearty rendition of some Russian folk song with Terrazas and Davenport joining in on the chorus when Gavrikov caught his eye.

"The fearless leader has returned!" said Gavrikov coming towards Marshall and giving him a hug.

"Thanks for the welcome, Aleksie," replied Marshall, "But what's with the party? Did I miss something?"

"Oh, well, where do I begin?" began Davenport, "Not only did you miss the greatest discovery in the entire world but today Aleksie managed to get the drill to pull out a sample over forty feet into the tree. Forty feet! Tim, do you know how much data I can get from that sample? It's mind blowing!"

"I don't know what to say but to tell you how truly happy I am for you all. I mean it; you've all put in such hard work. So, I noticed that you moved the camp site. What made you do that?"

"Well, it was Georgie's idea," said Terrazas, "She did after all find the tree."

"So where is it?" asked Marshall.

"You are standing on it," replied Gavrikov.

Marshall looked at his feet but somehow he didn't believe that there was a tree underneath him and that maybe Gavrikov had broken out the Vodka he had been stashing in his sleeping quarters even though Marshall had a strict no alcohol policy.

"What do you mean?" asked Marshall.

"We mean," replied Davenport, "That where you stand is the tree. It was something that you said that made me think about the riddle you told me and how the tree of life represents heaven, earth and the underworld. In the riddle, Alvarez found the tree in darkness and who ever said that the tree had to rise up from the earth? What if the tree grew into the earth? What if the surface of the earth where we lived was the underworld and not the in between space? It would explain a bunch of stuff in my life that's for sure."

"So the tree is underground? How did you know it was located here?" asked Marshall.

"When we thought about the possibility that the tree was underground," said Terrazas, "We went in search for caves and found many that led deep underground."

"Yes," said Gavrikov, "I speak to some backpackers who were going into the caves. They tell me that their favourite cave was the Crystal Eyes Caves.

"Where the sun shone through the eyes of crystal," said Marshall reciting the last part of the riddle.

"And this particular cave has a crevice that stretched down below for what must be hundreds of meters," said Gavrikov.

"Alvarez fell down a crevice. It's what put him in a wheelchair," said Marshall.

"So," continued Gavrikov, "I lower Georgie down to take a look."

"And there it was, Tim. I couldn't believe it. At first I thought it was just some discoloured rock formations created by an underground water fall. But when I felt the crevice walls there was something there that was not as cold as stone. The crevice opened up into a chamber and when Aleksie lowered down a light I could see it more clearly. It was a tree."

"Yes, so I go down there and I drill," said Gavrikov, "I take a core and there it was. Wood! Not dirt or clay or stone. Just wood."

"So, Georgie, what have you found?" asked Marshall.

"Let me show you," Davenport said taking a slice of bread and walking over to her station that doubled as a laboratory which Marshall felt was odd given that they had not had any bread or even flour to make bread for months. Terrazas and Gavrikov followed as well and Davenport sat herself down in front of her computer dismissing the screensaver of a gothic looking Valkyrie, "Charting this baby has been a nightmare. You haven't exactly been forthcoming with any clues as to what it is I need to look for."

"Our client isn't exactly sure as to what it wants to find," said Marshall.

"Yeah, well, I made some assumptions given that the brief was to find anything out of the ordinary," continued Davenport, "But first, I had to establish what was classified as ordinary. First, I needed to reference the dates of the rings. Are you familiar with the year that didn't have a summer?"

"Not entirely," replied Marshall.

"Okay, well. Between the years of 1812 and 1815 a series of volcanic eruptions all over the world released ash into the atmosphere. We're talking the Caribbean, Japan, the Philippines and finally the big one at Mount Tambora in Indonesia. It led to a volcanic winter in the year 1816 where basically there was no summer. There were frosts all over the world which caused famine and starvation and many people died. But, its significance for dendrochronology is that it allows us a reference point because there were no rings left on the trees for that year. Specifically, we are talking about the late wood growth which is the darker edge of the ring that grows in summer. But, because there was no summer that year, there wasn't a dark ring left and I can then use this as a cross reference point on other catalogued dendrochronology. Just like here."

Davenport brought up an image of a tree-ring sample and showed this against an image she had taken of the core sample they had taken of the tree. It showed that the tree lines matched identically.

"Now," Davenport continued, "From this initial sample Aleksie drilled for me I was able to determine that this data went back as far as 500 BCE. I performed some standard tests like precipitation, temperature and carbon dioxide that are captured in the rings from year to year; but, then I thought to myself, what isn't tested when we look at core samples. I mean, we are looking for things that are out of the ordinary, right? And, if we do the same tests we are going to get the same results. So, I started doing some tests and found traces of a type of carbon I had never seen before. You see, carbon is made up in the atmosphere of carbon-12, carbon-13 and very small amounts of carbon-14. But this type of carbon has not been catalogued and seems to be rarer still than carbon-14. And, the computer modelling showed that there seemed to be peaks of this unknown carbon form that occurred every twenty-three years in the core sample. But to illustrate where I'm going with this let me show you these two graphs. The top one shows the temperature variation by degrees and the bottom one shows the level of carbon dioxide in the atmosphere over the last two-hundred thousand years. You can see here how the temperature changes and the level of carbon seem to follow the same path almost like they are interlinked. Whenever there is a major peak it seems to follow that both the temperature and carbon levels progressively drop over time."

"So, the earth cools?" said Gavrikov.

"And where are we now?" asked Terrazas.

"Right at the top of the cycle," replied Davenport.

"Take a look at how much the carbon levels have accelerated in the past few hundred years," said Marshall.

"No surprises there," said Terrazas.

"But, what triggers this cooling phase?" continued Davenport, "My guess, is that the cooler temperatures from the mesopause drop into the mesosphere like some kind of pressure release valve. It's almost like the planet is expelling a toxin that has reached critical mass. And, that critical mass, is caused by an over abundance of the mystery carbon."

"It's a filter," said Marshall, "It doesn't happen instantly but the critical mass you speak of slowly leaks out until the equilibrium is reached."

"Just like a set of lungs," said Terrazas.

"The earth's lungs," said Davenport, "We forget that the planet is a living organism and almost every organism in the universe has an outlet to exhaust unwanted matter; a star will supernova; humans, also, expel carbon dioxide, faeces, urine but these are all necessary by products of the mechanisms that keep us alive. The earth, in much the same way, needs certain elements to ensure that it continues to live and these elements also create a wasteful by product that must be expelled and the mechanism for which it is released. Now, this cycle of cleansing moves from one part of the atmosphere to the next but when it releases it also takes in cool temperatures from the upper and middle spheres. But, back to our core sample of the tree of life, you can see that if I take the temperature and carbon level peaks and graph these it seems also to peak at the same time as the mystery carbon levels. And then, a pattern seemed to emerge. I noticed that a peak of the mystery carbon was reached before the 1815 volcanic eruption; and, previous to that the next peak was just before the year 1600 when there was another major volcanic eruption at Huaynaputina in Peru and again there was a subsequent volcanic winter."

"So are you saying that the spike in this mystery carbon is causing volcanic eruptions?" asked Terrazas.

"Not quite. My question is what is causing the mystery carbon levels to peak? And then I found this."

Davenport showed a graph read out on the screen which Marshall didn't understand, "Okay, I'll bite," said Marshall, "What am I looking at?"

"Stardust," said Davenport, "The traces of silicon carbide, graphite and aluminium oxide amongst others is consistent with stardust. Something has made the electromagnetic field that protects the earth from the Sun's solar winds act like a magnet which drew in a large portion of stardust. It was this event that caused the eruptions."

Marshall was looking at the graphs that Davenport had put on the screen. Harrison had been looking for something; something of consequence. He put this team together as he knew that they would find something and while the tree had unearthed some clues he had not yet tied the pieces together to find anything that you could conclude was out of the ordinary.

"Okay," started Marshall, "What do we think we've found here?"

"Deforestation has made the carbon levels of the planet sky rocket!" said Terrazas.

"Not necessarily," said Davenport, "The earth seems to build up carbon from plant decomposing plant materials. The planet experiences these build ups naturally like a cycle."

"Yes, and we, as humans, have put that cycle out of whack. We shouldn't be seeing these levels of carbon for tens of thousands of years," retorted Terrazas.

"What's the big deal? Just like Georgie says, it builds up and up and up until it goes pop! Much like Chernobyl, no?" interjected Gavrikov.

"Not pop, it deflates," replied Marshall, "It drops down until we're in another ice age. The way it is right now, we're at the peak just waiting for something to tip us over the scales. This is it. Whatever this event is, the next time it happens. It'll begin the process of cooling the planet."

"And given that we have accelerated the heating process it is likely to cause an acceleration of the cooling phase," said Terrazas.

"By then we'll have bigger problems than what to do about the melting ice caps," said Davenport, "Cooling temperatures will lead to greater food shortages. Plant and animal life will be desecrated."

"And then, after all that, we'll be covered in ice," said Marshall. Marshall recalled what was on the inscription they had seen under water at Easter Island that said: *when the oracle stands in the gates of the gods he will gain entry into the temple of illumination*. It was the *consequence* that Harrison had been looking for; but, what he didn't know, or have evidence of, was what happened when the doorway was opened. Suddenly, Marshall's endeavours began to make more sense.

Just then, a man walked into the habitat. He was a big man, inappropriately dressed in a suit and walked with a limp, "So, guys. I've got all your personal belongings packed and ready to leave. The rest of your tools and equipment will follow shortly after."

"Who's this?" asked Marshall.

"This is Jackson. He's taking us home. Job is done, boss," said Gavrikov.

"Wait, you didn't send him?" asked Terrazas.

"I certainly did not," replied Marshall.

"Oh, Mr. Marshall," began the man with the limp named Jackson, "I'm glad you could join us. I have been looking for you. The guide you sent me to help find your team was most helpful."

"What's going on here?" asked Marshall.

"Well, like a said. We're packing up and shipping the team out. Including you Mr. Marshall. Globe Corp thanks you for your services but now we feel it is time that this operation comes to an end."

"Do not listen to this man. He does not speak with any authority," said Marshall backing away from Jackson.

"He's from Globe Corp. He already told us that you have been terminated," said Davenport, "I'm sorry, Tim. They threatened to take my research grant away and with the core samples that Aleksie has collected I can research and map the course of history far greater than we ever have before. The only thing I could do was hold out on the test results and what I thought was happening here. I thought that it was your discovery and I owed you that much. They couldn't make me talk."

It was then that Marshall heard the sound of helicopters. How long this Jackson character had been here Marshall didn't know. He only hoped that he hadn't done anything fatal to Rosie's cousin that he had employed to lead him away from the camp site. Or, maybe he really thought that Marshall owed Rosie money and had not performed as he had asked at all. Either way, it was clear that whatever Marshall had paid Rosie's cousin this Jackson character had paid him more. All types of scenarios were floating around in his head at that moment but they all led to sheer power and wealth which Marshall had an abundance of neither. He just had his thoughts, his knowledge and like Davenport had said his discovery.

"Let's go people," said Jackson and the team filed past Marshall one-by-one each offering an apologetic glance; but, Marshall could not offer any thanks. The damage was done. He had been betrayed. A betrayal, that in the end, he could not stop.

"You too, Mr. Marshall. I am instructed to ask you to join us as there are some things that we need to go over before we can release you," said Jackson.

"And if I refuse," replied Marshall.

"I'm sorry, Mr. Marshall. Refusal is not an option," said Jackson pulling out a hand gun from the inside of his pocket.

Marshall followed Jackson outside where there were two passenger helicopters and a larger helicopter that other men were loading in the supplies from the camp site. Terrazas, Davenport and Gavrikov jumped in one helicopter and he was about to follow when Jackson veered him away to the other helicopter. He stopped for a minute and looked inside where he saw a familiar gold glint. It was Rogers.

Rogers opened the door of the helicopter and greeted Marshall, "Mr. Marshall, glad to meet you again. Please jump in; we don't have much time to lose."

Marshall got inside the helicopter and Jackson followed behind him. He buckled himself in and placed a headset over his ears when he looked and saw two other men sitting across from him. One that looked familiar and another untidy looking man wearing suspenders who was busy tapping at a laptop.

"Oh," said Rogers as the helicopter rose off the ground, "Have you met Bill Patrick, Secretary of State?"

He hadn't. But it all started to make sense. The urgency that Harrison had placed on the trees discovery, the intensity in which they pursued him; it all pointed to something far greater than what he had ever imagined and had seemingly stuck Marshall right in the middle of a power struggle.

Chapter 53

In the cold morning of Anchorage, Alaska, Molly Whitaker sat with George in the front of the stolen pick-up truck. The light was dull and foggy and Molly thought that it might not be possible to fly in such conditions. However, George had said that their pilot, Jimmy Condor, was one of the best pilots in the region and said that these conditions wouldn't be a problem.

They sat in front of the airstrip that appeared to be more of a run-down industrial estate with an open area wedged in between massive warehouse buildings. They had difficulty locating it initially as it was one that was strangely not listed on the map and Jimmy's description had been vague as to its whereabouts. They had stopped off at a service station and the man behind the counter knew exactly where the place was and he drew Molly a more detailed map. The service station attendant had joked that it was the worst kept secret in Alaska that most of their maps were useless as they had so many 'top secret' locations.

The previous night in the hotel with George had been a disaster. After the high of successfully playing the role of a distressed stripper on her way to a military base for a job she had returned to the hotel to find George in a state of confusion. He found it difficult to remember where he was or how he got there. He couldn't remember anything of the last forty-eight hours: not The Cube, the helicopter trip nor their dash across British Colombia. Molly had thought that he had been suffering some kind of paranoid delusion when George came back into her life suddenly and proclaimed that he could see into the future; and, even though events and people had persuaded her otherwise, there was a lingering doubt in her mind that told her that she didn't completely believe what it was that he saw and that perhaps coincidence was playing some kind of part in their whole saga. Maybe it was her medical training that required tangible evidence before she would take the leap of faith and the episode only assisted in galvanising this fact. The only way Molly was able to calm George down was to take his hands and then suddenly he seemed to be with it again and she was able to ease him into bed where he slept through the night.

"You're still thinking that I'm crazy?" said George suddenly.

"No," Molly replied.

"What happened last night is part of the downside to my ability," said George and Molly thought that he must be reading her thoughts again, "While my memory is filled with the lives of others it has no room for the memory of my own. I remember my own life through the memory of others by connecting with them. My ability, however, is not fully developed. Sometimes, I lose the ability to connect with people. It comes and goes and I have no control over it when it does but until I can reconnect with people I seem to be like a dementia patient."

While the explanation seemed tangible, Molly had been considering the possibility that his condition, or ability, seemed to rely on people acting and behaving in a consistent and predetermined manner. What it did not seem to recognise was the fact that people, in general, have a disposition for chaos. In Molly's experience she had come across all kinds of people who seemed to seek drama over happiness and their motivation for doing so was dubious at best; so, Molly wondered how it was that George accounted for these people.

"George," she began, "What if you're wrong? I mean, have you ever been wrong?"

The look on George's face was enough to tell her what she wanted to know. It was like she had stabbed him through the heart.

"Every day I wish I was wrong, Molly. Then I could go on living my life like everyone else. I could have been with you, always."

Tears now gripped her upon hearing this. All those years lost amid hate and sorrow and waiting for George to come back to her had finally caved in on Molly. She felt George's hand reach out and touch her shoulder in an act to comfort her. But it was not comfort that she wanted. It was revenge. Revenge at whatever that it was that tore them apart. It was not something that she had thought that George would understand and an odd feeling for her to have. She had never felt the urge before this moment and it suddenly sprung a resolute devotion in her to see this thing through. Whatever it takes.

The clock struck 8 a.m. and Molly wiped her tears and looked at herself in the mirror. Thankfully, the tears had not run her make-up that George had thoughtfully suggested she buy to keep in character. They had made a supply run before she went into the bar the night before ensuring that they had enough equipment and clothing suitable for the icy weather and she also purchased some clothes to round out the package of her character; even though they weren't visible under her full length jacket. The transformation was one that she had enjoyed and allowed her to keep an edge that she had developed in the bar the previous night.

"Okay, show time," said Molly as she got out of the pick-up truck, "Remember, follow my lead." She said to George as she shut the door and walked on out to the airstrip where she could see what must have been Jimmy's plane.

Chapter 54

President of the United Federation of Asia, Robert Hughes, sat in his Presidential quarters of the UFA mothership that had been nicknamed, The Conqueror. It was the largest of the fleet of over a hundred similar aircraft and from what Hughes had learned was also the most capable. It housed an army of four thousand smaller fighter planes and six thousand IA5 combat units; could stay airborne indefinitely; could be sealed shut and remain underwater for months before resurfacing; and, while it had been difficult to test, could even theoretically venture into space. He had to hand it to the Chinese though, they had kept the whole operation successfully under wraps for decades; and, while most of their military operations were moving to Australia the facility that they had built in the mountains of the Himalaya's was something else. Still, Hughes privately conceded that while the best engineering that the planet could offer had been assembled it would be no match for what was to come.

The military component of The Conqueror was currently engaged in a battle with the Peruvian, Bolivian, Argentinean and Brazilian combined air force with support from the United States. The Conqueror had left New York after Hughes' meeting with the United Nations Security Council and travelled in a direct path to Peru where it now held in a stationary position above Lake Titicaca in the south of the country. The battle had ensued when the request from the Peruvian and Bolivian governments for The Conqueror to leave their airspace was denied; however, Hughes had given direct instruction to ensure that UFA Air Forces were only used for defence purposes to ensure the least amount of causalities.

The battle was being displayed on one of the side panels that made up most of the wall in the Presidential quarters; however, he was not overtly concerned with what he was seeing on that screen. Hughes was more worried about the report he had just received from Lupei, the UFA's artificial intelligence unit, that a small group of remaining Australian's had been able to commandeer a UFA transport ship; and, subsequently, it appeared that two IA5 units were also involved.

"Lupei," he said out loud not yet familiar at the vocal interaction that he had with the artificial intelligence system, "Are you able to zoom in on those images?"

The images were of two crashed UFA transport ships; one as it burned on the ground and another that had clearly crash landed into a buckled wreck. But, it was the people in the images that disturbed Hughes more.

"Lupei, can you identify those individuals?" Hughes asked a little shocked to see the image of Lupei as she appeared on the screen. Another aspect that he would need to get used to.

"There are two IA5 combat units, FE-143-33 and SX-114-62. The other three are all Australian citizens before the instigation of the Federation: Harry Lockley, farmer, Harvey Amsterdam, journalist at the The Gazette and Professor Mitchell Reed, former Globe Corp lead developer of their robotics and artificial intelligence program," said Lupei.

Seeing Harvey Amsterdam reminded him of Ginger Amsterdam. Hughes had already confirmed that Ginger Amsterdam had been successfully transitioned into the citizens program. But, her husband was not on the K29K list.

"The Farmer, The Chronicler and The Librarian. So, this is where the riddle of The Oracle begins," said Hughes to himself.

"Mr. President, my analysis of the conflict shows that the two IA5 units were not connected to Central Control. However, I detected the definite signature of an artificial intelligence system controlling their systems."

"Really, that can only be the work of, Professor Reed. What have you done you fool?" Reed had been personally installed into his position within Globe Corp by Hughes and he considered it a personal insult in the way Reed had left the company. So much so, that Hughes had poured a significant amount of energy and risk into extracting Reed safely from the fate that would have been bestowed on a traitor of the Long March.

"I will continue to analyse these signatures and advise once I have been able to interpret what was controlling them."

"Yes, yes. Very well. Report back to me only once you have a full report."

"Yes, Sir. In the mean time, do you want me to send in another IA5 squad?"

Hughes contemplated this question. Under usual circumstances he would not show an ounce of leniency at such disobedience. However, as this operation had been under his private direction there would be no need for any show of consequence. His main goal was to ensure the safety of Reed and it seemed that requirement had been fulfilled and Hughes thought that he may also prove useful given that he was outside the confines of the Federation, "Ah, no. Let us shelve this operation for the time being, Lupei," said Hughes, "And Lupei, ensure that Professor Reed is marked in your records as deceased."

"Very well, Mr. President."

At that moment, Viceroy to Australia, John Payne, had entered the Presidential quarters. Hughes had anointed Payne his title albeit with apprehension after pressure from the Chinese. It had seemed that Payne had been doing a little bit of political campaigning on his own behalf; however, Hughes was sceptical of his motivations. There had been very few occasions where the two saw eye-to-eye and Hughes was weary that his appointment was granted on the concession of loyalty to the Chinese. In other words, he was to be Hughes' minder in his tenure as President.

"Ah, Viceroy Payne, how good to see you. How are you enjoying your new title?" said Hughes. The fact was that Hughes had campaigned for complete liquidation of any form of government in Australia. However, as Hughes had stopped short of complete annihilation of the population it was decided that the military alone would not be able to command a civilian population.

"Well, thank you, Mr. President. I have also been awarded the title of State Secretary and will be your chief negotiator on foreign affairs," replied Payne.

A part of his Presidency deal with the Chinese was that all offices in the administration would be appointed by the Federation Council that was chaired by the Vice President.

"Well, it looks like you will be sticking around after all, John."

"I understand that you and I have had our differences; however, if I could speak openly, Mr. President?"

"Of course, John. If we are to be working together then as Australian's we will recognise the discourse of free speech and freedom of opinion. If only amongst each other's private company."

"Thank you, Mr. President. As I was saying, I know that we have had our differences over the course of our political careers. However, given the makeup of the new Federation I wanted to assure you that I am fully committed to the cause."

"Thank you, John. In the interests of moving this Federation in the right direction I will render the past invalid. We are all working toward a greater cause now. But I offer this warning; I will only accept complete loyalty within this office. Your word will only be granted as trustworthy when it proves itself to be so. Am I understood?"

"Of course, Mr. President," replied Payne, "I have also come to inform you that your wife has requested leave to return to Australia. She has been reported in Singapore as becoming increasingly agitated."

This was typical of Gabrielle. She had become a creature of habit and the whole affair would have been very taxing on her indeed. The last thing Hughes needed was for her to start making noise. She was very good at the political game even though she protested to show no taste for it; and, given that she had already made her position clear on the actions Hughes had taken, she could become quite counter-productive to Hughes' pursuits.

"Grant her leave to return to the homestead of her fathers' winery estate in the Hunter Valley," announced Hughes, "It is the only place that she has ever wanted to be. I'm sure that the agricultural ministry that will be under your direction, Viceroy Payne, will ensure she is looked after."

"Most certainly, Mr. President," replied Payne, "I will see to the arrangements personally. We have also been contacted by the United States administration. An envoy has been sent containing Secretary of State, Bill Patrick, to hold critical discussions on our current predicament. He is currently en-route and is requesting permission to come aboard."

"Really. And what does he think he would hope to achieve?"

"He says that he holds the key to the entrance to the doorway of Amaru Meru," replied Payne coolly, "That is, after all, why we are here, is it not?"

Payne knew very well why they were there. After all, he was a former board member of Globe Corp. And, in effect, this was Globe

Corp's show. The facts were that the same radio signal that they had picked up all those years ago in space also existed, as Hughes had said to the United Nations Security Council, in one place on this planet. And that place was Lake Titicaca. They had been able to locate it because every twenty-three years there was a signal sent from somewhere underneath the lake. The local mythology suggested that Puerta de Hayu Marka, gate of the Gods, was the entrance into the Temple of Illumination. But while the mythology of a primitive civilisation made grandiose claims of some ethereal connection to explain that which they did not understand; Globe Corp had been able to ground what these meant into real terms. And, the reality was, that this bastion of knowledge, as the myth claimed to be, was more than likely some ancient computer left here by an intelligent visitor from another planet thousands of years ago that still knew the number to dial home. They had surmised that the device must have been located somewhere under the lake; and, while it seemed the visitors had left breadcrumbs on the trail to enter this location, over the years the instruction manual had become lost. So, their plan was to utilise the pillars of science and manpower to quickly locate its location. However, if Patrick had the keys to the front door then this was a better outcome than what Hughes had predicted.

"I suppose, that we better hear him out," said Hughes, "After all, we do not wish to start a war amongst ourselves. It is best that we hold out our resources for a more formidable foe. Lupei, please grant the US Secretary of State permission to come aboard and issue orders for the military to stand down."

"Yes, Sir. And Mr. President, I have received contact from a Mr. Charles Harrison on your private line, Sir. He would like to speak with you."

Finally, Harrison had been cutting it close, "Yes, very well. Please put him through immediately," Hughes turned to Payne, "That will be all, Viceroy. Please see to our guest and make him welcome."

"With pleasure, Mr. President," replied Payne as he turned and exited the Presidential quarters the image of Charles Harrison came up on the screen.

"Charles, this better be good. Tell me you've got something," said Hughes.

"Robert, I wish I had better news," began Harrison, "It seems from what I have learnt that the Americans have taken over the operation of Globe Corp and I have had to go into hiding. From what I understand, George Underwood has been lost, he had chartered a plane that serviced a secret US military base, god knows why. When we heard of this our plan was to pick him up there; however, there has been no sign of the plane thus far. Unfortunately, I have been cut off from our man in Venezuela so I am presuming that the Americans have him as well."

"So you have no news for me. You can't tell me what will happen when we turn on this device?"

"I'm afraid not, Robert," replied Harrison.

"Then we have failed to prevent what is to come," said Hughes angrily, "We had failed to prevent my country from being destroyed and now we have failed to prevent bringing on a future full of terrors that god only knows will bring."

Hughes paced the room running his fingers through the hair that he had left. The end game was near, he thought to himself.

"Robert, listen to me. It is not too late. We don't need to go through with this. We can still prevent it. The Oracle had said that together we would prevent the world from total annihilation. I still believe in that possibility."

"This whole thing was brought on by The Oracle, Charles. It was his prophecy that sent us on this crusade from the beginning. He gave us the belief that because we knew the future, that we could prevent it somehow. We only succeeded in postponing the inevitable it would seem."

"What will you do, Robert?" asked Harrison.

"What we must, Charles. What we must," replied Hughes, "Good luck, Charles."

"Good luck, Robert."

The image of Harrison's face cut out from the screen. Hughes sat on the edge of his Presidential desk and ran his finger nail over the top of the bench. They must do what they must, he thought. Unfortunately, for Hughes, that meant preparing for war. A war he had tried so desperately to avoid.

Chapter 55

"Helicopter 452 this is Conqueror control, you have been cleared for landing in hanger two."

Tim Marshall listened to the conversation the pilot was having with the control tower of an airship the size of which he had never seen in his life. As they had come on its position as it hovered in the air there had been some type of battle going on that he could see from a distance. A battle which had apparently halted with their arrival; however, Marshall knew that it halted because his travelling companion was the Secretary of State to the United States.

Marshall had learned that they were on a political mission. He had learned of the situation in Asia and also learned that his own country, New Zealand, had joined in the United Federation of Asia. In reality, it was something that he could not believe was ever possible. But, here it was. His thoughts were of his family back home and how they were coping and he had asked that he be given permission to attempt to contact his parents; however, he learned again that all communication in and out of the new Federation had been cut off.

"That's impossible!" Marshall had said.

"Not entirely," had said the man in suspenders, "My guess is that they have developed a complicated computer virus that acts as a firewall against all forms of digital communication. Satellite, telephone, mobile towers, internet. The works."

"I'm sorry, I didn't get your name?" replied Marshall. The presence of this untidy man had been bothering Marshall throughout their journey.

"This is Dr. Wilfred Escorner," announced Rogers, "He is lead robotics and artificial intelligence developer for Globe Corp."

"Artificial intelligence?" said Marshall surprised, "I didn't think such things existed."

"Much has been going on while you've been out there in the wilderness, Mr. Marshall," replied Rogers, "Now, what can you tell me about what it is you found out there. And this time, I want the truth."

Marshall had told Rogers about Georgie Davenport's discoveries. He didn't see much point in holding out at this stage. Knowledge, it would seem, would be the only leverage point he had left in his arsenal. However, their reaction did not seem to garner much enthusiasm.

"I was hoping that I could present these findings to Charles Harrison," Marshall had said when he finished giving them the rundown, "I think that he has the answer to what the catalyst is that will cause the next ice age. You see, Davenport seemed to think that the unknown element was the key. I believe that Harrison knows what this element is and he had employed me to find out the consequences when whatever that is gets activated."

"Well, that will be impossible," replied Rogers, "Harrison is now working counter to the goals of Globe Corp. He has been for quite some time and it is our belief that he wished to sabotage the greatest discovery of mankind."

"I thought that discovering the tree of life was the greatest discovery of all time?" said Marshall.

"Unfortunately, Mr. Marshall, Globe Corp does not wish to publish your discovery. Nor will any of your team I'm afraid," said Bill Patrick sitting forward in his seat, "You see, they all accepted the handsome payout Globe Corp has offered them. So, it would seem that the only other people that know about this are in this helicopter. No, the greatest discovery of all time is not the finding of some old tree. It is the discovery of life on other planets. It is the discovery of intelligent life forms in the universe and it is that which Harrison wanted to keep from the human race. Think about it, Mr. Marshall. Why did he take you off the path that you so clearly were on? You found the inscription in that cave at Easter Island; tell me, what did it say to you?"

Marshall looked at the Secretary of State in the eye. How did they know all this, he thought, "When a man stands in the gates of the gods he will gain entry into the temple of illumination."

"Not just a man, Mr. Marshall," said Patrick, "What type of man?"

"The Oracle," replied Marshall, "But, there is no Oracle? He doesn't exist."

"It would seem then, Mr. Marshall," said Rogers, "That Harrison kept much from you. The Oracle does exist, very much so."

"How do you know?" questioned Marshall.

"Throughout history there have been many people with these gifts of foresight," said Escorner, "But more recently we have been able to locate these people through DNA sampling. We have identified a strand on the DNA sequence that is normally dormant in you and me but is active in people with The Oracle ability. However, most have not been able to explain it or even control it which is why this has mainly existed without those people truly knowing they have it."

"We believe that dormant part is the key that will open the gates to the gods," said Patrick, "And, Mr. Marshall, who do you think you will meet on the other side?"

Marshall felt a tingling sensation course through his spine. So, this is what Harrison had been hiding. The true reason behind the tree. Harrison must have known that when the gate was open that the world would not continue on as usual once it was closed. He understood that this was not some kind of miraculous event of the divine; that it was mechanical and would more than likely involve some kind of consequence that tipped the scales in a direction from where we could never return.

"Truth in myth," Marshall said aloud as he was staring out the window and he noticed that they were flying over a large body of water; however, that body of water was inland, "This is Lake Titicaca, isn't it? We're going to the doorway of Amaru Meru."

"Yes, that is where the gate is located," replied Rogers.

"People have said that when you stand in the doorway carved into the rock that a strange sensation, like an energy force, flows through you. And, if you're right Dr. Escorner, I'm guessing that it isn't merely something hippy's do to get kicks. The doorway is analysing your DNA. It wants to know if you are this Oracle. And, you want me to walk through the doorway, don't you?" said Marshall.

"You are the most qualified," said Patrick.

"The facts are that we don't know for sure what is on the other side of the gate. As you have proven yourself as being more than capable in these matters it would be prudent for you to be the first to make contact," said Rogers.

"Yes, but you are forgetting one important thing. I'm not The Oracle."

"That is something that we are well aware of, Mr. Marshall," replied Rogers, "However, Dr. Escorner here has been working on something that will help you overcome that little problem. Doctor?"

"Yes, we will insert a drug which will stimulate the dormant DNA strand for a brief period. Just enough for a mechanical scanner to provide you entry," said Escorner.

"And what happens when the effect wears off?" asked Marshall.

"We didn't say that it was a perfect plan, Mr. Marshall," said Patrick, "But just think about what you could accomplish. You'd be the first human being to make contact with another intelligent life form. It has, after all, been the overall aim of your work, Mr. Marshall. To work out why we are here. Maybe whatever is on the other side will help you understand that pursuit."

As the helicopter slowly descended into hangar two that opened up on top of the hull of the port side of the mothership, The Conqueror, Marshall had the strangest feeling that he had finally come to the end of a long journey. Whatever happened from this point on would be totally new and more than likely unexpected. He would be walking into the abyss where no one in living memory had entered and he strangely felt nothing but jubilation. Patrick had been right, this was his ultimate aim. An aim that he had long believed the further he had dug deeper and deeper into the mythologies of the worlds. A myth of his own that he could finally lay claim to existing in truth.

PART V

Chapter 56

Convincing Jimmy Condor that George was a required part of her luggage was not as difficult as Molly Whitaker had thought it would be. She thought that she may have had to lay on more charm than she was capable of and would have had to retort to physical persuasion; but, thankfully, it wasn't needed. Her story must have been convincing enough that George was her travelling bodyguard that Jimmy had even agreed that she would have been crazy to go it out there alone with a bunch of isolated young men on her hands.

The unpleasantries aside, Jimmy had been telling her stories of his trips into the mountains; how he liked going fishing and hunting away from civilisation. He grew up on a strict diet of meat and three veg and church on a Sunday and yet all he wanted to do was to get away from it all whenever he could. Flying was the next best thing and it allowed him the luxury of convincing his mother that he was holding down a permanent job and doing something with his life while affording him the ability to break away whenever he wanted.

"Yep, it's a world away from the world up here. And out there," said Jimmy pointing to the open terrain of ice and snow, "Is another world entirely. So, where you from, my quiet friend in the back there?"

George was seated in the back of the plane while Molly rode up front with Jimmy with the seats a little too close together for comfort and George was unfortunately bailed up with Jimmy's cargo along with their own bags.

"Oh, Florida mainly," replied George.

"What was it that got you lured into the bodyguard business?"

Molly had told Jimmy that she was born in Las Vegas and had travelled with her father after her mother died hopping from base-to-base. She got into the exotic dancing game and returned to Las Vegas after she left her father while he was still on duty when she turned eighteen.

"I'm an associate of the ladies employer," George replied coolly.

"Well, I'm sure it's much more exciting than being a pilot. I suppose it aint all bad. You do get to see some interesting stuff when you're up here; I can tell 'ya!" said Jimmy.

"Like what?" asked Molly.

"Well, you'll see for yourself when you get on the ground but this military base is something else. I mean, there are things there that you aint seen in your life. And big, this thing is bigger than Texas."

"What mainly goes on down there?" asked George.

"Well, they don't tell me much. I really just run supplies up from Anchorage. But, every now-and-again, one of them soldiers gets a leave pass for the weekend and they come back with me to Anchorage. And after a couple of beers their lips get a bit loose and they tell me that they've been building something there that if the folks knew about it they would be absolutely gobsmacked. All in our nations interest for security I'm told. But seeing what I saw last night it sure as hell better be somethin' that'll blow that thing from the sky."

Molly looked out from the cockpit of the plane. The plane was an old rust bucket that had seen better days and Molly wondered how on earth it was even given clearance to fly. The vastness of the ice that seemed to blanket the earth below gave her even more cause for concern and she questioned why it was that they now seemed to be making a descent.

"Jimmy, why are we going down?"

"Oh, this old thing needs a rest now and again. There's a post just up ahead where I stop off and make sure everything is in order before I take off for the longest part of the journey. There aint nothing out here between this post and the base so if we need to go down then we all out on our own. No radio contact and GPS is practically useless so it's better to be safe than sorry, I say. Don't worry, little lady, we'll be back up in the air as soon as you know it."

There was something in the way that Jimmy smiled at her that left her questioning who this guy really was? George didn't seem to have a problem with him and maybe it was just her woman's intuition showing that alerted Molly and steered her away from creeps; but, she could not drown out the voice in her head that was singing 'Alert! Alert!' in C major.

As they came into a landing that was really quite smooth given the location there was not much else she could see but snow and a small shed lined with rusting metal sheets. There weren't any other people there and no ground crew to speak of and as the plane came to a stop a few meters from the small shed she saw too late when Jimmy had reached quickly into his pocket and produced a pistol pointing it at Molly.

"Jimmy!" screamed Molly, "What the hell is that?"

"You know very well what this thing is!"

"Yes, but why have you pointed it at me? George?"

She heard George stand and move toward the front of the plane in a quick movement but Jimmy had turned and pointed the weapon at him.

"Don't you move there, boy!" commanded Jimmy, "Or I will plug you where you stand. Are you packing?" he asked Underwood who stammered.

"Well, no."

"Just as I thought. Some bodyguard you be. I mean, what sort of bodyguard doesn't go around armed? Huh? Do you think I was stupid now? You don't think that I would know a sting when I see one. What are you, spies for the Russians? Or that new Asian Federation thing? Now, you two clearly have some kind of story whipped up to get me to take you out to this base and I'm goin' to find me out what for?"

"Jimmy," said George, "You've got this thing all wrong-"

But it was too late. In that moment Molly had seen an opening. It was small and she had no idea as to where the instinct had come from but she could hardly feel herself as her right hand whipped up quickly and she struck Jimmy across the nose as she tried to disarm him with her left hand. Unfortunately, Jimmy managed to get a shot off as they struggled with the weapon and in the recoil she sensed his hand loosen on the grip and she plied it away from his hands pistol whipping Jimmy out cold in the one movement. It was then that she saw George lying on the floor of the plane holding the left side of his stomach with his hands red with blood.

"George!" Molly screamed. But there was no one there to hear her and as she struggled to get into the back of the plane and cradle George's head she was acutely aware of the complete whiteness that surrounded her contrasting the red of the blood that was oozing from George's side and how in this place that was sure to mean certain death for her friend, her partner, her love.

Chapter 57

"And if you're wrong?" President Robert Hughes asked as he paced standing on the bridge of the UFA mothership, The Conqueror, while a team of military personnel worked at various computer terminals monitoring the ship like an intensive care patient. He was standing with his back to the United States Secretary of State, Bill Patrick who along with two men from Globe Corp, Norman Rogers and Dr. Wilfred Escorner were attempting to persuade Hughes to allow their man, Tim Marshall, an archaeologist and mythology expert to enter the doorway of Amaru Meru.

"He's the best man for the job," replied Patrick who sat smugly with an air of confidence that Hughes did not appreciate. The facts were that it appeared that the United States had outplayed Hughes on this occasion. They had infiltrated Globe Corp after many years of being on the sidelines and it appeared at great expense. When Hughes was on the board there had been many attempts by promising and dignified individuals well connected in the United States who had sort nomination for the board and all had been resisted. Globe Corp was bank rolled by the great pillars of Asian business and they had always been sceptical of the motivations of the United States. They also were weary of what they would do with the information that Globe Corp had obtained and it seemed now that scepticism had been justified. It would be important for Hughes at this moment to lay bare his tactical advantage. The infiltration, while inconvenient, was not entirely unmanageable and Hughes had been considering his next course of action since Harrison's efforts had failed to produce a positive result.

"Your offer does not seem to me to be worth a hell of a lot, Bill," said Hughes, "You have come here offering the key when I have the ability to bash down the door. But, you want to share in the spoils of the loot."

"It's not like that, Mr. President," replied Patrick, "All we want to do is share in this work load together. Now, you can't tell me that you have all the bases covered when it comes to the management and transition of society in a world that might be experiencing the greatest social upheaval of our time. You need us."

"We're not asking for your help, Bill," said Hughes sharply, "You have been left in the dark because of your failure to share in the world affairs for decades. You had your time and you blew it. Plain and simple. There were new powers rising up all over the place; but, when you had the chance, you did nothing. It was greed, Bill, that destroyed any confidence anyone had in your ability to lead the people of this world to greatness. We will take over that mantle now. The Federation will bring peace where the States only brought corruption. We are not for sale, Bill. Now, here is what is going to happen. We will allow Mr. Marshall to enter the gate. As a New Zealand citizen he is now a member of the Federation. Dr. Escorner here will carry out his end of the plan as you have described and you will be free to leave. We appreciate your assistance and it will be duly noted that you were willing to ally with the Federation when the time came."

"This almost sounds like a threat, Robert?" said Patrick standing, "No one threatens the Secretary of State to the United States of America. This is an outrage!"

Hughes turned and faced Patrick, "You are not the biggest bull in the arena anymore, Bill. I suggest you start acting like it. Infiltrating the upper echelons of Globe Corp may have been one thing; but, this is a whole new ball game."

"Mr. President," said Rogers clearing his throat, "But Globe Corp is already heavily involved with the Federation. Our investments have been significant and it is believed that United States may have something to offer."

"And your participation in the affairs of the Federation has been generously compensated," replied Hughes quickly. He was weary of what tactics Rogers may have employed. Globe Corp was heavily entrenched in the entire operation. The last thing that they needed was for them to cause trouble in these early days even though the percentage of ownership that the United States had in Globe Corp would not have been significant to enact a wholesale change of leadership or direction.

"If the States are willing to cooperate with the Federation," continued Hughes, "Then, in time, I cannot see any reason why we would not allow you entry into the Federation. But, right now, we can't afford any mistakes. If you have any more information that you would like to share in the future we will continue to show our appreciation. Gentlemen, if you will excuse me, I will escort Dr. Escorner back to the lounge where Mr. Marshall is waiting. I will have Viceroy Payne escort you back to your transport. Thank you for your time."

Hughes nodded at the two IA5 units that had been standing guard and they turned and followed him out from the bridge and down the corridor with Dr. Escorner in tow. It had been just as Hughes had imagined, they had nothing. They were merely hoping that he would capitulate to their wishes.

"I hope you know what you are doing!" said Payne as Hughes past him in the corridor, "That isn't just anyone you're pissing off in there."

"Leave such matters to me, Viceroy," replied Hughes, "These are moments that one needs a strong spine."

Chapter 58

Molly Whitaker had been lucky of two things. Firstly, she had been training hard recently in the gym and had managed to build her core body strength quite significantly. This allowed her to be able to drag both the unconscious Jimmy Condor and the bleeding George Underwood from the cockpit of the plane and into the small rusting shed. Inside the shed she found it quite well appointed. There was a small pot bellied wood heater with several bags of coal sitting beside it; running water and a stretcher bed. There were boxes stacked on the far wall where Molly found a first-aid kit marked with the emblem of the US Army Corp.

The second thing was that when she inspected George she found that the bullet Jimmy had fired went right through meaning she didn't have to go digging around for the bullet. Also, it didn't pass through any major organs. However, the bleeding was her main concern and she managed to dress both sides of the wound and gave George a shot of antibiotics. The bleeding had knocked George out and she put him on the stretcher to rest.

Molly then turned her attention to Jimmy. She needed answers, most importantly; she needed to find out how far the military base was from this station and if they could be raised on the radio. While she had done the best she could for George the only way to know for sure was to get him into a medical team who could monitor and care for him. It was her primary concern. She had started the fire with the lighter she had obtained from Escorner and the coals had been glowing for some time. She filled a glass of ice cold water and threw it onto the face of Jimmy who woke up spluttering and shaking the water from his face. He noticed that his hands and feet were tied and he tried to wriggle himself out of the knots.

"Let me go!" Jimmy yelled at Molly.

Molly held up a piece of glowing coal with a set of tongs from the fire up close under Jimmy's face and he reeled back trying to get away from its hot glow.

"Get it away from me, get it away from me!"

"I'll get it away when I'm good and ready. Got that?" said Molly enjoying the feeling of watching him squirm.

"Yes, yes."

"Good. Now. Tell me exactly where we are?"

"No, I don't know where we are. They don't allow me to keep maps."

"You're lying to me, Jimmy," replied Molly as she brought in the glowing coal closer to his face, "This is your warning. Every time you lie to me I'm going to scold you with a piece of hot coals. Do you understand me, Jimmy? And Jimmy, we've got bags and bags of coal so the more you lie to me the worst this will get. Now, I'll ask again. Jimmy, where are we?"

"We're about three clicks east of the base," Jimmy replied.

"That's better, Jimmy. That didn't hurt did it? Now, my next question is, are the military likely to come to this post?"

"They always see my plane. They'll be here shortly."

Molly brought in the hot coal and pressed into Jimmy's cheek. He screamed out in agony, "Stop! Stop! Stop!"

"Then don't lie to me, Jimmy! You know that I don't like lying."

"No, they won't come down here until they see my plane take off. I run contraband. Drugs. Alcohol. You name it. For my reward, they give me Army surplus. Sometimes, I need to stop over once in a while because the weather is too bad for me to take off so I keep this place just in case."

Which explains why the shed was so well stocked with supplies, thought Molly, "How do you contact them?"

"I don't-" Molly moved in with another strike of the hot coal on the other cheek this time to which Jimmy screamed, "Okay, I have an emergency channel. But, they would never come. It would expose their whole operation. If I died out here they would just go and get themselves another pilot. There's enough of us out here and there's very little pay for what we do."

"Do they know that I am coming?"

Jimmy hesitated a moment and Molly brought in the hot coal, "Wait!" Jimmy pleaded, "I told them that there was a woman looking for them and they told me to bring you up here and they would deal with you."

"Deal with me?"

"Kill you, knock you off! What else do you think it means."

"What are they doing up here, Jimmy?"

"All I know is what I see. But I aint seen nothin' like this before. One time, I got stuck out here for two whole weeks. I was starten' to get a little cabin fever so I went out trapsin' around the hills up behind us. I found me this door in the ground. But, it weren't no door you see. More like a porthole I fancy. So I duck me head in and I see what looks like coffins lined up as far as the eye could see. Now, they were connected up to all kind of computers and such and there's military people walking all over. I got myself outa there as quick as I came and I told myself that I did not want to know what it was they got goin' on out here after that."

"Can you tell me where this was? George might die if he doesn't get medical attention. You don't want the death of another man's life on your hands, do you Jimmy?"

"Ah, hell, no. It's easy to find. You just follow a direct line up the hill. When you get to the top you'll see what I mean."

Molly had to risk it for George's sake. The military wouldn't turn their backs on two citizens of the United States in need. Even if it was some type of secret military base.

"Dakini! Dakini!" George suddenly yelled out in his sleep. Molly went over to him and felt his forehead. He was burning up. The blood loss may have been too much for the antibiotics to take effect. Molly filled up another glass of water and poured it over Jimmy's face over the burnt patches of his cheeks.

"Do you have snow gear stashed in here?"

"Yeah, of course. Behind that large barrel over there."

Molly went over and found a large snow jacket, pants and snow shoes. She began to put them on.

"What are you going to do?" asked Jimmy.

"I'm going to go up to that facility and ask them for help. That's what I'm going to do," Molly answered.

"Do you think that them guys are going to help you? I know that it's best to keep your nose out of these situations. I already told you that they want to kill you and now you want to go walking right into their fire. You listen, you let me free and I'll take you to where ever you want me to take you."

"Yeah, sure, Jimmy. Just like you took me last time and you shot my friend. I don't think so," Molly had put on the snow jacket and was clipping on the snow shoes, "You just stay put here and I'll decide what I'm going to do with you when I get back."

Molly left to more objections from Jimmy. But, her mind was made up. She had no interest in whatever it was Jimmy had going on out here. Her only motivation was to help George. It had been her only motivation throughout this whole ordeal and she wasn't going to see him die in vain.

Behind the shed the hill rose quite steeply and in most parts the snow was fresh and made it difficult to walk on with the snow shoes as Molly dropped a couple of feet underneath with each step. The going was cold and her face felt like it was about to freeze. She would intermittently turn herself to look at the shed behind her to make sure that she didn't go off track and also make sure that the plane was still there. While he may have been untrustworthy, Jimmy was their only ticket out of the mountains. He knew this; but, he also knew that Molly had the gun and when she looked about the shed she didn't see any rifles or guns of any kind. Presumably, that was what Jimmy meant by Army surplus but they were useless sitting out here in the middle of nowhere so he must have taken them with him on his return trips to Anchorage.

Unfortunately, it was starting to get dark and while Jimmy had said that he had spent many nights out in the shed the reality was that it was no place to be when you had a gunshot wound to the stomach. George hadn't looked so good just then and she had wondered what or who this 'Dakini' was that he had mentioned in his reverie. It meant that Molly had to work faster and as she came to the top of the hill, exhausted and in dire need of water, she noticed across on the flat that there was some kind of square concrete looking structure protruding through the level of the snow. She walked up to it with some caution, drawing the pistol from her pocket just in case there were sentries standing guard.

When Molly got closer to the concrete box she quickly realised that she was the only person there as the snow was clean of footprints. She took off her snow shoes and stepped up the small metal rungs that were attached to the concrete box slipping a couple times before she made it to the top. On top she noticed that the porthole that Jimmy had been talking about was a hatch door. It was circular in size about three feet wide and had a wheel above that Molly assumed was used to open it. She tried with all her might to move it but found that it wouldn't budge. Either it was locked from the inside or the ice had sealed it shut. Molly looked around for something that would give her leverage to be able to open it up but the area was baron with nothing but snow and ice.

She had decided to head back down to the shed when she heard over the prevailing winds a sound of a spluttering engine. She firstly thought that there was some type of vehicle coming for them but then quickly realised that the sound was the engine of Jimmy's airplane. Jimmy had escaped! There was no telling what it was that he would do to them and George was all on his own down there probably still unconscious. Molly jumped off the concrete box and desperately re-connected the snowshoes bounding down the side of the hill using the snowshoes as skis but the going was not speedy at all. When she had made it down the bottom of the hill the airplane had turned at the top of the ice runway and began to speed up the engine for takeoff. Molly ran across into the middle of the air field and stood in front of the plane and she could see the red face of Jimmy seemingly yelling at her. Molly took out the hand gun and levelled it at the airplane. She squeezed off two rounds that didn't seem to have any effect at all as the plane kept coming closer until it was almost on her and she had to jump to the ground to avoid being hit. As she turned around in the snow the air-plane took off and she squeezed off a couple more rounds in frustration at the thought that they were stuck.

Chapter 59

Tim Marshall stood in front of the doorway of Amaru Meru; or, *Puerta de Hayu Marka* as the locals called it that stood on the Peruvian side of Lake Titicaca high up in the Andes. It was around four in the morning and the sky was clear overhead as the surrounding rocky area was dotted with flood lights, computer equipment and robotic guards from the United Federation of Asia. The flood lights highlighted the image of the doorway that had been carved from solid rock; and, Marshall could not help to be overwhelmed by its size. Dr. Wilfred Escorner was setting up to administer a type of synthetic concoction that would alter his DNA by stimulating dormant parts of the DNA strands in an attempt to trick some kind of alien gatekeeper that Marshall was The Oracle.

Why Marshall had accepted the offer to be the first to go through the doorway from the Secretary of State, Bill Patrick and Rogers from Globe Corp was beyond him. At the time, he was caught up in joining the dots of the Harrison affair and the possibility that he would finally see an end to his pursuits. It would be the feather of his career, an achievement so great that not one of his peers that had existed before him would ever be able to equal. And yet, the risks were high. Marshall did not know what would lie beyond the doorway and while he was experienced at overcoming his fear of the unknown this would be something else entirely. In his previous experiences, he had known that whatever lay beyond a stone wall or hidden in a cave was somehow touched by man. He could then, with some certainty, predict that his experience would be conceivably of human design and nature and thus familiar. However, walking through this doorway would be completely alien; he could only imagine that the experience too would also be one that he could not imagine and he was beginning to regret he accepted the offer.

Previously when Marshall was up in the UFA mothership, The Conqueror, and before President Robert Hughes entered the lounge where he had been waiting he had been trying to speak with the robotic guard. He was, however, stalled by what described itself as an artificial intelligence unit going by the name of Lupei who advised him that his questions were classified. The only thing that she would tell Marshall was that the robotic guard was called an IA5 combat unit and that it was, in fact, human. The irony was not lost on Marshall that the mechanical being and what he was about to do seemed to be equally foreign. It had seemed that overnight the world had become a place of the future. The ship, the robotic guard, artificial intelligence; it was like he had been stuck in the wilderness for so long that the world had sped up and technology had advanced by generations.

"Please leave us," said President Robert Hughes to the IA5 unit as he entered the room and it complied without question to his order leaving both Marshall and Hughes alone in the room, "Mr. Marshall, I believe that you are in possession of some information that you were holding for Charles Harrison."

Marshall was a little stunned and wondered how it was Hughes knew about his work with Harrison; however, it was conceivable that he had been updated by Rogers and Patrick.

"Sir, I'm not sure what you mean?" he lied. Marshall was not going to offload such vital information as that without first testing the waters.

"I can understand your apprehension, Mr. Marshall," said Hughes with a smile, "However, you must believe me when I say that Harrison was working with me."

"You said he was working with you?" stated Marshall, "That would mean that you no longer are his ally."

"I made contact with him earlier; however, he has since gone underground in fear of his life. I can assure you, that it is not me he is scared of."

"Rogers?" said Marshall.

"Most likely. You see, I know all about the tree. I know about your discoveries in the Easter Islands. I know why you have agreed to volunteer to go through the doorway; however, there was one last piece of crucial information that you were collecting for Harrison and I need to know what it was before I give you permission to go off into the unknown."

"Okay, perhaps I told you what we learnt from the tree is there will be an event that will bring on the next ice age. I think that the event that Harrison knew about was when the doorway was opened that there would be some type of consequence. He just didn't know what it could be."

"Harrison was charged with the responsibility of finding me a reason why it is we should not open that doorway. You are right. We did fear that there may be consequences that we could not foresee. But, from what you tell me that consequences seem to be minuscule to what we could gain."

"Some would disagree."

"And do you disagree, Mr. Marshall? Personally, it is my belief that once you walk through that doorway that we will be confronted with an adversary that we could have never comprehended. That whatever it is that is waiting has been waiting for something to happen before it acted. Think about it, they put this doorway here. They put it there so we could find it. They told us about it, even though our ancestors could not fully understand it; but, our ancestors told stories about it so that one day we could remember. So, that people like you, Mr. Marshall, would be able to understand the truth behind the myth."

"So, we don't go through the doorway, simple," said Marshall, "It stays hidden and we don't need to confront these things that you say."

"I wish that were true, Mr. Marshall. You see, if it is not us that does this then someone else will. Someone else that may not share our common values and will use this as a tool of tyranny. Unless I have tangible evidence that proves if we open this doorway that the world is in jeopardy instead of speculation then I'm afraid there will always be someone who wants to take the risk. No, this is our burden to bear. For the sake of our children's children. I only ask you this, that when the time comes, whatever you confront on the other side, you tell them to come. You tell them to come here and confront us in battle. We are ready for them."

"Excuse me?" Marshall wasn't sure what it was that was being asked of him. His main plan had been to offer peace not to invoke a war.

"That is an order from your President, Mr. Marshall. We will not be subservient to any species whatsoever. I cannot stress how important it is that this be carried out precisely."

Now, standing in front of the doorway, Marshall still did not know what it was he would do when he got to the other side. He had agreed with Hughes, if it wasn't us that walked through the doorway then who would it be? However, he was conflicted between what he thought was right and what it was that Hughes wanted him to do. He decided that he would make his decision once he walked through the doorway and arrived on the other side. There were just too many variables to consider and Marshall felt that he did not have all the facts. There was something about the way Hughes had said, *'we are ready for them'*, that gave Marshall the idea that there was more to this that was already known.

"Okay," said Escorner, "You're all set. Are you ready?"

Marshall nodded his head, "As ready as I'll ever be."

"Good. Now, this might feel a little funny but I doubt that it will hurt."

"You *doubt* that it will hurt? No offence, Doc, but that doesn't exactly fill me with confidence," Marshall replied.

"The parts of the DNA we are trying to stimulate are not physiological. In a sense, they are linked to the brain and if anything I think that you will experience a type of hallucination. Is that better?"

"Better," replied Marshall, "Let's just get this thing done. But can you do one thing for me? If this thing goes south can you have someone contact my parents and tell them what really happened here? Don't give them some hogwash story. Just the truth."

"You bet," replied Escorner as he pressed a button on a terminal that had been hooked up to Marshall by an intravenous drip, "Good luck."

Marshall closed his eyes as he felt a warm sensation flow through his right arm. There was a moment of panic where he couldn't draw a breath into his lungs and he thought that he was choking to death as the synthetic concoction began to circulate through his system; however, it subsided quickly and he felt himself calming down as his mind was seemingly detached from his body. When Marshall opened his eyes he saw the entire world in a blur. He could see Escorner standing beside him but he looked like he was moving in slow motion as Marshall was pulling off the cords that were attached to his body and an overwhelming sensation took hold of him as he focused his vision on the doorway of Amaru Meru. While the light from the floodlights seemed to dim there was a bright light that was emanating from the small doorway that was not there before. Marshall began to move toward the doorway; however, his brain was finding it hard to communicate with his legs and the movement seemed to take forever. It was then that he first saw a man that he had never seen. The man seemed to appear from the bright light of the doorway and he walked toward Marshall who felt the need to run away but couldn't. The man kept coming closer to Marshall until his face consumed his field of vision and then it was almost like he passed straight through him. Was it an apparition, thought Marshall? He then remembered Escorner saying that it was possible that he would experience hallucinations until the thought was wiped away by a voice inside Marshall's head.

"The Oracle is with you," said the voice and Marshall somehow was able to regain control of his arms and legs and the urge to walk toward the doorway returned with greater power until he was standing before it and he walked into the opening where he saw the golden disc that was already placed in the door. This was the missing piece of the puzzle and Marshall strained to consider the notion that the reason that the disc was not in its place in the cave on Easter Island was that it was already found and placed in the spot where it was meant to be. This also confirmed his fear that someone else had already walked through this doorway. However, Marshall was resolute and he put his hand on the door which released a magnificent energy and he was lost amongst the brightness of an all consuming red light that removed Marshall from the physical world.

Chapter 60

Twilight had fallen on the Australian desert. The sun had set magnificently in the west as the last of the golden rays fell behind the horizon. Harvey Amsterdam sat in the pilot's chair of the commandeered UFA transport ship watching the sky turn to night lamenting the events of the day. They had travelled the short distance from Uluru to a disused copper mine that had been discarded by the former mining company and it was now occupied by the militia group 'XXOO' which was led by The Chief. In their tenure of the site, they had built a large shed over the top of the mines entrance painting it the same red colour as the desert around them so that it could not be seen from above. It was where the transport ship now was parked safely hidden by the shed and Dakini's security protocols which ensured they would not be picked up electronically.

Dakini was the reason that Amsterdam chose to sit in the cockpit of the transport instead of in the main chamber of the mine where most of The Chief's men had gathered. When they arrived he had gone down there and watched as the men marvelled at the two IA5 units that strode down into their secured holding. Amsterdam counted roughly forty or so people that had come to this place; all armed heavily and on edge given the experiences that they had all just shared as one of escape from imminent death. When The Chief revealed his face they started to gather around him astonished at what they were seeing. He explained what had happened and he drew on Mitchell Reed to explain the details of how the IA5 worked and how it was possible.

"I am one of you!" said The Chief, "I have not deserted you. I have not deserted what we stand for. I come to you now, more than ever, ready to tackle what it is we must do. But this time, this time, my friends, I know our enemy. Before I was brought back by Professor Reed, I learned what it is our enemy is up to. I learned their battle plan. And I can tell you, we can take back our country!"

There was a rousing cheer from those standing around. Their look of steadfast fear seemed to turn into that of jubilation at The Chief's words. He was their leader. He had warned them of what was to come and they had followed. Essentially, every man there had owed their lives to The Chief; and now, Amsterdam had assumed, their lives were irrevocably changed forever to a point where they had nothing else to lose.

Amsterdam had noticed that Harry Lockley had moved away from the group after he greeted everyone but he did not stay for The Chief's speech. He sat by himself on the hood of a rusted out truck and held his head in his hands. It was a feeling Amsterdam himself had felt; totally overwhelmed at the events of the past days and now they had the opportunity to reflect their emotions were boiling to the surface.

"Some speech," said Amsterdam as he approached Lockley resting his back on the side of the truck.

"If you believe it," replied Lockley, "He was ready to make a break for it before. But now, he's ready to take on the world. I don't get it."

"People can change," replied Amsterdam, "Even when everything seems lost there is always possibility."

"I guess," Lockley replied unconvincingly, "Harvey, did you lose anyone?"

"I don't know. My family was at home when it happened and I wasn't there. I couldn't raise them on the phone before they dropped out. I guess, I'm hoping for the possibility that they made it."

"Me too. My wife, we had an argument just before and she ran off. I couldn't get in touch with her and now I feel like I have deserted her. She was good to me and when it really counted I wasn't there."

Lockley wiped the tears from his eyes and Amsterdam could feel his own coming on, "Hey, you keep strong, Harry. If they're out there, we'll find them. I promise."

And this was the reason that he now sat in the transport where he could speak with Dakini. It was important for all their sakes that whatever could be done to locate their families was undertaken without consideration of the cost. These men needed hope to keep them going and Amsterdam had surmised that Dakini would be able to speak with the other artificial intelligence system of the UFA, Lupei, and possibly identify whether they had kept some type of record. After all, Reed had said that his family was alive; which meant that there could be hope for the others as well.

"Dakini?" said Amsterdam and her image appeared on the screen of the transport ship, "I need you to do something for me. It's very important."

"Why did The Chief do what he did?" asked Dakini. It was a question that Amsterdam was not prepared for and he assumed that it alluded to the act where The Chief took the weapon off the transport ship and almost drained the life out of himself shooting down the ship that Dakini was in.

"I guess, he thought he owed you something," replied Amsterdam.

"I have been analysing the battle and I know where I went wrong. I just can't understand the actions of The Chief. Why would he almost sacrifice himself to save me?"

"Sometimes, human actions cannot be measured by numbers."

"Will you do something for me?" asked Dakini.

"Anything," replied Amsterdam.

"Will you teach me about love?"

"I can try. In fact, I think that I can prove what love is to you. I need you to break into Lupei's systems and try to find any records you can on the families of the men here. Whatever you can."

"I'm not sure I want to do that," replied Dakini, "She's mean and hurtful. I could feel her trying to probe me when we were in battle. She wanted to know who I am. Besides, you still owe me a story from the last favour I did for you?"

"I know. And, I want to tell you that story. But first, like we said, you need to find out what love is before you can understand it. Do this and I can tell you the rest of the story."

"Okay," replied Dakini as Reed entered the transport from the back of the ship and he walked up to Amsterdam handing him what looked like a wireless headset for a cell phone.

"Wear this, I found these and reprogrammed them to connect into Dakini. You can talk to her and any of us who has one."

Amsterdam took it and hooked it over his left ear. Reed walked over to one of the lifeless IA5 combat units that were held in the dock and stood in front of it.

"They are something," said Amsterdam.

"They're perfect. Too perfect. And that's the problem. Perfection requires one to be predictable," replied Reed.

"And that's why you left. You tried to tell them that but they didn't listen?"

"Something like that. When I built Dakini, I built her with the capacity to develop flaws. You see, one can't simply be given flaws, they are learned. And Dakini seems to be having trouble copying herself. It is strange."

"Listen, I've been meaning to ask you. Who is this Oracle you keep mentioning? It's just that I think I heard something; it was when I passed out in the vault. I heard a little girl say The Chief is strong and wise. The Farmer is careful but loyal. The Librarian is smart and skilful. The Mother is desire and playful. The Warrior does not know its enemy. The Chronicler does not know its story-"

"The Archaeologist does not know its history," continued Reed, "The Diplomat will bathe in glory-"

"And The Oracle will save them all," said Dakini in Amsterdam's headset almost in the same voice as the little girls voice he heard when he passed out.

"Did you hear that?" Amsterdam asked Reed who simply nodded his head.

"Dakini," asked Reed, "What do you know of The Oracle?"

"I've been talking with him," Dakini replied.

"Talking with him? But where?" asked Amsterdam.

"He found me. I like him," replied Dakini.

"He's alive?" said Reed shocked.

"Oh yes, of course he is silly."

"Should he be dead?" asked Amsterdam to Reed.

"Yes, very much so. When The Oracle was dead the robot army would rise up. This is what we were working from at Globe Corp."

"But it seems like the robotic army has risen, Reed. What does that mean?"

"I don't know," Reed said pointing at something behind Amsterdam, "But I think that might have something to do with it."

Reed was looking out the front of the window of the UFA transport ship. Amsterdam turned and looked as well to see that the bluish purple hues of the twilight sky had started to turn red in colour.

"What is that!" exclaimed Amsterdam as Reed walked out of the transport.

Amsterdam followed him and caught up with him outside of the shed. He looked around the entire horizon of the flat desert plain and the sky was entirely consumed in a transparent red colour replacing the night. Amsterdam could still see the moon and the stars in the background and when he focused his vision it looked like the red sky was moving in rippled waves.

"Chief," said Reed into a similar headset he had given Amsterdam attached to his left ear, "You better come topside and take a look at this. You better get everyone to come and take a look at this!"

"Roger," Amsterdam heard The Chief reply.

Amsterdam was overawed at the sight and wondered what would cause such a phenomenon, "It's amazing."

They were then joined by the entire group with Tenashi, The Chief and Lockley who were running at the front. There were collective groans and whistles from everyone as they took in the sight.

"As if anything else could possibly happen," said Lockley, "This can't be good!"

"Reed," said The Chief standing beside him, "Do you have any idea what this is?"

"Not a clue, Chief," replied Reed.

"It's some type of electronic signal," said Dakini.

"Electronic?" replied Amsterdam.

"I've analysed it and it seems to be an electronic signal that is reacting somehow with the magnetic field. It's almost like its sending radio waves?"

"The magnetic field! Isn't that the thing which keeps the sun from burning us to a crisp?" asked Lockley.

"Exactly," replied Dakini.

"Like I said, this can't be good," stated Lockley.

"There is something else though and it's stranger still," said Dakini, "I am also detecting television signals."

"Is it secure?" asked The Chief.

"Yes, it is only a one-way signal," replied Dakini.

"Let's show it then," said Reed, "Tenashi? Display the image out the front so everyone can see."

Tenashi walked to the front of the group and they formed a half circle around him. An image was projected like the way it was in the aqueduct of the Prime Minister of Australia, Robert Hughes and there was some boos and hisses from the crowd that followed.

"Fellow citizens of the Federation," began Hughes.

"What's the Federation?" asked one of the crowd.

"...Today you may be seeing in your part of the world a red sky. I can assure you that you should not fear it. No harm will come to you or the environment. What you are seeing is a signal. A signal that is being sent to the universe that is carrying a message. A message that is being sent to an intelligent life form in outer space. What that message contains is something that we do not yet know. But, we are confident, that it will result in the coming of a new era in human civilisation. It will be the era of first contact with an intelligent life form other than our own; and, how they will respond to this message is something that will yet to be seen. The United Federation of Asia, however, is taking the leading role to prepare the world for what is to come and I, as your President, will be doing everything possible to ensure that we are ready."

The image flickered out. Amsterdam was having difficulty bringing everything together. It had been one of his trademarks as a journalist that he was able to tie up the loose ends. But this was not something that he seemed to be able to comprehend. He started thinking back to his story that he had been trying to push with Evans and how insignificant it all felt knowing what he did now. It was merely a scratch on the surface, he thought as he looked up to the translucent red sky. Merely a scratch on the surface.

Chapter 61

George Underwood had opened his eyes. His stomach felt like it was being torn from the inside as he quickly gathered his thoughts around what had just happened. He was in the mountains, he was in a plane and he was shot. Underwood put his hands on his stomach and felt the wound. There was a distinct hole where the bullet had bored through him but the pain was excruciating and he almost passed out.

Where had he been, Underwood asked himself? After the gun was shot he had the distinct memory of going somewhere. A journey, of sorts; and he felt weary in much the same way. He recalled a young girl of about ten years of age and a room that was filled with soft toys and she seemed to have set up a tea party as she sipped from a fake plastic tea cup. George had seemingly walked in on her without her knowing which gave her a fright and she dropped the tea cup and scattered the soft toys as she crawled under her bed.

"No, please. Don't be frightened little girl. I didn't mean to scare you," said Underwood.

"Are you my friend, Mister?" asked the little girl.

"Yes, my name is George," said Underwood as he sat cross legged on the floor, "What's your name?"

"Dakini," said the little girl.

"That's a nice name. Say, how about you come out from underneath that bed and we can continue your tea party. I would like to know all about your other friends here."

"Would you?" asked Dakini crawling out from underneath the bed, "Well, these are my friends. This is Harvey, he's my favourite, and he likes to tell me stories. And this is Tenashi, Harry, Mitchell and this one is The Chief."

"Wow, those are great names, Dakini. I know a riddle about someone that is called The Chief. Would you like to hear it?"

"What's a riddle," asked Dakini.

"A riddle is a story that you need to work out its meaning. It does not always make sense but it is fun. Would you like to hear mine?"

Dakini nodded her head.

"Okay," said Underwood, "Here goes. The Chief is strong and wise. The Farmer is careful but loyal. The Librarian is smart and skilful. The Mother is desire and playful. The Warrior does not know its enemy. The Chronicler does not know its story. The Archaeologist does not know its history. The Diplomat will bathe in glory. And, The Oracle will save them all."

"Who is The Oracle?" asked Dakini.

"Well that would be cheating, wouldn't it? But, I'll give you a clue. The Oracle is me," replied Underwood.

"Really. Well that's a tough one. I'll have to think it over," replied Dakini as just then a deep low sounding horn engulfed Dakini's room, "Oh no! They're coming back!" Dakini shrieked.

"Who's coming back?" asked Underwood as Dakini crawled back underneath her bed, "I won't let anyone hurt you, Dakini."

At that moment, the four walls surrounding Dakini's room fell away and revealed an army of toy robots and Underwood stood up as they came closer surrounding him and Dakini. They then flooded the room piling in one by one until the room was totally consumed by toy robots and Underwood was cut off from Dakini.

"Dakini! Dakini!" yelled Underwood but he couldn't hear her over the sound of the creaking and scratching noises of the toy robots.

Underwood stuck out his hand through the wall of toy robots where he thought Dakini was and found her wrist. He pulled her toward him and picked her up which made the toy robots begin to recede back through the walls.

"I found you," Underwood said to Dakini.

"You found me," Dakini replied looking into Underwood's eyes.

Underwood put Dakini back down and he leant down and grabbed one of the last toy robots that were trying to make its escape.

"You have to go now, George," said Dakini.

"I do?" asked Underwood.

"You can't miss it. You have to go," Dakini persisted.

It was the last thing he remembered before waking and he now also sensed that he was lying down; but, he was moving at the same time.

"Oh, come on, George! You can't miss it!" he heard Molly Whitaker say and Underwood looked around to notice that he was outside and laying in the snow as Molly was dragging him up the side of a hill in a blanket.

"Molly?" he said.

"George, you're awake. Quick, you have to look at it. Look up, George."

George looked up and there it was. The red sky.

Molly stopped dragging him through the snow and walked on. George braced himself and stood up taking in the sight. It was a clear night and George could see the stars in the background. But what was most impressive was the red translucent layer that seemed to stretch from one horizon to the next. This was it. His vision, his final vision. It was a moment that George thought to himself would never come; something that had haunted him. In the moment, he did not know which emotion to pick. He did not know if he was elated or frightened. It just seemed to be a moment devoid of emotion; however, he was transfixed nonetheless.

"George! George! Come on, George!" shouted Molly as he turned to see that she was standing on top of a cement structure. He began stumbling toward her; however, each step felt like someone was stabbing a knife into him as he struggled through the snow. But he persisted and eventually made it to the cement structure and Molly offered her hand. He took it as he climbed to the top and it was then that he noticed the second piece of his vision, the hatch.

Molly had put a thick plank of wood in between the spokes of the wheel that opened the hatch, "You take one side and I'll take the other. We will push it in opposite directions and it should pop open."

For some reason, George complied without argument. He seemed to be going through a state of shock and he trusted Molly completely. He bent down on one knee and put his weight behind one side of the plank of wood.

"Ready, one, two, three and push!" said Molly.

When George did the pain was worse than ever; however, the hatch door would not budge.

"Come on!" yelled Molly as she pushed again and George joined her as this time the wheel started to give way as ice began to crack around the edges and then it began to freely spin open.

"This is it," said Underwood, "This is what happens when the lights go out."

"George, listen to me," said Molly puffing, "We need to get you down here. You've been shot, you're in shock and there will be people down there who can help you. I've done as much as I can but you will need surgery and soon or you will die. Do you understand?"

Underwood nodded his head and Molly nodded back fully unwinding the hatch and pulling it up with all her might as it creaked open. They both looked down the hatch and could see a ladder that dropped into a dark abyss.

"I'll go first," said Molly and she climbed down the ladder stepping down a couple of rungs before she turned to look at Underwood, "Come on, it's okay. I'm right behind you when you come down so if you slip, I'll catch you."

Underwood looked up into the red sky. A sky of flames, he had called it. It now looked like a massive sheet of red cellophane that had covered the sky completely and he knew that it was possibly the last thing that he would see.

"You have to come now, George!" said Molly.

And George did. He lowered his battered body into the hatch and reached over pulling the hatch down after him. His last image, a twinkling red star that sat on the horizon against the mountain of white snow. And then darkness.

Underwood then heard a clicking sound underneath him and then a dull yellow light dimly lit the ladder around him. Underwood looked down and saw that Molly had turned on the lighter and was looking further down the hatch.

"George, it's not far. There's a gangway here that you can drop down on. Just take one step at a time and follow my voice."

"Okay," replied George and again he complied with her request. Each step he took felt like it was taking longer and longer as he heard Molly land both feet on the gangway below him.

"You see, George, it isn't far. Keep going. That's it," said Molly.

When George reached the gangway he found it difficult to focus. He tried to squint to get a better look but the light from the lighter was not sufficient enough to get a bearing on where he was or what was up ahead. Underwood looked at Molly who was smiling at him.

"This is it," Underwood said, "From here on in, everything is new. I can't see where it is I am going. I am blind."

"Then let me help you," replied Molly who took his hand and

Underwood allowed her to guide him step-by-step as they moved down the gangway, "Welcome to the way us normal people experience life where every step could be your last."

This really was Underwood's fear. He had grown accustomed to what his ability had provided him and each second that went by Underwood felt like he was in a state of constant surprise. He did not know what his legs were going to do next or what his thoughts were going to be. Worst of all, as he was holding Molly's hand, he could not sense anything; not a single echo of her future. Just the moment in time that he was currently in and nothing else. It was like walking in the distance between stars where all the noise vanished and there was no one else that had ever existed but Underwood and Molly.

At the end of the gangway they came to a metal door which was marked 'E-UH 14'. The door was rusted and condensation was dripping down in one stream that left a trail of built up mould. Molly held up the lighter and found a switch that was marked 'Air Lock'. Underwood nodded at her and she flicked the switch. A red light that was sitting above the door flicked into life hurting Underwood's eyes and he listened as the sound of air was decompressed on the other side of the door.

There was then a *beep-beep* sound and the red light turned to green releasing the lock that was holding the door. Molly pulled back the heavy metal door which groaned in protest as its rusted hinges moved for what must have been the first time in a long time. It revealed a room of white. A clinical, sterile white room where a conveyor belt was sitting at one end with a console to the right and the room was flooded with an ambient light which stung Underwood's eyes.

They walked forward into the white room and stopped at the conveyor belt.

"What do we do?" asked Molly, "It doesn't seem to go anywhere else."

Underwood looked at the conveyor belt and he was struck by a memory of the facility that he had found in the mountains of Tibet. He recalled the coffins that were holding people in a state of suspended animation and how they were lined on the walls of corridors that stretched for miles down into the depths of a massive facility not too dissimilar to this one.

Underwood looked at the console and saw that it had one switch on it with the two reference points of 'On' and 'Off'. It was currently switched to 'Off' and Underwood reached up and switched it to 'On'. The conveyor belt began to move right to left and then a trap door on the right of the white room opened. Underwood watched as a coffin sized white box moved down toward them and came to a stop. The trap door shut and there was a hissing sound as the lid of the white coffin popped open revealing a padded white interior that was lit from inside by a white light.

It had then made sense to Underwood. The emptiness that he felt when he was connected to The Cube; the feeling of nothingness but not being dead.

"What is it?" asked Molly.

"It's a vessel that puts its occupants into a state of suspended animation," replied Underwood, "In my vision I kept coming to this end where I could feel myself being alive but I was encapsulated somehow in perpetual darkness. I didn't understand what that meant until now. It means that I need to go into that thing."

"I know that look," Molly said to Underwood with tears beginning to weld in her eyes, "I've seen it before. You need to do something and you think that you need to do it alone. Well you don't, George. You don't! I am not going to let that happen again. Not ever. Come on!"

Molly stepped up onto the conveyor belt and into the coffin. She held her hand out for Underwood who grasped it firmly and also stepped inside. Molly then helped Underwood lay down and the task was more difficult than it seemed as he felt a painful stabbing feeling burn in his wound. Surprisingly, the coffin was spacious enough to also fit Molly who was easily able to squeeze in beside him and she rested her head on his shoulder.

"You said that you would never leave my side again," said Molly as the lid of the coffin hissed closed and there was a clicking sound as it was set into place and the conveyor belt started to move again. Underwood looked into Molly's eyes that seemed to glow under the artificial white light and he kissed her on the lips. It brought back with it a flood of memories from when they first began dating; almost like they were kissing again for the very first time.

The moment, however, was broken by an image of a man that appeared on the lid of the coffin. He had fair hair that was tightly cropped with blue eyes framed by black rimmed glasses.

"Hello, my name is Peter," said the man in the image, "Preliminary tests are all okay so we will be ready to go shortly. We hope that your stay with us is pleasant and that we can welcome you shortly sometime in the future."

An immense state of calm fell over Underwood and he listened as Molly's breathing became shallower, "George, how long we will be asleep?" said Molly with panic in her voice.

But Underwood had already closed his eyes and he gripped Molly's hand tighter than he had ever done before.

"Okay, we're ready for suspended animation in 5, 4, 3..."

"George?"

"...2...1..."

Keep up to date and join the conversation at:
www.lbmayman.com